MIKE THE WEREWOLF

HOWLING MAD MONSTERS

BOOK 1

RICK GUALTIERI

COPYRIGHT © 2025 RICK GUALTIERI

Visit the author at:
www.rickgualtieri.com

ACKNOWLEDGMENTS

For Falkor and Axel, my own personal *wolf* pack.

A huge shoutout of thanks to my awesome Patreon supporters - James G., Chris, Angela, James C., Gary, Tina, Simon, MRB, Stephen, Randal, Mark, RE Carr, Sean, Blix, Jen, Ashley, Gordon, Cherry, Wendy, Shaun, Lee, Jeff, Stephanie, Eric, Dylan, Allen, Rachel C., Timothy, Dawn, D.M., Susan, Alisia, R.E., Geri, Peggy, Zack, Jude, and Christopher!

Series / Universe Note: This story takes place roughly two weeks after the events of *The Liching Hour* (Bill of the Dead – 4).

Have a question about a series, reading order, sequels, spinoffs, or more? Visit the author's Series Status page.

https://rickgualtieri.com/series-status/

PROLOGUE

THEN...

You ever open your eyes, only to realize you have no idea where you are, how you got there, or whether you're even awake?

That was me right at that particular moment and I had a feeling it had nothing to do with a weekend bender gone wrong.

My vision was all fuzzy around the edges, hinting this was quite possibly nothing more than a bad dream, but if so, it was more vivid than any dream I'd ever experienced. Heck, I could feel the cold clamminess of the stagnant air and the slick, grime-covered floor beneath my feet.

Just for the record ... *Eww!*

The space around me was dimly lit, bathed in an eerie green glow like some cheap Halloween haunted house. It was enough to see by, but that wasn't really a plus in my favor.

Thick stone walls stood on all sides, with rusted metal pipes running through them at seemingly random intervals. Muck, mold, mildew, and God knows what else covered much of it, making me wish this *dream* came equipped with a gallon of bleach and rubber gloves.

Whatever this place was, it was old and neglected, as if it had been abandoned centuries ago – like some sort of steampunk dungeon.

This was no time to stop and marvel at the *sights*, though, as I heard movement from behind me. I turned through no conscious will of my own, only to spy a group of people nearby. They were all dragging their feet in the muck, slowly shuffling along toward some unknown destination.

I tried to ask if any of them knew what was going on, yet the words refused to leave my lips. Heck, my lips didn't even move. Instead, my muscles grew tense as if in reaction to some unrealized danger.

Or maybe not as unrealized as I thought, as a moment later one of them partially turned my way, revealing eyes black as coals and canines that would've given my family dentist a minor coronary.

These weren't people.

They were vampires.

Such a revelation should've given me pause, except I recognized this particular vamp's face. It took a moment for my muddled brain to make the connection but then I remembered he'd been with me when…

When what?

Before I could follow that train of thought back to its depot, all the hairs on the back of my neck stood up. A shiver passed through me as some instinct from deep inside screamed a warning, insisting this creature was my enemy.

Even as I tried to process that, I crouched low, my intent seemingly clear. I, or whoever was at the switch controlling my body, was prepared to fight back if this vampire, this *thing*, made a move against me.

I held that position for several long seconds, unable to do otherwise, but no such attack came. Nor was that likely to change because it was painfully apparent there was something seriously *off* about this vamp and all his buddies.

Well, okay, more off than being a walking, blood-sucking corpse.

That's when it hit me. His face, heck, *all* of their faces. They were blank slates, devoid of any emotion. The lights were on but no one was home, almost like they were ... sleepwalking.

Guess it was contagious.

Either way, the entire group continued walking past me as if I wasn't even there.

That wasn't the only thing weird about them. Far from it.

Each was carrying a heavy armload of raw, bloodied flesh, as if the world's worst discount butcher was holding a huge clearance sale nearby.

Despite their burdens looking the exact opposite of appetizing, my stomach rumbled nonetheless and a sliver of drool dripped unbidden from my lips.

It was kinda like that dream I used to have about Grandma's rhubarb pie, except infinitely grosser.

Nor was that the end of the weirdness.

I scurried toward the nearest of the vampires, nothing more than a spectator within my own body. Then I reached out, seemingly intent on claiming their gory meal for my own.

Okay, time to wake up! I really don't want to know what that tastes like.

I only paused once my own hand came into view. It was drenched in blood, same as the vamps now marching away from me.

Wait. Does that mean I was also...?

My vision panned downward, scanning the floor

around me, only to discover a similar pile of innards now lying discarded upon the ground.

Hold on. Had I been doing the same thing as those vamps, carrying around piles of rancid meat like some zombie *Door Dasher*?

And if so, for what purpose?

Of equal importance was why I was somehow now awake when all the others clearly were not.

Despite being grossed out beyond belief, I needed to investigate further. There had to be some reason behind this madness.

If I follow these guys, maybe it'll lead me to…

Sadly, my body apparently didn't give a damn what my intent might be.

Instead, I felt a euphoric numbness deep inside that began to rapidly spread to my extremities. It was the space of an instant for me to understand what was happening.

Seriously? That's only going to make it worse!

If any part of my rogue body heard my thoughts, it gave them no heed. In the next instant, any protest I might've made was drowned out by the *crackle* of my bones rearranging themselves. Then came the sound of fabric ripping along with the subtle *schlup* of muscles growing larger and denser, all of it reverberating within my ears as they too changed.

Everything took on extra sharp relief within the dim light. Myriad colors replaced the dull green glow as I began to *sense* the varying temperatures of everything close by.

A snarl escaped my lips as the change neared its completion, the sort of thing you'd expect to hear from an angry dog.

It told me I was about to attack. I wasn't sure who, what, or even why. All I knew was I was powerless to stop it, no matter how hard I…

A veritable tsunami of odors slammed into my freshly upgraded olfactory nerve, sending my senses reeling. Sitting atop it all was the stench of dirt, decay, death, and no small amount of human excrement.

The sewer! I'm in a freaking sewer.

Mind you, that and five bucks would buy me a cup of coffee – not that I'd want to drink anything in this filthy place. Not to mention, knowing my general location was the least of my concerns as my legs tensed for action I could do nothing to stop.

However, where I might've had no power over my own body, whatever my nostrils picked up next most certainly did.

What the…?

I stopped dead in my tracks, trying to make sense of whatever was currently dirty dancing all over my ultra-sensitive sense of smell.

Alien. Totally, inexplicably alien.

That's the only way I could describe it without scream-ing. This scent was like nothing I'd ever encountered before. My mind, a veritable Wikipedia of foul odors, was unable to identify it beyond that.

Whatever it was, it was old, as in *impossibly so*. I don't know how I knew it. I just did. Same as I somehow understood this strange and terrible scent was not of this world.

More importantly, I instinctively realized this was for the best. That this was the sort of knowledge that could drive a guy irrevocably mad.

Though instant insanity didn't seem to be on the table, thank goodness, the growl within my throat immediately turned into a mewling whine.

Whatever the heck it was, my body was as terrified of it as the rest of me.

In the next instant my transformation abruptly

reversed. Sights, sounds, and, mercifully, *scents* became muted as I once more became myself.

Sadly, that primal fear remained.

I felt panic starting to grip my entire being, even semi-detached as I was from the situation. Gone was my body's former aggression, replaced instead with the overwhelming need to flee.

Take a deep breath, I told myself. *Calm down. Don't do anything stup...*

So, of course, I turned and ran.

It didn't seem to matter the direction, so long as it was away from wherever here was. Caution was thrown to the wind as my now bare feet slipped in ungodly crud while desperately seeking purchase.

Don't think about it. I repeat, do not think about it!

I spied more people ahead. Humans or vamps, it didn't matter as I careened into them, knocking them aside in my race to escape.

It was the fastest way to get past them, but perhaps not the smartest. Even as I sped up again, I saw their eyes turn my way – hostile awareness replacing the blank stares.

That's not good.

Seconds later that became more than apparent as I came upon yet another group. Gone were their placid expressions, however. They dropped their bloody cargo and turned my way, ill intent etched upon their faces.

Still in a blind panic, I turned down a narrow side tunnel to avoid them. There, the eerie green glow was considerably muted, dissipating the terror a tiny bit as I...

Oof!

Probably should've paid better attention. Instead, I slammed into something massive in the diminishing light, rebounding off and landing on my butt in the grimy muck,

I squinted to see whatever was blocking the way, only to immediately wish to God I hadn't.

The creature was the size of a grizzly bear, held up by three pairs of spindly legs while a gleaming carapace covered its backside.

Don't look up. Whatever you do, don't...

Needless to say, I looked up.

No less than three pairs of glowing red eyes stared down at me from atop a vicious set of mandible jaws that looked sharp enough to cleave bone.

It was some kind of nightmare cockroach, the spawn of an insane prehistoric wet dream. It was also apparently way too much for my over-burdened brain to handle. I felt my tenuous grip on consciousness begin to mercifully fade. The fuzziness at the edge of my vision closed in again, slowly erasing this fever dream.

Just a nightmare.

It was only a nightmare.

The knowledge of where I'd been, what I'd seen, and most importantly what had caused me to run, began to fade away, leaving only...

"Oh, fuck me with Hobart's fat, hairy dick!"

What the?

The voice had sounded like my own, but the words most certainly weren't.

As my awareness continued to fade, I once more vaguely wondered where I'd been and how I'd gotten there, but there was also one other nagging question.

Who the heck am I?

Because I knew one thing for certain.

Whoever was now crying out, using a voice eerily similar to my own, wasn't me.

1

HAIR OF THE DOG

NOW...

What in Spud's name?

A moment ago I was surrounded by chaos with a capital C. I was on a beaten down dock in Manhattan fighting alongside vampires, a witch, and a woman I wasn't sure about other than she had freaky glowing eyes.

I probably should've asked her about that when I had the chance, but there hadn't been time, mostly because that's when things had gotten really *weird*.

A massive sea monster, bigger than anything Herman Melville ever imagined, picked that moment to explode out of the Hudson like some Japanese monster movie. That alone should've been cause enough to soil my pants, but then it had inexplicably started talking to me inside my own freaking mind. We're talking the bastard love child of *Godzilla* and *Charles Xavier*.

Yes, I know how it sounds. As I said, *weird*.

And it's not like it hadn't already been a night to remember. This new development, however, had taken the cake.

Not to be pessimistic but I was certain that was it —

my story was about to end right then and there. After all, I'm not delusional enough to think I can throw hands with a two-hundred-foot psychic dinosaur.

Except I didn't die. At least I don't think I did.

All I know was I blinked, only to find night had turned into day. Gone were the vampires along with the Manhattan skyline. As for that time-lost dinosaur looming over me like a hungry kaiju, it had been replaced by ... a potbellied pig?

I blinked again to make sure I wasn't seeing things. Yep, still there and grunting curiously at me as if I were the weirdo here.

Don't get me wrong. I hadn't yet ruled out I might actually be dead. But if so, this was an afterlife they'd overlooked back at Sunday school.

Now, just to be clear, neither drugs nor booze had any hand in this crazy train, even if part of me was starting to wish it had. I likewise realize I probably sound pretty blasé talking about vampires, *Devil Dinosaur*, and green-eyed voodoo women.

After all, learning that beasts from myths and movies actually exist wouldn't normally be something to gloss over.

These were far from normal times, though.

Besides which, there's a very simple reason why real-life monsters don't particularly faze me.

I'm one of them.

My name is Michael Hunter Walden, Mike to my friends, and I am an honest to goodness werewolf. So are my parents Lloyd and Ginny as well as a fair number of the folks I grew up alongside, even if none of us realized it until fairly recently.

Sounds nuts, I know, but trust me, this rabbit hole gets a whole lot deeper.

I'll get to all of that, but for now let's talk about my somewhat unique *condition*.

You see, Hollywood would have you believe being a werewolf involves terror, self-loathing, and avoiding the silverware at holiday dinner. Depending on the film, you might also find them hanging around high schools and picking up underage girls, but the less said about that the better.

Anyway, I fully admit that being cursed to transform into a slobbering hell beast would probably suck. After all, you'd have to be a real jerk to enjoy waking up to the possibility of having slaughtered half the countryside while wolfed out.

And believe me, I do feel bad for the non-jerks who have to deal with it.

Regardless, that's not an issue for me because, unlike most of the werewolves in town, I have full control over my actions when I change.

Not gonna lie. That little detail makes all the difference.

True, learning I was a monster required a few lifestyle changes, but it mostly came down to figuring stuff out and incorporating it into my life.

Don't get me wrong, I was seriously weirded out the first time I changed, which may have resulted in a few poor decisions on my part. But I'm also pretty sure most people would be thrown for a loop if they found themselves unexpectedly transforming into a massive wolf creature under the light of the full moon.

Thankfully, it wasn't long before I had my head screwed on straight and was able to start making sense of it all.

True, changing into a hairy beast of the night sometimes entails dealing with primal instincts of a baser nature but, aside from that, I have both hands firmly on the steering wheel.

Or at least that had been the case before I woke up in my current situation.

I'd never had what you might call an out-of-body experience, but as I took in the space around me, I began to wonder if maybe that was something I needed to start worrying about.

Aside from the rather curious pig still staring at me, the first thing I noticed were the scents or lack thereof. Cliché as it might sound, when you're a werewolf your sense of smell tends to be a big part of everything. Anyway, the last thing I remembered was a mix of unpleasantness – dirt, gravel, pee, and of course the Hudson River, although it was a fine line between those last two. Oh, and there was also the overpowering briny stench of an impossible beast that almost certainly didn't belong there.

Needless to say, stuff like that is hard to forget.

But all of it was now gone, replaced by cheap carpeting that reeked of floral scent *Febreze*.

Mind you, the floor covering was far less interesting than the fact I was down on my hands and knees for some reason. A quick look confirmed I was back in my human form, absolutely filthy, and naked as the day I was born.

Great. Because a lack of pants always makes things better.

As freaky as my abrupt change of venue was, however, that's when things went from strange to downright terrifying.

I tried to stand up, only for my body to not respond. Instead I remained on all fours as my gaze involuntarily returned to the pig, obviously someone's pet as it was clean and well-cared for, unlike me. It continued to grunt and snuffle as I bared my teeth. A snarl escaped my lips, a pathetic sound compared to what I could make when fully transformed, but the threat behind it seemed clear all the same.

The pig let out a squeal in return, although whether it felt threatened or angry, I had no way of knowing.

I opened my mouth, meaning to... *Wait. How do you reassure a pig?*

What came out instead was an inarticulate growl as I shuffled forward, my body moving with a mind all its...

Ugh! The most horrific feeling of déjà vu slammed into my brain like a speeding truck, a fleeting memory of a dark place and being trapped inside my own body.

But ... but that was just a dream.

Maybe so, but right then it was more like a waking nightmare.

Step by step, I inched toward the chubby little porker, doing everything I could to stop myself. But it was no use.

Don't even think about it. I repeat, do not...

I pounced. It was an ungainly, inelegant move on my part, made in a body that wasn't meant to be quadrupedal. Hell, I'm sure it looked pretty darned ridiculous, at least up to the point where I descended upon the confused piggy, a tendril of drool escaping my lips as I silently screamed in protest.

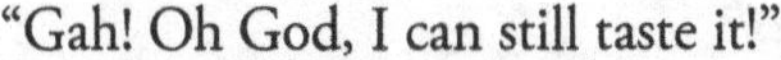

"Gah! Oh God, I can still taste it!"

It's probably not surprising to learn my senses became greatly heightened while in my werewolf form. We're talking sight, smell, and hearing, not to mention my tastebuds.

So, thank whatever gods existed that I was currently human. Nevertheless, let it be known that raw pig wasn't something I was liable to forget anytime soon.

Uggh!

This was no ham sandwich. Quite the opposite.

It was vile to the point where I didn't care if I was using a stranger's toothbrush to try and rid my mouth of the awful aftertaste. And no, I really didn't want to think about that either. I'd already gone through half a tube of toothpaste and yet still the taste of raw pork lingered.

Blecch!

Sadly, the knowledge of what I'd done was even worse. The brave little piggy had put up a hell of a fight, partly helped by my body forgetting it had opposable thumbs. But in the end it had fared no better than a plate of Grandma's homemade breakfast sausage.

Great. Now breakfast is ruined forever.

All of that should've had me retching my guts out, yet everything seemed to be staying down just fine, which wasn't exactly helping my state of mind.

Worse, it made me think of my own pet. Spud was a seventy-pound pit bull mix, as sweet as his stubborn noggin was thick. I couldn't even imagine doing something so barbaric to him. Although, in all fairness, he'd probably have slightly better odds than a chubby little piglet.

It was only after I'd finished the last bite, feeling the meat and gristle slither down my throat, that whatever spell I was under let go and I once again found myself in control of my own body.

Wait a second ... a spell?

Was all of this somehow Myra's doing?

Myra Wallanger was my ex. Just a few months ago we'd been thick as thieves, so sweet on one another we'd probably given cavities to passersby. Heck, I'd even started to mull popping the question.

In retrospect, it's probably a good thing I hadn't because right about then everything changed, and I mean for both of us. I discovered flea baths were now an option, while Myra suddenly displayed an uncanny ability to perform magic above and beyond card tricks.

Turns out she was a witch, a powerful one at that. More importantly, she was aware of this fact, something that, oddly enough, had never come up in the year and a half we'd dated.

Thing is, dangerous and unpredictable as she'd become since her power awakened, or *reawakened* as I eventually learned was the case, I could think of no good reason why she'd want to hex me to eat someone's pet. Like seriously, why would anyone do that?

Unfortunately, that didn't mean I could rule her out as the cause. The truth was, that girl's head hadn't been screwed on right as of late.

Of course, neither was mine considering I still had no idea where I was or how I'd gotten there.

I spat out another mouthful of toothpaste, repressing a shudder as it ran down the drain. The entire sink was now stained a reddish brown, as was everything I'd touched since regaining control of my body.

It would've been disgusting enough even had I not known what I'd done, the sort of thing that had my OCD twitching for a gallon of bleach and a *Costco* sized pack of paper towels.

I glanced at myself in the mirror, seeing a ghoul

covered in blood, slivers of pork fat, and no small number of bite marks.

Go figure, but when cornered, potbellied pigs can put up a heck of a fight.

It was almost laughable to think that, under different circumstances, I was pretty normal looking. Aside from the whole werewolf thing, I was just a twenty-eight-year-old guy trying to figure out his life. Beneath all the gore was light brown hair above a six-foot frame and a pre-piggy weight of about two-hundred pounds. True, I didn't exercise as much as I probably should've, but my job as a trash collector with the Harris County Public Works Department kept me in decent enough shape. I was no gym stud but was still a far cry from the horror show staring back at me.

Heck, I could've passed as the last survivor in some gory slasher flick. I was bloody, scratched to hell, and my left eye was involuntarily twitching for some reason.

At least nobody could claim my opponent hadn't taken its pound of flesh before giving up the ghost.

I wasn't sure if there was a pig heaven, but if so, I had no doubt this one was arriving at the pearly gates with one heck of a story.

Alas, it was too late for the little porker. All I could do now was worry about myself and what to do from here.

That last one was an easy choice. I pulled open the shower curtain and turned on the faucet. Figuring out where I was trespassing could wait until I was clean. Skulking about looking like an unhinged serial killer would almost certainly not help my cause.

As for my wounds, I wasn't too worried. Painful as they appeared, they'd be healed by...

Now that I stopped to think about it, I had no idea of the time, other than it being daylight. Oh well. Yet another mystery to add to the list.

But first things first.

I looked at the man in the mirror once more before stepping into the shower, meeting my eyes as they stared back at me. "What the hell is going on with you?"

"You mean other than being a dipshit hairless ape?"

I nearly jumped out of my skin at the voice that answered, having seemingly come from nowhere.

"Is – is someone there?" I asked, peeking out the bathroom door. The other room, however, was just as I'd left it, copious blood stains and all.

"Gods damn, you really are a massive pussy."

I spun back around, the voice sounding as if it had come from right beside me. Won't lie. I fully expected to find someone else had ... I don't know, maybe materialized out of thin air. Trust me when I say that's not the weirdest thing I've seen.

But no. The bathroom was still empty.

"Who said that?" I asked, fearing I might be going crazy. First my body had acted of its own accord and now this. What other explanation could there possibly...?

"Hold on just a sec. Can you actually hear me?"

Movement caught the corner of my eye as the voice spoke again. I turned to follow, feeling more terror than I'd felt since the day I discovered my true nature. "I did ... I mean I can," I stammered. "Clear as day."

"Well, ain't that a kick in the balls," my reflection replied. "It's about goddamned time too."

2

THE BEAST THAT BURDENS

Back in high school, my buddy Dallas managed to sneak a twelve pack of Michelob from his old man's liquor store over on Beaver Dam Road. My parents were out of town helping Grandma after her hip replacement, so it had been the perfect time for two friends to hang out and get trashed.

Or so I'd thought.

The next thing I knew, I'd woken up with my head in the toilet and an unflushed turd floating maybe an inch away, like a catfish gone belly up. To make matters worse, neither of us could remember who'd launched this brown torpedo or when.

At the time, I'd thought it was the weirdest thing that could ever happen to me. In retrospect, however, it seemed downright quaint, almost a fond memory.

"So, are you just going to stand there like a stupid shit-kicker or what?"

The voice was my own but somehow also not. The inflection was rougher in pitch as well as intent. Stranger still was the feeling I'd heard it before, although I had no idea when or where.

18

Barely believing this was happening, I touched my face to confirm my mouth was actually moving.

"Who are you?" I asked.

"Think of me as ... your former prisoner," *I* answered. "Emphasis on former." Sure enough, my lips were forming the words seemingly all on their own.

"I ... don't understand."

"No shit, jackass."

I clenched my teeth to see if I could stop it from happening, only to find myself partially successful.

It was like my own body was fighting against me in some insane tug of war for control, until finally the other voice managed to spit out, "You ... know, it's ... really ... fucking hard ... to talk ... when you do ... that."

I tried to reply but ended up biting my tongue instead. "Ow!"

"Don't like it when the shoe's on the other paw, eh?" my reflection replied. "Then maybe take that as a hint to knock it the fuck off."

I nodded, tasting blood ... well, okay, *more* blood. "Fine, you win. I'm sorry. This is just ... really weird."

"This is weird for *you*?" the intruder within my skin replied. "How do you think *I* feel standing here in this mange-ridden body?"

"Mange-ridden?"

"Duh! You're like one giant bald spot. And goddamn, is it always this fucking cold being you?"

What? None of this made any sense. "Back up a bit. What was that stuff about being a prisoner?"

"Former prisoner," they ... I corrected.

"Whatever. I still don't know what that means."

"Like hell you don't."

"I'm serious. This has been a really stressful day and I honestly have no idea what you're talking about ... or how you're even talking."

"Wait, for real?" My reflection raised an eyebrow. "Are you seriously trying to tell me you don't remember locking me up?"

I nodded.

"Well, *I* do. That night, gods, I remember it so perfectly. It was like waking up from a dream that seemed to never end. After years, maybe *decades*, of perpetual slumber I was finally free to stretch my legs. Gods damn, that was a good night."

Wait. Is he talking about...?

Instead of giving voice to those thoughts, I let the voice continue as I watched myself in the mirror. I wasn't sure what they were rambling about, but bits and pieces of that last part had struck a chord. I needed to hear more, though, before I could risk jumping to any conclusions.

"Too bad that was the *only* night," he continued, my voice dropping in pitch until it was nearly a growl. "After that, I was still awake, still aware, but it was like being penned with a collar around my neck."

"Penned?"

"Did I stutter? I don't know how you did it, but somehow you stuffed me into some kind of ... I don't know, *brain cage* and there wasn't shit I could do about it. What a fucking joke. To think your pansy ass could crate *me* like a newborn pup, and yet that's what fucking happened ... at least until I broke free."

"Hold on. I don't even know what a brain cage is."

He wasn't finished ranting, though. "Every single time it should've been me out there running wild, instead it was you. When I wanted to rip and claw, you swatted me on the nose and told me to pipe down. When I wanted to show those other mutts who was in charge, you ignored me and treated them with kid gloves. By the way, how'd that work out for you? Let me guess, that knuckle dragger

Hobart is still calling the shots while you're here mewling like a free-range bitch."

I felt my mouth go dry. "You know about Hobart?"

"Of course I do!" the voice barked. "I know about him, that two-faced bitch Myra, and their shithead lapdog Jeb. I know about Larry, Edna, Dallas, you name it. Hell, I even know about the braindead drool snack you let loaf around that shithole you call a home."

"Drool snack?"

"Yeah. What do you call that runt ... Scud, Skat?"

"You mean Spud?"

"Yeah, that's it!"

And just like that, more pieces fell into place. I began to visualize the picture this puzzle was starting to paint.

"I can see from the somewhat less stupid look on your face you're finally starting to get it."

"Our face," I said. "It's *our* face."

"No need to be insulting. This pile of useless pink flesh is all yours, bub. Our *other* face is mine — or as I like to think of it, your better half."

I stood there letting the hot water rinse away the blood. God, there was a lot of it. Why couldn't these people have owned gerbils instead? Not that I had any desire to munch on live gerbils, but still.

Fortunately for me, the intruder inside my body didn't have any objections when I, needing a moment to clear my head, stepped into the shower.

Mind you, that my mouth kept snapping at the water like some over-stimulated Golden Retriever was a little distracting.

Except this thing inside of me is no dog, not quite anyway.

Somehow, I'd been having a conversation with my *inner wolf*, and yes I know how crazy it sounds. But what other answer could possibly make sense?

Farfetched as it might be, I'd been diligent in my *research* these past few months. The idea of werewolves having a human half as well as a feral alter ego was a concept that popped up here and there in the lore, even if I'd since dismissed it as nothing more than Hollywood bs.

Shame on me for jumping to conclusions. Maybe I needed to go back and rethink some of the source material I'd been cramming in the three months since this all started.

That's not entirely true, though, is it?

Three months earlier something had happened to change the status quo. But there was more to it than that, a truth I'd suspected but had never really dwelled upon — that all of this, everything I was dealing with, actually started long before I was even born.

I should probably explain.

Remember when I mentioned being a werewolf? See, the catch is, I wasn't bitten by some fell beast while traversing a forbidden forest at midnight. Nor did I make any deals with the devil, at least none I'm aware of.

Far as I can tell, I was born this way and I wasn't the first, not by a long stretch.

The problem is, none of us realized it until recently.

I had a decent upbringing as the only child of blue-collar parents. Mom still waits tables at the local diner, while Dad recently retired from his job as a mechanic. I was raised in a small Pennsylvania town, went to school, made friends, et cetera. If it sounds mundane that's because it is.

There's only one small catch, something I would've never even considered had events played out differently.

Growing up, many of us in town had a recurring get-together me and my friends used to call *the ritual*. That might sound ominous, but it's just a name we gave it to make it seem cooler than it was. In truth it wasn't that big of a deal. Heck, it wasn't much different than the local Elks lodge or the Baptist church over on Danton Street.

That's what others in town thought too, that it was merely some private group gathering, aka none of their concern.

Never discount the power of hiding in plain sight.

Anyway, once a month, just like clockwork, a bunch of us, maybe a tenth of the local populace, would gather at town hall. It was always the same people, no invites allowed. Now, don't go thinking this was some kind of cult. Sure, we had our share of weirdos, like old man Spitzer who liked to sit on his front porch and have shouting matches with the crows in his trees, but most who attended were just regular folk.

Once we were all gathered, those in charge would take roll call, then bring us up to speed on any local news of interest, like zoning changes, road closures, and whatnot. Pretty dry stuff for a kid but it usually didn't last too long. Everyone knew *why* we were there, so there wasn't any of the usual bickering that went on during normal town meetings.

Once all that stuff was out of the way, we'd line up just like they do at church. But, instead of communion, we'd each be handed a pill and a cup of water. It wasn't by any priests either. No. The people running this part were always out-of-towners. They'd stay just long enough to see things through then leave until the next month.

I never knew who they were, save they weren't local. I didn't make the connection until I was older, but most of them dressed like characters straight out of *The Matrix*. We're talking trench coats and mirrored sunglasses, even though the ritual always took place after dark. They were never mean to us, but they weren't friendly either. It's more that they were *efficient* – always making sure the line kept moving, checking off names, and ensuring there were no stragglers.

Anyway, I'd swallow my pill like I was told and that was it. The meeting would adjourn, the strangers would leave, and everyone would go back to their lives until the next month.

Like I said, I never even thought to question it.

It was merely a part of my life since the day I was born. Same with my parents and their parents before them. To this day, I have no idea how far back it stretched, save that I've yet to meet anyone who could remember a time before it.

After, however, is a completely different story.

It all came to a rather abrupt end one month about five years ago, when the pill-bearers didn't show up. There was no sign of them or the ominous black vans they came to town in. We gathered as normal only for the mayor to adjourn things early.

What we didn't know then was that was the last ritual any of us would ever attend.

A whole week passed before folks started to freak out. We had no idea what it meant. The ritual had been a part of our lives for so long, something we'd never questioned, and then suddenly it wasn't.

There was a lot of panic at the time. Rumors were flying. People were at each other's throats. And, sad to say, more than a few, the mayor included, went so far as to check out on their own terms, if you catch my drift.

But then that too passed.

A few more months went by and absolutely nothing

changed for those of us who'd decided a noose around the rafters wasn't the ideal solution. Nobody got sick and nobody went crazy, at least not anyone who wasn't already halfway there. Life in Harris County simply went on.

The ritual ended and it was like it had never even mattered.

Sure, there was plenty of speculation. Heck, my buddy Dallas became convinced it was all a massive social experiment by the government – feeding us placebos to see how compliant we'd be at following orders. Crazy as it sounded, it wasn't much different than any of a hundred other loony theories that people would expound upon after a few beers come Friday night.

Despite all the talk and bluster, the only thing we knew for certain was something which had once been a pillar of our lives was over, yet nothing had changed for us.

The problem, as it turned out, was we were wrong – *dead wrong*.

3

BARE-LY FUNCTIONAL

"**I**s it always so goddamned cold being you? Like seriously, how the fuck do you not freeze without fur?"

"Because I don't walk around naked, that's why," I snapped, continuing to dry off. A quick look in the mirror confirmed the shower had worked wonders. I finally looked *human* again.

I wasn't, though, not really. Amusingly enough, the voice continuing to harangue me from my own freaking body only served to further drive that point home.

The fur remark at least cemented my theory. Either I was possessed by some sort of *Cousin It* demon or the thing speaking to me was my inner beast. Neither sounded particularly sane, but the latter seemed slightly more plausible. Or that's the conclusion several werewolf movies I'd binged seemed to suggest. And yes, that pretty much amounted to the *research* I'd mentioned.

Seriously, what else could I use? It's not like I could walk into the library and ask if they had any reference books on the subject.

If this voice did represent my inner wolf, though, the bigger question was why he was speaking up now. After all, I'd come to grips with my condition months ago, accepted what I was and that this was my life now. Yet this was the first time I'd been given even the slightest inkling I wasn't alone in my own skin, that there might be something else lurking inside of me, something with a serious attitude problem no less.

Except maybe that wasn't true. I'd mentioned those instincts and urges while in my other form. However, I'd never once thought to question where those had come from. Call me an idiot, but I kinda figured it was just part and parcel of being a werewolf.

It's not like this curse came with an instruction manual.

Curse. Before this day I'd never had much reason to consider it that way. But now, with an intruder inside my noggin with a taste for household pets, maybe it was time to reconsider.

There was also the issue of this creature's claims of being some sort of prisoner inside my mind. Let's just say I had some doubts there. Heck, I didn't even like to crate Spud, preferring to come home to him asleep on the couch.

Crap, Spud!

When last I'd seen him, he'd been with my folks. That was right before I was forced to take an extended sojourn to New York City in order to avert a war Hobart and Myra seemed intent on starting.

Talk about a hot mess.

I'd rented an apartment in Brooklyn to keep tabs on things, commuting back and forth for nearly a month since it's not like I could afford to lose my job.

Things finally came to a head in a block-wide supernatural scuffle before finally leading to Manhattan, where I'd gotten mind-zapped by the Loch Ness Monster's uglier cousin.

The problem now was twofold. I had no idea whether my efforts had been successful, nor any clue how much time had passed since. It could've been a week, a month, or much longer.

Safe to say, I needed to find a calendar and then figure out a way to get my butt back home.

Unfortunately, I had a feeling it would all be that much more difficult until I got a handle on this voice inside my head.

That meant it was time to be proactive.

I focused once again on my reflection. "Who are you?"

My left eyebrow rose curiously in response. "Is this some new age, self-affirmation shit or are you talking to me? Kinda hard to tell on account of you being a fuckhead."

"I'm asking *you*," I replied. "And do you have to keep doing that?"

"Calling you a fuckhead?"

"No ... yes! I mean, cursing like a sailor every time you speak."

"A sailor? Oh wait, aren't they those guys who live in the water?"

I shook my head. "Not quite. They work on ships and submarines."

"Oh, that's real helpful, especially since I have no fucking idea what that is!"

"You don't know what a submarine is?"

"Have you been on one since I've been awake?"

I had no idea how to answer.

No doubt taking my silence as a cue, he continued, "Then how the fuck would I know what one is?"

"See?" I replied, throwing my hands in the air. "That's my point. Not the submarines, the cussing. Do you need to be so crude about everything?"

"Seriously, *that's* what you're most worried about? Are you a fucking puppy? Because I sure as shit ain't got no teats for you to suckle on. Gods, it's no wonder your bitch ass got dominated."

I raised an eyebrow, my other eyebrow that is. "What did you say?"

"I said you got dominated. You remember that thing in the water, don't you? Big and ugly, hard to miss, probably not a sailor either."

My breath caught. "What do you know about it?"

"More than you, dickless. Far as I can tell, that fuckup is the whole reason I was finally able to break out of my cage. And before you ask, no, I ain't going back. In fact, if I have any say in the matter, I'm gonna do the same damned thing to you that you did to me."

What?!

The waterfront in Manhattan. It was my last clear memory before everything went blank.

The night had begun in Brooklyn, where I'd been renting an apartment from a vampire named Bill Ryder – supposedly a bigwig amongst their ranks.

Things had quickly escalated. Hobart had decided this particular vamp was in possession of knowledge he wanted, and he wasn't about to take no for an answer. I still wasn't entirely sure of his reasoning, but it apparently had something to do with the ritual.

See, what I know now that I didn't know then is the ritual wasn't the only thing that came to an abrupt end five years ago. That's also right about the time when all magic was supposedly banished from our world.

Coincidence? I doubt it.

And no, I'm not exaggerating. Back then the world had seemingly gone crazy. All at once the news started treating nonsense like vampires, witches, and even Bigfoot like they were real – claiming they were battling each other out in the open in major cities like New York and Boston.

They called it the Strange Days. In truth, I figured it was all some *War of the Worlds* ratings grab, a way to make the evening broadcasts interesting for a change. It worked too. Heck, folks would gather over at Jasper's Pub every night just to place bets on what madness would be reported next.

Then, just like that, it all ended. Everything went back to normal, with no acknowledgement from the authorities that anything strange had ever happened. It was like a countrywide Mandela effect.

I still don't know the actual specifics behind it all. Heck, I didn't even believe magic could ever be real until Myra started conjuring fireballs from thin air. All I can say for certain is something significant happened that altered the course of life for those living in Harris County, including for yours truly.

We just didn't realize it at the time.

Mind you, had that actually been the end of things, then I wouldn't be standing naked in a stranger's bathroom talking to myself. If anything, my life would've probably turned out pretty mundane.

I would've remained ignorant of my true nature, perhaps not entirely a bad thing. Myra and I might still be a couple, for better or worse. Poker night at Dallas's would've continued as usual. And I certainly wouldn't have gotten caught up fighting my fellow townsfolk, some of whom I still considered friends, as they tried to turn Harris County into a den of murderous moon beasts.

That wasn't the case, though, because for some reason whatever door was slammed shut five years ago didn't stay closed.

"Hey, don't cover that up. I might need it."

"What are you yammering about?" I slid into a pair of jeans, or tried to anyway. Getting dressed was easier said than done with half my body fighting me every step of the way.

At least the voice had backed off on the threats. For a moment there I was afraid I might either fall unconscious again or, worse, somehow end up in that brain cage they kept talking about.

Fortunately, no such thing had happened. Whereas when I'd first woken up, I'd found myself a prisoner within my own body, now it seemed the worst they were able to do was fight me for control of my left half.

It wasn't an ideal situation, but it could've been worse.

On the upside, the room I'd woken up in turned out to have an adjoining closet full of clean clothes. They weren't a perfect fit, but beggars couldn't be choosers.

"I'm talking about my dick, dickless," my other half replied, dragging me from my thoughts. "What if I see a hot bitch and decide to mount her? How in hell am I supposed to do that with my prick trapped behind these ... metal teeth?"

"You mean the zipper?"

"Stupid name, but I guess so."

"First off, I'm not running around with my penis hanging out, because that's both gross and illegal. Secondly, you're not mounting anyone. We ... *I'm* going to finish getting dressed. Then I'm going to figure out where I am and how to get back home."

"Is that so?" he replied, clumsily trying to undo the clasp with my left hand. Too bad for him I was a righty.

"Yes, it is," I said, slapping it away. "And then afterward ... I dunno. Maybe I'll look into therapy to rid myself of the voices inside my head."

"Oh yeah? Well, I can get some therapy too."

"Do you even know what that is?" I asked.

"Of course. It's ... um. Is it like those submarine things?"

"No. Now stop fighting and let me get dressed."

"This stuff itches."

"You're the one who said he was cold. So what's it gonna be?"

There came a faint snarl from my lips, but then my left side stopped working against me. That made the rest a whole lot easier.

I put on a pair of boots a size too big, lacing them up extra tight. Clean and dressed, I was finally ready to start looking for answers.

A cursory search of the pig room yielded an alarm clock which had fallen behind a dresser, probably while I was busy *pigging out*. Turned out it was a little past three pm. That was one mystery solved. A quick peek out the window likewise told me I was on the second floor.

Now to figure out the rest.

"Are we good?" I asked before stepping out the door. Won't lie, the thought of stairs while half my body was flailing about didn't strike me as fun.

"We are far from good, shit stain," my inner beast said, "but I'll let you take the lead, *for now*. You're just lucky I'm dog tired."

"Is that a joke?"

"No. Why?"

"Never mind." I opened the door, finding myself at the top of a landing.

Here goes nothing. "How can you be tired?" I asked, hoping to keep him distracted while I made my way down. "I just woke up."

"Exactly. *You* woke up. I've been doing all the grunt work while you were snoozing away."

"What kinda work?"

"Who the fuck do you think freed us?"

Huh? "From where?" I replied, taking each step slowly.

"Not from where, from *what*. I'm the one who saved our ass from the fucking monster that snagged your feeble excuse for a brain."

I stopped halfway down. A dim memory flickered in the back of my mind, me in a dark, dirty place. But then, just as quickly, it was gone again.

"You did? How?" I probably should've been whispering, but so far there'd been no other sounds from inside the house. Besides, my fight with that pig had been anything but quiet. Either the owners were out, or deaf as a post. "I mean, what happened?"

"As if you don't know."

"I don't!"

"Sucks to suck, kibble for brains," he replied with a chuckle as I reached the bottom no worse for the wear. "If you don't remember *the what*, that's your problem. But as for the why, that's easy. I'm a *Dominant*. Shit-heels like yourself get mind mounted, but I'm the son of a bitch who *does* the mounting."

I opened my mouth, trying to pick from a dozen different replies, but the words died on my tongue as I turned a corner into the *living room*.

And I use that term loosely.

I'd been wrong about this place being empty. The presumptive owners, a man and a woman, were indeed home. The reason they hadn't made so much as a peep, however, was as plain as the nose lying on the floor in front of me.

They'd been torn to shreds, their remains splattered across the room as surely as if they'd both been run through a woodchipper.

What the hell had happened here while I was out?

4

DOMINANT TRAITS

It wasn't too long after my first transformation when I learned there was someone else like me in town – another werewolf who remained in control when he changed.

Hobart Callahan was the younger brother of our former mayor, the one who'd ended his days swinging from a rope after the ritual ended. And yeah, it was safe to say old Hobart had a chip on his shoulder ever since.

Don't get me wrong, a part of me couldn't blame the guy. I'd probably be messed up too. But with Hobart it went deeper. He'd always been a nasty character – bad tempered, quick to anger, happy to bully anyone he thought was an easy target. His brother's death, however, only served to amplify those traits.

What I didn't know then, what I'm only starting to understand now, is that whatever allows us to retain control when we change also gives us power over those lacking said control. Sadly for me, Hobart was far quicker to realize this.

While I was still dealing with Myra dumping me like

35

ten pounds of you-know-what in a five pound bag, Hobart was busy asserting *dominance* over the werewolf pack that now called Harris County home.

I remembered the night he tried to do the same to me, as well as the surprise on both our faces when it failed.

Then...

The woods felt alive as I raced through them, nimbly vaulting over roots and sidestepping low hanging branches. I swear, it was like I could hear every cricket and chipmunk crawling through the underbrush.

I was still getting used to the sheer power of my new form. I'd never been afraid of the woods before, but I'd always had a healthy respect for them. But now, well, it was hard to explain except to say the forest almost felt like home, like I practically owned the place.

It was a heady experience that left me...

What the...?

Speaking of heady, I skidded to a halt as my head began to tingle. It felt kinda like the shock you might get from a poorly grounded light switch, save it was entirely inside my head, like a fly buzzing within my brain.

Submit. Don't try to resist. It's just the natural order of things.

Except this *fly* had a voice attached to it.

Freaked out, I gave my head a good shake, wondering if maybe there'd been a few bad mushrooms in the gravy I'd had with dinner.

The strange buzzing subsided as quickly as it hit me, leaving me wondering what could have caused such a...

That's when I saw *him*. A black-furred werewolf was leaning against a nearby tree, the expression on his rottweiler-like face nearly as surprised as my own at having been snuck up on so easily.

Where did he come from?

Whoever he was, he was as tall as me but broader, both in shoulder and his pronounced gut. A werewolf with a beer belly should've been funny, but all the hairs on the back of my neck were standing straight up, no small feat.

The other werewolf's body abruptly began to shrink, the crackle of bones rearranging themselves easily audible to my ears. Claws, fangs, and fur all receded as he changed back to his human form.

Hold on! He can control it too?

From those few who'd been willing to speak about the change they'd experienced, I'd come to the conclusion there was something different about me. Far as I was aware, I seemed to be the only one capable of changing at will.

What Dallas had described, for instance, sounded more like a typical Hollywood werewolf. He knew something had happened to him, but it was like a wet dream, his words not mine. He had a few fragmented memories leftover from his transformation, but nothing more.

That first night of the full moon, the forest had been nearly bursting with freshly transformed werewolves running wild like mindless beasts. It was a small wonder no one in town had gotten hurt. Fortunately, folks living in Appalachia seemed to have a sixth sense for knowing when it was best to lock their doors, close the shades, and ignore the strange sounds coming from outside.

Since then, I'd mostly had the woods to myself, seemingly the only monster in town not tied to the lunar cycle. Sure, I'd caught the occasional scent that left me wondering, but had chalked it up to still getting used to my new senses. Either way, the monthly cycle had been a small mercy to the others, limiting the chaos they could cause.

Or so I'd thought.

The other werewolf finished his transformation, his corpulent, six-foot-three frame causing my eyes to open even wider once I realized who it was.

Of all people, why did it have to be him?

"Well, ain't this a kick in the balls," Hobart Callahan declared, standing there naked as a meaty jaybird.

I followed his lead, changing back as well, until both of us faced each other buck-ass nude like it was the most normal thing in the world.

"That you, Mikey?" he asked, raising a thick eyebrow. "Goddamn, now this here is a real surprise. No offense, but I would've never suspected the kid who picks up my trash every Monday and Thursday would have the chops for *the gift*."

I decided to ignore the dig. "What gift?"

"To be able to control it, boy, what else? It's a rare thing to be blessed with the gift of dominance. Rare enough where I didn't expect to run into another in these parts." He let out a chuckle. "I admit it, you caught me off guard."

"The gift of ... dominance?" I echoed, my confusion no doubt evident.

"Exactly. I've got it and now it seems you do too. How else could you ignore the call when everyone else has fallen in line?"

"Hold on, are you talking about that buzzing in my ear?"

"That weren't no bee buzzing in your bonnet, Mikey. It's more, far more. We're talking instinct, pheromones, maybe even a little psychic hoodoo."

"Is that supposed to make any sense?" I asked, curious how he seemed to know so much while I was still standing on the starting block. Of course, he could've just been drunk for all I knew.

Hobart turned his head and spat. *Eww.* "I'm sure it will soon enough. See, you and me, we're a cut above the rest, a different breed, chosen by providence itself."

"To do what?"

"To dominate, of course! We lead and the rest follow. Just as nature intended."

The rest? I inclined my head. "You're talking about the other ... um ... werewolves, right?"

Hobart laughed. "Don't go saying that word like we're monsters, kid, because we ain't. This is just who we are, who we were born to be."

"I don't know about you, but I sure as heck wasn't born like this."

"That's where you're wrong, kid. You just didn't know it back then. None of us did."

"You're losing me."

"It's a long story, son." He paused to scratch his nether regions as if I needed to see that. "Too long for me to bother with. All you need to know is the Top Coven ain't got no sway over us anymore. We are finally free to be ourselves."

"Top what now?" *Oh yeah, definitely soused.*

"They're the ones who've kept us on a leash. Us, our parents, and all those who came before," he snapped, spittle flying from his mouth. "They kept us from knowing the truth about ourselves." He stepped forward and poked me in the chest. "It's why you and the rest are just figuring it out now. But that's all behind us. They've been gone going on five years now, dragged off to Hell along with all the wonder in the world."

I had no idea what he was going on about. More and more I was beginning to suspect he'd had one too many shots down at Jasper's before coming out to the woods.

"I'm talking about the Strange Days," he continued, no doubt sensing my confusion. "That's what they called it back then. You remember, right? Everyone was talking about all the weird shit going on. Monsters up in Boston turning people into trees, vampires duking it out with witches in New York, like the world had gone mad."

I nodded, remembering it all too well. It was like that old show *The X-Files* come to life. Heck, half the town had been convinced the world was about to end.

Except it hadn't.

"I remember there being a lot of nonsense thrown around," I replied. "One day the world was drowning in chaos, the next it was back to normal, like none of it had ever happened."

"Because that's what *they* wanted us to think," Hobart said. "Except something did happen. Most were too blind to realize it, but the world became a little bit dimmer afterward. Not for us, though. True, most didn't realize it at the time, but the end of the Strange Days marked the end of our servitude. No more gatherings, no more pills. You know what I'm talking about."

I nodded but held my tongue. The ritual's end was followed shortly after by his brother Merle checking out at the end of a noose. It was probably best not to say too much regarding those days.

"But now," Hobart continued, "all that was lost is back again. The wonder that is. I'm talking magic, *real* magic. I don't know how. Don't really care either. All I know is we're finally free to be our true selves and there ain't nobody who can say different."

Part of what he was saying made sense, but there was an unhinged quality to his tone, as if he knew something I didn't.

"But now's not the time to sit around licking our balls.

We gotta act and soon. If not, then our newfound freedom might be for nothing."

"What do you mean?" I replied, trying real hard not to envision him grooming himself.

"I've been hearing rumors from those in the know, that the bastards who kept us caged are back as well. It's not like it was, though. They ain't strong like they used to be, not yet, but they will be before long. We can't let that happen."

"And who are *they*?"

"The outsiders, Mikey, the ones who peddled those pills while acting like they were doing us a favor. You probably never realized it, but those weren't people."

Now I was certain alcohol was involved. "They weren't?"

"Nope. We might not be monsters, kid, but that doesn't mean the same ain't true for them. They're leeches in human skin, sucking dry everything they touch."

"Wait, are you saying they're...?"

"Vampires, boy! Do I need to spell it out for you?"

"Oh," I replied, glad he'd interrupted since I'd been going somewhere completely different. Still, I was already well aware werewolves were real, witches too. Why not vampires as well?

"Anyhow," he continued, "word's reached my ear they've got themselves a new leader, someone they think will usher in a new golden age. They call him the Progenitor and he's been working to ensure the old ways are made new again. You know what that means, don'cha?"

I didn't. Heck, I was still trying to process everything. It was a lot to take in from a naked guy rambling in the woods past the midnight hour.

"It means it's only a matter of time before they turn their attention our way again, force us beneath their heel once more. I don't know who this Progenitor is yet, but I will soon. I got people working on it. From what I hear, he might even have kin in these parts. If so, we can use that."

"Who exactly is telling you all of this?"

A sly grin crossed his face. "Never you mind. What matters is I aim to keep us free. We ain't never going back to the way it was."

"You keep saying that like we were in prison."

"That's because we were! 'Cept there weren't no bars. I'm talking about those gatherings, you hare-brained fool. Merle knew what they were, what they *really* were about, except he never had the balls to fight for us. But I do and now I've got the power to back it up."

"You need to slow down, Hobart. No offense but you're starting to sound like one of those online conspiracy nuts."

He let out a sigh. "Maybe you're right. Hell, I can't even blame you for thinking that way. Only reason I know as much as I do is because I found Merle's files. Had a whole safe full of papers he'd been hiding, secrets passed on to him by our daddy and his daddy before him."

I couldn't help the surprise on my face. "What kind of secrets?"

"Pages upon pages of pagan learnings, stuff that would make Preacher Roscoe gouge his own eyes out. And there was lots about our history too, our *real* history, not the bullshit we've been taught." He turned and spat again. "I'm starting to think I spoke too soon. Maybe I *do* need to start at the beginning, tell it to you nice and slow so you understand what I'm getting at."

At the very least he had my undivided attention. "Okay, I'm listening."

"Good, but first I need your word."

"No problem. I can keep a secret."

"I mean your word that you'll join us." He swung his arms wide, gesturing to the woods around us. "I'm talking about the pack, son. I've been gathering them since day one. Nearly got the whole lot following me. First, I tamed their beasts, made them heel to my command. But afterward I spoke with them, same as I'm talking to you, and most agree with me."

"Did you say *most?*"

Hobart let out a short laugh. "There's always gonna be a few knuckleheads who don't know what's best. Whatever. They're free to do as they please during the day. I ain't got no beef with that. Come nightfall, however, I can't abide any dissent. It's simply the way it's got to be if we want to remain free – just like the gods of old meant us to be."

By that point my mind was reeling. All I'd meant to do was enjoy a run in the woods. Instead, I found myself having a conversation with a madman as he spouted off about vampires, pagan rituals, and now primal gods.

Sadly, I was starting to suspect I'd listened for too long to back out easily. "I ... I'm willing to hear what you have to say, Hobart, but I can't promise anything beyond that."

He grinned at me but, despite being human, there was a predatory gleam in his eye that made me feel far too exposed. "That's fair, I suppose. There's just one little issue we gotta take care of first."

"And that would be?"

"Us, Mikey. We're special, *Dominants*, just like I told ya. Problem is, a pack can only have one leader. It's the way it's gotta be to ensure we stay on the right path. You get what I'm saying?"

I was beginning to. Good thing I wasn't looking to start a fight. "I think so."

"Do you now?"

I nodded. "Means you're the boss. Fine by me. I've got no interest in that sort of thing. Heck, Stucky offered to make me shift supervisor a few months back but I turned him down flat."

"Glad to hear it, kid, but I'm still gonna need a small act of supplication, something to show the rest you've submitted."

"Now hold on, I didn't say I was…"

"One oughta do it. I'll let you choose. Left or right?"

That caused me to cock my head. "Left or right what?"

"Testicle."

"What?!"

"Your balls, boy!"

"Hold on. You want one of my…?"

"By rights it should be both, at least from the history I've read, but you're still young. Might want to have kids someday. So, I figure one should be enough to satisfy tradition."

"What kind of nutjob tradition is that?"

"It's the way of our people. As has been written, a pack can only have one Dominant. Normally we're supposed to fight, but I figure we can skip all that nonsense. The gelding ain't optional, though."

"Gelding?!"

"Yeah. Sorry, son, but it's the way things gotta be. Now, I don't expect you to know this, but back in the old days the winner would geld the loser with his teeth. Fuck that shit, I say. We can do it just as easily with claws or a pocketknife."

"What? No!"

He stepped forward. "Ain't no backing out now. It's too late for that. Was too late the second I realized what you are. The pack needs to understand you've been humbled, but mere words won't do. I gotta show them proof, then I have to eat it while they watch. It's to signify your power is now mine, or some bullshit like that.

Honestly can't say I'm looking forward to it, but I'm willing to make the sacrifice if it means keeping us strong."

He wants to eat my left nut while a bunch of drooling werewolves watch.

It was so absurd it should've been hilarious.

Sadly, there was nothing funny about the look on Hobart's face as a pair of distant howls filled the night air, telling me we weren't nearly as alone as I'd thought.

5

DOA IN THE HOA

NOW…

"Earth to dipshit. Don't fall asleep on me. I already told you I'm too tired to properly steer this meat wagon you call a body."

I tried to say something, but the words wouldn't come. I was too utterly horrified by the carnage before me. What had been done to these people was … inhuman.

"Hold on, are you actually sobbing?" my inner wolf asked disgustedly. "Are you fucking for real? That's it. We're going to the kitchen. I need a knife so I can cut your dumb ass out of me."

"I'm not crying," I snapped, anger replacing shock. "I'm just … it's … look at what I, what *we* did!"

"We? There ain't no we in this equation, dickless. This is all me. I came, I saw, I turned these assholes into meat confetti."

"But why would you do something like that?"

"Why do you even care? They're just humans. They were in the way and I wasn't in the best of moods, not to mention kinda hungry. Do the math."

"Y-you *ate* them?" *You.* That was a good one. The truth was, if he'd done it, then that meant *I* was party to it. It

46

was so much worse than I'd imagined. I hadn't just chowed down on someone's pet pig, I'd helped myself to some of the *long* variety too.

I wanted to retch but once again my horrific meal seemed content to stay down. Damn my werewolf constitution.

"Not all of them," my inner demon continued, as if nothing were amiss. "I mean, look at all that's left. Shit, you could probably still make a full person if you glued all the pieces together."

"That's not funny."

"Fuck if it's not. Oh lighten up, pupcake. It was only a few mouthfuls at most. Frankly, you humans taste like shit. But not real shit. That tastes like…"

"I don't want to know!"

"Fine. Be a crying little pussy. See if I care. Besides, it's not like it mattered anyway."

"How can you say that?"

"Because it was too late by then."

"Of course it was too late! You … shredded them."

"I'm not talking about these assholes, shit for brains," my obviously deranged alter ego replied. "I meant me. I've been running on fumes for the better part of a day. Putting all those miles between me and that roach motel of a city takes a lot out of a wolf."

"I have no idea what that even means," I replied, unable to look away from the mess before me.

He let out a sigh. "Why do you think you woke up when you did? It's because I couldn't hold my form anymore. Hell, I just barely had enough to chow down on that succulent meat log upstairs before you started in with your bullshit."

I tried to ignore his callousness, a fairly easy thing since I was busy envisioning the multistate manhunt that would soon be looking for me. "Oh God, what are we gonna do?"

"There you go with that *we* shit again. What's done is done. No point in crying over spilled entrails. So, stop your whining and start acting like you deserve to be a part of me."

"Don't give me that! You murdered these people."

"And?"

"And ... you can't do that!"

"I can and will, especially when they fucking deserve it."

"What?" I replied. "Just because you think they're..."

My left hand clamped shut over my mouth, muffling the rest of what I had to say.

I was still trying to pry it off with my right when it released its hold.

"Are you calm now?" The creature inside me had dropped the aggression in favor of a patronizing tone.

"No, I am not calm. Far from it."

"That's nice, but do us both a favor and shut the fuck up anyway, okay? It's time for me to talk and you to listen."

"I..."

"Or I could just bite our tongue in half and be done with this conversation. Your choice."

It was an effort, but I managed to keep my comments to myself.

"Good, because I'm being serious here," he said after several long moments. "Breaking free from that *thing* in those tunnels took a lot of effort, and that's not even counting how many of its minions I had to cut through getting away. Talk about a mess. Then it took me forever to figure out the... What do you call them? They've got these metal bars on the ground and these big ... tubes on wheels running through them."

"The subway?" I replied.

"Sure. That works. Anyway, getting through the subway was a real bitch. First of all, it's like the whole place smells like one giant ass. Secondly, those tubes aren't the only thing living down there. So, I had to slice and dice my way through those too."

"Are you talking about rats?"

"Do rats normally grow bigger than people?"

"No, not really."

"Then probably not rats."

"Okay, and the point of this trip down memory lane?" I asked, trying my damnedest not to gag at the reek starting to permeate my nostrils.

"My point is it took a lot out of me. More than I thought and believe me that ain't something I care to admit. All I was trying to do was get back to someplace familiar, my territory."

"Your territory?"

"Yeah, you know. The woods near that shithole where you live. Problem is, the sun came up before I could make much headway."

"So?"

"So, it's harder to maintain my true form during the day."

"It is?"

"Of course it is, you dumb fuck. Wait. How have you not noticed that yet?"

"I ... actually haven't had much reason to change forms during the day."

"Seriously?"

"I mean, once or twice in front of the mirror maybe."

He sighed disgustedly. "My point remains. And no, don't ask stupid questions like why that is. I don't fucking know. It just is, okay. Anyway, I reverted into this pink skinsuit you call a body."

"I don't remember that happening."

"Of course you don't. You weren't awake yet. Hell, you were quiet as a mouse, probably stuck in some happy little dream about Hobart cornholing you good and proper."

I gritted my teeth. "You have about thirty seconds before I find a phone and call 9-1-1."

"And yelling out random numbers does what?"

"It's ... never mind. Just keep going."

"I will. Now shut the fuck up and let me finish," he said. "Where was I? Oh yeah. I was in this body but still in full control. Won't lie, I'd thought that was it, that you were locked away in the same brain cage I'd escaped from. Ah, such a nice fantasy."

I tried to take control of my mouth, but he kept talking over me.

"Relax. I'm getting back to it. So there I was, walking along the side of the road, trying to get my bearings because this nose of yours ain't worth shit, when suddenly one of those ... um ... station wagon things pulled up alongside me."

I was tempted to ask how he knew what a station wagon was but not a subway, but that probably wasn't super important right then. "You were on the side of the road after changing back? Wearing what exactly?"

"Just this hairless flesh suit. Why?"

"Forget I asked." Guess I could add public indecency to my growing list of crimes.

"So, the pair of monkeys inside rolled down the windows and asked if I was okay. I was still figuring out what to say, being that talking is a relatively new concept for me, when they unlocked the doors and told me to get in."

"Just like that?"

"Yep. They said they'd give me something to eat."

"So, you just got in the car with them?"

"Sure. Why wouldn't I?"

"I'm gonna assume you've never heard of stranger danger."

"That a friend of yours?"

"Just keep going," I said, stifling a sigh.

"They stopped at one of those convenience stores you humans seem to like. I stayed in the car with the male while his bitch ran inside..."

"Woman."

"That's what I said. A few minutes later she came out with a bag of food and handed it to me."

I shook my head. "Let me guess. You ate it without question?"

"Of course. Can't say I'm a fan of the way you monkeys like to ruin meat, but I was starving by then."

I finally let out the sigh I'd been holding, having an inkling where this was headed. "What happened next?"

"I got sleepy, so I curled up in the back and took a nap."

Unbelievable. It was like listening to an overly trusting toddler. "And then?"

"I woke up right here, except I was stuck. I couldn't move because they had me tied to a chair."

"Is that when *this* happened?" I gestured toward the carnage.

"Not quite. I was still waking up when these two chucklefucks sauntered back in dressed like vets."

"As in soldiers?"

"As in veterinarians. You know. Blue gowns, masks over their faces, that sort of thing."

"You mean like doctors?"

"Sure, whatever. Anyway, the male starts waving a knife in my face while his mate explained how they were going to slice me up and feed my dick to Cuddles, whatever the fuck that is. Now that I think about it, they might've been trying to scare me."

"Ya think?" I replied. "Let me guess, it didn't work."

"What do you think, genius?"

I forced myself to take in the grisly scene, all of it this time. Sure enough, scattered among the gore and viscera I spied splintered wood and snapped wire ties. Further in, I spotted the blue-grey remnants of a shredded surgical gown followed by the glint of metal from within a puddle of congealed blood, a knife blade.

Holy crap. He's telling the truth.

As for *Cuddles*, well, I had a feeling that was who I'd met upstairs. "What happened next?"

"*I* did," he said. "I still didn't have a lot in me, but that little nap must've recharged me a bit."

"It wasn't a nap. They drugged you."

"Who gives a shit? Either way, it was enough to change back to my true self, for a few minutes anyway."

"That's why you did it," I said mostly to myself, feeling a tiny amount of relief. "You were acting in self-defense."

"Yep. Don't get me wrong. It was loads of fun too. Gods, you should've seen the looks on their faces ... for the two seconds it took me to tear them off."

And of course he had to ruin it.

"As for what happened afterward," he continued, "I'm guessing whatever they put in that food to mess with me must've somehow had the opposite effect on you."

"Oh?"

"Like I said, I just barely had enough strength to hold my form for the time it took to puree these two. After that... You know the rest."

I actually didn't, but could put two and two together. After he finished here, he'd must've heard something upstairs – Cuddles the pig I'm guessing. He went looking for it and must've changed back in the process. That must've been right around the point where I started to come to.

I'd missed the main event, thank goodness but, lucky me, had managed to catch the encore.

Although, considering the horrors still waiting in the living room, the more important question was how long it would be before the cops showed up for my final curtain call.

6

HOUSE CLEANING

If I was hearing things correctly, a pair of serial killers on the lookout for their next victim had managed to pick up a psychotic werewolf instead. Talk about a plot twist. Honestly, this was the sort of lazy writing that would cause me to turn off a horror movie halfway through.

And yet it had apparently happened.

I had no way of knowing how much matched what my inner wolf described. After all, he seemed the very definition of an unreliable narrator. All the same, there was no denying the slaughter staring me in the face contained enough *clues* to substantiate his claim.

The truly insane part, though, was this was starting to feel like a best-case scenario.

I mean, what if the people who'd picked him up had been regular folks with kids? Mind you, I'm not sure why anyone with a car full of children would stop to pick up a naked stranger on the side of the road.

Regardless, even if these two had been a modern-day Manson Family the fact remained, I was in way over my head.

"What do we do?" I asked, knowing I'd probably regret it.

"You really have a fondness for that W word, don't you?" my inner demon replied.

Speaking of which, I really needed to find something better to call him, although that was low priority for the moment.

"I don't know what *you're* going to do," he continued, "but I've got my part all figured out."

"And that would be?"

"Simple. I'm gonna curl up in our shared noggin and get me some shuteye."

"What? You can't do that!"

"Watch me."

"But ... why?"

"I already told you, pupcake, I'm beat. Much as I'm certain you're gonna fuck this up for us both, I can barely keep my eyes open, or at least the one I seem to have control over."

"But we have to find a way to..."

"I'm not asking, numb-nuts, I'm telling you. It's either sack out or pass out, but since one of us needs to be awake to deal with this shit, I guess that leaves you. And no, I'm not happy about it either."

"That makes two of us."

"Just try not to fuck it up *too* badly." He fell silent for several long seconds before adding, "Oh, but first a warning. I am a real light sleeper these days. You try to stuff me back into that brain cage, hell you do *anything* to tick me off, and I will tear off your arm and beat your half to death with it. Am I clear?"

I wasn't even sure how to respond to that. I had no idea how I'd stuffed him into this so-called cage to begin with, so it's not like I had the first clue how to do it again.

Don't get me wrong. He deserved it. This wasn't like

when I'd first gotten Spud and didn't have the heart to crate him. This creature sharing brain space with me was quite obviously a psychotic monster.

A monster...

But was that truly who he was or because I'd somehow kept him locked up against his will? It was a classic nature versus nurture problem.

I let out a heavy breath. If this was actually my fault then didn't I owe him more than locking him back up and throwing away the key? Didn't he deserve a chance to prove he could be more than a murderous animal?

I glanced once more at the blood and guts painting the living room, shuddering despite myself.

Regardless, the fact remained. I had no idea how to lock him away again and figuring it out didn't seem like the wisest use of my time.

"Fine," I said at last. "You win."

I am so gonna regret this.

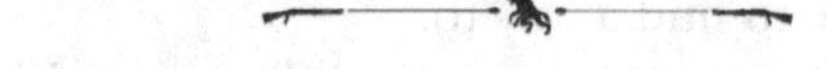

It's hard to describe the sudden change other than I felt *normal* again, like I was simply me, the guy I'd been before ... whatever happened back in Manhattan.

In some ways it was like being in a crowded bar and not realizing how loud it really was until you stepped outside.

In short, I was once again alone inside my own head.

To test this theory, I hopped up and down on my left leg before sticking the index finger of that hand up my nostril, all of it with no resistance.

Then, a scant moment later, I realized how stupid I looked while a horrific crime scene sat barely a dozen feet away.

A part of me wondered how light a sleeper my inner wolf was. Like, what could wake up a creature who existed only within my own subconscious? Would physical stimuli do it – pain, noise, or some combination of the above? Or was it all mental, as in I should be careful not to think too loudly?

If so, that could be problematic as my mind wasn't exactly a quiet place these days, especially not there smack dab in the middle of Murder Mansion.

I had neither answers nor desire to test those boundaries. Problem was, I also had no frame of reference. Was I expected to walk around on eggshells, like the parent of a newborn? That didn't seem particularly expedient considering my current crisis.

That settled it.

He'd caused all of this, only to leave me high and dry to deal with it. I took it as my cue to worry more about myself and less about showing consideration to a napping werewolf.

If he wakes up, that's his problem.

Okay, it *was* still mine too, but I could only worry about so much. And right then, I had a far more pressing issue to deal with. I needed to get the hell out of there in a way that wouldn't leave me the prime suspect in a massive manhunt.

But how to do so without...?

I stopped dead in my tracks, no pun intended, as I realized that maybe death was the answer I was searching for. No, I didn't mean jumping in front of a bus. I meant the two *victims* splattered about the living room, or more precisely their original intent.

Good thing I'd watched *Dexter* back when it first aired.

If my inner beast was telling the truth, the couple

who'd picked him up were stone-cold killers. After all, the way they'd abducted him – *us* – told me this probably wasn't a spur of the moment decision on their part. Again, assuming he wasn't making things up, it pointed to the high probability they'd done this before.

Sick as that was, it might also be my salvation. Because if so then surely that meant they had the means to cover their own tracks.

That seemed a logical assumption to start with. Good thing too, since I had absolutely nothing else to go on.

I got supremely lucky in the back of the pantry, finding a hidden stash of latex gloves, masks, more surgical scrubs, and a few gallons of overly-caustic cleaning solution.

Either these guys were even bigger germophobes than me or I was right. Whatever the case, not only did I feel far less skeeved out with another layer of protection between me and the ick, I had enough supplies to get started.

Tempting as it was to try, I didn't have time to scrub this place from top to bottom. The mess still *congealing* in the living room was beyond anything my experience as a trash collector had prepared me for.

What mattered more was erasing any trace that I'd ever been there. However, while that might've made my task easier, it was still no walk in the park.

It wasn't long before the air became thick with the reek of acid cleaner. Not the healthiest stuff to breathe, but I didn't dare risk opening any doors or windows.

Instead, I took several breaks to keep from passing out, giving me the opportunity to be a little nosy.

One thing you quickly learn working as a garbageman, other than most people are disgusting slobs, is how careless folks can be when it comes to throwing important stuff away. Over the last few years, I'd found social security statements, checks, credit cards, and more just sitting at the top of people's trash cans. Good thing for them I was an honest guy.

That said, some discarded mail in the kitchen seemed to confirm the owners, Robert and Nora Chadworth, were the only ones living there, aside from Cuddles of course.

The Chadworths. Tell me that isn't the perfectly normal sounding name a pair of psycho killers would have.

While on the surface things in their unhinged little home appeared mostly normal, the closer I looked the darker things became.

Heavy blackout curtains were hung from every window on the ground floor, giving the place a claustrophobic feel. Paranoid too, as a few quick peeks from the upper floor suggested this house of horrors was situated far back on a secluded lot.

Further exploration revealed an attached garage opposite the living room. Inside sat the vehicle my werewolf had mentioned. Smart. The Chadworths had been able to drag his unconscious butt inside with no risk of being seen.

Won't lie. I stared at the car for a good long while, imagining just driving away from this nightmare. Heck, the keys were easy enough to find, hanging from a friendly little hook next to the front door. However, leaving no trace that I'd been here was going to be tricky enough without also adding grand theft auto to the mix.

Instead, I used the opportunity to wipe down the back seat for prints.

That still left the living room itself. Already I could feel my left eye twitching, although not because of my inner beast this time.

I wasn't sure how much of a problem fingerprints

would be in the utter disarray left behind, but I spied tufts of brown fur lying in the congealed pools of blood.

Could those be traced back to me? I had no clue, but there was no way I could take any chances.

Instead, I grabbed another gallon of acid cleaner while hoping Rob and Nora knew what they were doing when it came to destroying evidence.

It was vile, disgusting work, made even worse by the thick fumes. But it was also cathartic in a strangely disturbing way. Cleaning up a mess introduced order into chaos. It was one of the reasons I'd become a trash collector to begin with.

As far back as my childhood I'd never liked germs or filth. Heck, playing in the mud had totally skeeved me out. But eventually I came to the realization that I could either spend my life wrapped in plastic and slathered in hand sanitizer, or I could choose to tackle my fears, desensitize myself in a bid to keep my phobias under control.

The best part? It was a strategy that had worked. Or at least it had until I found myself ankle deep in Robert and Nora Chadworth.

GAH! So disgusting!

The loss of life was bad enough, but it was like my inner beast had acted like a giant toddler in a highchair – playing with his food in the most horrific manner possible.

Don't imagine what they tasted like. Don't you dare!

Much as I wanted to run screaming back to the shower, though, I couldn't stop. I needed to see this through so I could finally get out of there.

Sadly, I still had no idea where *there* actually was.

Sure, the Chadworths probably had a cell phone somewhere, but it's not like I was about to search through their gooey remains looking for it.

That meant waiting until dark, then hoping there were no neighbors close enough to spot me making my escape. My best bet would be transforming into my wolf form and then...

I paused in the middle of sweeping a pile of intestines into a plastic bag.

What if changing woke up my inner wolf? More importantly, what if he ended up in control again?

If there were any neighbors nearby, I could easily end up in this same situation again – except next time my victims might not be serial killers.

No. I can't test it out unless I'm sure it's safe.

The only problem was I couldn't be sure that was a promise I could keep.

My wolf form was stronger, faster, and had the advantage of being able to see in the dark. In order to make a clean getaway, I might have to...

Clunk.

I inclined my head at the sound the push broom made as it hit the floor. *What the*? Curious, I lifted my foot and took a step, once more hearing a hollow *thud* from below.

As drenched in blood as everything still was, I couldn't just ignore it.

Don't think about what you're about to do, just do it.

I bent low, then used the fingers of my double-gloved hand to feel along the floorboards until... *There*!

It wasn't much, just a shallow indentation with a small lip for a handhold. A trapdoor!

Judging by the overturned end table close by, it was easy to guess it was probably normally hidden from view.

The bigger question now was where it led to and whether I was going to be stupid enough to press my luck and investigate.

Oh, who am I kidding?

I could either keep mopping up a crime scene I had zero chance of fully concealing, or see if maybe there was something below I could use to my advantage.

At this point what else did I have to lose?

7

THE PLUNDER DOWN UNDER

I wasn't sure what was worse – the open trapdoor leading down into inky darkness, or the congealed blood on the floor which immediately started to dribble down into it, making it seem more like a hungry mouth.

Needless to say, that wasn't helping my motivation to see what might be down there.

I took a deep breath and tried to push the fear away. This was ridiculous. I was a freaking werewolf, one of the so-called things that go bump in the night.

In the past couple months I'd faced off against others of my kind, my witchy ex-girlfriend, and even an economy-sized sea monster. Sure, that last one hadn't gone in my favor, but that wasn't the point.

I was the predator here, *me*. Not the two dead psychos who owned this house, and certainly not the well-fed porker they'd kept as a pet. A cellar wasn't something to be afraid of.

And yet I wanted nothing more than to shut the trapdoor and forget it ever existed.

Stop acting like an idiot.

I took a deep breath and steadied myself, glad my inner wolf was taking a catnap. He would've surely had no shortage of opinions, none of which would've helped the matter.

I tried to logically assess the situation instead. A narrow wooden staircase led down below. The light up here didn't penetrate far, illuminating nothing more than a patch of concrete floor at the bottom.

That wasn't so bad. It didn't look much different than any other basement or root cellar, minus the pooling blood of course.

More importantly, I couldn't detect any sound from below. I took a moment to sniff the air, but that just made me cough thanks to all the caustic cleaner.

It was a pointless endeavor anyway. My human nose was somewhat more sensitive than a normal person's, but it was nowhere close to its intensity in my alternate form.

As a werewolf, scents weren't just heightened they were a whole new dimension of input. One whiff would create a kaleidoscope of colors and images in my brain, vivid enough to navigate by. Heck, sometimes it was almost more information than I could process.

Changing was out of the question, though. Not only was there the danger I'd mentioned before, but my other form was simply too large. When fully transformed, I stood over a foot taller with about three hundred pounds of muscle added to my frame.

I had no idea where that extra mass came from or returned to once I changed back, but had a feeling the answer was the sort of thing that would give a physicist a stroke.

Regardless, no way was I fitting through the opening as a werewolf.

On the flipside, heading down as I currently was brought a definite risk of slipping in the blood and breaking my neck at the bottom. I wasn't sure whether that would kill me or not, but it would almost certainly ruin my day.

For a while anyway.

I'd seen other werewolves grievously injured, only for them to quickly recover a short time later. Not only were we pretty durable, but the change from one form to another seemed to trigger an enhanced healing burst – one capable of fixing even major wounds in mere minutes.

I was pretty sure there were limits, though. For instance, Hobart's *generous* offer to eat one of my testicles had come with the implication it wouldn't be growing back afterward.

Then...

"Don't take any offense at this, Hobart, b-but ... I think I'm gonna pass."

"Come again?" he replied, as if we were having a pleasant dinner conversation rather than standing naked in the dark woods.

I let out a nervous sigh, sensing he was trying to bait me. Into what, though, I wasn't sure. Regardless, hearing the howls of other werewolves, ones that should've been powerless with the full moon still three weeks away, had unnerved me. I was beginning to suspect I was in over my head.

All the same, following Hobart's rant about dominance, I had a feeling that showing any weakness would be tantamount to handing over my left nut.

"You know darned well what I mean," I said, hoping to impress upon him that I was no threat, "but I'll spell it out if you need me to. I have no interest being in charge of anything, much less out here. But that doesn't mean I'm letting you eat my balls."

Are we really having this conversation?

"I want you to think real hard on this, Mikey," he replied, dropping the friendly cadence. "We ain't like the rest. Our gift comes with power the others in the pack don't have, but with that power also comes a terrible burden. Think of it like a beehive. Can only be one queen. No exceptions."

I had no idea whether that was true or not, but it's not like I had my phone to check Wikipedia. "Fine. You want to be the queen, be my guest. I'll buzz off somewhere else, but you ain't eating my honey."

Hobart raised a quizzical brow, probably trying to make sense of my nervous pun vomit. Then his gaze became hard as stone. "I think I'm beginning to understand."

"You are?"

"Yeah. You might have the gift, but you ain't got the stones to use it. Because if you did, you'd feel the call, same as me. Hell, it's no wonder Myra ditched you like a bad habit."

His words hit me in the gut like a bowling ball, the pain of our breakup still way too fresh. "Myra doesn't have anything to do with this," I warned. "She and I ... well, it ain't none of your bee's wax."

Okay, maybe it was time to drop the bee puns. The moment had passed.

"You may think that's true, Mikey, but it's not. See, Myra's got what you and her sisters don't, ambition."

"You do know she's an only child, right?"

"Her coven sisters, you idiot. You think she's the only witch in these parts?"

"Wait. How do you know she's a...?"

"Power knows power, kid. I've got it, so does she. She

sees what you don't, that these last few weeks represent a chance for us to rewrite the status quo, to change our lot in life. You might be content to empty my trash twice a week, but she and I intend to grab that brass ring and ride this fucker to the very top."

He was losing me again. I had no idea what he was talking about, but the fact he and Myra had come to some sort of understanding seemed clear enough. As to what that might entail...

"You hear them, don't you?" Hobart asked, cocking his head as another distant howl echoed through the night air. "You do know what it means, right?"

I actually didn't. Before this night, I'd thought myself the only one who could change at will. Then, seeing Hobart, I figured it was just the two of us. But now...

He grinned, no doubt enjoying my confusion. "I know what you're thinking, boy. How is it any of the others are out here with only half a moon in the sky?"

He wasn't wrong, but it seemed unwise to admit my ignorance.

"That right there is *my* doing, kid. I'm the one who set them free."

"You did?!" I tried to make my response sound casual and failed miserably. Heck, I probably wouldn't have sounded more surprised had he claimed to be my long-lost sister.

"Yep, and you could probably do it too, that is if you weren't some slack-mouthed pretender to the throne."

"Hold on. There's no need for name calling..."

"But doing it by myself takes too much time," he interrupted. "It ain't quick like I need it to be."

"What isn't quick?"

"But it will be soon enough," Hobart continued, talking over me. "Myra's working on a way even as we speak. She thinks she knows how to make it happen, to unleash them all at will."

Unleash them? All at once it made sense. The other werewolves. Hobart could somehow force them to change outside the cycle of the moon, but it sounded like it took some effort. That's why I was only hearing a couple of them out there. But if Myra was working on a way to fix that...

"She's a clever one," Hobart explained, his voice dropping an octave, "far more clever than you ever gave her credit for. Ain't too hard on the eyes either. That's why I'm letting her join the pack."

"What?"

"I could use a lieutenant, especially one who knows the things she does. Her sisters, on the other hand, well, I'm starting to realize they ain't got what it takes. And that means they gotta go. *Shame they ain't the only ones.*"

I wanted to ask what he meant, but the gravelly tone of his voice in those final words made it crystal clear. Mere moments later, his body began to change once again, growing larger, stronger, and infinitely more deadly.

I was never the fastest learner but I wasn't a complete moron either.

Realizing any hope of talking this through was over and done with, I reached inside myself and triggered my own change.

Sadly, Hobart had a head start. He finished the transformation from man to wolf beast while I was only at about three quarters of the way there. It wasn't a huge advantage, but it was more than enough as he charged forward with a snarl.

I was vulnerable and he knew it.

Good thing I did too.

My power might not have been on par with his yet, but I was still a lot stronger than I'd been just minutes earlier. I just barely sidestepped his attack, managing to give him a shove as he raced past, using his own momentum to send him careening into a bramble patch.

Argh!

It was a good try on my part. Too bad I'd caught a pair of claw slashes in the side for my troubles. Trust me when I say those did not feel wonderful.

Thankfully they were nowhere close to fatal as my own transformation completed itself.

Every instinct inside of me screamed I should launch myself at Hobart and tear him to pieces while I had the chance.

I ignored them all and took off running instead.

He must've taken exception to that because it wasn't long before his shouting voice followed after me, my super sensitive ears catching his words despite the distance I managed to put between us.

"You'll keep running if you're smart, boy! You ain't no Dominant! You ain't nothing! These woods are mine. You cross me again and I'll make sure you regret it!"

Now...

I chuckled, despite there being nothing remotely funny about the memory. I'd stood up to Hobart that night, and it hadn't been the last time either. And yet there I was, refusing to face the *terror* of a simple set of stairs.

Hobart and Myra were both still problems I needed to deal with, but in order to do that I needed to get back home.

That's what finally got me moving. Steeling myself best I could, I slowly made my way down the stairs on legs that felt like rubber.

The scents finally began to change once I'd descended

far enough for my head to be below floor level. There was still the caustic stench of cleaner, true, but beneath it all, just barely perceptible to my human nose, was something else, a rottenness which sent a shiver down my spine.

I paused in my descent, unsure if I wanted to go further. However, that proved to be my saving grace as I spotted a pull chain barely a foot away.

Thank goodness!

I grabbed hold and gave it a yank. The darkness instantly retreated as a high wattage bulb flared to life, leaving me feeling more than a little foolish.

As I reached the bottom, nearly slipping on the now slick concrete floor, I took in my surroundings. The basement was unfinished, mostly concrete and support pillars. The floor was only broken up by a double wide French drain covered by a stainless-steel grate.

In front of me stood a heavy worktable. A large duffel bag was shoved into one corner, but it was the space above it which caught my eye. Rows of hooks ran the length of the wall, from which hung a seriously unhealthy collection of knives, chisels, and sawblades.

A spigot protruded from the wall right next to the workspace. A contractor grade hose was attached to it, one almost certainly meant to work in conjunction with the drain.

Oh boy.

To my left were the only other items of interest in sight, but they were more than enough to paint a gruesome picture. First was a column of metal shelves attached to the wall, upon which stood rows of gallon-sized plastic bottles.

Please be detergent and fabric softener.

No such luck as I spied labels warning of the dangers of hydrofluoric acid.

Then, next to the shelves, rounding out this nightmare, was, of course, a stack of quicklime.

Yeah, it was probably safe to say the Chadworths hadn't been using this room for arts and crafts.

That appeared to be it. Far as I could tell, the only way out was back up. Much as I didn't want to dwell on it, I had a feeling this space had seen double duty as both prison and torture chamber.

A prison... That's it!

Crazy as the idea sounded, it dawned on me this place might represent an opportunity to test my transformation without the risk of anyone getting hurt. Or at least anyone who hadn't already been hurt.

There's only one way to find out.

Rather than risk overthinking things and realizing what a stupid idea this probably was, I clambered back up the stairs intent on closing the trapdoor, only to notice something odd.

Why is the lock on this side?

Everything about this basement screamed inescapable prison, so then why put the keys to freedom on this side?

The only ones who could answer that were scattered in bloody chunks upstairs. Far more important was the latch appeared to be solid.

That, combined with the narrowness of the stairway, would hopefully hinder my escape just in case my worst fears proved true.

Good as I'm gonna get, I suppose.

Crossing my fingers, I locked myself in, the heavy *clack* of the deadbolt telling me it meant business. Whether it was enough to hold an enraged werewolf, however, remained to be seen.

I looked around once more, debating whether I needed to do anything else. Hopefully my inner wolf wasn't stupid enough to chew on bottles of corrosive acid.

Werewolf constitution or not, that didn't sound like fun.

Realizing it was time to crap or get off the pot, I undressed — stripping off first the gloves and surgical smock, then the clothes I'd purloined, all of them now liberally stained with gore.

I set them on the work bench alongside the duffel bag, not quite wanting to know what was inside.

Last chance to back out.

Sadly, this was a question I couldn't afford to not know the answer to.

Would I still be myself afterward, possessing the precious control that stood between me and becoming yet another of Hobart's minions? Or was I destined to learn he was right all along, and there was room for only one Dominant in Harris County?

It was time to find out one way or the other.

8

TUNNEL OF TERROR

My buddy Dallas had explained to me what it was like when he changed.

He said that looking at the full moon was like staring right into the face of God himself. He explained it as a moment of pure rapture, the light growing ever brighter until it consumed everything he could see, hear, and smell. After that, there was nothing but bits and pieces. He'd wake up with some memories, but they were like a vivid fever dream.

It wasn't disturbing, though. Instead, he found it strangely satisfying – like being constipated for several days, then finally taking a good dump.

Again, his words not mine. Dallas is a good guy, but a poet he is not.

And yes, that is one hundred percent at odds with what Hollywood would have us believe. To them, the process of turning into a werewolf was both painful and traumatizing. If that were the case, though, then I'd have expected the suicide rate around Harris County to have skyrocketed in the last three months. Except it hadn't.

Regardless, the change was somewhat different for me.

For starters, I was awake and aware as my body shifted forms. Won't lie. I did it in front of the mirror once or twice and it sure as heck looked painful. Except it wasn't, not entirely. There was a little discomfort, don't get me wrong, but it was heavily numbed.

I'm no scientist but my personal theory was the change was kicked off by my brain releasing a boatload of chemicals: adrenaline, endorphins, stuff like that. Enough to dope me up until my body finished rearranging itself.

Or maybe it was just magic. It's not like I could call a doctor and ask. All I knew was it didn't hurt and at no point did I lose consciousness.

At least that *had* been the case. I had no idea what to expect now. My only solace was hoping I was boxed up tight.

From what I'd observed, regular werewolves required one of three things to initiate the change.

A full moon was obviously one of them, a small mercy for those who wanted to cause as little chaos as possible.

The next method involved Dominants such as myself, or so Hobart had claimed. I'd never actually tried it myself, but he was able to, through sheer will alone, force others to transform outside the lunar cycle. Thankfully, it was supposedly an arduous process, something he could only do to a few werewolves at a time.

Had that been all, my worries wouldn't be so ... worrisome.

However, not too long after that first confrontation with Hobart, Myra had apparently made her breakthrough.

Magic.

She'd somehow figured out how to whammy up an

illusion of a full moon in a way that set off the change for everyone present. Needless to say, the fact she seemed happy to cast this spell at Hobart's whim had done little to mend the growing rift between us.

But, once again, it was different for me. Heck, it wasn't even difficult for me to get it going. I merely focused and willed it to happen. It wasn't quite as easy as flipping a light switch, but it wasn't some torturous *American Werewolf in London* ordeal either.

I'd stalled long enough. I took a deep breath and tried to force my fear away as I focused on the things which seemed to make it easier for me – envisioning the moon, the woods, and that heady feeling of running free.

Change.

For a moment nothing happened, making me wonder if I was now beholden to the same rules as the rest. But then I realized I wasn't nearly as focused as I was pretending to be.

All right, take two.

A few more deep breaths to clear my head and ... this time I could feel it happening. First came a rush of brain chemicals, making me feel all tingly inside. It was followed by the crackle of flesh and bone rearranging itself, growing ever louder as my senses increased in acuity.

My perspective began to change as my body grew in height and weight. Fortunately, my strength in this new form was more than enough to offset the difference.

It was a pity I couldn't be this strong all the time. Would make bulk pickups at work a heck of a lot easier.

My job was the least of my worries, though. If I was going to lose control, it would be right ... about ... *now!*

"*Achoo!*"

However, rather than black out, I sneezed.

"*Achoo!*"

Then I did it again.

Crap! Totally forgot about that.

Before today, there'd been only one downside to me being a werewolf – discovering I was allergic to my own fur.

I kid you not. It's like fate had a sense of humor.

Fortunately, it only seemed to affect my human nose. As my body continued to change, the sneezing mercifully dried up while the myriad scents of the basement became magnified – assaulting my nostrils with far more detail than I was able to discern just moments before.

It was the space of seconds for me to understand.

You freaking monsters!

This basement wasn't a prison so much as a garbage disposal, used by the Chadworths once they were finished with their victims. The stench rising from the drain confirmed this, acid mixed with a disgusting *puree* of human remains, too melded together for me to tell how many or for how long this had been going on.

It made me want to vomit. It was even worse than...

Wait. I'm still me.

That realization helped push away thoughts of the horrors in the drainpipe below.

I was still in control, still conscious.

To make sure, I spun around, swung my arms, and even jumped – smacking my head against the ceiling. *Ouch!* Yeah, I probably needed to remember I had a lot less headroom in this form.

I waited a minute, then two, taking stock of myself. Thankfully, everything felt like it should've, my mind, my body, and my...

Crap! Spoke too soon.

Even as I rejoiced, the hair on my arms began to slowly recede, as if I'd willed myself back.

What the heck?

The second I refocused on it, though, it stopped, reversing until I was fully a werewolf again.

That's when I realized I could *feel* it.

There was a strange weariness deep inside, hovering at the periphery of my conscious mind, an impulse to change back to my human form, almost as if what I was doing was somehow ... *unnatural.*

It wasn't overwhelming, but it was there all the same, making me realize my body could potentially change back on its own. Heck, it seemed as if it wanted to.

Panic began to set in as all thoughts turned to the sleeping monster inside my head, wondering if this was him telling me my mind wasn't welcome in this body, that from this day forward I was destined to be...

Day!

Just like that, I remembered what he'd told me earlier about how it was harder for him to hold this form, *his form*, during the day. It had been some time since I'd started cleaning, but I was fairly sure the sun was still out, albeit probably not for much longer.

There was also the fact that before today I'd never really changed into my werewolf form during daylight hours for more than a few minutes at a time. I mean, it seemed an unnecessary risk, especially in an apartment just barely big enough for me and my dog. Not to mention, Spud seemed to think I was a giant chew toy in this form.

He was a great pupper but not the sharpest tool in the shed.

Outside of that, though, transforming at night had simply felt more ... natural.

All right, calm down. Crisis averted.

I was still me, still able to think, and still in control of my actions.

The question now was what that meant for the voice inside my head. Was he still there waiting to wake up? Or was it too much to hope he was maybe gone for good – a one-time quirk brought about by whatever that monster in the Hudson had done to me.

All I knew was I currently felt like myself, with no alien presence hovering over my shoulder to...

What the?!

I spun as my senses abruptly blared a warning.

Heck, I wasn't even sure what I was reacting to. It was simply ... instinct, I suppose. Instinct or not, no one was there. I was still alone.

Great. Hopefully I wasn't dealing with ghosts now. Talk about more crap I didn't need.

That's when I noticed it, a slight current across my fur, barely perceptible but there nonetheless.

Hold on. Is that fresh air?

I took another sniff, pushing past the acid and the rot until... *There!* Beneath it was grass, trees, dirt, and more. But from where?

I forced my mind to go blank and let my senses take the lead. It was .... coming from ... the direction of those shelves of acid? Much as I didn't want to, I turned that way and took a good long whiff.

The fumes were strong but thankfully not nearly as bad as I'd have guessed. It was another instant for me to realize most of the containers were either empty or close to it. Either the Chadworths had an aversion to recycling, had recently gone on a crazed killing spree, or ... they were decoys.

Another scent caught my attention. Beneath the acid, invisible to anyone who didn't have a werewolf's olfactory prowess, was another odor, a familiar one.

WD-40?

But why would someone need to lubricate a shelf set into the wall?

Unless...

As I stepped that way, I noted the smell of lubricant was heavier on one side.

Oh yeah. This was getting more suspicious by the moment.

I grabbed the *unscented* side and gave a quick pull, noting it had no give. Fortunately, I had more oomph at my disposal than most people.

I put my back into it and there came the squeal of metal, but it wasn't from the shelving itself. It was more like ... a latch giving way. There came a metallic *pop* and suddenly the *shelf* swung open on well-oiled hinges, scattering plastic containers in every direction.

I spied the now broken lock, telling me there was probably a hidden release I hadn't noticed. Oh well, patience wasn't a virtue I had in ample supply right then.

Someone had chiseled a wide hole in the concrete behind the hidden door. Beyond, a claustrophobic-looking dirt tunnel led off into the darkness. Wooden support beams had been hammered into place every dozen feet or so to keep it from collapsing. A string of low-wattage Christmas lights likewise hung from the ceiling.

I had no idea how long it continued, save I couldn't see the end. It either angled at some point or the exit was hidden from view.

None of that mattered, though. Wherever this led to, my nose confirmed it let out into the open at some point.

I'd found another way out, one that was almost certainly better than using the front door.

9

ESCAPE FROM PSYCHO MANOR

Despite being considerably larger now, I still maintained much of my former dexterity. That was good, because I had no intention of resuming my human form until I was far away from this hell hole.

Once the police discovered this nightmare, and I had no doubt they would, I had to make sure it was as difficult as possible for them to connect the dots back to me.

I'd done my best upstairs and in the garage to destroy any evidence of my passing. As for down here, perhaps it was best to let them think a wild animal had broken in.

To that end, I grabbed the hose and turned it on full blast, rinsing all the blood from the trapdoor, stairs, and surrounding floor before turning the powerful stream on the clothes I'd worn, not stopping until the water running down the drain was clear again.

My nose was still able to pick out the blood on the fabric, but it was heavily muted now. I grabbed them anyway because, washed or not, no way was I leaving them behind as evidence. But then my eyes fell upon the bag still on the table.

Screw it.

I unzipped the top, meaning to stuff the bundle inside without looking, only to realize it was already full of clothes – both male and female. That wasn't all, though. Curiosity got the better of me, so I took a closer look. Beneath the clothing were two fat stacks of cash, a pair of flashlights, two burner phones, some water bottles, and a loaded gun.

I didn't need to be a CSI detective to recognize a bugout bag when I saw one.

It was the final piece of the puzzle.

The Chadworths had obviously been ready for a quick getaway in case the police ever paid them an unexpected visit. That was the reason for the tunnel. It was also why the trapdoor's latch was on this side. It was to give them as much extra time as possible to traverse the same escape tunnel I was now planning to use.

I took a closer look at the hidden door. Sure enough, a deadbolt was welded on the back, one that could be slid into place from the other side.

If I hadn't been convinced they were seasoned serial killers before, I sure as heck was now.

Insane as it was, my inner wolf had seemingly done the world a favor. I doubted he would've cared, but there were almost certainly people out there who'd been spared the future heartache of loved ones vanishing without a trace.

Heady stuff, but perhaps best saved for another time.

For now, I considered the bag's contents. I was no thief. I'd been raised better than that. But I was smart enough to know I still needed a way to get home. That settled it.

As for whatever was left over, well, I could figure that out later. Heck, who was to say I wouldn't need it for rent and groceries? I still had no idea how much time had passed since my adventure in Manhattan, but there was a very real chance I'd return home only to find out I'd been fired.

Wouldn't that be a kick in the pants?

Once again, though, that was a problem for future Mike.

I stuffed the wet clothes in with the rest, zipped it back up, and then slung it over my shoulder – the duffel bag no more than a fanny pack against my much larger wolf form.

Unfortunately, that was going to make this next part uncomfortable, but first things first. I made it a point to trash the place – scattering everything and scratching up the walls to further drive home the idea an animal was to blame.

That done, I finally turned my attention toward the exit.

Unsurprisingly, the tunnel hadn't been built with werewolves in mind. I just barely fit inside laying on my belly. It was a good thing I had no intention of closing the door behind me because there was no chance of that happening.

Instead, I used my claws to inch forward, something neither pleasant nor quick.

After roughly an hour of crawling, getting stuck repeatedly, then crawling some more, I craned my neck to look up. The scent of fresh air was stronger than ever, but now there was an undercurrent of death and decay.

The way out appeared to be covered by an old wooden door camouflaged with leaves and branches. More importantly, the dim light filtering down from above, coupled with the fact my body was no longer trying to change back, seemed to indicate that dusk had finally descended, a point in my favor.

My patience at an end, I clawed my way upward until

I could finally reach the exit. Then I shoved it open, revealing treetops and the sky above.

About freaking time!

Feral instincts whispered to me as I stood up, free at last. I threw back my head ... and just barely caught myself before I started howling like an idiot.

Needless to say, that wouldn't help my cause.

Being a werewolf could be a heady experience, but now I had an inkling where those instincts were coming from.

Speaking of which...

I cocked my head and waited as I stood half-concealed by the Chadworth's escape tunnel. However, those urgings quickly silenced themselves, leaving me alone inside my head and still in full control of my body.

Thank goodness!

It wasn't all wine and roses, sadly. The scents I'd noticed below were now stronger than ever, impossible to ignore. I was now deep in the woods, at least a couple hundred yards from the house those nutjobs had called home, but still the stench of death lingered.

I sensed rotting bones and marrow mixed in with the soil all around me. It was hard to tell how many, but my nose painted a gruesome picture of unlucky victims killed by monsters wearing human skin – their flesh dissolved in the basement while whatever was left got dumped out here.

It was almost enough to make me sick as I climbed out, the stench so overwhelming I failed to notice another scent until I'd managed to step free – that of well-oiled metal.

Sadly, it was at the same moment my foot landed atop the bear trap hidden there, setting it off with a heavy crunch of steel meeting bone.

Son of a...!

I couldn't help but scream. Had I been human, it would've likely been laced with no small number of expletives, but in my current form, it came out more like the roar of an angry lion.

No doubt about it. If the Chadworths had any neighbors nearby, they were almost certainly wondering what on Earth was roaming the woods this night.

I bit my tongue against the pain of metal teeth digging into my ankle. Had I not been a supernatural monster, I'd surely be sporting a broken leg.

Call me paranoid, but I had a feeling it was no accident this trap was here.

First things first, though. I bent down, grabbed hold of the heavy iron jaws, and pried them open. Thank goodness for opposable thumbs.

Freed, I quickly tested out my injured leg. It hurt like a mother, no question there, but it was able to support my weight. That was good because I'd just about had my fill of crawling. Instead, I grabbed hold of the sprung trap and twisted with all my might.

When I was finished, the beartrap was bent in a way to ensure it would never be usable again. I reared back, meaning to throw it away, but ... instead clonked myself upside the head with it?

Oof! What the heck?

My mouth opened of its own accord and a rumbling growl came out, except I somehow understood its meaning.

"What the fuck did I tell you about waking me up?"

And just like that my situation went from bad to worse once again.

10

STRANGE BEDFELLOWS

"Um, sorry, didn't mean to wake you." Or that's what I tried to say. What came out of my mouth instead was a series of chuffs and grunts.

"*What?*"

Whereas my words were completely unintelligible, my inner wolf's seemed to make perfect sense for some reason.

Weird. I tried to speak again, but he interrupted before I could finish.

"*I'll stop you right there, dipshit. The problem as I see it, is you're talking like a human bitch, something my mouth obviously isn't built for. So, if you have something to say, either say it correctly or shut the fuck up so I can kill the shit outta you!*"

Frustrated, as well as slightly terrified, I tried to replicate what he'd just said, but it came out as nothing but growling gibberish.

"*Okay, I see this is pointless,*" he remarked. "*Time to gut your stupid ass.*"

How the heck am I supposed to talk to him like this?

"*Maybe try learning the language, idiot. Werewolf, moth-erfucker. Do you speak...? Wait a second. Do that again.*"

I grumbled nonsense in response, which earned me another smack upside the head with the bear trap.

Ow! Stop that, I mentally cried. *I don't know what you're asking me to do.*

"*Well, what do you know? You can't speak for shit but somehow I can still hear you yammering inside my head.*"

You can?

"*I just said that, didn't I?*"

He swung the trap once more, but this time I caught it with my right hand – surprised to find I still had control of that side. Before he could try again, I yanked it from his grasp and threw it into the bushes.

"*How the fuck are you able to do that? This is* my *body. I'm in control now.*"

No idea, I just did. Then, feeling spiteful, I added, *So, let's see if I can do it again.*

I drove a fist into the left side of my own face, stag-gering myself.

Okay, maybe that wasn't the brightest move. On the other hand, I'd definitely felt it, but the blow was muted, as if the nerve endings on that side were only sending a partial signal.

Good to know, but probably not something I should make a habit of.

"*The fuck do you think you're doing?*"

You hit me first!

"*If you think that hurt, just wait until I carve your whining ass the fuck out of me.*"

The next several minutes found my right-side wrestling with my left, which I'm sure looked quite the sight. A werewolf with multiple personality disorder. Who'd have ever guessed?

We fought back and forth, each of us trying to wrest control from the other. All the while, my inner wolf growled nonstop invectives at me while I ... thought mean thoughts back at him.

Yeah, it was probably a good thing no one else could hear me.

Who knows how long this strange dance of death would've gone on for had we not inadvertently stepped into yet another trap the Chadworths had *helpfully* hidden there.

The snare was obviously designed for a normal human, not a seven-and-a-half-foot tall wolf beast. It pulled me off my feet but that was it – leaving me lying on my backside with one leg dangling in the air.

However, it did serve to momentarily halt our infighting.

"*I am so gonna gut whoever put that there,*" my inner wolf growled.

You already did. The Chadworths set it.

"*The What-worths?*"

Those two nutjobs who gave you a lift.

"*Oh. Then maybe I should go back and shred them extra hard.*"

And what is that going to accomplish?

"*I don't know, but it might make me feel better about being woken the fuck up!*"

Ask a stupid question...

All right. Let's take a deep breath and calm down. Fighting isn't accomplishing anything. Who knows how many traps they have lying around here?

What ensued was my right and left halves attempting to take a breath out of sync which, needless to say, was a seriously weird sensation. But at least our brawl seemed to be over for now.

Instead, we ended up fumbling with the rope around our ankle for the next two minutes before I finally thought, *Time out! This isn't working. The snare's on your side, so ... I'm going to give you control. Okay?*

In truth I neither thought that a wise idea nor did I have any clue how to do it. However, he'd managed it back inside, so I knew it was possible.

Possible and easier than I'd have guessed. In the end, all I had to do was relax and let go. He hesitated for a moment, as if debating whether to throttle me again, but then started working to free us without any input from me – a rather unpleasant thing to experience.

Years back, I'd read a story called *Locked In*, in which victims of the zombie virus effectively became prisoners within their own bodies. They were fully conscious, but unable to do anything as their shambling forms ravaged the countryside looking for victims.

It was a notion I found infinitely more terrifying than the zombies themselves.

If that was indeed what my wolf had meant by being locked in a *brain cage*, then perhaps he was due more sympathy than I'd originally judged.

Mind you, it's not like I'd been on the hunt for human brains during that time. If anything, his main complaint so far seemed to be that I wasn't killing nearly enough people to make him happy.

Either way, it was the space of seconds for him to slice the rope around our ankle. Freed, I did a little test as we scrambled back to our feet, wiggling my fingers just to make sure I still could.

Phew!

"*What was that?*" he asked.

Um, nothing. Just happy to be free again.

"Fucking pussy," he grumbled before asking, *"So, what now?"*

You mean do we go back to fighting?

"Tempting as that is, no, dumbass. I mean, what's the plan?"

Hold on. Are you actually asking me?

"What does it sound like? You obviously had something in mind when you dragged us out here. Unless, that is, you were planning on those metal teeth biting my leg off."

No! That was just an accident.

"You'd better hope so because if you wake me up again, I swear..."

He trailed off, the threat obvious.

It had been a little over three hours since he'd disappeared into my subconscious to take a nap, which I guess explained why he'd woken up extra cranky. If he was still tired, then maybe he intended to go back to sleep. If so, that would make my – *our* – escape that much easier.

Rather than play games, I quickly filled him in on what had happened, as well as my plan to get my bearings and make it back to familiar territory.

My other half was silent for several long seconds after I finished, but then he said, *"Fine. Give me control."*

Control? I was almost afraid to ask. *What for?*

"So I can get us the fuck out of here. What else? You've already shown you can't be trusted to watch where you're going."

Oh, come on. It was one time.

"Here's what I'm proposing," he said, ignoring me. *"I'll get us past whatever surprises those assholes left lying around, then you leave me alone so I can go back to sleep. Deal?"*

I mean, I guess that would...

"Let me just point out, the alternative is me bashing your side of our skull against a rock. Your call."

All things considered, it wasn't the worst deal I'd ever been offered.

I was both impressed as well as envious at how adept my inner wolf seemed to be when in control of our werewolf form.

Don't get me wrong, I didn't consider myself a slouch. I'd never felt uncomfortable adapting to either the strength or speed of this body. But the way he moved when in charge, well, it was something else. It was like his mind and senses were completely in tune as he neatly side-stepped boobytrap after boobytrap – stopping only to pee on one as I guess a sort of farewell to the Chadworths.

Eh, whatever worked.

It was only when he started digging that I became a little concerned.

What are you doing? There's nothing here.

"Untrue, pupcake. There's a tasty pile of bones beneath us. Figured I could use a snack."

What?! No!

"Why not?"

Because those are people, that's why.

"So?"

So, we don't do things like that! It's … wrong.

"No. Starving is wrong, especially when there's tasty morsels just within reach."

Not wanting to start another fight, but also not wanting to wolf down human remains, I tried to think quickly. *I … I'll get you something else to eat. I promise.*

"When?"

I don't know. Soon as I can.

"But I'm hungry now."

You just ate a full pig!

He scoffed. "*That little thing?*"

It was all I could do to keep from screaming. *Just don't, okay? I swear, I'll ... make it worth your while.*

He let out a grumble, but at least he'd stopped digging. "*You'd better!*"

I had no idea how I was going to make good on that promise, but I'd cross that bridge once we were far away from here, as well as any people, living or otherwise.

Finally, my inner demon declared us to be in the clear. Aside from the bag still hanging from my arm, the Chadworths were now officially in our rearview mirror, which was no small relief.

Ten minutes later I was back in control. Won't lie, I was kinda envious how quickly the savage beast inside my noggin was able to conk out.

Back in the driver's seat once again, I craned my head toward the sky – the only real sense of direction I had to go by. I wasn't a survivalist, but knew enough to spot the North Star.

Once I had an idea which direction was which, I turned west – relying on my senses to guide me, a task made much easier now that I no longer had to worry about boobytraps.

Why west? Call it a hunch. I didn't have much to go on, but my other half had been trying to get back home when the Chadworths picked him up. Assuming he hadn't gotten turned around, that meant he'd probably been heading west away from the city. So long as his would-be killers hadn't ended up on an extended road trip with him passed out in the backseat, it seemed a safe assumption that we were still somewhere east of Harris County.

And if I was wrong, well, there was enough cash in their bugout bag to afford a plane ticket.

I pushed that thought away as I started running, trying not to imagine an angry werewolf waking up in a crowded passenger jet at thirty-thousand feet. Instead, I passed the time thinking up names for my inner werewolf.

Sure, there were far more pressing matters to dwell upon, but I figured I'd earned a small break from things dark and disturbing.

Spot, Rover, and Rex were the obvious low-hanging fruit, but those all felt cliché.

Wolfie? Nah, too cutesy.

I'd always told myself that if I got another dog, I'd name it Mater to go along with Spud, but I doubted that would go over well.

Our relationship was already pretty adversarial. There was nothing to be gained by kicking that particular hornet nest.

Something out of a horror movie was probably more fitting anyway. Talbot or maybe Lucien.

Both were solid choices, but they sounded a bit too hoity-toity for my tastes. I didn't want to insult the creature taking up residence inside my noggin, but saw no point in feeding his ego either.

Not to mention, there weren't many Luciens to be found in a place like Harris County.

No. I needed something simple, something honest and every day. Something like...

An idea hit me just as my nose picked up the lingering scent of burnt rubber and exhaust fumes. It was coming from the south – a road, a decent sized one from the smell of things.

There was more too, a kaleidoscope of scents giving me a sense of the bigger picture. Beyond the road were railroad tracks, and past that moving water. A river.

I immediately turned that way, curious to see what I'd find.

Though the woods were both dark and dense, I felt no fear. My nose had already cataloged the wildlife that called this stretch of forest home and found nothing worth worrying about.

It was probably arrogant of me to say that, but I didn't see the local bobcats trying their luck against a full-grown werewolf.

There!

I spied a break in the trees up ahead, and past it asphalt.

There was a lane going in either direction, not a major highway but not a tiny country road either. I followed it as it curved westward, staying out of sight until I finally spotted a marker.

Yes!

I was on Route 120, Renovo Road. That meant the river I'd sensed was the Susquehanna. I knew exactly where I was. If memory served me right, this stretch was right outside of Cooks Run.

If so, I was two counties from home – a daunting walk for a person, but nothing but a good workout for a werewolf. Heck, I could probably run back to Elk County faster than an Uber could get out there to pick me up.

From there, it was a reasonably straight shot back home.

That was one mystery solved.

Problem was, I had no idea what was waiting for me there. I still had no sense of how long I'd been gone, meaning there was no way of knowing how much mayhem either Hobart or Myra had caused in the meantime.

No.

Much as I wanted to get back home, grab another shower, then fall asleep in my own bed, I needed to do some recon first.

And that meant taking a slight detour.

11

WHO PREYS UPON THE PREDATORS?

Despite its name, Harris County was merely a township not a whole county. As the story goes, its founder, a trapper by the name of Nathanial Harris, had big plans for it, but his vision never quite panned out as he spent his final years going slowly mad from a combination of syphilis and wood alcohol.

Anyway, by the time folks realized that Harris County wasn't destined to become a Mecca of backwoods commerce, the name had stuck. Referendums to change it popped up from time to time in the local elections, but they never passed. People were comfortable with what they knew, and if any outsiders scoffed at it, well, that was their problem to deal with.

Bottom line was we were too far from the beaten path to be useful for travelers, other than maybe as a quick pit stop at Larry Parker's *Gas & Go* station.

On the other hand, Harris County's remoteness and proximity to the Allegheny forest ended up making it the perfect home for a pack of werewolves. Or perhaps it was perfect for those attempting to *hide* a pack of werewolves from the rest of the world, as the question of the ritual's origins was still unanswered, at least as far as I was aware.

Back when Hobart first confronted me about being a Dominant, he'd mentioned a mysterious group he'd called the Top Coven.

My first inclination, after having time to collect my thoughts, was he must've been talking about witches.

However, as time wore on and I became slightly less ignorant of matters, I learned that was wrong. The group he'd erroneously labeled as the Top Coven had in fact been called the *First Coven*, and they weren't witches. They were vampires, the top dogs amongst the undead as a matter of fact.

That certainly explained Hobart's mad-on with vamps and their so-called *Progenitor*, a vendetta he'd pursued all the way to Brooklyn – ultimately leading to my current predicament.

As for why he was convinced that vampires were responsible for drugging us, I still had few answers.

All I knew was the road that led to our standoff in New York started with the harassment of a man named Jacob Vesser.

Jacob was a Harris County lifer, known to most in the area. He had a home just outside the city limits on a large, wooded lot, where he'd lived by himself ever since his wife passed and his step kids moved out. He was a good fella, even if he mostly kept to himself.

Jacob had never been part of the ritual, but neither had lots of other folks in town. He was also no vampire, having seen him out and about many times during the day.

In short, there didn't seem to be any logical reason to target him, but Hobart and logic had never been kissing cousins.

It had started with Hobart's inner circle haunting the

woods around Jacob's house, mostly trying to spook the poor guy into giving up some information he supposedly had. It was definitely creepy, don't get me wrong, but it could have been way worse.

At first, I tried to avoid getting involved. So long as the pack kept their distance, I kept mine. They were all firmly under Hobart's thumb by then. Outnumbered as I was, I had no interest in tangling with them if it could be avoided. Needless to say, his threat regarding my balls still hung heavy in my thoughts.

Sadly, it was a stalemate not destined to last.

One night, company came calling at Jacob's place, except they weren't the normal type a fella might keep.

When Hobart started his harassment for the evening, they made it a point to confront him.

Things went downhill quickly from there.

Then...

What in Spud's name?

I was up in a tree way back in the woods, maybe thirty feet off the ground – close enough to make out Jacob's backyard but not enough to be seen.

Or smelled, thanks to the scent control agent I'd hosed myself down with earlier. Amazing the stuff you could buy online.

Anyway, my goal was to keep an eye on things, nothing more. For the past week, Hobart and his crew had been out here harassing the poor fella – calling to him from the woods, demanding information about the so-called vampire Progenitor, but never approaching.

I wasn't sure what connection, if any, a guy like Jacob Vesser might have to some bloodsucking messiah, but Hobart seemed convinced of it. Either way, it was obvious he was trying to unnerve Jacob into giving him some bit of information he wanted.

I'd hoped this night would end no different than the previous ones, with them giving up after a few hours. I didn't like what they were doing, but so long as they kept their distance, I saw no reason to get involved.

Tonight wasn't like the rest, though. Jacob had visitors. I didn't know who they were or what their relationship to him was, but they seemingly had no interest in letting this harassment continue unchecked.

Two of them, a man and a woman, had taken up watch in the backyard. Both were armed, but that wasn't what had set my warning bells off.

I shook my head several times to make sure I wasn't seeing things, but there was no mistaking it. The woman's eyes were aglow with an eerie green light.

I wasn't sure whether she was a witch like Myra or something else, maybe one of those vampires Hobart had told me about, but something was seriously off about her.

Too bad I wasn't the only one who'd noticed.

Things quickly took a turn from there. Unlike on previous nights, Hobart and some of his thralls, Myra included, actually stepped from the tree line and approached these newcomers.

An escalating war of words ensued, both sides going back and forth threatening each other, until the woman with the glowing eyes seemingly had enough.

"Listen up, assholes," she cried. "I don't know what you dickheads want and I don't care. The only thing I give a shit about is that you're trespassing and pissing me off. So, I suggest you go back to whatever bar you stumbled out of, put on a pair of sweatpants, and stay the fuck away from here." She lifted the comically oversized revolver in her hands to give her threat extra emphasis. "Or else I can guarantee something bad is going to happen."

I knew at that moment things were about to get worse, but even I couldn't have guessed what was going to happen next.

Without any warning, there came a flash of light and then the woman vanished without a trace.

A witch. She has to be, I told myself, gobsmacked at the raw display of power.

Or maybe not.

Confusion seemed to reign in Jacob's yard, even among the woman's companion. Whatever had just happened, it didn't appear to have been planned.

More back and forth threats ensued until finally Jacob himself made an appearance, stomping around the side of his house with flashlight in hand and...

What in God's name?

An undulating blob-like *thing* was slithering along by his side. Stranger still, Jacob was giving it no heed, as if it were the most normal thing in the world.

Needless to say, it was all I could do to keep from falling right out of the tree. What the heck had I stumbled onto?

"That you, Hobart?" Jacob asked a few moments later, as if the pack's presence was the only weird thing going on.

Rather than comment on all the craziness, however, Hobart simply said, "I'm sorry you had to see my face, Jacob."

I knew at that moment any chance of a peaceful resolution had vanished along with the strange woman.

I was preparing to climb down, trying to figure out what to do, but then the other fella spoke up. He was nothing special to look at, a bit overweight and wearing glasses, but he had an attitude that seemed to match his lady friend's.

"Back the fuck off. Last warning!"

My first thought was his mouth was writing a check

his body couldn't hope to cash, but then Jacob's flashlight beam fell upon him.

That's when I saw his black eyes and elongated canines.

He was a vampire.

Hobart was right all along. They were real.

Now...

The vamp in question was the same Bill Ryder I'd ended up renting an apartment from some weeks later, not that I'd known at the time. More importantly, he wasn't the one Hobart was looking for, not that it mattered. Just his presence alone was enough to set the pack off.

What followed was an all-out brawl between monsters, the likes of which I'd never seen before. In the end, I'd had no choice but to intervene. By then, two of the pack were dead, something I hadn't thought possible, while Jacob and his *guests* had been forced to flee.

Things had spiraled in the days afterward, ultimately leading to where I was now – attempting to find my way back home with no clue as to how long I'd been gone.

The memory served as a reminder that I needed to check on Jacob again at some point. After all, he might have chosen to run, but I knew the man. He was a stubborn S.O.B. It was only a matter of time before he returned to his home, no matter how foolish it might be.

Although, considering the *friends* he apparently kept, perhaps it wasn't as foolhardy as I made it out to be.

It was yet another on a long list of things I needed to do, but all that would have to wait for now.

First, I needed to take a detour and check in with some *friends*.

Hopefully they'd be able to fill me in, so I didn't end up walking back into Harris County completely blind.

Barley Hills was situated just a few miles south of Harris County, but it wasn't what you might call our sister town. Harris County might've been small but it was a melting pot, home to different faiths and creeds – not to mention species.

Barley Hills, however, was somewhat more *homogeneous*. On the surface, it was a quiet Mennonite settlement, one of the few outside Lancaster County. They were humble, hardworking people who, much like their kinfolk to the east, mostly made their living off the land. Unlike their more agriculturally minded cousins, however, this particular sect was focused on hunting and trapping. It was how they put food on the table and money in their pockets.

It was such an ingrained part of their culture that the settlement had even received a special allotment from the state, allowing them to hunt year-round – making them the envy of sportsmen far and wide.

The townsfolk were friendly and welcoming to outsiders, provided they didn't stay past dark. Because once night fell, these simple, God-fearing folk stalked the woods with a purpose they took as seriously as any other, but one that wasn't to be found in any Bible I'd ever heard of.

The sacred mission of the Mennonites of Barley Hills, the one which kept them isolated from their sister sects, was something known only to them and a few others.

They hunted werewolves.

Okay, that was probably a gross oversimplification. After all, if that were the case, then I'd have to be a few candles short of a birthday cake to be heading there now.

It was more like their job was to hunt any werewolves who strayed too far outside Harris County. And no, that didn't make what I was doing sound any saner, but trust me on this.

I knew what I was doing ... mostly.

As I finally closed in on the midway point between the two towns, my nose began to pick up a whole plethora of different scents. Many were human, some were not. Most were old and lingering, but a few were disturbingly fresh.

Unfortunately, fast as I was moving, it wasn't fast enough. The owner of one of those *fresh scents* must've likewise picked up on mine, because I sensed them changing direction to intercept me.

Give yourself a kewpie doll if you guessed the owner wasn't human.

Damn it!

There was no full moon tonight. That meant this was either Hobart's or Myra's doing.

Can't say I was surprised either way.

In the weeks following our first confrontation, Hobart had gotten bolder and more paranoid with regards to the pack.

What should've been nothing more than a monthly worry had quickly escalated. Word on the street during the day, when people weren't beholden to his will, was that he'd become obsessed with making sure Harris County never fell under the thrall of vampires for whatever reason.

One of these days I needed to figure out what was in those files he'd gotten from his brother, but for now it was enough to know that even before our battle in Brooklyn it had become increasingly rare for the woods surrounding my town to ever be werewolf-free come nightfall.

Guess some things haven't changed.

It was reckless and dangerous on his part, especially since most of the pack were little more than monsters once they changed.

Case in point as my keen eyes caught sight of the werewolf racing my way. It may have looked like me on the outside, but I sincerely doubted it had any thoughts running through its bestial mind other than to kill me in the most brutal and vicious manner possible.

12

FANGS AND FLYING FUR

Far as I've been able to tell, every living thing had its own unique scent. Think of it like an advanced form of fingerprints. Two creatures could be close, but there were always underlying differences.

Mind you, this wasn't obvious unless you either had preternatural senses or happened to be born a bloodhound.

Further complicating matters was the fact some creatures had more than one. For instance, shapeshifters like me could have a completely different scent depending on their form. I mean, sure, some things might carry over. If someone was wearing, say, *Old Spice* on the night of the full moon, it's not like that would magically disappear once they grew fur.

Unfortunately, matching up someone's human form with their wolf-half wasn't that easy, and it's not like I'd had time to go door to door smelling everyone in town like some kind of butt-sniffing Jehovah's Witness.

Best I could tell, the beast tearing butt my way was neither Hobart nor his second in command Jeb. It wasn't one of my parents either, thank goodness. Beyond that, it was anyone's guess. Since most of my encounters with the pack had been more hit-and-run than anything, that hadn't left a whole lot of time for casual sniffing.

The monster bearing down on me could've been anyone associated with the ritual. Too bad none of them were accommodating enough to wear nametags.

That was okay, though. I was too preoccupied with trying to stand my ground as the slobbering beast barreled toward me.

See, real life werewolves weren't like the movies. Sure, superficially they kind of resembled the beasts found in *Underworld* or *Dog Soldiers*, but there was a realness to them that Hollywood films lacked.

Movie werewolves tended to all look alike, doubly so if they'd been created with CGI. More importantly, there was a certain neatness to them. Movie lycanthropes all had perfect fangs, ears, and luxurious coats of fur uniformly covering their bodies.

People weren't nearly so neat in real life, though. Alas, Harris County wasn't home to a population of perfectly sculpted underwear models.

There was a certain *messiness* to these monsters that somehow made them far more terrifying. We're talking bald patches, missing teeth, scars, beer bellies, you name it.

The beast closing in on me now was roughly seven feet tall, a bit shorter than me. In truth, his face looked more like that of a nightmare rottweiler than a movie werewolf, possessing a heavy head with wide jaws that meant business. Further driving home the danger were hands and feet which terminated in three-inch claws.

Though black fur covered most of its body, there were ragged patches here and there, as if it were fighting off a case of mange, culminating in an ugly, hairless, rat-like tail protruding from its backside.

I'd once sat through the *Twilight* movies with Myra and, well, won't lie. I'd have much sooner faced their oversized canines than the creature headed my way.

Too bad beggars couldn't be choosers.

As for any chance of talking this through, well, maybe my inner wolf could've understood the snarls and foaming growls coming from the beast's mouth, but far as I was concerned it was little more than a rabid monster.

Sadly, that was all the time I had to think this through as the enraged werewolf slammed into me like a freight train.

Oof!

I caught a quick glimpse of his shame, erect and on view for all the world to see. *Yep, definitely a he.* Mind you, that fact along with five bucks would buy me a cup of coffee, as we both went tumbling end over end, only for me to land on my back with him on top.

I wasn't sure whether this jerk was attacking on Hobart's orders or had simply identified me as an intruder, but ultimately it didn't matter. After all, it's not like I was filming a nature documentary.

No, I was far too busy keeping him from tearing my throat out as he slashed me with his claws before leaning in with a set of chompers that would've made Spud jealous.

The bleeding wounds now crisscrossing my upper body were painful but superficial, nothing that would slow me down. Instead, I managed to grab hold of his jaws before they could further ruin my day, forcing them shut and then shoving him off me, gaining enough breathing room to roll back to my feet.

Whatever made me a Dominant had fortunately come with a few extra perks. I was a little larger than your average werewolf as well as a fair bit stronger. My fur was also brown for some reason, whereas the majority of werewolves in Harris County were closer to black.

Hair color wasn't going to win this fight, though. Sadly, neither was the so-called gift of dominance, since I had no clue how to use it. I mean, heck, it's not like I could even talk to the clown currently circling me with murder in his eye.

Speaking of murder, I needed to be careful on two fronts. The first was obviously staying alive against a beast that would've gladly spilled my entrails across the forest floor. The other was making sure my inner wolf didn't inadvertently wake up mid-fight.

He was too much of an X-factor. Not only did I have no idea how he might react at the sight of another of our kind, but I likewise didn't relish what it might do to our ability to fight if I was trying to zig while he wanted to zag.

No. He needed to stay in dreamland for now.

I glanced at the scratches on my chest, realizing how lucky I'd gotten. They stung, sure, but it was nothing like that bear trap. I needed to avoid anything worse, a feat easier said than done as my foe crouched down on all fours and leapt.

The action was swift and savage but there was zero thought behind it. I sidestepped the snarling beast with room to spare, then grabbed hold of him from behind and locked his arms in a full nelson. That solved the issue of having my face bitten off, at least for the moment, but now I had to figure out what to do with him.

I also needed to be quick about it. This wasn't like restraining a person. The werewolf went absolutely nuts in my grasp. It was more like wrangling a four-hundred-pound alley cat. I was barely able to keep my footing as the beast let out a roar of rage while trying his damnedest to shake me loose.

This was a losing strategy at best. It's not like I could stand there for the rest of my life holding this nutjob, but he'd be all over me in a heartbeat if I let go.

That ultimately was part of the problem. In being able to think and strategize, I held the advantage, but only in theory as...

Oh no. Not that!

Something wet splattered my legs. In the werewolf's struggle to break free, he was quite literally raining on my parade, except with pee.

Gross!

If there was one thing I hated about being a monster of the night, it was all the bodily fluids. Why oh why couldn't Hobart devote his time to something worthwhile, like housetraining all the werewolves under his command?

Gah!

My stress levels were peaking, which I realized might not be conducive for keeping the beast inside my brain from waking up. So, I did the only thing that came to mind.

I started singing lullabies inside my head.

Rock-a-bye werewolf ... um ... in the dense trees. Please keep on sleeping ... you big bag of fleas...

Would that actually help? I had no idea. But my inner wolf could apparently read my thoughts in this form, so, I figured it couldn't hurt.

What *could* hurt, however, was the freaking monster still snarling, snapping, thrashing, and peeing as it tried to break free.

Ewww!

How freaking big was this thing's bladder?!

I had to do *something*. Problem was, my best option — snapping this werewolf's neck — was also the one I didn't want to take.

The beast might've looked and acted like a rampaging

monster, but deep down he was still a person – someone I knew.

And yet, if I didn't do something, he'd eventually break free and cut me down as soon as look at me.

As much as I hated to admit it, mercy was a conceit I could ill afford in this strange new world of the weird I'd been dragged into, more so because I couldn't expect any to be shown in return.

Hobart and Myra had already proven that in their bid to take down that vampire and his friends. Both in Harris County and later in New York, they hadn't hesitated when it came to collateral damage. The battle in Brooklyn in particular had been a brutal affair as they'd unleashed the pack on a street full of civilians, not caring how many were torn to shreds in the process.

Holding back was a recipe for disaster.

And yet still I persisted, even as my grip began to slip bit by bit.

Sadly, creatures such as myself weren't built for restraint. All the tools at my disposal, whether teeth, claws, or super strength, were those of an apex predator. The simple truth was werewolves were built to kill, not slap each other around like kittens.

There was also our durability to take into account. I'd seen others put down in ways that should've been lethal, only for them to heal once they changed back. Conversely, I'd also witnessed some who hadn't been that lucky.

I simply didn't know where that fine line between incapacitated and doomed lay when it came to my kind.

Pity, I was also the only one who seemed to be worried about it.

The werewolf suddenly crouched low, causing me to bend over to maintain my grip. Then, before I realized what it was doing, it kicked off with its feet – launching us both backward until...

Oof!

I was the first to hit the tree trunk, followed immediately afterward by the creature I'd been trying to restrain – our combined momentum knocking the wind out of me.

Maybe this beast wasn't as dumb as I'd thought.

Too bad I was forced to split my attention between defending myself and practically screaming lullabies inside my head.

Hush ... little werewolf, please don't wake up. Mama's gonna, I dunno, give you a pile of raw meat or something.

A songwriter I was not.

I risked taking a moment, both to catch my breath and see if my mouth was about to start cursing me out of its own accord.

Needless to say, it was not the best time for introspection.

The other werewolf tried to spin around to get at me. Fortunately, with us still pressed up against one another, that made it an awkward move at best.

With my back against the proverbial wall, I did the only thing I could. I shoved him away with everything I had, sending him flying a good fifteen feet to land face first in the dirt.

Impressive as it looked, such a fall wouldn't have stopped a pup much less an adult werewolf – not that I'd ever seen any werewolf puppies.

Heck, I wasn't even sure they existed. For all I know our condition didn't manifest until a certain age. As I've said, it's not like this curse came with an instruction manual.

Now was not the time to dwell on such trivial things, though. I had moments at best to catch my breath and figure out my next move.

By then, the other werewolf was already rising and

turning to face me — his red eyes glaring with feral malevolence.

All right. Let's try that again. I'm ready for you this time. That wasn't entirely true, but a little positive thinking never hurt.

Regardless, I braced for the inevitable attack. However, rather than charge me as I expected, the beast raised his head and took a deep breath.

Oh crap!

Call it werewolf instinct or just plain common sense, but I immediately understood what he was about to do. Though I hadn't done much more than toss him around a little, the beast had come to the realization I wasn't going down as easily as a scared rabbit.

And what did a lone wolf do when it came to that conclusion? Well, if he was part of a pack, he'd probably howl his fool head off calling for reinforcements.

Oh, this is not good.

I was too far away to stop him. If he succeeded in alerting any others, I'd quickly end up outnumbered. That meant either becoming more brutal in my battle tactics or making a run for it.

There was no real choice in the matter, because staying also meant a near certainty the narcoleptic monster inside my head would wake up.

I wasn't ready for that to...

BOOM!

A thunderous report echoed through the forest, loud enough to feel like an icepick through my brain. I covered my ears and winced, praying the blast didn't double as an alarm clock.

The sharp whine of pain that came from the other werewolf, however, caught my attention. I looked up to find copious amounts of blood dripping from an ugly wound that had appeared on his right arm.

Realization set in even as my head continued to throb. He'd been shot. Then, a mere moment later, smoke began to rise from the bloody wound, causing the beast to whimper even louder.

Smoke?

The werewolf's ears folded back and his ratty tail drooped. It was a look I knew all too well, similar to the one Spud liked to guilt me with if I so much as raised my voice. Hot urine splashed to the ground between the werewolf's legs as I watched all the aggression drain from its face, only to be replaced with raw naked fear.

An instant later it turned and ran, yelping like a kicked dog.

It took a moment for the implication to sink in. *Someone shot it with a silver bullet.*

It was the only explanation that made sense.

Silver. When it came to the precious metal, Hollywood had it both right and wrong.

It wasn't a magical anti-werewolf MacGuffin that would destroy us if we so much as picked up the wrong salad fork. However, there was something about silver that caused it to react *negatively* with our bloodstream. It was less a poison, though, and more like shoving a lit road flare into the wound.

I'd had the displeasure of being grazed by a silver slug not too long ago and could attest it hurt like a mother-lover. I had no intention of letting it happen again.

Make that doubly true as I realized who was responsible for this shooting, as well as the fact they almost certainly had ammo to spare.

So, I made the only logical choice.

I put my hands up and surrendered.

13

HUNTER'S MOON

Please be someone I know.

I stood there with my hands raised, not moving, not even daring to change back into a human. Probably a good idea on that last point as I'd dropped the bag containing my clothes during the fight.

Now wasn't the time to go looking for it, though.

No, right then I needed to focus on not getting shot. I wasn't afraid for my life, per se. I knew the hunters had a strict policy of wounding first whenever possible to deter further conflict. However, even if the pain of being shot didn't wake the beast within me, there was also the agony of feeling my blood boil thanks to the silver in their bullets.

No way even a narcoleptic wolf could sleep through that.

Would my inner wolf then try to run, as my opponent had, or would he take a more aggressive stance?

I didn't care to find out the answer.

Long minutes passed. The only change to my surroundings, so far as I could tell, was the scent of

113

recently expended gunpowder. It was one of the few things even the hunters couldn't control.

Where my nose failed me, however, my eyes and ears served as the first indicators I'd made the right choice in surrendering. I picked up the faint crunch of foliage, two pairs of footsteps. Not surprising. The hunters seldom operated alone. It was too risky against the sort of prey they stalked.

The faint glimmer of lantern light caught my attention from a few dozen yards away. I turned my head to see two shambling mounds of rotting vegetation rise from the surrounding foliage and start walking my way. One held a lantern, while the other had a rifle trained directly on me.

Though at first sight their appearance was gruesome, I knew better. My eyes cut through the darkness well enough to recognize their ghillie suits – allowing them near perfect camouflage against the forest around them.

Fortunately, the upside of being one of only two werewolves able to maintain control was it made me easy to recognize.

"Don't ye dare move," the one holding the lantern cried out. "Only warning ye get. We've seen the witch's devilry, so don't think us easily fooled."

Or maybe not. I wasn't sure what devilry they were talking about but had a feeling I knew the witch in question. Myra. Far as I was aware, she was the only one from her coven who'd aligned with Hobart.

Being I still had no idea how long I'd been missing, I could only hope the situation hadn't changed for the worse.

Guess I'd find out soon enough.

The one with the lantern approached, finally drawing close enough to bathe me in its light.

"Dear Lord, that looks like..."

"Looks mean nothing, Amos," the other cautioned,

"not when that witch's magic can cloud the minds of men. Use the charm and be quick about it."

The first one, Amos – a name I vaguely recognized – reached his free hand into a hidden pocket and produced ... some weird *Blair Witch* type fetish made up of corn husks and old housekeys. He tossed it at my feet.

I glanced down at it, then back at the two men, unsure if I was supposed to pick it up or do something else.

Amos waited a beat, his eyes darting between the object and me. "Change back. If ye are who you look like, then do it. If not, we'll know ye as a deceiver."

The threat was quite clear.

I knew witches like Myra were capable of creating illusions so lifelike you would never guess until it was too late. Still, illusion or not, I was standing there calmly with my hands raised, something regular werewolves were mostly incapable of.

Oh well, I could either comply with their orders or risk eating a bullet. The choice was an easy one.

I once more focused internally – this time grasping onto a mental image of my human self, my humanity. As before, euphoric numbness spread through me in the moment before my body began to shrink.

"Achoo!"

Pity those wondrous brain chemicals didn't also keep me from being allergic to my own fur.

A sneezing fit overcame me as my fur, tail, and fangs all receded – making it extremely difficult to keep my hands raised.

"It's him. I told ye so. He's back!"

"Stay yourself awhile. We don't know for certain yet."

"The charm is right there, Elijah. If there was any devilry about him, it would've been dispelled."

"Maybe."

"No maybe about it."

I ignored their argument as my sinuses continued to protest. Finally, the sneezing jag began to subside enough for me to see that Amos had removed his ghillie suit and was approaching while Elijah held back, gun still raised.

Now that I could see his face, I definitely recognized him. Not one of the hunters I knew well, but we'd conversed a few times.

"Your name," Amos asked, no doubt playing it safe.

"M-Michael," I started, trying to ignore the tingle in my nose, "Hunter Walden."

That seemed to do the trick. Amos's demeanor instantly became more relaxed. "Aye it is. I see you're still allergic to yer own fur, Michael."

"Lucky me."

The one named Elijah pulled the hood of his suit down and lowered his rifle. "My apologies to ye, but that witch has been getting clever as of late."

"Myra?" I asked to which he nodded.

Amos then replied, "Enough of that for now. I've got two questions for ye. Where have you been and do you have any britches stashed in yer bag over yonder?"

I followed his gaze to the discarded duffel bag, on the ground with its strap broken. I nodded my gratitude then stepped over and unzipped it. The clothes I'd worn back at the house were still soaked, but there was more and I already knew their former owner was a close enough fit to make it work.

"That first one is a long story," I told them, pulling a pair of jeans on, "one I don't have all the details for. But maybe you can answer something for me instead. How long have I been gone?"

Amos and Elijah exchanged a glance, making me fear the worst, that it had been months or longer.

"It's been two weeks since the night you disappeared

with those nightcrawlers. I swear, Hannah's been out of her mind with worry."

I barely heard that last part. *Two weeks?*

In truth, it was a lot better than I'd feared. Heck, if that was the case I might even still have a job. My manager Stucky, not his real name obviously, would no doubt work me like ... a *dog* in retribution, but he was also the type to hold a job for a friend in need.

I let out a chuckle that my first thought was regarding my employment status. What a strange thing to fixate on now of all times.

"Something funny, Michael?" Amos asked.

"No. I was just afraid it had been a lot longer."

"You mean you didn't know?"

I shook my head. "I literally just woke up a few hours ago." At their shocked expressions, I added, "Like I said, long story."

"Best save it for Isaiah then," Amos said. "He's going to want to hear it awhile. For now let's get ye back to Barley Hills."

Elijah nodded. "Especially since yer pal Hobart is going to realize you're back soon enough. And when he does, he's liable to send reinforcements. My apologies. If I'd known it was you, I would've done more than wing that fell beast ye were fighting."

"All things considered, I'm glad you didn't."

Once again the two men exchanged a glance until Amos said, "Ye say that now, but I have a feeling tis a decision we might all soon regret."

14

ISAIAH HOOD – MEN-IN-ITES

The sect that called Barley Hills home was as mysterious as the ritual's origin. All I knew was the town had been there as long as Harris County, maybe longer. The local history texts confirmed as much.

Mind you, those same history books said nothing about werewolves, witches, and other monsters, so perhaps it was best to take them with a grain of salt.

Growing up, it had been common to hear gunshots coming from the direction where Barley Hills lay. Heck, some nights, back when I was a child still afraid of the dark, I found it downright comforting – telling myself nothing could be stalking the nearby woods so long as the hunters were nearby.

Little did I know how prophetic that would prove to be.

Following the big scuffle at Jacob Vesser's place, I'd taken to patrolling an ever-widening circle around Harris County. I wasn't trying to provoke a fight, mind you, merely being vigilant in case Hobart's crew decided to harass anyone else.

As it turned out, I wasn't the only one in the woods keeping an eye out for trouble of the werewolf variety – not by a long shot, pun fully intended.

That fact became painfully apparent a few days later when I found myself surrounded by enough firepower to put a hole in the moon.

Then...

I was patrolling about two miles outside the Harris County city limits, as if the word city even applied. My mind was still reeling from what had happened at the Vesser place, both the weirdness of the battle itself along with the fear it might happen to someone else.

My senses were on high alert keeping an eye out for any of Hobart's thralls, because that's what they were once they changed. They might still be themselves during the day, folks I knew and respected, but come nightfall they were his to command.

Unfortunately, I had no idea how to fix that. Best I could do, for now anyway, was act as a spoiler if they tried that crap again.

Mind you, I doubted anyone else in town was secretly friends with vampires, but who could say. I still had more questions than answers. Too bad Jacob had made himself scarce ever since, not that I could blame the guy.

I was running along, keeping my nose and ears perked for pack activity, but thankfully there didn't seem to be much going on this night.

It wasn't uncommon to sense a few werewolves out and about on any given evening – Hobart no doubt flaunting his influence. However, being as they were all about as smart as Spud on a good day, they were easy enough to avoid.

That was fine by me. It was more the bigger gatherings I was interested in, making sure there was no one else on Hobart's personal hit list.

I'd stopped in a clearing to catch my breath. My ears picked up the sound of foliage crunching but I didn't think much of it. This was the forest. Something was *always* moving around, going about its business. The important thing was I hadn't smelled anything off.

I was just about to resume my patrol when the ambush happened.

Flashlight beams cut through the darkness, momentarily blinding me. By the time I could see again, it was already too late. It was as if the bushes and shrubs had grown legs and surrounded me. Talk about freaky, but the fact all of them had rifles pointed my way was enough to rattle my nerves even further.

Nothing! I'd smelled nothing. How the hell had they gotten the drop on me so easily? Unless ... they were using a descenting agent similar to the one I'd used to spy on Hobart.

Damn it! It had been stupid to not figure my own trick might be used against me.

"One chance."

I turned at the sound of the voice to find a man in camo fatigues stepping out from behind a tree. He appeared to be in his sixties, with a long greying beard and a wrinkled brow. Definitely not one of Hobart's crew.

But then who?

It was the severe look etched upon his face, however, that really caught my attention. He was staring me down, showing neither surprise nor an ounce of fear.

This was the face of a man who knew he was in charge.

Unsure of what to do, I turned his way – slowly, as being riddled with bullets held little appeal.

"One chance," the old hunter repeated. "If ye be a

man as I suspect, then surrender and let us speak. Otherwise..." He let out a grim chuckle as he gestured toward the armed men in their ghillie suits.

I glanced around, momentarily weighing the odds. I was strong and fast, but not stupid enough to think I could take them all.

So, rather than do something I would almost certainly regret, I raised my arms over my head.

Now...

The walk back to Barley Hills was quiet and slow, same as it had been on that night months ago.

Unlike my first encounter with the hunters, though, I didn't mind this one in the least. The company, while not super talkative, were pleasant enough. And by that, I mean they shared some water and beef jerky instead of forcing me to eat a live pig or constantly berating me for every little thing.

Go figure but I'd discovered a newfound respect for people who weren't jerks.

Most of the hunters living in Barley Hills were simple folk living a traditional lifestyle. Amos and Elijah were no exception, even barring the sleek new rifles both carried — in stark contrast to Amos's old oil lantern and the obviously home-woven ghillie suits both men wore.

We collectively decided it was best to save any questions until we got back to the settlement and the elders could be roused.

Can't say that bothered me, as it gave me time to consider what I was going to tell them, since blathering about the last few hours alone would almost certainly paint me as a crazy person.

I did, however, warn the two hunters that things had

been ... *off* with me ever since waking up, urging them to keep some space between us as a precaution.

It was probably a safer plan than telling them my wolf half had gained sentience and could not only talk but seemed to have dominion over the left half of my body.

Yeah, that was going to be a fun conversation with the elders.

Thankfully, my inner wolf continued his slumber party as the lights from the town came into view.

Despite its quaint citizenry, Barley Hills had plenty of modern amenities – electricity, running water, and even cable TV. Strange as that might sound for an insular religious sect, when your job involved hunting werewolves, you used whatever advantages you could get.

As we entered the town proper, I spied sentries patrolling the streets, as if this were a medieval keep. Their readiness was warranted, though, as the last thing they wanted was to drop their guard once the sun went down.

Soon enough, with additional eyes now aware of my presence, Amos took off running – no doubt to make those with a need to know aware their long-lost prodigal werewolf had returned.

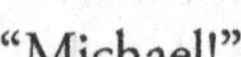

"Michael!"

I turned at the familiar voice, glad my escorts had been good enough to let me get dressed before bringing me to town.

Hannah was the eldest daughter of Isaiah Hood, the town's overseer. She was two years my junior, practically a spinster in a settlement where women were usually long since married and popping out little baby werewolf hunters.

That wasn't the only thing different about her. The men of Barley Hills traditionally served as the hunters, with few exceptions allowed, but Hannah was one of them. Being the daughter of the town overseer almost certainly played a part in her being granted special treatment. However, hers was no mere pity posting. Physically, Hannah could hold her own with the best Barley Hills had to offer. Standing just shy of six feet, she was tall, graceful, and strong enough to wrestle a bear.

Seriously, if she was ever in need of a job, I had no doubt Stucky would put her on the rotation in a heartbeat.

Won't lie, she was kinda cute too, although, I had a feeling mentioning that aloud might cause her father to rethink his thoughts on our *alliance*.

Hannah was dressed in a housecoat covering a long nightgown, with her brown hair falling freely around her shoulders – having obviously just woken up. Her appearance was no big deal to me, but borderline scandalous amongst the townsfolk as Elijah was quick to avert his gaze.

"Hannah, yer ... dress."

"Oh hush yerself awhile," she replied before stepping my way. For a moment, I thought she was going to give me a hug but she stopped short instead. "As for yinz, Mr. Walden. You had us all a might worried. Care to explain yerself, or should we assume you've been sowing yer wild oats over in the big city?"

"It's ... a long story," I said, ignoring that last part. "Probably best to hear what your father has to say about it first."

She folded her arms in front of her, holding my gaze with her blue eyes as if she were debating beating the information out of me.

In truth, I didn't favor my odds in such a matchup,

but it was best not to tempt fate with a monster slumbering inside of me.

Fortunately, she quickly adopted a more relaxed stance. "Fine, keep yer secrets then. See if I care."

"It's not like that. It's just..."

She stopped me with a quick jab to the arm. "I'm teasing you, you squirrel-brained fool. Truth is I'm glad you're okay. Although I imagine not quite as glad as a certain someone."

I inclined my head, unsure whether she meant her father or...

She turned, put two fingers in her mouth, and let out a shrill whistle.

I winced, afraid my inner demon might awaken, but he wasn't the canine I should've been worried about. A moment later a big headed, brown and white missile shot from the door Hannah had stepped from – his tail wagging so hard he almost knocked himself over.

Spud?!

It was him all right. I would've recognized the big, sloppy brute anywhere. I bent low to greet him and was almost knocked off my feet as he eagerly plowed into me.

But why was he even here, and since when did he come when someone else called for him?

That could all wait as my surprise was quickly overcome with the emotion of finally seeing the one creature on this planet who I knew, without a doubt, I could one-hundred percent count on.

I grabbed the drooly pit bull in a big hug as he slobbered all over me, whining and rumbling with happiness. Finally, he let up, allowing me to stand and wipe the tears from my face.

"Got something in yer eye, Michael?" Hannah asked with a grin.

"Just glad to see *another* familiar face." I looked down at Spud then back at her. "But why is he here?"

"You can thank your father for that."

Dad? That was ... odd. I hadn't told anyone in Harris County that I'd been working with the hunters, especially not my parents. It was too risky. By day they might've had free will, but once transformed they were practically Hobart's slaves.

I hadn't wanted to risk him forcing any information out of my folks – assuming he could understand werewolf better than me, a big if but not one I cared to risk.

However, I also realized that cat was almost certainly out of the bag, and I'm not talking about the wolf Amos and Elijah had let get away.

The Hunters had been there in Brooklyn too, fighting alongside me. In fact, their presence had effectively turned the tide, allowing me and the others to escape when we had.

They'd stayed behind to cover our tracks and provide a distraction, which meant they hadn't followed us to Manhattan and subsequently been enslaved by a monstrous sea serpent. Good for them, but it also meant Hobart had been given two weeks to figure things out, more than enough time even for him.

No doubt prompted by my silence, Hannah said, "He drove out here two days after you vanished, announced who he was, then begged Da for parley. I don't know what was said between them, but he left this fine fellow behind." She scratched Spud's rump, something the chonky mutt was more than appreciative of.

Dad. Before the fight in Brooklyn, I'd left Spud in his and Mom's care. Under normal circumstances, they would've left him locked in the basement with water and kibble once the sun went down. Something must have changed.

Perhaps I should've gone home first after all.

"All right, that's enough," Hannah barked. "Back to bed with ye." She made a clicking sound with her mouth. Spud looked up at her, wagged his tail, then went happily trotting back inside.

"How did you...?"

"He's a dog, Michael," she replied. "And dogs can be trained ... by someone who knows what she's doing, which is most obviously not you."

Her tone was playful, but it made me wonder if maybe she was right. Don't get me wrong. I loved Spud like he was my own child, but I could barely get the stubborn pittie to sit on command, much less what she'd just done.

However, this was not the time to dwell on my inadequacies when it came to doggie daycare, as the sound of approaching footsteps caught my ear.

I turned to see a large group heading my way. Six older men dressed in traditional garb stood in the middle, their faces unreadable. They were flanked by an equal number of hunters, all armed.

At their forefront stood Isaiah Hood, overseer of Barley Hills and leader of the hunters.

He was dressed like his fellow elders, a white button-down shirt with black overcoat and pants. A simple straw hat sat atop his head, but it did nothing to dispel the piercing gaze of the man himself.

"Michael," he greeted, his voice sheathed in the iron will of a man comfortable in his authority. "Though it fills my heart with gladness to see you hale and hearty, ye'd best get to explaining your long absence."

15

BUILDING BARNS,
BURNING BRIDGES

I tried not to let myself be too intimidated, although it wasn't easy. Isaiah's position required him to be imposing to outsiders, to leave no doubt whatsoever as to who was in charge.

It went beyond that, though. He had a sort of presence about him. I can't really explain why, but if he were to, say, order my butt to start shucking wheat, then I'd probably start shucking wheat – despite not being sure whether wheat even needed to be shucked.

Hannah gave me a reassuring smile as I was marched into the longhouse that served as Barley Hills's meeting space. Then I was on my own. The elders may have granted her an exception to be a hunter but that didn't mean she was privy to their business.

Though I was led past a light switch and could plainly see fixtures hanging from the ceiling, the only illumination in the room came from lantern light. No doubt there was a ceremonial aspect to what was going on.

Pity there was nothing quaint about the high-powered rifles the hunters carried. I had no doubt they were all loaded with large bore silver cartridges, more than enough to turn me into a greasy silver smear where I stood.

I tried to calm myself as Isaiah and the other elders stepped to the far side of the room where they turned to face me.

I'd already figured out that enough pain could reawaken my inner wolf, but I guess now it was time to test whether stress could play a factor as well.

Isaiah nodded to the guards and they moved to leave, but not before two of them transferred their weapons to the elders at the far end of the procession. Oddly enough, I found myself split on the matter. As much as I preferred to not be threatened with loaded weapons, a part of me felt better knowing they weren't left unprotected.

Y'know, just in case.

"Michael Walden," Isaiah began, instantly causing me to stand a bit straighter. I tell you, the man had missed out on a great career as a drill instructor. "Two weeks ago we accompanied ye to the city on a quest to contain the Callahan pack."

Is that what they're calling it now? If so, I bet it made old Hobart happy as a fat clam.

"We risked life and limb for ye," Isaiah continued, "but more importantly we risked exposure. The outside world cannot know of our sacred mission. To do so endangers us as well as all others who have been tasked with our calling."

Wait. Others? Was he saying there were more trigger-happy Mennonites out there somewhere?

Wild as that thought was, I had a feeling it wasn't what I should be focusing on right then.

"Two weeks we have thought ye dead. Two weeks we have wondered what hath befallen ye. And now you appear here from seemingly out of the blue, having riled the pack yet again. Explain yerself."

I opened my mouth, not quite sure where to begin, but Isaiah wasn't finished yet.

"And I caution ye to tell the truth. Know, Michael Walden of Harris County, if ye should tell a falsehood or omit facts I shall know. Not because of devilry or witchcraft, but because of the sharp eyes and ears the Lord hath seen fit to bless me with." He paused for a moment to add, "And I also know thee to be a terrible liar."

Isaiah didn't want me to omit anything. Problem was, I only had so much to share.

He already knew the events which had led up to that night – Hobart tracking that vampire to his home in Brooklyn, me renting an apartment to keep an eye on things, and then eventually reaching out to the hunters for help once it became apparent the pack was about to do something stupid.

I hadn't been wrong on that matter, but I'd sure as heck underestimated the scope of how bad it might be.

Hobart, subtle as ever, had basically declared war on that vamp and his friends out in the open for all to see. Endangering outsiders was bad enough, but doing so in a city where literally everyone had a cell phone camera at their disposal defied all logic.

That summed up Hobart to a tee. He was big, strong, and terrifying, but was in no danger of splitting the atom anytime soon.

In the end, the battle came down to a choice of either leading Bill and his friends away or staying and fighting – knowing that even if we won, we'd all end up as losers.

In truth, that had been the easiest part of an otherwise chaotic night. Isaiah and his hunters had been there laying down cover fire for that express purpose – so we could scatter before our faces were plastered across the news, social media, and every wanted list in the country.

However, Isaiah had made one point clear beforehand. He and his people were there to contain Hobart's pack, not announce their existence to any vampires, witches, or whatnot. Hence our escape had ultimately fallen to me.

I recounted to him our journey from Brooklyn to Manhattan, trekking through the subway tunnels beneath the city and nearly jumping out of my skin at every noise we heard.

Next, I told him of making our way to the docks on that vampire's say so, where we met up with a wizard who lived nearby. An argument ensued for some reason I wasn't privy to, but it was cut short the moment a giant psychic dinosaur burst from the Hudson.

And no, it didn't sound any more believable hearing it from my own lips.

I paused there for a moment, lost in the terrifyingly bizarre memory.

It had all happened so fast. I'd stood there wide-eyed as this wannabe beast from twenty-thousand fathoms surfaced – debating between facing it alongside my newfound *acquaintances* or doing the smart thing and running for my life.

Perhaps that made me a coward, but fighting a real-life kaiju was more than I'd signed up for.

In the end, though, it had been a moot argument, because that's when it all went blank. I felt it somehow reach into my mind and then ... nothing.

I told the elders all of this with growing dread, not because of how insane it sounded, but knowing it was the easy part of my tale.

As bonkers as all that surely sounded, it was still the part least likely to get me shot, because up until that point I was still the Michael they knew.

After my first run-in with the hunters, earning their trust hadn't been too difficult. For starters, Isaiah had proven to have a surprisingly open mind. It also hadn't hurt that Hannah had been a prominent voice in convincing the younger hunters of my good intentions.

It was obvious I was different. Not only could I control my transformations, but I was willing to stand with them against Hobart's pack.

In truth, I'd expected to be put on some sort of werewolf probation, perhaps a warning that stepping out of line would earn me a bullet. Instead, Isaiah seemed willing to work with me from the start. Heck, it was almost as if he hadn't needed much convincing.

Why? I honestly still wasn't sure, but had figured it best to not question my good luck.

Standing there now, though, I was slowly coming to realize that keeping their trust wasn't going to be nearly as easy.

Had this been a horror movie, I'd have probably lied about the next part in an ill-conceived attempt to protect us both. Too bad that never seemed to work. Besides, I wasn't so naïve to not know how dangerous it could be to keep my allies in the dark, especially when dealing with powers beyond the ken of normal folk.

Mind you, telling the truth came with its own risks. What if they heard me out, only to decide I was no better than a rabid dog waiting to snap? I'd seen *Old Yeller* more than once. Trust me when I say I didn't want to relive the ending with me as the titular hound.

As much as I feared that outcome, though, I still found myself hesitant to lie. What if not telling them the truth left Isaiah and his people unprepared? What if my inner wolf then decided he didn't like the company I kept? More importantly, what if I couldn't stop him?

I considered Isaiah and Hannah to be friends. Heck, they'd taken in my dog despite having no reason to. I had no desire to see any harm come to them or the other hunters – even the ones who didn't like me very much.

Indecision gripped me as the seconds ticked by, Isaiah's raised eyebrow telling me he suspected I was floundering with something important.

Screw it.

Back in fourth grade I'd been assigned to do an oral report in front of the class. The very idea had terrified me for some reason, enough to cause me to freeze up like a deer in the headlights even when practicing in front of the mirror. Thankfully, my teacher Mr. Bickle had noticed my apparent stage fright.

One day he pulled me aside and said that whenever I felt myself freezing up, I should bite the inside of my cheek and not gently either. Then, while I was distracted by the pain, I needed to start talking, to let the words fly and trust my own mind to do its job.

It was advice that had saved my butt in more than one classroom.

And now it was time for it to save me again.

I crunched down on the side of my cheek hard enough to draw blood. There was no time to regret the pain, however, as I started in again, telling them about the murder house, its owners, my escape, and, most importantly, discovering I wasn't alone inside my own skin.

Once the words started flowing, it was like a dam burst. I found myself recounting every detail I could remember, even a few I probably should've kept to myself like the fate of that poor piggy.

"Wait," one of the elders, a fellow named Abram, said. "Ye ate someone's pet?"

"Not by choice," I replied. "I had no control over…"

"Huh-ugh … he didn't do shit." My lips sputtered for a moment before I somehow managed to talk over myself. "*I* did. And it was no accident."

Oh no!

"The same way," my inner beast continued, "it's gonna be no accident what happens here if any of you fuckers so much as look at me the wrong way."

16

SHEEP IN WOLF'S CLOTHING

In my haste to ensure I omitted nothing, I must've accidentally bitten the side of my mouth harder than I realized. Either that or my inner wolf had the absolute worst timing in the world.

Whatever the reason, things had just gone from manageable straight to dumpster fire.

Isaiah's lips narrowed until they were pencil thin. Behind him, the two elders acting as ceremonial guards raised their rifles.

Can't say I blamed them.

"Go ahead and try," my inner beast warned. "I'll rip those stupid beards off and shove them up your assholes before you can even..."

"No!" I cried, wresting control of my vocal cords. "You can't."

"I can and will. Now shut up and enjoy the show because shit's about to get messy."

I debated how best to fight my own body, but my werewolf apparently had different plans.

I felt the stirring from deep inside, a flood of brain chemicals numbing my nerves and inducing a state of

134

mild euphoria. He was doing it. He was forcing my body to conform to his will. Guess that answered yet another question about how much control he could exercise.

Even as I watched in horror, the hair on the back of my hands began to grow courser and thicker.

No!

Two could play at this game. I gritted my teeth and looked inward, envisioning an effigy of myself in my human form. I grabbed hold of that image and embraced it with every ounce of will I could muster.

Amazingly enough, that managed to reverse the change as the fur on my hands and arms receded until they were normal hair follicles again.

"The fuck are you doing?" he cried.

"Stopping you!"

"You do realize these chucklefucks are pointing their boom sticks at you too, right? Or is that some human kink I'm not aware of?"

"I ... that doesn't matter," I told him. "Besides, you started it."

He let out a disgusted sigh. "You know what? Fuck it and fuck you. If you think you've got what it takes to stop me then bring it on, pupcake!"

He doubled down on forcing the change, once more turning the warring tide inside my body to his favor. My bones crackled as my clothing grew taut around me.

Once more I tried to match his effort, this time focusing not only on myself but also everything I held dear in life – my parents, Spud, Dallas, even my job.

I managed to stalemate him again but was pretty sure that was it. I was using everything I had but it was night out now, the time when beasts stalked the woods. I could sense my body wanting to side with his will.

He didn't have a huge advantage, probably on account

of it not being a full moon, but it was enough to give the beast the edge in our struggle.

There was only one option left.

I had hoped that given time I could reason with my inner wolf, come to an agreement of sorts. But now I saw there was no chance of that happening. For the very first time my condition truly felt like a curse.

I had no reason to want to die, but my life wasn't the only one at stake here. If I lost control and killed the elders, who was to say how much damage I'd cause, how many lives would be lost before the rest managed to stop me?

I had no intention of finding out the answer.

"*Do it,*" I cried, the words slurred thanks to my teeth rapidly becoming fangs. "*Shoot me. You have to stop him!*"

In another second or two human speech would become impossible. However, the elders still had time to react. Though the change itself didn't take long, I was vulnerable during it.

Fortunately, the Barley Hills council wasn't just made up of geezers who'd spent their lives churning butter while others faced danger. Each had earned their place, rising to the top through experience, cunning, and fortitude.

Mind you, I wasn't sure how much relevant experience they actually had as, far as I was aware anyway, there'd been no werewolves for them to hunt before three months ago.

Not a comforting thought as my body began to bulk up.

Fortunately, the two armed elders wasted no time in lining up their shots.

This was it, the end of my story.

Mom, Dad, wish I could've told you goodbye and how much I love you both. Dallas, you're the best bud a guy could ever hope for. Oh, and sorry about that ten bucks I never paid back...

"Hold," Isaiah said, raising his hand.

What?!

That single word might as well have been a commandment from God as far as the others were concerned. They didn't question, didn't hesitate, they merely shouldered their weapons as told.

Amazingly enough, I felt the change within me pause as my head cocked to the side.

"Aye, that goes for ye as well," he added, talking *at me* yet obviously not *to me*.

"*Why should I?*" my inner beast replied with a mouth no longer entirely human.

This was a new sensation for me, the transformation stopped halfway between man and wolf beast – something I hadn't realized I was capable of.

Can't say it was particularly comfortable. My muscles and bones were in the process of shifting and growing, stuck in positions they were never meant to be stuck in. And with the stew of brain chemicals starting to subside, this halfway form would quickly go from uncomfortable to downright painful in short order.

"Because I acknowledge thee," Isaiah said. "You are clearly not only a fearsome foe, but an intelligent one at that."

"*No shit*," my inner beast responded, sounding perplexed.

"Alas, intelligence is both blessing and burden," the elder huntsman continued. "To have it means one's eyes are open to the truths of this world." He shrugged. "And one of those truths is being forced to acknowledge one's own mortality."

"*Mortality?*"

"Indeed. Take me for instance. Though my love of

God is strong, I have no desire to meet him before my time. I trust the same is true of ye."

What is he playing at? I wondered.

"Like you have any chance in hell of making that happen."

"I merely acknowledge the possibility I could die if we continue this course awhile. All I ask is ye acknowledge the same."

"And why's that?"

"Because the weapons ye see here are not all this humble village has to offer. We might seem simple folk to ye, but our craftsmanship for silver runs deep."

"That a threat?"

Isaiah shook his head. "Merely the truth, as I think ye might already understand."

He was right. My inner werewolf had told me as much back at the serial killer house. Though I hadn't realized it, he'd apparently been awake this whole time – watching things through my eyes. If that were true, then he already knew the hunters were not to be taken lightly.

"You think I'm afraid of you ball lickers?"

Or maybe not.

"Not at all," Isaiah replied. "I merely believe we would both prefer to live."

"Let's pretend for a moment that's true. What then? You expect me to sit down for a spot of tea while we sniff each other's asses?"

Isaiah cracked the ghost of a grin. "Nay. I merely wish for us to converse."

"You want to talk?" the beast grumbled, as if all of this were nothing more than a test of his patience. *"Then talk, but make it quick. My stomach's rumbling. Trust me, that's not something you want while you're standing there looking all edible and shit."*

"Food can be provided."

I felt my ears suddenly perk up. "*Why the fuck didn't you say that to begin with?*"

Sensing the possibility for violence had perhaps dropped a notch, I grabbed control of my mouth. "*Can we maybe change back first? Because this halfway form kinda hurts.*"

"*Sure, why not? Beats listening to you whine like a pussy.*"

Ten minutes later found me tearing into a smoked ham much as I'd done with that poor pig, all while the elders looked on in silent judgement. At least this time the pork was cooked.

Unfortunately, my inner werewolf had the table manners of a wild animal.

After a while I stopped fighting and let him have at it, focusing instead on making sure we chewed before swallowing.

I can only imagine how I looked, ripping apart hunk after hunk of pork while talking to myself like a madman.

Needless to say, this had potential to complicate future Sunday dinners with my folks.

"I trust the food is to yer liking," Isaiah said after several minutes, the barest hint of amusement in his voice.

"I prefer it still squealing, but this'll do," my wolf grunted, coming up for air long enough to talk.

"S-sorry about this," I added, trying not to choke.

"Calm yourself awhile, Michael. I know ye to be a good man. That still holds true."

"Good for nothing you mean," my inner wolf replied with a combination belch / cackle.

"Yer welcome to your opinion, of course," Isaiah said

before adding, "Speaking of which, I don't believe we've had the pleasure."

"That's because I don't fuck humans."

Son of a...

"Not quite what I meant," the elder hunter replied, displaying the patience of a saint. "I merely wished to know your name."

Huh. I held my tongue, curious to see where this was going,

"My name?"

"Indeed. Yer an intelligent being, one gifted with a tongue for speech. Tis common for those who converse to address one another by their names. Ye know mine, yes?"

For a moment I was sure another insult was incoming, but my other half merely said. "It's Isaiah."

"Indeed it is."

"Don't sound so surprised, shit-licker. When you're trapped in a dipshit's skull with nothing to do but watch and listen, you either pay attention or go insane."

"I'm not," Isaiah replied. "Nor was my question meant to condescend."

"Really?" my inner wolf replied dubiously. "Why do I find that hard to..."

"Yer name, beast," another elder, David I believe, demanded. "We'll not ask ye again!"

My eyes narrowed, or one of them did anyway. "Say that again, asshole."

"Peace to ye both," Isaiah quickly said before turning to the others. "If you'll excuse us awhile, I'd like to speak with our guest *alone*."

The rest of the elders, David included, looked none too happy with that. But Isaiah held each of their gaze in turn. The battle of wills was over before it even began.

Within a minute, they all filed out of the longhouse. They definitely didn't seem pleased with this development but none appeared ready to challenge Isaiah. Like I said, the guy had a certain force of will to him. In another place, another life, he could have been a politician ... or maybe a cult leader. It was probably for the best that neither had come to pass.

The last of the elders handed his rifle over to Isaiah, which he accepted. He might've had some plan for pacifying the beast inside of me, but he was no fool.

"About time," my inner wolf mumbled, tearing off another hunk of ham. "Those piss stains were starting to ruin my digestion."

"Hold no ill will against them. They're all good men."

"They'll be dead men if they fuck with me," he replied just as our eyes settled on the rifle in Isaiah's hands. "Try not to forget that."

"Does this frighten ye?" the elder hunter asked, glancing down at the gun.

A laugh escaped from my throat. "Hells no. It's just nice to see you're not as stupid as you look."

Isaiah must've found that funny because he chuckled too, before shouldering the weapon. "Now, back to that which we were speaking of. I would hear yer name if ye have one. Calling ye beast is unbecoming."

"I'm not a beast, I'm a *Dominant*," my inner wolf growled. "So the only thing you should probably be calling me is *master*." Mind you, the implied threat was immediately undone as he began gnawing on the ham bone. There came a crunch as I'm pretty sure one of my molars cracked.

Ow! "You've had enough," I cried, yanking the bone from my left hand and tossing it away.

"Hey, I was eating that!"

"No, you were breaking *my* teeth on it. I don't expect you to understand, but my dental plan is good but not *that* good. Besides, trust me, you're already full."

My stomach gurgled as if in response, making me wish I had a few antacids to follow the ridiculous amount of ham we'd just scarfed down.

Then, realizing I was interrupting whatever had been going on, I handed the ball back over to Isaiah again. "Sorry about that. You were saying?"

As crazy as all this was, the wizened hunter seemed to take it in stride. He nodded before his expression changed, just enough to let me know he was no longer focused on me – or my half anyway. "I'm afraid the only master I acknowledge and serve is our good Lord in Heaven. But if there is something else I may call ye, I would know it."

"Yeah, it starts with *fuck* and ends with *you*," the beast replied.

Isaiah remained undeterred, though. "Do ye have a name or not?"

"I..." He gritted our teeth. "No, I don't. Are you happy now?"

"Why not?" Isaiah asked patiently.

"You probably won't understand this as a dumbass human, but us higher lifeforms identify each other by scent. Pretty simple stuff for those of us who aren't hairless apes. Now where did that bone go?"

"A higher lifeform ye say? And yet I see a man sitting before me."

We clambered to our feet before I could stop myself. "Say that again to my face."

If the huntsman was intimidated he didn't show it. "I speak only the truth, friend. You stand before me as a man not a beast. Do ye deny this?"

"Fuck yeah I do," my inner demon growled. "The only reason I look this way is because of the beta bitch I'm unfortunate enough to share this skin with."

Hey!

"Yes, but said skin is that of a man."

"I could *change* that if you want."

Isaiah met and held our gaze. "Tis merely an observation, nothing more. You wear the face of the man I call Michael, yet you are not he and he is not you."

"Fuck no we ain't."

"Then if ye not be Michael, who...?"

"I already told you! I don't have a..."

"It's Winston," I blurted out.

If my left eye had been capable of shooting from its socket to glare at the rest of me I'm certain it would have.

"The fuck did you say, pupcake?"

My reply had just sort of popped out. Regardless, it seemed I was back in this conversation whether or not I wanted to be.

17

THE NAME GAME

"**W**hat the hell did you call me?"

"Um ... Winston?" I replied sheepishly.

"What the fuck is a Winston?" my other half snarled, "and you'd better hope I like the answer better than I like *you*."

"Listen. Isaiah has a point," I said. "In fact, I was thinking the exact same thing on the way over here. I can't just keep referring to you as my inner wolf."

"*Your* inner wolf?"

"You know what I mean," I replied, realizing it was entirely possible he didn't.

"Yeah. You think of me as some sort of fucking pet. Well, guess what, butternuts, I can do a whole lot worse than shit on your carpet."

This was veering into dangerous territory. I needed to try and right this ship before he did something stupid.

"My *point* is you need a name others can refer to you by. It's just the way things work in human society."

"Like I give a flying fuck about human society."

I felt my temper start to fray. "Yeah, well, some of us

do. And since you haven't offered up any suggestions, I'm giving you a name – *Winston*. There. It's settled."

"The hell it is," my inner ... Winston replied. "I don't like it. Sounds stupid."

"It's not stupid. It was my great grandfather's..."

"If you're about to say the name of his dog, then I'm about to see how many layers of skin I need to peel before you shut up for good."

"Not his dog," I quickly replied. "It was *his* name."

"Don't care. The answer is no."

"Not to mention, also my favorite *Ghostbuster*."

"I have no idea what the fuck that even means, but now it's definitely no. Suckle my teat if you don't like it, but under no circumstances are you to *ever*..."

"Michael's right," Isaiah interrupted. "Tis a good name, proper and sound. More importantly tis a *strong* name."

My head immediately cocked to the left. "How strong?"

"Tis a name that implies stature," the hunter continued, his tone suddenly mollifying. "It brings to mind respect, *dominance* even."

He can't possibly think this brute is dumb enough to...

"Is that so?" Winston replied.

On the other hand...

"Of course," Isaiah said. "It be a name any of my hunters would be glad to claim for themselves. However, if ye still think it doesn't suit ye..."

"Hold on! I didn't say that."

No way! He'd just fallen for reverse psychology that not even a child would buy. Winston, however, was apparently *not* smarter than a fifth grader.

"Don't get me wrong," he remarked, "I'm still not convinced, especially since nutless here came up with it.

But maybe I'll give it a try ... for now. I'd better hear some goddamned respect, though."

I let out a mental sigh, unable to believe he'd been so easily baited, but that wasn't the only realization to dawn upon me.

Winston had been able to pick up on my conscious thoughts while we were in our other form, but there'd been no indication he'd heard any of my commentary just now. Otherwise he would've surely lost his temper.

Did that mean I was safe inside my own head, or my portion of it anyway, while we were human?

Talk about no small relief. The last thing I needed was an emotionally unstable werewolf cherry picking every stray thought running through my mind.

Alas, that was all the time I was allowed for introspection.

"Tis a pleasure to make your acquaintance, mighty Winston," Isaiah said, nodding his head in approval. "Now with that bit of business out of the way, perhaps ye can enlighten my humble self as to the missing parts of Michael's story, and how a dominant soul such as yours managed to endure such tribulations."

It was amazing to see the change in attitude once Isaiah called the other elders back in. My experience with the leaders of Barley Hills was their word was considered law. Those who didn't show proper respect were quickly put in their place.

However, following a brief word in private by their leader, they'd gone from browbeating us to complimenting Winston, even mollifying him as they encouraged him to tell his side of our tale.

It was obviously meant to feed my inner wolf's not inconsiderable ego. Regardless, it was seriously weird to see coming from a bunch of werewolf hunters. Winston may have been fooled, but I wasn't quite so naïve. Isaiah was playing chess while my werewolf half was still figuring out the rules to Old Maid.

Little by little they coaxed from him what had happened while I was mind-whammied by that sea monster, leading to a far more detailed retelling than the two minute recap I'd been able to deliver.

The problem was that with every detail Winston recounted, I once again experienced an awful sense of déjà vu – experiencing strange flashes of memory I had no recollection of.

Winston had awoken somewhere deep underground, within the New York sewer system.

The space around me was dimly lit, bathed in an eerie green glow like some cheap Halloween haunted house.

He'd gained consciousness in a strange place alongside people he didn't recognize, all of them laboring toward some purpose he couldn't quite articulate.

My vision panned downward, scanning the floor around me, only to discover a similar pile of innards now lying discarded upon the ground.

Wherever he was, Winston had been both confused and frightened to find himself suddenly free of whatever mental prison he'd been stuck within.

He didn't quite describe it that way, mind you, filling his tale with obviously false bravado I doubted anyone in the room believed.

Whatever the truth about his feelings, he'd gotten lucky. At first, the others didn't seem to notice he'd broken free of whatever control they were under. They were too focused on the gruesome task they'd been set to.

That's when it hit me. His face, heck, all of their faces. They were blank slates, devoid of any emotion. The lights were on but no one was home, almost like they were ... sleepwalking.

Isaiah raised an eyebrow, possibly noticing me twitch as I experienced the shock and terror of these bizarre flashbacks while Winston recounted his story. However, he said nothing, gesturing for my other half to continue, which he did.

Whatever confusion he'd felt upon awakening quickly gave way to rage. The way Winston explained it, he'd had every intention of clawing and slashing everything in sight – either not knowing or caring those others were likely victims too.

I felt a euphoric numbness deep inside that began to rapidly spread to my extremities. It was the space of an instant for me to understand what was happening.

"And then what?" Isaiah prodded after Winston paused in his retelling.

"I changed my mind," he said.

"Truly?"

"Yep. Not much sport in gutting mindless drones. So, I decided to leave instead."

That was a lie. I wasn't sure how I knew it. I just *did.*

Alien. Totally, inexplicably alien.

That's the only way I could describe it without screaming. This scent was like nothing I'd ever encountered before. My mind, a veritable Wikipedia of foul odors, was unable to identify it beyond that.

Winston had smelled something which spoke of worlds other than our own, places that were hostile, wild, and completely unlike anything either of us had ever experienced.

I wasn't sure of much beyond that save for one thing –

it had utterly terrified him because that was the point when he'd turned his focus toward escape.

That alone was enough to give me pause. Werewolves didn't frighten easily. In my dealings with the pack, I knew it took either overwhelming odds or injury to make them rethink their actions. But that wasn't the case here.

It was fear, plain and simple – not that he was about to admit it.

Winston instead focused on the details of his escape, which mostly involved gloating about effortlessly slashing his way through countless enemies standing between him and freedom.

I squinted to see whatever was blocking the way, only to immediately wish to God I hadn't. The creature was the size of a grizzly bear, held up by three pairs of spindly legs while a gleaming carapace covered its backside.

From deep within my subconscious an image began to take shape of some ... monstrosity, inhuman in a way that made werewolves almost seem mundane.

"No!"

It was only the curious stares of the elders which made me realize I'd said that last part out loud.

"No?" Winston replied. "You calling me a liar, asshole?"

"It's not that," I backpedaled. "It's just ... I got caught up in the emotion of it all."

"Sorry if my retelling is too badass for a pussy like you. Oh wait, no I'm not."

What he'd described as a kick-butt adventure through New York's underground was in reality a desperate escape. I don't know how I knew this, just that I did – almost as if some small part of me had been awake enough to remember.

More important was the question of what had triggered our shared primal fear. It may well have been that kaiju-sized monster from the river, but somehow I didn't think so. All I could seem to remember was an eerie green glow and then smelling something *that didn't belong*, a scent strong enough to induce pure terror.

There wasn't much more to Winston's tale. He kept running until he was far from the city, and that's apparently the point where the Chadworths decided to make their appearance.

I tuned out the rest. There was no need to relive it.

Won't lie. A part of me was glad I didn't fully remember that underground prison. Just hearing Winston talk about it was enough to give me the willies.

However, it did serve to confirm what I already suspected. The weirdness in Harris County was only the tiny tip of some much larger supernatural iceberg.

Sure, I'd known about vampires and witches, but there was more out there – a *lot* more. How much? I had no clue nor did I really want one. All I knew was that history was full of myths and monsters, plenty of whom were much higher up on the food chain than lycanthropes.

We're talking demons, devils, demigods, and more. A whole wide world of terrors.

I'd once thought I had a handle on what was real versus what was imaginary. No more.

The only thing I was certain of were my limits with regards to how much I could take. There were things out there that were more than I'd signed up for, something I wasn't ashamed to admit.

I wanted to keep Harris County and its people safe. That was it, the limits of my ambition. I saw now that I'd overreached in traveling to New York to confront Hobart. If anything, my ordeal beneath the streets of Manhattan was quite possibly the universe's way of telling me to keep my snout out of situations that were none of my business.

If so, I intended to heed its warning, especially having caught a glimpse of what awaited out there.

The strangest thing was, I had a sneaking suspicion Winston felt the same way.

The question now was whether we'd have any say in the matter.

18

SECRETS AND LIES

I wasn't quite sure how to explain my fears to Isaiah without setting Winston off in the process.

Sure, I'd sensed that same fear from my alter ego through the bits and pieces of memories I had. But where I wasn't afraid to admit I was in over my head, I had a feeling my wolf half wouldn't be quite so accommodating.

Call it ego or a massive inferiority complex, but if someone were to ever, say, challenge Winston to prove his bravery by diving headfirst into molten lava, well, I'd best be wearing asbestos underwear.

I stood there debating where to begin, only for a massive yawn to escape my lips instead. Odd since I was wide awake. Hell, after spending two weeks asleep inside my own body, I wasn't particularly eager for some shuteye.

"Gods damn," Winston groused, "You fuckers are even more boring than I realized."

"That was you?" I replied. "Didn't you just wake up?"

"Save it for someone who cares, bitch boy. And maybe next time pick more interesting company than these rubes." He yawned again, taking my half along for the ride.

Ahead of me, Isaiah grinned knowingly.

"Yer of course welcome to rest awhile," he said. "Please do enjoy our hospitality."

"I'd ... enjoy ... gutting you more. But ... maybe ... later."

The way Winston slurred his words told me he was fading far faster than I would've expected.

Don't get me wrong. I understood boredom. Stucky loved to share his fishing stories whenever it was slow at work. He was a nice guy, but he couldn't spin a yarn to save his life. He could've been out on Loggerhead Lake battling Moby Dick himself, but somehow he'd make it sound as exciting as watching paint peel. Still, he'd never conked me out quite this fast.

"Be ... a good ... pupcake," Winston continued, the left side of my face drooping with fatigue, "and don't fuck around. Remember, I ... know where ... you live."

I wasn't sure if that was meant to be a threat or joke as my left side suddenly went limp, causing me to stumble. Fortunately, I managed to regain my footing before I could eat floor. I stood up again, not sure what had just happened, other than being certain I was once again alone in my own head.

I either shared a body with the laziest werewolf ever or something else was afoot. The fact that Isaiah's body language instantly changed from overly friendly back to his typical severe self, clued me in that it was the latter.

"The beast is asleep, yes?"

I nodded tentatively.

"He will be awhile, although I fear not long enough. He's frightful strong, and the night calls to his kind."

Won't lie, the instant change in demeanor scared me, albeit not nearly as much as those memories from my time in New York. "What did you do to me?"

"Not ye, only he." Isaiah turned toward Abram and nodded.

"The ham," the other elder explained. "'Twas dosed with a tincture that affects wolf not man."

"You drugged him?" Even as the question left my lips, I realized how stupid it was compared to what he'd implied. "Hold on, you can do that?"

"Indeed."

Holy crap! I'd confessed my dual personalities to them barely an hour ago. Now, I was no science whiz, but didn't it normally take whole teams working for months if not years to formulate vaccines, antivenoms, and the like?

What the heck kind of chemists were Barley Hills hiding that could specifically target a split-personality werewolf in less time than it took to watch a movie? Unless...

"I'm not the only one. Am I?"

"Only what?" Isaiah replied.

"You know what I mean," I snapped, momentarily finding my backbone against the elder huntsman. "There are others out there like me, aren't there? Dominants whose wolves have somehow become conscious."

Isaiah raised an eyebrow at my outburst but said nothing.

However, David was quick to fire back. "Mind yer tongue before your betters, boy."

Betters? It was a good thing Winston wasn't awake as I had a feeling he'd have an opinion or two to share.

"That will do," Isaiah interrupted before either of us could say more. "Be at peace, Michael. Yer among friends. But to answer yer question, nay. Neither I nor any of my fellows have met another like ye."

"Then how come he's asleep and I'm not? You can't just tell me it was a lucky guess."

"I claim no such thing. What we did was purposeful."

"I don't understand."

"Nor are ye meant to." He let out a sigh, as if debating whether to say more. "I understand yer confusion. Truly I do. To have yer whole life upended a few short moons ago, not to mention that of yer kin, has to be nothing short of terrifying. But yer also young, where this world is not. What might seem strange and new for yinz, is ancient history for those with a better understanding."

David, despite being admonished moments earlier, turned to him. "Our oaths, Isaiah. I will remind ye..."

"I need not be reminded of my duty, brother. Though I may not be as quick in body, trust that my mind remains sharp. Sharp enough to know that, though our fealty remains, those we swore our oaths to do not."

"But..."

Isaiah waved him off. "I am quite aware of recent happenings. But until we are presented with proof the old words haven't been forgotten, we shall stand as judge of our own actions." He turned to address the others. "You are all aware the natural order has been upset, perhaps irrevocably so, are ye not?"

The elders looked among themselves but none of them spoke against him.

"Good. Then I say we shall honor our oaths while also acknowledging these changing times. The world has moved on. We cannot allow ourselves to be dragged down by refusing to move with it."

I had no freaking idea what he was talking about. That said, while I wasn't holding my breath to be taught their secret handshake, I got the impression Isaiah was trying to clue me in more than his fellow elders were comfortable with.

"Is any of that supposed to mean anything?"

"Not to ye, Michael. But I will tell you this much. Your knowledge of yer true nature is only due to events no one, be they witch or seer, could have foreseen. But yer actual story is far older than ye will likely ever suspect."

He held up a hand before I could ask. "Alas, tis a story ye will not hear from my lips. Just know my people have long prepared for a time we thought would never come to pass. But now that it has, we find ourselves as ready as any man could hope to be. And yet, despite our preparations, we also find ourselves adrift same as ye. Tis truly strange days we live in."

I waited for him to continue, but he'd said his piece.

While I couldn't pretend to be terribly enlightened compared to five minutes earlier, there were some things I was beginning to suspect – assuming I was correct in reading between the lines.

If so, then the people of Barley Hills and Harris County were similar in that none of us had actually seen a werewolf prior to three months ago. But where I'd been raised to think the boogeyman was make believe, the folks here had been taught otherwise via some hidden knowledge passed down from generation to generation.

I couldn't help but draw comparisons to the ritual, nor wonder who had originally set both towns upon their respective paths. Were they the same people, or two groups diametrically opposed to one another?

One town full of hidden monsters and another of hunters training for the day when those monsters might appear, all of it stretching back to the distant past. I didn't know how far, but at this point couldn't rule anything out.

Heck, for all I knew, those ships which landed at Plymouth Rock four centuries ago could've been carrying pilgrim werewolves.

Gah! It was ... simply too much for me, a sanitation worker from rural Pennsylvania, to process. If there was anyone ill-prepared to handle the idea of a centuries long supernatural standoff, it was me.

What the heck kind of crazy world had I stepped into? And more importantly, how the hell did I get out of it and back to my life?

19

BRAND NEW DAY

"Time to pay the piper."

"What's a piper and why aren't we ripping him to shreds instead?"

I let out a sigh. "It's only a saying."

"Which means what?" Winston asked.

"It's ... something people say that doesn't really mean anything."

"That's pretty fucking stupid. And yet you humans consider yourselves the dominant species. What a joke."

"Whatever. I was just talking to myself, okay?"

"Then I suggest shutting your meat hole so I don't have to hear it."

I suppressed a yawn as we waited near the outskirts of Barley Hills, but this time it had nothing to do with werewolf hunter alchemy.

Sleep had been a long time coming after the elders finally decided they'd browbeaten me enough. They didn't want me to risk another confrontation with Hobart's minions, so they found me a spot in Isaiah's barn instead. The accommodations were a little rough but I'd had worse. It was more an issue of my brain refusing to turn off.

Not only did I have way too much to think about, but I couldn't easily dismiss the fear of closing my eyes only to wake up and find another two weeks had passed.

I'd been hoping for the elders to fill me in on everything that had happened whilst I was on my extended catnap, but they'd remained tight-lipped after Isaiah's speech. The best I could glean was that a sort of unspoken demilitarized zone had been established between the two towns.

So long as each faction stayed on their side, things remained at a low simmer.

Can't say that was bad to hear. Following the debacle in Brooklyn there was no way Hobart wouldn't have known about the hunters' true calling. So the fact I hadn't returned to outright war between our respective municipalities was nothing to sneeze at. Although now that I was back, there was no way of knowing whether the peace would hold.

Regardless, I'd finally drifted off, only to awaken a few hours later, upright and pantless as I stood in the open doorway of the barn blissfully relieving myself.

Thankfully, it had only been number one, but it was enough to realize that whatever they'd drugged Winston with had obviously worn off.

Now, with the sun up, my butt once again covered, and with my purloined bugout bag over my shoulder, I was waiting for my ride home. Hopefully, the early hour would give me a chance to settle in before...

"Is it true?"

Huh? I spun, much quicker than was warranted. A snarl escaped my lips, followed by, "Who the fuck are you? Not that soon-to-be dead bitches need a name."

Hannah raised an eyebrow, showing far less surprise than I would've expected from Winston's violent and vulgar outburst.

"No," I cried. "She's a friend."

"She ain't *my* friend."

"Not with that attitude," she replied, her voice calm as a summer breeze, the rifle slung over her shoulder and six shooter at her hip no doubt contributing to her confidence.

She wasn't alone either, even if the bulky pit bull by her side looked far more confused than menacing.

"I see it's true then," she said after a moment.

"Um, what is?" I remarked, trying to play it cool.

"Calm yerself, Michael. Da told me."

"He did?"

"Indeed, but not before swearing me to secrecy. I think they're still pondering awhile on what to make of this ... development." She looked down at Spud. "Anyway, did ye forget someone?"

I actually hadn't. I loved Spud with all my heart, but things had changed. I was no longer fully in control of my own body. The fact that Winston had been able to take control while I was asleep told me I could no longer trust myself.

"Hannah, he..."

"Has been looking forward to his rightful home and master, as I'm sure ye can guess."

"Yeah, but..."

"Fuck it," Winston interrupted. "Just about time for breakfast anyway."

What?! "No," I snapped. "There will be no eating Spud. He's family."

"Is that some kind of half-assed dog joke?"

"No. It's just..."

"Michael's right," Hannah interrupted. "Spud's family. He's part of yer pack."

"What in the seven Hells are you yammering about?" Winston replied, baring our teeth.

"Ye claim to be a Dominant do ye not?"

"I don't *claim* anything, bitch. I lead, others follow. That's all there is to it."

"Indeed. A leader needs followers, a pack, and what is a pack if not extended family?"

"Okay, and...?"

"Michael here is part of ye, whether ye like it or not, and he claims Spud as his own. That makes him one of yours."

"No, it fucking doesn't. My pack is ... well...," Winston trailed off as if at a loss for words. "Gods damn it! This is why we should've gutted Hobart when we had the chance."

"Except he didn't, and neither did ye," Hannah continued, pressing her luck. "I won't tell ye how to deal with yer business save to warn ye. If ye stroll back into Harris County like ye own the place, it won't end well."

"You saying I can't handle that fat prick?"

"Yes, that's exactly what she's saying," I snapped. "Because it's not just him. Hobart controls every werewolf in Harris County."

"Not after I kill his ass."

"A feat made exceedingly difficult if he gets word of yer existence first," Hannah added.

"What do you mean?"

"Hobart isn't afraid of Michael. That I'm certain of."

Winston let out a bark of laughter but she wasn't finished. "Tis neither joke nor meant to offend. The simple truth is he considers ye more nuisance than threat." She held up a hand before either of us could respond. "Tis a good thing, but a status quo that could change in an instant if he learns of yer ... partnership."

"Partnership?" my alter ego replied dubiously.

That set him off on a rant, unsurprisingly, but I ignored his tirade, reading between the lines of what

Hannah had said. I'd thrown a few monkey wrenches into Hobart's plans, true. But the truth was, I hadn't done much to actually threaten his authority. Heck, I'd even told him upfront I didn't want to be in charge. However, the same couldn't be said of my inner demon.

I realized now that could be a problem.

Before I'd disappeared, Hobart had been making it a point to keep the pack's business separate from the town's. He seemed content to let pack members go about their lives so long as the sun was up. But that could change if he felt his position was threatened.

The implication was clear. If I waltzed into town with a Winston-sized chip on my shoulder, not only would it be dangerous for me but others could suffer because of it.

The problem was, I doubted my other half would care. That meant I needed to spin this in a way he would agree to.

"I don't give a shit what either of you fuck nuggets think," Winston continued to rant. "If Hobart wants a fight, I'll shove my paw so far up his ass he'll..."

"He can't know about you," I interrupted. "Not yet anyway."

"Why? Afraid he'll beat your ass while I'm beating his?"

"No. I'm afraid he'll sic the entire pack on us."

"Which just shows you have no fucking idea about any of this. One Dominant challenges another. That's the way it works."

"Maybe under normal circumstances," I replied, as if anything about this was normal. "But I know Hobart. And I'm telling you, if he catches wind that something's changed, that you're free from your ... brain cage..." I caught Hannah raising an eyebrow. "Don't ask. Long story. Anyway, if he senses things are different now, I guarantee the rules will go right out the window."

"Michael's right," Hannah replied, catching on quick. "Strong and brave ye might be, but one against many is a fight neither of ye can win. Ye need to bide your time, gather your strength. There's no shame in a bit of strategy so long as ye win in the end. And ye won't be alone either."

"You're talking about this dipshit dog, aren't you?" He pointed a finger at Spud. "Don't lick my hand, stupid!"

Hannah shrugged. "I meant Michael too."

"You've gotta be fucking kidding me."

"Not at all. Tis a small pack perhaps, but a pack nonetheless."

"Yeah, but..."

"One that's yours to lead and grow as ye work to claim yer *rightful place*."

I felt my left eyebrow rise as Winston no doubt considered this. Hannah was her father's daughter after all, able to honey her words just as well when necessary.

If Winston had one weakness, it was definitely his ego, and right now she was stroking it like a pro.

Perhaps not the best way to word it, as he replied, "I kind of like this one, pupcake. She ain't much to look at with that pasty skin, but if you want to mount her I won't object."

Wait, what?!

———— ❧ ————

"You can't say stuff like that!"

"Why not?"

"Because women don't like it, that's why."

"Maybe they would if you actually mounted them instead of whimpering like a little shit kitten."

We were once again alone, save for Spud who was busy alternating between sniffing our right and left legs, looking mighty confused as he went about it. At least Winston hadn't objected when I'd taken his leash from a very red-faced Hannah.

Needless to say, we were lucky to not be peppered with silver slugs.

There was no doubt I'd be back here at some point. Maybe by then Isaiah would even be in a talking mood. However, I had a feeling it might be best to keep Winston away from Hannah until I figured out a way to civilize him.

Assuming that was even possible.

For now, I was just happy to be on my way. Even so, I was still somewhat surprised Isaiah had let me go so easily. I hadn't expected them to take me prisoner, mind you, or at least I'd hoped that wouldn't be the case. Regardless, they'd swallowed the pill of my split personality much easier than I'd expected.

I was no Rhodes Scholar, but at this point had zero doubt they knew more than they were letting on.

It made me wonder if my case wasn't as unique as I'd originally thought. Heck, maybe there'd been a few Winstons scattered amongst those pilgrim werewolves after all.

I pushed those thoughts to the side as a familiar vehicle turned the corner and headed my way – a 2005 Ford Crown Victoria that continued to chug along despite its advanced age.

"Remember what we talked about," I said as the car approached. "The less people who know about you the better."

"Yeah, yeah. I got it. Just don't go pretending you and your pet snack are my packmates. I wouldn't want to die of embarrassment before gutting Hobart."

It wasn't quite the level of cooperation I'd hoped for,

but it was as good as I was going to get as the car pulled up and the passenger side window rolled down.

I leaned down to greet the sole occupant, or tried to anyway.

"You need to give me control," I hissed beneath my breath, a second before I felt the muscles on my left side relax.

Oh yeah. No way was this not going to end in disaster. For now, though, it was time to pretend all was right with the world.

"Hey, Dad, I'm back."

20

O, FATHER, WHERE ART THOU?

"Try to behave," I muttered, opening the rear door of the sedan.

Fortunately, Winston opted for discretion as I tried to coax Spud inside. Sadly, my dog wasn't in as accommodating a mood as my inner werewolf. Talk about a reversal of fortune.

Can't say I even blamed Spud. First, he'd been dropped off with total strangers, albeit welcoming ones. Then I'd returned after a two-week absence only for him to find me drastically *changed* from the experience. Not only was I talking in a cadence and tone unfamiliar to him, but from the way he kept nosing my pants it seemed my left half smelled different from my right. That could potentially be a problem if any of the pack decided to get too nosey around me. Yet one more thing to worry about.

Spud whined and planted his feet until I was forced to hoist his butt into the car, buckle him in, and shut the door. All the while, my father sat silent behind the wheel.

I debated tossing my *luggage* into the trunk but I just wanted to get home, the sooner the better. So I climbed into the shotgun seat and put it on the floor.

"You have no idea how good it is to see you," I said as Dad put the car in reverse and performed a k-turn.

He glanced my way out of the corner of his eye but again said nothing.

Guess I'm getting the silent treatment.

My father was usually slow to anger and quick to forgive. But that was before I'd disappeared for two whole weeks after causing a hell of a ruckus in New York City – one I hadn't told either of my parents about beforehand, fearing Hobart's hold over them.

However, me keeping secrets from them should've come as no surprise, since it had been their idea to begin with.

Then...

"I swear, if I live to be a hundred, I will never get used to waking up outside, naked as the day I was born."

"I can think of worse things to wake up to," my father replied with a lecherous grin.

"Michael doesn't need to hear that kind of nastiness," Mom chided, a smile curling the corner of her mouth nonetheless. "That's not the sort of talk decent folk have at the dinner table."

"It's fine, Ma." I spooned a pile of mashed potatoes onto my plate, focusing on the food in front of me. My parents' sex life wasn't something I cared to dwell upon, but I also wasn't a kid anymore.

"Oh well, I suppose Margie Summers had it worse," Mom continued, shifting gears.

Dad let out a laugh. "Why? Did someone leave a mirror lying around for that old prune to find?" He looked my way as if seeking backup but I made it a point to keep my mouth occupied with pot roast.

"You be nice, Lloyd Walden. Margie can't help the way she looks. What I meant was the poor dear was covered head to toe in rabbit fur and entrails." Mom lowered her voice as she turned my way. "She's a vegetarian, y'know. Imagine the shock."

I nodded, feigning concern, but secretly pleased she was feeling comfortable enough to gossip. Of my two parents, she'd been the one I was most concerned about in terms of adjusting to this new monster lifestyle.

"The old biddy needs to get over it." Dad replied, taking a sip of beer. "Ain't no such thing as a vegan werewolf."

"Vegetarian not vegan. And you don't know any such thing."

"I'm just saying, Gin. Last I checked, the legends weren't exactly full of monsters raiding carrot patches."

"Legends? You mean those silly movies, don't you?"

"Same thing far as I'm concerned."

"Well, isn't that just dandy," Mom scolded. "Maybe I'll tell Margue she needs to *get over it* because Hollywood hasn't seen fit to make any movies about vegetarian werewolves."

Dad let out a sigh then glanced my way again. "How'd things go for you, Mikey? *Out there*, I mean."

I shrugged. "It was fine. I was just keeping an eye on things."

"You didn't get too close to anyone, did ya? You know we can't control ourselves like..."

"I know, Dad. Trust me, I was careful."

"You're sure?"

"Yes, sir. Found a cozy spot near Canal Street and mostly kept watch, making sure nobody wandered into downtown."

"All right, just so long as you mind yourself. Those

things... *We're* nothing to fool around with. We might as well be rabid dogs beneath the full moon."

"Don't say that, Dad."

"We sure as heck aren't begging for treats like your Spud. All I'm saying is to be careful."

I nodded not wanting to argue.

"Especially if that bastard Callahan is lurking about."

"Lloyd! Language."

"I'm just telling it like it is, Gin. That greasy son of a ... gun was in my head. I know it. I can still feel his grubby fingers rooting around my brain."

"Well, I can't," Mom replied. "It's all a blur to me. One I'd just as soon forget until next month."

"Unless he makes it happen sooner." He and Mom locked eyes as if in a battle of wills. "Don't look at me like that. We both know he can do it."

"Yes, but he hasn't," she said dismissively.

"Doesn't mean he won't try."

Mom had no answer to that, but Dad wasn't done yet. "I know you and Hobart have unfinished business, son."

"I... It's not like that."

"Don't lie to me, Mikey. You never were any good at it. I know you say you're just out there making sure nobody gets hurt, but I ain't stupid. You've got a good head on your shoulders, even if it's sometimes filled with rocks."

"My grades were never *that* bad."

"You keep telling yourself that. All I'm saying is I know you. You're gonna do what you think is right. That's the way you've always been, even if it ain't smart. And we both know you're *different*, just like he is."

I opened my mouth to protest, but Dad held up a hand. "I don't mean it like that. We didn't raise you to be a jackass. What I mean is you're still you, no matter what skin you're wearing. I don't know how. Don't really care either. All I know is secrets like that don't last forever, not in a small town like Harris County, which makes what I have to say all the more…"

"He already knows," I blurted before I could think better of it. Maybe Dad was right about good intentions not going hand in hand with common sense.

"What?"

"Hobart. He knows about me."

"For how long?"

"Since last month."

"And you didn't think to tell us?" Mom replied, wide-eyed.

"I didn't want you to worry."

"Didn't want to worry us?" She leaned forward, almost knocking the gravy boat over. "How did it happen? Who else knows? What are you doing about it?"

I shook my head, realizing I should've kept my mouth shut. There was a certain bliss in suspecting versus knowing for certain, serving as a security blanket against the harshness of reality. And I'd just stupidly ripped that bandage right off.

"I … I'm being careful," I said. "I'm keeping my…"

"No," Dad interrupted.

"Seriously, Dad, I've got it under control."

"I don't want to hear it. Neither does your mother." He took another sip of beer, longer this time. "That probably came out harsher than intended, Mikey, but I'm serious. I was going to say this before you let it slip, but now it's even more important. You need to stop telling us what you're up to in your other form. That means me, your mom, Dallas, and anyone else you're friendly with."

"But…"

"Hear me out. I don't think Hobart's got that big a hold over us, least not while the sun is out, but I also can't say for certain. Hell, I don't think anyone can." He met my gaze. "Unless you know something I don't."

I shook my head again. The truth was I didn't.

"Okay then," Dad continued. "So we should assume the worst. We know for sure he can control us when we change. I don't remember much from my time in the woods, but I can sense that much. And I think your mother can too."

Mom clenched her jaw for a moment, no doubt wanting to disagree, but then she nodded.

"And therein lay the problem," Dad said leaning his head on his fist. "He can force us to change and then command us, but we don't know if there's anything else he can do. I wish I could remember more, son, I really do, but it's all static like watching an out of tune TV station."

"It's okay..."

"No, it's not, least not for you. What I'm trying to say is, I don't know if our other bodies remember our human lives or if Hobart is even capable of understanding them if they do. But so long as we don't know, you need to assume the worst. That means whatever you say to us, you're potentially saying to him too."

"I know you would never try to..."

"Except you don't!" Mom cried. "Listen to your father for once. Of course we'd never willingly betray your trust. But that's not to say he couldn't ... force us to."

Dad got up and stepped behind her, putting his hands on her shoulders. "You need to listen. Until we know for certain, which might be tomorrow or never, you need to start keeping some stuff to yourself. It breaks my heart to say this, but you can't trust anyone in the pack. And that includes us."

Now...

Hearing him out had broken my heart a little, but I'd also understood. Being different was destined to be lonely business so long as I had enemies out there.

Fortunately, it hadn't been quite the doom and gloom my dad had warned of. After all, being a werewolf was only part of our lives. Once the sun was up, I put on my pants and went to work the same as anyone else. Sure, I might've asked Stucky to keep me off route C, which serviced Hobart's neighborhood, but that was about it. There was no point in tempting fate after all.

My point is, I'd been working to find a balance without becoming some sort of town pariah. Mom and Dad both understood that. Nonetheless, it was one thing to keep a lid on things during dinner, quite another for me to outright disappear for two weeks.

In the backseat, Spud continued to whine, not helping the already tense mood. As for Winston, I had no idea what he might be thinking, other than being certain he was enjoying my discomfort.

Guess it's up to me to break the ice. "Listen. I know you and Mom were worried sick. I get that. Trust me, I didn't disappear off the face of the planet because I wanted to. Things just got ... weird."

Dad glanced at me, one eyebrow raised, but again said nothing.

"I'm not sure how much I can say. Heck, I'm not entirely sure how much of it was real and how much was my imagination."

He gave me some more side-eye but that was all. Suddenly I felt like an eight-year-old who'd just gotten caught breaking the living room window with my football.

"I got caught up in something big, okay? And no, I can't really explain it other than it was scary and weird as all heck. The important thing is I'm done with it, along with any nonsense going on in the city. None of it is any of my business. I know that now. So, there's no need to worry."

Dad inexplicably let out a laugh. "Oh, you are so dead wrong it's almost fucking hilarious."

My eyes opened wide, but it wasn't because the silent treatment was finally at an end. No. The words may have come from my father's lips, but it hadn't been in his voice.

The pitch was too high, too feminine. In fact, it almost sounded like...

Spud's whine turned into a growl as the air around the driver's seat began to shimmer and distort. In the space of seconds, as the illusion finally dropped, my father's greying hair became a luxurious mane of bright red, while his body became considerably more ... voluptuous.

The woman who'd replaced him, an all too familiar if unwelcome sight, turned to me and grinned.

"Hell, this party's just getting started, lover."

Myra!

21

HEX WITH THE EX

"What are you doing here?"

"Giving your pedestrian butt a lift, obviously."

"Where's my father?"

The shapely enchantress let out a cackle. "Probably at home wondering who stole his car."

"What?! But that's... Never mind. Pull over."

"Aww, but we just started rolling."

"I said pull over."

"Okay, okay, relax. Hold your dog collar. I just need a second here."

"I said..."

"Give me a minute, will ya? I got something I need to do first."

"What?"

"This," she replied, taking one hand off the steering wheel and tapping it to my head. I felt a jolt, like a static shock, and saw a brief flash of bright yellow.

"What the fuck?"

The words came from my lips, but they weren't mine. *Great!* Winston had lasted all of five minutes before deciding to announce himself to the world. Albeit I suppose the circumstances were anything but normal.

"Ooh, look at you using big boy language," Myra said, still grinning.

"That wasn't me. I mean it was, but..." *Crap*! I hadn't meant to sputter like an idiot, but I could somehow feel Winston stirring within me. I didn't know what Myra had done to us, but he was apparently taking exception to it. I needed to take control of this situation before he did something we'd regret, like ruining Dad's leather seats. "Calm down. I've got this."

Myra glanced my way, one eyebrow raised. "Honey, in case it ain't clear, I am cool as a motherfucking cucumber. You, on the other hand, ain't got nothing 'cept a handful of shit."

"Do you have to be so vulgar?"

"Seriously, that's your biggest fucking issue right now?" Winston spat.

"Will you shut up already!"

Myra stared at me, head cocked. Then she let out a laugh as if she found the whole thing hilarious. "Jesus, Mike, I didn't zap you that hard. And yet they say I'm the one who should be in the loony bin."

"It's ... can you please keep your eyes on the road?"

She refocused on driving just in time to avoid wrapping us around a tree, giving me a moment to gather my thoughts.

Myra Tabitha Wallanger had never been what you'd call a meek girl. Growing up, she'd hung with a different crowd, one that never gave me so much as a second glance. They weren't exactly what you'd call mean girls, but they very much kept to themselves.

I didn't know it at the time, but part of the reason for this was because her friends were all witches like her, the offspring of a small coven that had secretly established itself in Harris County.

I had no insight into how long they'd been there. Heck, I couldn't even say whether it was sheer coincidence they'd chosen to settle in a place also populated by latent werewolves. Myra had never seen fit to grace me with that knowledge, and by the time I had a clue, things had already gone sour between us.

I've mentioned how everything changed roughly five years ago. Well, that goes for Myra too. While many of us were dealing with the end of the ritual, Myra and her coven found themselves without magic for the first time in their lives.

I have no idea what such a dramatic change in lifestyle would do to a person, but I can't imagine it was pleasant.

Though I'd never been morbid enough to check the obituaries, I would've bet good money these ex-witches accounted for some of the suicides from around that time. As for the rest, I'm guessing they eventually learned to adapt to a world without magic. Myra was one of them.

All I knew was she eventually landed a job at McNalty's Realty and started saying hi to me whenever we'd run into each other during our respective lunch hours.

Quick hellos turned into short chats. Chats turned into hanging out. And eventually romance bloomed.

Sadly, this particular flower's season wasn't meant to last.

The Myra I'd fallen for was a far cry from the cackling siren sitting in the driver's seat. She was sweet and friendly, not to mention marginally sane.

The return of magic had changed all of that. All at once, I was no longer worth her time, but it turned out I wasn't the only one. At some point during the intervening years, Myra had a serious falling out with her coven – one bad enough to turn her against them.

Whatever happened between them, it couldn't have been pretty because, far as I was aware, it was a scant three months after magic's return and there was no longer any sign of Myra's old crew to be found in Harris County. It was possible they'd simply packed up and left, but somehow I didn't believe it.

If you'd asked me back then, I'd have told you the Myra I'd known and loved, the one who'd enjoyed many a weekly dinner at my folks' place, wasn't capable of such things. The Myra sitting next to me now, though, was not someone to be underestimated. It was a real pity, since that's exactly what I was doing, sitting there and talking to her like this was nothing more than a blind date gone bad.

Winston, however, wasn't having any of this. Just as Myra started to slow the car down, my extremities went numb.

No! Not now!

Myra was no longer my girlfriend. Heck, she wasn't even in the friend zone anymore. I knew for a fact she and Hobart were up to no good and needed to be stopped.

But that didn't mean I wanted her dead.

I thought back to the Chadworths and the absolute mess made of them. Winston might as well have run them through a woodchipper ... *twice*. Angry as I might've been with her, I didn't want to see her splattered across some living room like human paint. Such a thing was *inhuman*, a heinous crime only a true monster would commit. And I was no monster. Not yet, and not ever if I could help it.

As the flood of euphoric brain chemicals coursed

through me, I tried to stop the change the same as I'd done at Barley Hills.

Except, a moment later I realized there was nothing to stop.

The rush of chemicals was meant to dull the pain of transformation, except no transformation followed. My body didn't begin to swell, my hair didn't grow, and none of my bones started rearranging themselves.

I was just sitting there, same as I'd been two minutes earlier, save I was now enjoying one hell of a natural high.

Whoa. Had I known my own brain was capable of this kind of rush, I wouldn't have bothered with all those weekends soaking up suds down at Jasper's.

"What ... the ... fuck?" Winston asked. I think he meant it as a snarl, but it came out as more of a giggle.

"Let me guess," Myra replied, just as we pulled into a shallow turnoff on the side of the road. "You were trying to change, right here in the front seat of your daddy's Ford, weren't you? 'Cept ain't nothing happening."

"You bitch," Winston spat.

His remark only caused Myra to grin even wider as she shut the car off. "You know something? I kinda like this new you. Shit, maybe that wild beast you got inside is finally rubbing off a bit." She slowly lowered her gaze to somewhere south of my chin. "Well, will you look at that. Seems to me like something else could use a bit of rubbing."

I was about to ask what the hell she was talking about when realization hit. That flood of brain chemicals had caused another unintended side effect, one that was pitching a solid tent against the interior of my jeans.

No. She couldn't possibly think...

Behind us, Spud once more began to whine.

"You hush now," Myra told him, sliding her seat back.

"Adults are talking, although not for much longer." She reached beneath her skirt, then slid her panties off.

No way! Uh uh. This is not happening. I tried to unbuckle my seatbelt but found my fingers too numb to work the latch. "Wha-what are you doing?"

"*You*, stupid." She clambered across the front seat, straddled me, and began working the buckle of my pants.

My left hand raised in response, curling into the shape of a claw.

Oh crap! "Don't do it!"

"Come now, honey bun. Your lips say no, but your stick shift is most certainly saying yes."

"I didn't mean..."

Rather than throttle her as I feared, Winston grabbed the collar of her shirt and ripped it away, taking most of her bra with it.

What the hell?

"Goddamn," Myra whooped. "Now this is what I'm talking about." She pressed her lips to mine and forced her tongue into my mouth, not that there seemed to be much resistance. My other half bit down on her, drawing hot blood, but that only seemed to encourage them both.

Things were getting weird way too fast. I needed to stop this before it went any further, so I reached up to push Myra away with the hand I still controlled.

"I don't think so, stud."

My body erupted in blue sparks instead, leaving me unable to do much more than flop like a fish in the front seat, which didn't seem to dissuade her in the least.

Myra leaned back, eldritch energy crackling up and down her body as her voice became a throaty whisper. "That's more like it. Now listen here and listen well, cowboy. I'm aiming to ride you until your head explodes. Which head, mind you, depends entirely on how nicely you treat a lady."

No doubt about it. She'd gone completely around the bend.

I continued to struggle, only to realize half of me wasn't making any effort at all to resist. My left side seemed quite fine with what was about to happen. What the hell was Winston doing?

All at once, I understood. For all his obstinance, aggression, and insistence that he found humans disgusting, the sick son of a bitch was enjoying this as much as she was.

This was no longer just about me and Myra. I was now stuck as the unwilling participant in the world's strangest threesome, powerless to do anything but sit there and take it.

22

ROACH MOTEL HELL

"Hot damn, Mike, when did you learn to fuck like such an animal?"

"I don't want to talk about it," I said, pulling my pants back up while trying not to think about how wet and sticky everything now felt. I swear, would it have hurt my father to keep a pack of wet wipes in the glove compartment?

"Is this a werewolf thing? Is it insensitive for me to ask? I mean, shit, we didn't even do it doggy style." Myra let out another cackle as she finally slid back over to the driver's seat. "Don't get me wrong, sugar, the sex wasn't bad before, but *that*... No offense, but if you'd hammered me like that back then, I might've stuck around a bit longer."

"'I gotta admit," Winston blurted out, "that wasn't half bad for an ugly hairless bitch."

Oh crap.

"Say what now?" Myra's eyes lit up with magical energy.

"I said..."

"You shouldn't have ... taken advantage of me like

that," I interrupted, wresting control of my mouth from the moronic beast inside my head. "I … I'm sorry. I didn't mean to be hurtful with my words, but … it's just … I'm not some piece of meat."

Myra smirked. "Aww, does little Mikey need to cuddle-wuddle?"

"No! It's just…" What I really needed was for Winston to shut up, so I lowered my voice to a bare whisper. "Remember what we talked about. *No one* can know."

Myra raised an eyebrow as she continued straightening her clothes. "I see someone's got a high opinion of himself. Just for the record, lover, it was good, but not good enough to brag about. You owe me at least one more orgasm for that."

"Think I'll pass."

"Your loss." She leaned forward and stared at me hard, the grin never leaving her face. "Now don't be sitting there all pouty. Sometimes you gotta give your inner devil his due, consequences be damned. Although if it'll make you feel better, we can stop at Ketchum's Pharmacy so you can pick yourself up a *Plan B*. Y'know, in case you're worried about catching pregnant with pups or something."

I cocked my head, forgetting for a moment she'd just used me as her own personal sex doll. "What are you yammering about?"

"Ain't that a werewolf thing?" she replied with another cackle. "I seem to recall reading about it in a book somewhere."

"Seriously, are you on drugs?"

"Why? You got some?"

"No, it's just…"

I needed to turn this around. I didn't want to hurt her and it's not like I could anyway, not without changing. But she'd walked all over me enough for one day. "I think you should worry less about bad fiction and more about what Hobart's gonna do if he realizes what you've been up to. What do you think he's going to say if he smells me all over you?"

She shrugged. "I don't see why I should care."

"Are you seriously telling me your new boyfriend's not going to have an *opinion*?"

Myra threw back her head and laughed. "Hobart and me are business partners, but that business ain't got nothing to do with my coochie. I'm insulted you'd think otherwise."

"No? Then how come..."

"Good idea," Winston replied. "We should find out if Hobart's got any other bitches and mount them too."

Jesus! "Will you shut up already?!"

Even as the words came out of my mouth I realized my mistake. The look on Myra's face said as much.

"Did I zap you too hard back there, Mike?" she asked, studying me like a bug under glass. "Because not only do you have a whole new vocabulary, but it sounds like you're having a sidebar with whatever voices you got in your noggin."

I couldn't help my eyes opening wide in surprise. I knew she was just spouting off but she'd come way too close to the truth for my liking.

Myra leaned in close enough to kiss her had I wanted to, which I didn't. "What happened after you disappeared?"

What? "Listen, Myra..."

"Don't give me any of that *Listen Myra* bullshit. You aren't mansplaining your way out of this. I know something happened to you. You ain't the type to vanish off the face of the Earth, not without telling that burnout friend of yours."

"Dallas isn't a burnout."

"It's funny you knew exactly who I was talking about

without me even needing to mention his name, but that ain't neither here nor there. They got to you, didn't they?"

Huh?

"Let me guess," she continued. "They fucked your brain over real good with mind magic, maybe not as good as I fucked you, but they worked you over nonetheless."

"Mind magic?"

"You heard me. It's not just for keeping a fella in his rightful skin." She gritted her teeth. "I'm guessing they were happy as clams to filet your grey matter trying to figure out what you are and why their precious archives barely make any mention of you."

"I have no idea what you're talking about."

She waved me off. "Of course you don't. They would've fucked with your memories too. That's what they do. And why not? To them, you're nothing more than an animal, just like those bloodsuckers. Subhuman trash to be used and abused."

"Pretty rich coming from someone doing the abusing."

"Oh, honey, what you call abuse, I call rocking your world. You're just too much of a prude to admit it."

"I am not a..." *Okay, deep breath.* She'd gone off on a huge tangent, one that sounded kinda important. Now was not the time to change the subject.

Spud picked that moment to sit up in the backseat, having had the audacity to fall asleep while Myra was having her way with me. So good to know I could count on man's best friend. Regardless, I reached back and patted his head. It reminded me to treat this situation with kid gloves since I wasn't the only one here that Myra could vent her crazy upon.

"All right, let's back up a bit. Who are *they* and what did they do to me?"

Myra finally scooted back behind the wheel of my father's car. "They really did a number on your noggin."

"Again…"

"Relax. I was getting to it. Hold your goddamned horses. You never were much for pillow talk." I made a hurry-up gesture, refusing to take the bait. "It's the same sons of bitches who've trapped us all here like rabbits in a cage."

Her words immediately brought to mind Winston's brain cage, although that was probably mere coincidence. "Not even remotely clearing anything up."

She cocked her head as if thinking about it. "Technically they're calling it a quarantine but potato, po-tah-toe."

"A quarantine?"

"For Harris County, Barley Hills, and all the space in between. Not that I imagine those trigger-happy Jesus freaks are even aware of it. Anyway, they said it's for our own good, so we don't cause no more trouble."

I had no clue what she was babbling about, but a cold fear began to creep up my spine that had nothing to do with my shirt being only half buttoned.

Myra was afraid that something had messed with my head. She was right on that front. All the same, I couldn't help but think we were talking apples and oranges. For starters, she kept referring to her unnamed boogeyman in the plural and, quite frankly, I didn't even want to think of the possibility there might be more than one psychic dinosaur residing in the Hudson. More importantly, I couldn't quite envision how or why such a massive beast might travel from Manhattan to Elk County Pennsylvania without everyone under the sun noticing.

It was time to stop playing guessing games and cut to the chase.

Myra opened her mouth, probably to spew more nonsense, but I reached over and put a finger to her lips – using my right hand just in case Winston decided to do something stupid. "Who are *they*, Myra?"

She rolled her eyes as she pushed my hand away. "The Magi of course, you dumb son of a bitch."

"The *what*?"

She let out a sigh. "Witches, wizards, and anyone else with the gift. That's what we're called. Figured you would've picked up on it since you saw fit to team up with a trash witch back in Brooklyn."

Trash...? Now that she mentioned it, one of Bill's friends *had* been a witch. Kelly if I recalled correctly. No idea what a trash witch was, probably an insult on account of her being strong enough to cancel out Myra's power during our ill-fated battle.

"Okay, and what do these *Magi* have to do with me?"

"Not you, *us*," Myra replied. "Sorry to say, but the world doesn't revolve around Mr. Michael Walden and his furry behind."

"His ass isn't furry, mine is..."

I broke into a cough to cover for Winston. "Sorry. Must be something in the air. Anyway, you were saying?"

She stared at me for a moment before continuing. "Seems one of the elite covens took exception to our little soiree in Brooklyn. Ain't nothing special about their magic, mind you. No, it's all about the moolah, just like everywhere else in the world." She rubbed three fingers together then let out a humorless laugh. "Ah, if only all that bullshit about turning lead to gold were true."

Myra's editorial aside, I was finally starting to understand what she was talking about. It wasn't surprising to hear that our actions had drawn unwanted attention, not with the mess we'd made. Heck, I wouldn't have been surprised had they sicced the National Guard on us too, but perhaps it was best not to tempt fate by speaking such thoughts aloud. "Maybe they didn't appreciate all the innocent bystanders you and Hobart killed."

"Fuck no. Those rich pricks couldn't care less about a

couple dead normies. It was more because we weren't exactly ... subtle about it. You can blame Hobart for that one. I told him not to start shit in the middle of a big city, but god forbid he listen to anyone with a set of titties."

I opted to ignore that last part. "Okay, so what happened?"

"What happened is, despite my best efforts to the contrary, they tracked us all the way here and were none too happy with what they found."

"And that was?"

"You! Or the pack anyway. Seems they weren't all that pleased to discover a bunch of nasties they were certain didn't exist."

That caught me by surprise. "What do you mean?"

"The Magi elite are big on their written history. Always have been. They like it all neat and clean, just the way they wrote it. So, when something pops up that threatens the established narrative they tend to react *badly*."

Hold on. Was she saying they didn't know about us beforehand? "How badly?"

"Bad enough to turn everything in and around Harris County into one giant roach motel."

"Meaning what?"

Myra shook her head. "Oh, you sweet blockheaded child. I bet they let you go knowing you'd head straight home like a moth to a flame. But now that you're here, you're stuck just like the rest of us – those of us with power anyway. You see, they let you check in, no problem, but there will be the Devil to pay if you think they'll let you check out."

23

DEAD END STREET

I should've gotten out and walked. Nothing good was to be gained staying with Myra. Of course, that assumed she'd let me go without a fight.

With daylight working against me as well as Winston's violent unpredictability, that made it a questionable endeavor at best.

Then there was Spud to take into consideration. I wasn't about to risk him being hurt. I didn't think Myra was so far gone as to actually use him for target practice, but it was best not to risk it.

So, I compromised. I pinky-swore to go with Myra to wherever she had in mind – which I'm guessing involved a meetup with Hobart. But first she had to take me back home so I could drop Spud off. Fortunately, she knew how seriously I took a promise. And even if I didn't, she was a witch. She'd found me once. She could do it again.

It wasn't exactly a win, but the ride at least gave me a chance to reflect on what she'd told me.

There was a whole community of witches and wizards out there, and some hadn't taken kindly to Hobart's antics. It wasn't because of the chaos we'd caused, so much as us shining a spotlight on the fact that monsters and magic were real – something they preferred humanity at large not know.

I guess that made sense. After all, prior to a few months ago I didn't have a clue things like me were real outside of movies and Stephen King books.

The first rule of Monster Fight Club was don't talk about Monster Fight Club. Duly noted.

However, the second rule was apparently not to start a war in front of a bunch of people with cell phone cameras.

She heavily implied this was the sort of thing that would earn literally anyone else in the supernatural under-world an automatic death sentence. But not the citizens of Harris County.

The only reason I was returning to my apartment and not a smoking crater was because somehow folks like me were oddities even among the oddities.

Seemed that secret history Hobart had hinted at was even more secret than I'm guessing even he knew. As a result, the Council of High Mentors, as Myra called them, upon discovering a town full of living, breathing were-wolves, opted to quarantine us instead.

As Myra continued to ramble like she was mayor of Crazy Town, I found all of this hard to believe. I mean, why on Earth would witches and vampires be surprised to discover that werewolves were likewise real?

Heck, there were plenty of myths and movies about all three. And since the so-called legends were based on fact for the rest of these *make believe monsters*, why was it so hard for them to imagine we might exist too?

If Myra had any insight, she either didn't know or wasn't sharing. She obviously understood more about the world of the weird than me, but she'd also lived in Harris County for most of her life. A jet-setting socialite she was not. That she was still under the impression these Magi

Mentors had been behind my two week *vacation* seemed to bolster that fact, and I saw no reason to correct her. Fortunately, Winston must've concurred since he mercifully kept his mouth shut for most of the ride.

Regardless of the method of my return, I hadn't sensed anything odd in the woods surrounding Harris County as I'd gotten closer, but according to Myra that was by design. The area encompassing our little town had apparently been ringed with what she called scrying wards – magical thingamabobs designed to activate if something inhuman tried leaving the quarantine zone.

As for what would happen if someone tried, Myra cautioned, "Fuck around and find out, honey."

Ominous as that sounded, I had to question why Barley Hills had been included within this magical minefield. Far as I was aware, everyone there was human. I said as much once we finally turned onto Chestnut Street, the road where I lived.

"You ever talk to a high Mentor, Mike?" she replied.

"Not that I can recall."

"Nor are you liable to. All you need to know is this – when one of those hoity-toity assholes gets a bug up their ass, you can be sure as shit everything in sight looks like a fly swatter."

"That makes no sense."

"Nope. And neither does warding Barley Hills since those bible thumpers can come and go as they please. But I ain't holding my breath for an explanation, especially since asking for one will put me on their radar, which is somewhere I'd prefer not to be."

She didn't explain further and I had a feeling pressing for an answer would be a waste of time. "So how long are we expected to be the bugs in their little ant farm?"

She let out a laugh as we pulled into the long driveway that led to my place. Returning home at long last should've been an emotional moment for me, but I was currently too caught up in our conversation.

"Something funny?" I asked.

"Just your optimism. I ain't gonna sugarcoat it for you, lover. This here quarantine is almost certainly gonna last until one of two things happens."

"And those would be?"

"Either they decide to nuke us from orbit, or we push back and give the bastards a bloody nose they won't ever forget."

Donald and Katherine Haversham were in their late seventies. He'd been a career army sergeant, she a nurse — both of them retired now. Neither were werewolves but they were longtime homeowners. A few years back they'd decided to convert the second floor of their detached garage into an apartment to bring in a bit of extra income.

Yours truly now called that cozy little space home.

It had been a pretty good deal even before realizing I was a monster. It was affordable, spacious, and gave me a place to park my old Jeep Wrangler. They also didn't mind if Spud did his business in their back yard, so long as I mowed in the summer months.

It was situated far enough away from the main house to ensure some privacy back in the days when Myra was prone to staying over. All in all, not a bad deal for a single guy in this day and age.

It was only after my true nature became apparent that I realized there were some perks which also made it were-wolf friendly. The Havershams owned a big lot, one encompassing a narrow stretch of woods running through its far end. Since the stairs leading up to my place wrapped around the rear of the structure, that meant I could come and go in my other form without being seen. Or, as in the case of my first few transformations, get back inside before anyone saw me running around buck-ass nude.

It likewise didn't hurt that Harris County was one of those towns where you could safely leave your doors unlocked, a major plus since werewolves didn't come with pockets.

I told Myra to stay in the car while I got Spud settled. I didn't need her coming up and causing trouble, nor did I have any desire to once again be the meat in a Myra and Winston sandwich.

There's a visual I could do without.

Fortunately, she was in an agreeable mood, a good thing since I doubted there was much I could've done if she'd decided otherwise.

I can't even explain the relief I felt at stepping foot into my apartment. Nothing had really changed, yet it felt as if a weight were lifted from my shoulders. Doubly so since it appeared everything was as I'd left it ... well, maybe minus a few extra cobwebs and dust bunnies.

Regardless, it gave me a few minutes alone to stop and catch my breath. Or it would've had I been anyone else. Sadly, it was the space of seconds for me to once again be reminded that *alone* was no longer an option.

"I can understand why you like mounting that bitch," Winston remarked as I tossed my bag onto the counter. "She's got a certain feral quality to her, despite all the bare skin."

"I really don't want to hear about..."

"But I gotta gut her anyway."

What? "No. She's not our enemy." Okay, even I didn't believe that one.

"The fuck she ain't. But that's not the reason why. It's not her, it's you. She brings out the pathetic in you extra fucking hard, and that sort of shit is just too embarrassing to deal with."

"What do you mean?"

"I mean *you*, shithead, acting like a poor whipped puppy desperate to suckle at her teat."

"I did not!"

"You forget, I was there. You couldn't have been more pathetic had she pissed on your leg and claimed you as her own. No more. And since I can't kill you without fucking up my day, that means the bitch needs to die instead."

I tried to wrap my head around his insane logic and failed badly. "I was only ... tiptoeing around her because of Spud." I looked over to see him already settling onto the couch as if he had no worries in the world.

"I didn't realize you were taking orders from the snack," Winston said.

"I'm not. I was keeping him from getting hurt. Also, he's a dog and dogs don't talk."

"I'll do you a favor and pretend that's not a thinly veiled insult. Anyway, you convinced me."

"I did?"

"Yep. Now I need to kill them both."

"There will be no killing Spud ... or Myra for that matter! Wait. Are you even listening to me?"

The answer was obvious as he forced me to crouch down onto our hands and knees right there on the kitchen floor.

"What are you doing?"

"All this talk is making me thirsty."

We started crawling forward, our destination: Spud's water bowl and the algae-ridden mess within. *What?!* "No!"

I managed to reassert control right before we could drown our sorrows, grabbing hold of the counter and hoisting myself back up. "We have these things called glasses, y'know."

"I can see just fine."

"For drinking out of!"

"Why bother when the water is right there?" he replied. "Besides, I like to keep my paws free in case of an attack."

"Who's gonna attack us in here?"

Our gaze turned back toward Spud, already asleep in his spot.

"Seriously?" I replied.

"You can't possibly tell me you trust that stupid thing."

Over on the couch, Spud let out a long fart in response.

"See what I mean?"

"I trust him a heck of a lot more than..." I meant to say *you* but realized that wouldn't help matters. "Than the witch waiting downstairs for us."

"Which is why I want to slit her throat. Duh!"

"There will be no slitting of any..." I trailed off as my eyes fell upon the bag still on the counter. *I wonder...*

"Any what?" Winston prodded. "Let me guess. Pussy got your tongue?"

I ignored him as I unzipped the bag, unsure if I really wanted to go down this route.

The truth was I didn't, but I was already at a disadvantage, and that was just with Myra alone. If she was taking me to see Hobart, as I suspected, that would only dig me deeper into whatever hole I was standing in.

I pushed past the clothes and rolls of cash to the handgun sitting at the bottom. I doubted it would be of much use, but if push came to shove the bullets would still hurt like...

What the?

The gun was no longer alone in the bag. An extra

magazine had been placed next to it, along with a hand-written note. I grabbed both, finding only a single line of text on the paper.

Just in case – Hannah.

Curious, I took a closer look at the magazine and the gleaming bullets that had been loaded into it – silver hollow points.

I so could kiss you right now.

"No killing, not if we can help it," I told my other half, eying the extra ammo. "But would you perchance be willing to settle for some proactive defense instead?"

24

ENEMIES AND ALLIES

I expected Winston to be old school when it came to weaponry, assuming he'd be all about the fangs and claws. But apparently any violence was good violence where he was concerned.

In fact, he was a little *too* enthusiastic, wanting to go downstairs, shoot Myra in the face, then hunt Hobart down and ... likewise shoot him in the face.

Needless to say, I made a note to keep the gun on my side to avoid him indiscriminately murdering everything in sight.

Speaking of which, I needed a place to hide it, so I took a few minutes to change into my own clothes, including my old bomber jacket. Oh wow. I can't even tell you the difference it made wearing my own stuff again.

I know it probably doesn't sound like much, but it finally felt like I was truly back home.

Sadly, this was not the time to relax and put my feet up. Myra was still waiting outside, and I had little doubt her patience was limited.

God, there was still so much to do. I needed to call my parents, talk to my job, check the mailbox, dust everything, and a thousand other tiny things just to get my life back in order.

That would all have to wait, though. I didn't even have time to sit down and crack open a beer. Instead, I settled for checking my voicemail.

Unsurprisingly, there were several from my parents. All of them were eerily calm and measured, as if they were being mindful of what they said – which they probably were. I didn't envy the self-control it must've taken to keep their emotions reined in. It ended with a mention from Dad talking about dropping some *stuff* off with an unnamed friend of mine. I was no codebreaker, but that was almost certainly about taking Spud to Barley Hills.

I tried my best not to get misty-eyed at hearing their voices, a feat made infinitely easier as I listened to the rest of my messages – most of them from my boss.

They started off well enough.

"Hey, Mike. Couldn't help but notice you didn't clock in today. Just checking to make sure all's well. Call me when you can."

They quickly went downhill from there.

"It's Stucky again. The fuck, Mike? We're backed up like crazy here, man. I swear to god if I find out you're down in Tijuana making it with a donkey while I'm running a triple shift, I will personally haul your ass into the compactor!"

No doubt about it. A lot of night shifts spent hosing out trucks were in my future.

Future being the operative word, though. Far as he was aware I was still away. It was best to let him think that until I'd concluded whatever business awaited me downstairs.

It was time to head back out before Myra hurled a fireball through my front window. I couldn't help the sigh that escaped my lips as I prepared to leave the apartment I'd just gotten back to. I might've technically been home but it still felt like I was deep in enemy territory, far from any help.

Or maybe not, as I stepped outside only to hear what sounded like a heated discussion coming from below. And it wasn't just Myra arguing with whatever demons were inside her head.

"I have every right to be here. It's a free country."

"You must've missed the sign out front. *Hoes Will be Prosecuted for Trespassing.*"

More important was the fact I instantly recognized the second voice.

Dallas!

"Now I know you're full of shit. As if your dumb ass can read."

"I can read the tire tracks on your backside just fine, you skank-ass... Wait. Is this Lloyd's car?"

"That's none of your concern."

"What the hell are you doing in it? You'd best get your butt out of that seat and hand over those keys before I..."

"And you'd best back the fuck off, Dallas Emory, or I swear I will hex you so hard your mama will thank me for forgetting your name."

I headed down the stairs, eager to see my friend, as well as to intervene before things got ugly.

Dallas and Myra had been cool back when she and I dated, but in some ways he'd taken our breakup even worse than I had. It was safe to say I'd gotten *custody* in the *divorce*. Fine by me since Dallas was the best friend a guy could hope to have.

We'd been buddies since we were kids, both at school and during the ritual. Yes, Dallas was a werewolf too. Unfortunately, he was a *normal* one, meaning he was totally beholden to Hobart in his other form. His human half, however, was solidly on Team Mike, something I was eternally grateful for.

That said, much like with my parents, a small part of me lived in perpetual fear that one day our friendship would be used against us, a fear I hoped would never come to pass. Of course, now I had whole new fears to worry about.

"I was wondering when your idiot friend would come sniffing around," Winston muttered.

"That's enough," I whispered back. "Remember what we talked about."

That was all the time I could devote to ensuring Winston played nice before I rounded the corner of the Haversham's garage.

Sure enough, my friend was standing alongside my father's car. At six foot four, Dallas was a tall drink of water who'd never quite grown into his gangly arms and legs. Dark skinned, with shoulder length black hair and seemingly permanent stubble – he wouldn't have looked out of place solving mysteries alongside *Scooby Doo*.

Upon catching sight of me, shock replaced the anger on my friend's face. "Holy shit! Is that you, Mikey?"

"In the flesh, bro," I replied, throwing him what felt like my first genuine smile since waking up with dead pig on my breath.

In the space of a second, he seemingly forgot all about his argument with Myra. He ran over, threw his arms around me, then backed away and slapped my arm. "Where the fuck have you been, man? Everyone's been worried sick." He turned partway, throwing Myra the stink eye. "Everyone who counts anyway."

"Least I *can* count, you dumb fuck," Myra threw back from the driver's seat.

Dallas shot her the finger over his shoulder. "Here's the only number I care about." He then turned his full attention my way. "Speaking of numbers, I've got three questions for you."

"Only three?"

"Yeah. Where have you been? When did you get back? And what is Sluterella doing here?"

"Um ... long story, just now, and she gave me a ride home after stealing Dad's car."

"I gave you a ride, all right," Myra shouted back.

Dallas clicked his tongue. "Please tell me you didn't reopen your account at the skank bank."

"Definitely not. Let's just say it's ... another long story."

"One we ain't got time to waste on the likes of you," Myra said, still hanging halfway out the car window. "Let's go, Mike. I held up my end of the bargain. Now it's your turn."

"Wait, what bargain?" Dallas asked.

I lowered my voice. "I promised I'd go with her."

"Where to?"

"Wherever she wants." I held up a hand. "Spud was in the car with us and I wasn't taking any chances. You catch my drift?"

"Spud? Is he...?"

"Upstairs, asleep in his favorite spot."

Dallas stared hard at me before giving a single nod of his head. He was more than aware of her and Hobart's invisible stranglehold upon Harris County. And now he was trapped here with them, along with everyone else with a penchant for howling at the moon.

"You really think she would...?" Even as he said it, I saw the lack of conviction in his eyes. I don't think either of us wanted to truly believe that Myra was the *Fatal Attraction* type, but our world had been turned upside down too much to risk it. "Yeah, I see your point."

"Which means you need to..."

"Go with you."

"No way. I'm not dragging you into this."

"You can't drag someone who's volunteering, Mike."

"She's taking me to see Hobart."

"Better than a cheap motel room infested with bedbugs, albeit not much."

"I heard that," Myra cried.

I ignored her. "You know what it means."

"Which is all the more reason you need someone there watching your back," Dallas said.

While my heart swelled at what a great friend he was, I just couldn't risk it. "And if he forces you to change?"

"Then we'll cross that bridge. But I ain't letting you disappear again. Your folks would never forgive me." A grin broke out across his face. "Not to mention what Stucky'll do to me if he finds out I let you get away. Dude's been going crazy backfilling your shift."

"So I've heard."

"Shit, he's even trying to get Kurt outta dispatch to help cover the load. You know how he feels about getting his hands dirty. Dude's even more of a germophobe than you."

I couldn't help but chuckle at the thought of that conversation. The moment was short lived, however, as Myra leaned on the horn.

There was no time for this. "Listen, man, I appreciate it. I really do, but..."

"You want in on this shitshow?" Winston interrupted. "You got it."

What?!

"Now you're talking," Dallas replied with a conspiratorial smile.

"Wait. I didn't..."

He was already heading back to the car, though. "Yo, Agatha Heartless. Unlock the door and don't even think about throwing any of that voodoo shit my way."

Son of a...

I spun around so the others wouldn't hear this next part. "What the hell are you doing?"

"Taking charge before you fuck something else up," Winston replied.

"You promised to..."

"Promise is a really strong word, cat litter for brains," he interrupted. "But you're right. Nobody else should know about me, at least not yet."

"Good, then..."

"Which is why you're going to do exactly as I say."

"No. That's not how this works."

"It is now, pupcake. I'm changing our deal."

"Let me guess. Pray you don't alter it any further?"

He cocked our head. "I was gonna say, better hope I don't crumple it up and shove it up your ass sideways, but whatever works. Anyway, since you won't let me gut your fuck puppy over there, you have a choice. You can either play along or we can tell her the truth."

"Are you insane? She's the last person who should know about us."

"Good," he said. "Then we're in agreement. And right now I say your fuckhead friend is coming along for the ride."

"But why?"

"Because of the gun bitch."

"Hannah?"

"Yeah, that's her. Anyway, she hit the kitten on the head. I need a pack if I'm going to stick it to Hobart. And I think it's high time I got started by making that buddy of yours my first recruit."

25

PRISONER WITHOUT A CAGE

I was at a loss for what to do. While I'd expected Winston to be difficult when it came to keeping our secret, I hadn't anticipated how quickly he'd turn it around and use it against me.

In truth, I'd begun to think of him as being sorta ... dumb. But I was beginning to realize I might've been wrong. Maybe he wasn't stupid so much as simply naïve when it came to human culture, coupled, of course, with him being psychotically violent.

It was the latter which worried me as I once again found myself in Dad's Ford with Myra behind the wheel. The only difference this time was that Dallas was in the backseat. Myra, for her part, seemed to be taking the scenic route, passing by my job almost as if to taunt me.

I stared out the window, watching as the sign for the Harris County Department of Public Works disappeared from sight. Never did I imagine longing so badly for the simplicity of picking up bags of trash.

"So where are we going?" Dallas asked.

"*Your* stupid ass ain't going anywhere," Myra replied,

203

taking her eyes off the road despite us being in the middle of town. "I'm giving *him a ride*, not you."

"Then I guess I won't be needing a shot of penicillin today."

Before I could warn that he might want to avoid taunting the unstable witch behind the wheel, Winston spoke up. "Here's an idea. Why don't the both of you shut the fuck up?"

"Damn, bro," Dallas said with a chuckle. "You kiss your mama with that mouth."

"No, I kiss *your* mom with this mouth. Right before I bend her over a stump and give it to her like a bitch."

"What?!" I cried, before attempting to cover it up as a laugh, easy enough to do as Myra let out a cackle. I had no idea what Isaiah had used to knock Winston out the night before, but I could've really used a dose right about then.

Fortunately, Dallas looked far more surprised than upset. No surprise there. I'd never been much for cussing, not even during my teenage years when I'd done almost everything possible to rankle my parents' nerves. Needless to say, Winston's colorful *vocabulary* coming from my mouth stood out like a sore thumb.

"Damn, bro. What happened while you were gone?"

Winston turned us to face my friend. "Let's just say I've seen some shit." We then glanced toward Myra. "Speaking of piles of crap, I assume you're taking me to Hobart. So what's it gonna be? Are we talking ambush, assassination, or are we gonna maul each other like civilized wolves?"

What are you doing?! Unfortunately, I was stuck with a choice of either thinking mean thoughts or yelling at myself like a madman, neither of which would...

"Damn, Mike," Myra said, derailing my train of thought. "When did you become such a drama queen?"

"Oh, I don't know," I replied, reasserting control. "It

might've been when my girlfriend dumped me because she was a witch. Or maybe it was after you and Hobart decided to run Jacob Vesser out of town. Or how about in Brooklyn when you two...?"

"Point taken, although you're a little out of date on old man Vesser."

"What do you mean?"

"Don't tell me Hobart actually grew a pair and hunted that old fuck down," Winston added much to my chagrin.

Myra let out another chuckle as if that were somehow funny. "Not quite, especially on account of us all being stuck here."

"She ain't kidding, man," Dallas said.

"I know. She told me all about the quarantine."

"Oh really? Did she tell you what happened to Trent?"

I raised an eyebrow. Trent Howser was another former disciple of the ritual, although that was as close to any kinship we might've shared. He'd been a few years ahead of us at school – big kid, a football player. Mean, too, as both of us had gotten our butts kicked by him back in high school. Later on, after flunking out of state trooper school, he'd ended up working nights as an orderly at Saint Bartholomew's three towns over. Or that had been the case before we'd all discovered our penchant for howling at the moon. "No. What about him?"

"Dumb old Trent," Myra muttered with a laugh.

"She ain't wrong," Dallas said. "Trent didn't take too kindly to being locked up. Thought it was all a load of horseshit, so he tried to leave."

"And?" both Winston and I prompted.

"And Hobart let him, the sadistic bastard."

"Sometimes an example needs to be made," Myra remarked.

"So what happened?" I asked.

"He got sent right back," Dallas replied. "Most of him

anyway, and it wasn't all to the same place. They found his legs north of town, his arms over on the east side, and his head lying atop a bale of hay over near the old Burford farm."

"Jesus," I hissed.

Myra turned my way. "Afraid not, honey bun. The good lord didn't have nothing to do with it. That was the Magi sending a message. Just be glad it was a sacrificial lamb who won't be missed."

I was about to protest that Trent was still a person, but Winston was a little quicker on the draw.

"Whatever. One less asshole taking up space. So anyway, back to that part about dating old men."

"Huh?"

"You were telling him about Jacob," Dallas prompted.

"Oh yeah. Well, seems the old fool decided to come back home. Made a big deal of showing up at Timber City Hardware and loading his truck with supplies. Guess he wanted folks to know he was back, ya know, in case something bad happened."

"You didn't..."

"Relax. The old coot's fine. Hobart's keeping tabs on him but that's it. We got what we needed from him so there's no reason to do anything else ... for now."

"And that was?" I asked.

"None of your beeswax, that's what."

I felt a growl rising in my throat, so I quickly deflected the situation by turning toward Dallas.

"Don't ask me," he said. "I'm about as far from that asshole's inner circle as it gets."

"Only when you look like this," Myra mocked.

"Yeah, well, maybe he told my *other half*, but if so he ain't talking."

An edge of bitterness crept into my friend's voice. Dallas had made no secret of being jealous of my ability to remain in control, although he'd probably be singing a different tune if I told him the truth. But that would have to wait as we pulled into the gravel lot of Callahan Hauling, the small freight business Hobart had inherited from his brother.

The intervening years had proven the werewolf Dominant to be a better truck driver than business owner. However, I couldn't recall ever seeing the lot as empty as it was now. Most of his crew were locals, though, including plenty who were also pack members. So, it stood to reason that Magi quarantine might be having an effect beyond merely keeping us contained. Alas, Hobart's P&L statement wasn't my top concern right then.

Callahan Hauling was located on a quiet road at the western end of town. It was fairly isolated, situated in front of a wide grassy field that led to the woods. That alone made me nervous as Myra drove around to the back of the building where she leaned on the horn.

This was it. I needed for Winston to let me handle whatever happened next, but there was no way to tell him without my two other companions thinking I'd gone round the bend.

Either way, it was too late. The back door opened and Hobart lumbered out, looking as tall, heavyset, and imposing as ever. It made me wonder if I was about to get another ultimatum about him eating my balls. And no, I still wasn't over that.

He was by himself, not that it meant anything since the depot was more than large enough to hide any reinforcements he might need. If this was a setup then I was already in way over my head.

Guess it's showtime. "Stay here," I told Dallas as I stepped from the car.

I expected Myra to follow, but she merely sat there

letting the engine idle. It gave me an unexpected moment of opportunity.

"Let me handle this," I muttered under my breath. "Do not. I repeat *do not* say or do anything stupid."

That was all the time I had to wrangle my inner demon before Hobart was looming over me. He wore a scowl upon his face, not exactly a new look for him.

"So, the periodical son returns," he stated, his breath reeking of cool ranch *Doritos*.

"Prodigal," I corrected.

"What?"

"Never mind." I wasn't there to start a fight, but it was entirely possible I was alone in that hope – *alone* being the operative word. I patted my jacket pocket, feeling the reassuring bulge of the handgun within. It was a last-ditch deterrent, nothing more, but it made me feel slightly less exposed.

"Been gone for a couple of weeks now, ain't ya?" Hobart asked as if we were discussing the weather.

"So it would seem."

He grinned. "Bet you got a hell of a story to tell." I held my tongue as his grin widened. "A story involving witches I'd reckon."

He was far closer on the Hell part, but still I said nothing, curious to see where this was going.

"Speaking of witches, I assume Myra brought you up to speed on our little ... predicament?"

"You mean the quarantine?"

"I do. That's why she brought you out here."

It was time to drop the tough guy act and talk straight. "Listen, If you think I had anything to do with..."

He waved me off. "Like you've got that kind of pull, kid." He let out a short chuckle before adding. "Like any of us do."

"So then why am I here?"

"Because you're back in Harris County, which means we're all in this together. It's why I asked for this parlay."

"Parlay?" I replied, unable to hide the surprise in my voice.

"Yep. I don't expect bygones to be bygones, not after all that's happened, but I've been thinking hard on it and have decided it would be in the pack's best interests if we agreed to a truce, at least until we can find a way out of this mess."

I'll admit, I was not expecting that.

Hobart apparently took my silence as a sign to continue. "I know you've just been doing what you think is right, no matter how misguided you might be."

"Hold on," I replied, ignoring that last part. "Is this some kind of trick?"

"No tricks, son. Just me realizing that us butting heads ain't gonna do jack to solve anything. We can go back to bickering after we're free again if'n you want, although I imagine we'll have bigger problems to worry about at that point."

"I..." Okay, I'll admit it. I was totally gobsmacked. I'd expected a lot of things after being practically kidnapped by Myra, but a ceasefire wasn't one of them. Maybe this Magi problem was more serious than I realized.

"And just to show I mean business," Hobart continued, "I'm prepared to release your folks from my servitude."

I raised both eyebrows, certain I'd misheard him. "You are?"

Hobart sighed as if he thought me a fool. "That thick-headed friend of yours in the car too. I hereby renounce my claim over them as their Dominant. Shit, I'll even throw in one or two more if you want, within reason of course." He held out a meaty hand. "So what do you say, Mikey? Shall we sit down and talk about this like men?"

I didn't trust him as far as I could throw him, not after all that had happened. But I also couldn't pass up an opportunity like this – not if it meant freeing my parents and Dallas from Hobart's grasp. Heck, at the very least, it would give me some breathing room to think things through in case he decided to renege later.

What could it hurt to talk? Despite my misgivings, I reached out to take his hand.

Sadly for me, my other half was faster.

In the blink of an eye, my left hand pulled something from the pocket on that side. I had a split second to register the glint of sharpened steel – one of my kitchen knives!

What the? "Where did you get that?"

I was too late with my warning, though, as my rogue half plunged the blade deep into the side of Hobart's neck, unleashing a veritable fountain of blood.

"Sit and talk like men?" Winston remarked as Hobart collapsed, grasping at his ruined throat. "Think I'll stand instead. Easier to piss on your grave that way."

26

NEW SHERIFF IN TOWN

I stared in horror as Winston laughed his insane head off. I wasn't sure whether it was at his own joke or the joy of committing senseless murder. Maybe both. The smart thing would've been to run, but I doubt I'd ever be convicted of making good choices in bad situations. Besides which, unlike the beast I shared skin with, *I* was no monster.

Mind you, the second smartest thing would've been to run back to the car and tell Dallas to call 9-1-1. However, that failed to take into account the distinct possibility of Myra reacting *badly*. True, I didn't want Hobart to die, but I also had little interest in joining him.

Instead, I dropped to my knees to see what could be done to help him. Hobart was still alive but rapidly bleeding out. I immediately recognized the knife still sticking from the side of his throat. It was from a cutlery set Mom had gifted to me when I'd moved into my own place. They were neither fancy nor expensive, but they were sharp. The serrated edge also guaranteed I'd do more damage yanking it out than Winston had done shoving it in.

As for how my personal *demon* had gotten hold of the blade, that didn't require a stretch of the imagination. I kept them in a holder on my kitchen counter. He must've grabbed one while I was distracted by the million other little things going on.

He'd used my body like a thief in the night while I wasn't paying attention. The implications were, quite frankly, terrifying. Albeit not as terrifying as going to jail for first degree murder.

"It ... it'll be okay," I told Hobart, lying my butt off. With the amount of blood gushing from his neck, saturating both the ground beneath him as well as my favorite jacket, *okay* was not part of the equation.

Don't think about the mess. There's more important things to worry about. Easier said than done as my humanity warred with an overwhelming desire to run home and lock myself in the shower stall.

This is crazy. I'd come here expecting the worst, only for Hobart to offer me an olive branch. It even made sense as the current situation in Harris County was probably best dealt with if we weren't at each other's throats – not shoving knives into them.

All of that was now a moot point.

"Why?" I whispered. Hobart's eyes opened wide with confusion, but my question hadn't been directed at him.

"Save it for after fuckhead here stops breathing," Winston replied.

"No," I hissed. "I'm not gonna let him die."

"*You* won't let him? Gods, you have no idea how much of a bitch you sound like."

Hobart opened his mouth as if to speak, only for a gurgle of blood to come pouring out instead. He didn't have much time. I needed to do something, but what?

The sound of car doors slamming caught my ear. Myra and Dallas had apparently noticed.

"All right," Winston said with a partial shrug, "as fun as this is to watch, I've wasted enough time on this pretender to my throne." My left hand moved to grab the handle of the knife.

I slapped it away. "No!"

"Jesus, Mike!" Dallas cried. "I thought we were just coming out here to ... urk!"

There came a sizzling *zap* and then Myra replied, "And *I* said you should've kept your nose outta other people's business. Maybe next time you'll listen."

I turned to see my friend on the ground, blue lightning coursing through his body – the same spell Myra had used on me earlier. *Crap!* I jumped to my feet, the dying werewolf leader momentarily forgotten, only to realize my friend was merely stunned.

I had no idea why Myra was choosing to attack Dallas while her partner was bleeding out, but there was no time to question her motives. Instead, I spun back toward Hobart, hoping Winston was done acting like a blood-thirsty maniac.

Go figure, he wasn't.

"Oh yeah, that's more like it. Now how do you use this thing again?"

Huh? Sadly, I'd once again underestimated my other half. While I'd been distracted by Myra's spell, he'd reached around and fished his hand into my right-side pocket, finding the silver-loaded handgun inside. "No, don't do it!"

"Never mind! Figured it out."

BLAM! BLAM!

Winston fired twice before I could hope to stop him. His grip was poor, his stance non-existent, but we were at point blank range. Two small holes appeared in Hobart's shirt as the silver bullets struck him dead center.

Blood began to spurt from the wounds, although not

for long. Already Hobart's eyes were glazing over. This was it. There was nothing anyone could do for him at this point.

"What have you done?" I muttered, still in disbelief at how quickly things had gone south.

"Not much. Just taking out the... Wait. What the fuck? Is this some kind of trick?"

"Trick?" I spat. "He's dead because of you!"

"I'm not talking about that, cat shit for brains. Look at the blood."

"I don't need to see it. You've done enough."

"Stop whining and pay the fuck attention," Winston snapped. "Where's the smoke, the sparks, all that good shit?"

Huh? Much as I didn't want to look, he was right. Hobart's corpse was a bloody mess, but there were none of the telltale signs that silver had been used against him. *No*. I couldn't let that distract me from what he'd done. Maybe it was because of the time of day or, I dunno, maybe Hannah had given me a bad batch of bullets. None of that mattered compared to...

My thoughts trailed off as the space around Hobart's body began to shimmer, like the air over a hot barbecue.

What the?

In the next instant, his form grew shorter and leaner. His unseeing eyes changed color from brown to green and his facial features became that of someone else entirely.

Bob? Bob Dobkins worked as Callahan Hauling's bookkeeper. He was an unassuming sort – quiet, well spoken, and usually happy to give a wave if he saw you around town. More importantly, he'd never been part of the ritual.

"The fuck just happened?" Winston demanded.

"Christ on a cracker, what a mess," Hobart's cried, except his voice hadn't come from the body at my feet.

I turned to see him once again step foot from the depot, just as he had minutes earlier.

No way.

"Gotta say, Myra," he continued, "I honestly didn't think Mikey here had the sand to do it, but you were right. Good call on the glamour by the way. I owe you one."

Glamour?

"Actually, you owe me twenty," she called back with a cackle. "Don't forget our bet."

"Worth every penny," he replied, turning my way. Behind him, three more men stepped out of the building – Jeb Ketchum, Hobart's friend and right-hand wolf, along with two other employees, both of whom I recognized as members of the pack.

Holy crap. She'd done it again. It was the same sort of illusion Myra had used earlier to make me think she was my father. Realization struck like a boot to the face. This had been a setup from the get-go. Though I had no way of knowing whether his offer of a truce had been real, one thing was obvious. He'd willingly sacrificed a man's life and didn't seem to care one bit about it.

"Poor Bob," Hobart continued, glancing down at the body. "Oh well. With business being what it is, couldn't really afford him no more anyway. No big loss."

No big... "You killed him!"

He cocked his head. "Nuh uh. Technically you did, thinking it was me no less."

Myra must've sensed my next question because she quickly cut in. "Remember what I said about mind magic? Well, those fancy dancy Magi ain't the only ones who got it going. Old Bob here might've been good with numbers, but the dumb shit had all the willpower of a dull-witted woodchuck. Maybe next time he'll learn not to stare at a lady's titties when answering a question about her taxes."

"Enough of that," Hobart cautioned, taking a step toward me before glancing down at the gun still in my hand. "Why don't you drop the peashooter, kid?"

"How about I jam it up your ass sideways instead?" Winston replied, raising the gun.

Crap! Before I could stop him, though, a burning hot lance of red energy engulfed my left arm.

"ARGH!"

I wasn't sure which of us screamed first, but it was as close to a group effort as we'd managed up until that point. Unfortunately, my inner werewolf might've controlled one half of our body, but my nerve endings were apparently still happy to share the pain.

The gun, its barrel now red hot and smoking, fell to the ground, but I barely noticed it against the smell of charred flesh and burnt leather coming from my hand and forearm.

"Sorry, Mike," Myra remarked as she pumped another stun spell into Dallas, "but you kinda deserved it."

I opened my mouth but the only sound that escaped was a pained whine, not much different than a dog might make.

"All right," Hobart said, clapping his hands together, "quit zapping that fool. I need him ready for what comes next." He turned my way again. "I'm sorry this is the way it's gotta be. I truly did hope we could come to an accord. Hell, I was even starting to believe you meant it when you said you didn't want the pack for yourself. What I get for being a big softy, I suppose."

He probably meant to sound regretful, but it didn't come across that way. Instead, his tone was that of a man looking forward to whatever was about to happen.

I had a sinking feeling I knew what that was.

Hobart unbuttoned his shirt then discarded it to the

ground next to him, just as Myra's body began to glow again – this time a sickly yellow color.

Hobart's muscles undulated and his body began to swell, while his partner in magic raised her hands. Moments later, the noonday sky filled with an exaggerated illusion of the full moon – so large you'd swear it was about to fall on all our heads.

What happened instead is that Jeb and the others began to change as well, and they weren't alone. At Myra's feet, Dallas began to writhe as the transformation took hold of his unwilling body.

I'd seen her do this before. The illusion itself was only part of it. After all, it's not like looking at the moon in a picture book did anything. No. In addition to looking ominous as can be, it also reached deep inside of folks like me, somehow convincing our bodies the time of the wolf was nigh.

Heck, I felt it too. It wasn't like with the others, though. I still had control, but that subtle pull to remain human I felt during the day was now gone, and in its place was a yearning to run free and howl.

Or there would've been had my hand not been cooked like a Christmas roast.

As for Winston, I couldn't say what was going through his mind, other than he'd fallen silent following Myra's attack.

Between that and the fact I was outnumbered, I managed to ignore the call of Myra's spell, tempting as it was. Instead, I turned and, against all inclination to the contrary, finally made the smart choice for once.

I ran.

27

WOLF HUNT

My instincts, upon reaching the tree line, practically screamed for me to give in to the headiness of Myra's spell and allow the change to happen, but I held myself in check, despite the pain causing tears to stream down my face.

In truth, I would've loved to curl up in a little ball and give in to the rush of brain chemicals that would make the hurt go away. But there was no way for me to change while running full tilt. And stopping wasn't an option, a fact I was reminded of as a series of rapidly rising snarls filled the air behind me.

Then there was Winston to consider. Myra's attack had hurt like hell, no doubt about it, but I got the impression he'd taken the brunt of it. Don't ask me how that worked since we shared the same body. All I knew was that I was still functional, whereas the only indication he was even conscious were the occasional whimpers which escaped my lips in between my own gasps of pain.

I couldn't be sure how he'd respond if I tried to change. Maybe he'd be okay with escaping, or he might decide to lash out like a cornered animal instead. Since our odds were currently six-to-one, the last thing I needed was to have to fight him too.

No. Running was by far my best bet. Besides, Myra might've been crazy strong, emphasis on *crazy*, but she wasn't all powerful. Though I didn't know the range of her magic, it was still middle of the day. Given enough distance, the werewolves under her and Hobart's thrall would revert back to their human selves. That would go a long way toward evening the odds.

The only problem was the very real possibility that I'd end up as bite-sized chunks long before then. My human legs were simply no match for a werewolf's speed. In my other form, I could easily beat a greyhound in a foot race, which meant those chasing me could as well. Heck, if anything, they should've caught up to me already.

That they hadn't was no comfort, though. Quite the opposite. I was starting to feel like a fox being hunted by some mighty large hounds.

In the past, Hobart had been content to drive me off. But that was before I shanked his doppelganger in the neck. Sure, it technically wasn't my fault, but with Winston using my body to do his dirty work, that didn't leave me with a lot of options for an alibi.

I needed to face facts. Hobart was out for blood this time and the only reason I wasn't dead yet was because he wanted to play with his food first.

I shuddered in pain and no small amount of fear as I stopped between two pine trees to catch my breath. Call me a cynic, but I had a sinking feeling Hobart wasn't about to settle for one of my balls this time. As the pack Dominant, he'd almost certainly want to be the one to strike the killing blow, but that didn't mean he wouldn't have his minions use me as a chew toy until he was ready to...

"Dallas."

Huh?

The word was barely a whisper, but it was enough to tell me Winston was still hanging in there. Although whether for good or bad, I dared not speculate.

Tempting as it was to lay into him, there'd be time for that later, hopefully.

Or maybe not.

I cocked my head as a low-pitched howl rent the air – Hobart loosing his *hounds* was my guess. Whatever head start I'd been allowed was over.

I forced myself to start moving again despite the pain. My only hope of outpacing Myra's spell before those were-wolves caught up was to find one of the many creeks dotting the area and hope that threw them off my scent. Sadly, it was a slim hope at best.

"What about Dallas?" I asked, attempting to stave off the terror threatening to overcome me.

"*It's ... it's not too late,*" he replied weakly.

"I know. That's why we're running."

"*No, stupid. I mean for him.*"

I stumbled over a tree root, almost losing my footing. "Can we maybe do this later?"

"*He can help us!*"

It was becoming increasingly difficult both fleeing and carrying on a conversation while in near blinding pain, but I tried anyway.

"No, he can't," I snapped, my anger boiling over. "He's nothing but a monster now because of *you*, because you decided he needed to tag along."

"And why the fuck do you think I did that?" Winston replied, his voice growing stronger with every word.

"No idea." I looked back. There was still no sign of the werewolves after us but I could hear them, like a snarling dog pack tracking their prey. "I have no idea why you do anything!"

"It's because he's not one of Hobart's, or at least he doesn't want to be."

"You think I don't know that? A lot of them don't. Doesn't seem to matter much, though."

"Were you even listening earlier? That asshole offered up your friend and parents in exchange for a truce. He renounced his hold over them."

"That wasn't Hobart!"

"Doesn't matter. You heard him back there, the real one, not the shithead I capped. The offer was real."

"I don't see how that helps us."

"It helps because the dumb fuck made it that much easier for me to bring them over to my ... our side, our *pack*." Gone was any trace of the grogginess of moments earlier. Guess Winston had finally shaken it off.

Regardless, I had no idea what he was talking about and there was no time to indulge his foolishness. "You do realize I don't know how to do that, right?"

"Of course not. You're an idiot. But fortunately for us both, *I* do."

I hadn't considered that possibility. Sadly, there was no time to discuss it as a twig snapped directly behind us. It was followed by a low snarl. *Crap!*

I turned, already knowing what I'd see. The werewolf was less than twenty feet away. It wasn't Hobart, but that didn't make it any less dangerous. Absolutely no humanity shone from its feral red eyes as it stood to its full height.

I didn't see the rest but that didn't mean anything. Maybe this was Hobart's game plan, sending them one at a time to wear me down. As if it even mattered. In my current condition, even one werewolf was one too many.

"I-I'm all ears," I stammered, backing up until I was pressed against the nearest tree. "If you know how to bring my friend back, then do it."

"Great," Winston replied. "There's just one small problem."

I let out a sigh. "Let me guess. That isn't Dallas?"

Winston let out a morbid chuckle as the beast closed in. "On the upside, you're not as dumb as you look."

It was small comfort as we stared death in the eye.

28

DOG RUN

"All right, enough of this shit. I'm gonna need your stupid, fleshy ass to step back."

"Step back?" I asked, pressed so tightly to the tree that I was in danger of growing bark.

"Yeah," Winston replied as the werewolf continued to stare at us, almost as if waiting to be given the go-ahead to tear us limb from limb. "It's simple. You want to keep breathing, then you let me handle this."

The tingle within my limbs, the momentary easing of the terrible pain, told me what he was trying to do. Despite not wanting the hurt to return, I put a stop to him.

"What the fuck, idiot?" he growled.

"We can't. Myra's spell. We don't know if she's..."

"Fuck Myra's spell. I already told you. I'm a Dominant. *No one* controls me, not you, not some big-ass sea lizard, and definitely not your hairless mount buddy."

It was the worst possible time imaginable for us to be having this discussion, especially since whatever invisible leash was holding the werewolf picked that moment to let go.

The monster snarled and charged forward.

"Give me control!"

There was no time to argue, so I went limp. Rather than crumple to the ground, though, I instead dove out of the way at the last moment. A second longer and I would've been crushed between the beast and the tree behind me. Instead...

Crack!

Leaves and limbs crashed to the ground from the sheer force of the monster's impact, painting a not-so-wonderful picture of what would've happened to my very much still human body. The upside was the werewolf hadn't fared too well either. It staggered back dazed, blood discoloring the fur at the top of its head.

Under Hobart's control it might have been, but that didn't mean it was any smarter than normal.

Now wasn't the time for a werewolf IQ test. I needed to make a decision – give Winston control and hope he was right, or fight him, knowing at the very least he was still a freaking psychopath. On the flipside, he claimed to have a plan, which was more than I had.

Stuck between a rock and a hard place, I didn't see much choice.

"About fucking time," Winston cried as I gave him full control. "Any longer and I *would've sliced your...*"

The rest was lost to a snarl as the change took hold. Fur began to sprout, muscles contorted, and bones rearranged themselves. My clothing abruptly grew tight around me before bursting at the seams.

My poor jacket. I'd had it since high school but now it was... "*ARGH!*"

Blinding pain cut through the haze of brain chemicals like a hot knife, nearly driving me to my knees just as a sneezing fit took hold.

"Achoo!" Winston had been wrong after all. Myra's

magic was cutting through our defenses despite his insistence to the contrary. But then, just as I was about to lose my mind from the combination of sneezing and hurting, I realized the agony wasn't coming from inside my head.

Sure enough, the mangled and burnt flesh of my left arm appeared to be rapidly regenerating. *The healing burst from the change*! I'd almost forgotten about it. I just wish it didn't hurt as much.

Sadly, it wasn't quite perfect either.

As the transformation and my sneezing fit both came to an end, I took note of my left arm again. It was missing most of its fur and the skin was a jumble of scar tissue. Still, there was no doubt it was a considerable improvement.

As I stepped from the remnants of my tattered clothing, Winston gave it an experimental flex.

"*Not too shabby,*" he grumbled, his unintelligible voice once again somehow perfectly understandable. "*Now to test it out.*"

Before I could ask what he meant, he launched himself at the still dazed werewolf and raked our claws across the beast's face. It let out a horrified yipe as its eyes were gouged from its head, leaving behind nothing but bloodied sockets.

Holy crap!

"*Calm your teats,*" Winston said. "*I didn't kill him. Just … slowed him down a bit.*"

A bit?!

It wasn't enough, though, as the wolf raised its head and let out a keening yowl, one answered almost immediately from the direction where we'd come.

"*You can shut the fuck up now.*" Winston backhanded the wolf, sending it flying.

Rather than finish it off, as I feared he might try, we

instead took off running again. Albeit this time it was at a considerably faster rate.

We'd gone maybe a quarter of a mile when I felt a twinge in my joints, the same sensation I'd felt in the Chadworth's basement. It was my body's natural impulse to revert to its human form, something Winston quickly put a stop to.

This was it. We were finally outside the influence of Myra's spell, a good thing as the sound of not-nearly distant enough snarls told me Hobart wasn't holding back anymore. He and the rest of his wolves were coming.

Do you think this will cause the others to...?

"*To change back?*" Winston interrupted as we turned to face the coming assault. "*Probably. They're not smart enough to resist, not unless that asshole forces it.*"

Can he do that?

"*Yep, but it'll cost him. This time of day, it'll take a lot of effort to keep even one or two in their natural forms.*"

I was tempted to point out there was nothing natural about raging man beasts, but philosophical discussions could wait. Besides which, I was far more interested in why Winston chose to step to the nearest bush, raise our leg, and ... pee on it.

Are you marking your territory?

"*Nope. Just a piss break before the fun starts.*"

Oh. Ask a stupid question... *So, um, what now?*

"*Duh,*" Winston replied. "*We circle around, wait for them to come after us, then pick off the fuckers one by one.*"

That's your brilliant plan?

"*About time you recognized my genius,*" he replied, my sarcasm obviously flying way over his furry head. "*Anyway, that scent mark will keep them focused on my trail. The dumb fucks won't be smart enough to realize it's a trap until...*"

Until what?

"*I gut the shit out of them, of course.*"

You can't do that.

"*The fuck I can't.*"

Dallas is with them.

"*Doubt it.*"

You can't know that for certain.

"*Sure I can. Your fuckwit friend is Hobart's leverage. The fat shit-sniffer might be an idiot but even he's not dumb enough to throw away his advantage so quickly. He'll have Dallas hold back for now.*"

And if he doesn't?

"*Then you get to make some new friends. Preferably ones with more survival instinct.*"

I was about to tell him what I thought of his plan when something else he'd said hit me. *Wait, what do you mean for now?*

"*Once he realizes that I'm ass-fucking his minions to the seven Hells and back, he'll send your buddy right in.*"

Why?

"*Because he'll assume you'll either hesitate or be blood-lusted enough to kill him by mistake. Either way, it'll screw shit up for you.*"

I was once again set to question his murderously insane strategy when another sound caught my ear.

"*Except that won't happen, because I'm running this... Wait. What the hell is that?*" Winston asked, noticing it too.

Sounds like an engine, I told him.

"*I know that, stupid. But what is it doing out here?*"

Listen to the hum. That's a side-by-side and I'm pretty sure it's heading toward those werewolves.

"*What's a...*"

Do we really have time for this crap now?

My first thought was it must be the hunters, that

Isaiah had sent a team to Harris County to keep an eye on things. I wasn't a big fan of being spied on, but in this case I could let it slide.

However, I quickly changed my tune as I realized the twinge was gone. I no longer felt a subtle urge to revert. If anything, my current form once again felt right as rain.

Crap! It's Myra!

"*Gods damn it all. Guess old Hobart planned ahead.*"

Ya think?

"*Well, that definitely complicates shit.*"

Talk about an understatement. We could no longer count on Hobart's focus being split by the effort to keep his minions all furry. Instead, he could remain dead set on hunting us down like ... well, a dog.

What now, genius?

"*I...*" Winston hesitated. It was only for a second or two but enough to tell me he'd been outmaneuvered. "*So, anyway, what was that plan of yours again?*"

29

OLD FACES, NEW PROBLEMS

If there was one upside to sharing headspace with a slobbering wolf monster, and believe me I hadn't found too many, it was that a shared consciousness allowed us to split up duties in a pinch.

Winston stayed focused on keeping us moving – making sure we didn't do anything dumb like trip over exposed roots, something I was forced to admit he seemed far more adept at.

With him steering the *ship*, I was free to brainstorm ideas for how to get out of this mess without ending up in a shallow grave minus my family jewels. Too bad I was coming up emptyhanded so far.

Whether through good planning or happy accident, Hobart and his pack buddies had put Barley Hills to their backside. There was no getting there without going through them first.

Unfortunately, taking the scenic route wasn't an option, as I had no idea how far that magical quarantine extended. Too far in either direction and there was a good chance I'd run afoul of it.

Sure, it was possible Myra had made the whole thing

up, knowing what was to come, but my gut told me that was one gamble it might be best not to take.

So what does that leave us? I asked silently as we vaulted over a stump, landing a good fifteen feet past it.

Winston merely let out a grunt, although I couldn't help but notice he'd stopped suggesting we simply murder our way out of this mess. Since I doubted he'd discovered altruism anytime in the last few minutes, that meant he understood how screwed we truly were.

Even if we somehow managed to get the upper hand against the werewolves still hot on our tail, there was Myra to contend with. She was the artillery to their infantry. One clean shot and it would be all over. Heck, even a glancing blow would probably be enough to ruin my day. Making a stand was out of the question.

What then? *Think, stupid, think!*

"Stop yelling at me!"

I'm not yelling. I'm trying to figure out a way to... That's when it hit me. It wasn't some grand plan or scheme, but it was better than anything I'd come up with so far. *Turn east!*

"Why? What's east?"

Main Street.

Winston made a grumbling sound but then abruptly changed direction. *"I think I get it. Good idea."*

Wait, really?

"Yeah, there'll be plenty of human snacks to keep those assholes busy. Then we can shred the fuck out of them."

Not what I was going for. We need to change back before anyone sees us.

"What good will that do us?"

For starters, it won't give everyone a crash course that we exist. More importantly, it'll keep us from getting shot by Sheriff Haskell.

"He tries it and I'll..."

No, you won't. Being arrested for first degree murder is not *part of the plan.*

"*Okay, then what is the fucking plan?*"

I swear, it was tempting to take control just long enough to smack him up his side of our head.

In truth, getting arrested was almost certainly in the cards for us, just not for Winston's reasons. After all, it's not like I'd had time to plan ahead in terms of bringing a change of clothing. We'd be strolling into the town proper naked as a jaybird. And while Deke Haskell had always been a reasonable fella, I had a feeling there'd be no talking my way out of that. On the upside, we'd be around plenty of people.

Considering the status quo appeared to be intact, and by that I mean the general populace didn't seem aware they were neighbors with werewolves, I had to assume Hobart would think twice before coming for us. It would give us a small breather.

I explained as much to Winston.

"*So let me get this straight, pupcake. Your plan is to walk into town all pink skinned and freezing, get arrested, but not for anything fun, and then have both our asses thrown into a cage?*"

Relax. I don't mean a brain cage. It's a... I let out a mental *Ouch* as he slapped my side of our face with a big meaty paw.

"*I know what the fuck a cage is. Same way I know how stupid it would be to let them lock me up in one.*"

Hobart won't be able to get us in there, I replied, fighting the urge to smack him back.

"*Maybe not, but your mount buddy might decide to turn it into a crater anyway, since we'll be stuck there like sitting pups.*"

Ducks.

"*What?*"

The phrase is we'll be sitting ducks.

"*Who fucking cares? What matters is they'll be able to fuck around however they please and there won't be shit either of us can do about it.*"

I... He was right. I hadn't considered Myra. Heck, even if she opted for restraint, a big if, we'd still be talking a night in jail.

Normally that wouldn't be a big deal, outside of the embarrassment it was sure to cause at work. But Winston had crossed a line by killing Bob Dobkins. He'd upped the ante immeasurably on this dangerous game we were playing.

Getting tossed in the clink would give us a breather, true, but it would also give our foes time to plot their next move while knowing I was locked up tight with no way to stop them.

They might use that time against me, or they might opt to use it against my parents.

Winston's motives for staying out of jail might've been fully self-serving, but that didn't make him wrong about it.

Damn it! So much for Plan A.

That once again left us in a bind. Any pack members I could turn to for help, my parents included, were ultimately under Hobart's thrall. The thing was, even if Winston could turn them against the pack leader, did I really want to use my mom and dad as foot soldiers in some clandestine supernatural war?

At least that one was an easy answer.

Finding help amongst my non-werewolf friends was similarly out of the question, as they too would be endangered. That left either circling the woods nonstop in the hope Hobart grew bored enough to call off his hunt, or crawling in a hole and hoping the monsters didn't find me. Neither sounded promising, unless...

Another idea hit me, crazy as it might be. There was

one person in Harris County who straddled both worlds, someone neither werewolf nor witch, yet more than aware that things in our little town were far from normal.

Change of plans. Keep heading north.

"This better not involve us rotting in a cage."

It won't ... probably. I'll fill you in along the way.

"You sure about this?"

Not really, I admitted.

"Fuck it. Beats running around like my tail's on fire. Besides, the old bastard owes us one."

I hated to drag Jacob Vesser into our mess but he was technically already part of it, whether he wanted to be or not.

Besides, Winston was right, sorta anyway. I'd saved Jacob, back on the night when Bill the vampire and his weirdo friends had stopped by for a visit, inadvertently setting events in motion with the pack.

Then...

As Jacob and his guests found themselves increasingly outmatched by Hobart's werewolves, they retreated to the detached garage, within which sat Jacob's old Ford pickup – a truck he was known to meticulously maintain.

Their plan of escape was blindingly obvious as I watched all this play out – debating whether I should get involved. However, if it was clear to me, then I had little doubt it was likewise clear to Hobart and Myra.

They were beaten and attempting to retreat. That should've been the end of it. But once I saw the pack encircling the garage I realized how wrong I was. Hobart, for whatever reason, had no intention of letting them get away.

I knew then that I had to step in and clear a path for them as quickly as possible before either of us could be overwhelmed.

Now...

Jacob and his friends had gotten away, but that hadn't been the end of things. Far from it. Hobart had then turned his attention toward Jacob's vampire visitor, tracking him all the way to Brooklyn. I followed, renting an apartment in Bill's building to keep tabs on the situation.

One thing led to another, and now here I was – back in Harris County, missing two weeks of my life and trapped with a bunch of nutjobs who wanted me dead.

Of all the things which had transpired in the short while since my return, Myra's mention of Jacob returning had been one of the most surprising. After all, far as I was aware, he was just a regular guy.

I understood him not wanting to abandon his home, but it's not like he'd left because of bad neighbors or a gas leak. To come back after being chased off by werewolves was ... not really normal. Jacob was either unreasonably stubborn or had decided to make a stand.

I was willing to bet on the latter as we neared the outskirts of his property.

The sounds of pursuit still rung in my ears, but was it my imagination or had they fallen behind a bit? More importantly, that twinge was back. We were once again outside Myra's sphere of influence.

Did that mean Hobart had been caught off guard by our direction, or was I reading too much into it?

Regardless, if he hadn't figured it out yet, he soon would.

Still, I didn't want to rush this. As we paused inside the tree line leading to Jacob's front yard, I took a sniff of the air. The picture it painted was not one I expected.

"There's no one fucking here," Winston grumbled.

Maybe he drove into town for supplies.

"Not what I'm talking about, shithead. Focus. No one's been here. All the scents, the human ones anyway, they're old, stale."

That can't be right. Myra said…

"And you believed her? What, you mount a bitch and suddenly your brain stops working?"

Technically she mounted me. Banter aside, Winston was correct about the human scents being stale, but his conclusion painted only half a picture. Even as doubts about my plan began to worm their way into my subconscious, I realized there was a lot more here to scrutinize – specifically odors that were far fresher: car exhaust, freshly cut boards, and more.

Peering out from the bushes, I took note of Jacob's house. It was the type of log cabin one might normally expect to be owned by a millionaire pretending to rough it, except in Jacob's case he'd painstakingly built it by hand – continually upgrading it over the years until it was a thing of beauty.

Though the drive took us out of the way of our normal route, I never minded picking up the trash here because it was so nice to look at, a work of art by a dedicated craftsman.

Unfortunately, it had also gotten pretty roughed up the night he'd fled. But, aside from a couple of boards still marred by claw marks, the structure standing before us now showed few signs of having undergone any such trauma.

Someone had been actively fixing the place up. It was all the evidence I needed.

We need to get closer, but not like this.

Winston let out a growling sigh, but didn't fight me as I gave in to the twinge.

Once more, pain flared from my damaged arm, enough to overcome those sweet brain chemicals. However, this time when the transformation finished my left arm was once again whole. Whatever the first healing burst hadn't fixed, this second one had apparently taken care of. Talk about things that were good to know.

"Not too bad," I muttered, testing it out. "All right. Let me take the lead for now. Jacob's probably going to be squirrelly after everything he's been through, and the fact that we're naked is going to make this weird enough."

"Be my guest," he said. "Just don't fuck it up."

"Relax. I've got this." I stepped from the bushes and onto the gravel driveway, the stones beneath my bare feet digging in uncomfortably. "Trust me. I know how to handle... OOF!"

I'd taken no more than two steps when there came a blur of movement from my flank ... in the split second before something plowed into me. I was sent sprawling onto the gravel, bruised, scraped up, and with the wind knocked out of me.

I rolled over onto my back still dazed, only to find a thin, wiry looking man glaring down at me.

"Figured one of you fuckers would show up eventually," he said. "It's about time we had a chat about private property, respecting boundaries, and the fact you shit-biscuits seem intent on being constantly up my ass."

Before I could ask what the heck he was talking about, his eyes flashed bright yellow and he bared his teeth, revealing a pair of elongated canines.

A vampire, one seemingly unbothered by the sun shining down upon us both.

30

HEY, WRONG SERIES, ASSHOLE!

I could feel Winston trying to take control, no doubt wanting to say or do something that would almost certainly make this situation worse, especially once the vampire pulled a shotgun from his shoulder and pointed it at our face.

Instead, I clamped down hard with my teeth, biting my own tongue in the process. It hurt like the dickens, but served to distract my inner beast while I attempted to make sense of this new development, only to realize I vaguely recognized our captor's face.

That's when it hit me. Bill, the vamp I'd rented an apartment from, was friends with this guy. Heck, he'd even introduced the two of us, shortly before things came to a head in Brooklyn.

So then what was he doing here?

Even as I finished that thought, my subconscious put two and two together, making me realize what a colossal idiot I was. Back when we'd met, we'd both been struck by the fact the other had seemed familiar – something he'd voiced but I hadn't. At the time, I'd dismissed it as him just having one of those faces.

That wasn't actually the case, though. He looked familiar because he *was* familiar, and not just from a few weeks ago.

God, what a moron I could be.

"You-Your name's Ed, right?"

If memory served me correctly, Jacob Vesser had two step-children via his late wife – Maggie and Edward. Ed had been a few years ahead of me in high school, meaning we hadn't hung in the same circles. I simply hadn't made the connection before now, probably because I'd never even thought to suspect one of Jacob's kids might be undead. Suddenly it made all the sense in the world why Jacob had vamps visiting him. Heck, Bill was probably Ed's sire or something like that.

Speaking of which, Ed raised a curious eyebrow. "Yeah, and you're that werewolf asshole who's been spying on us."

How did he know...? Okay, that wasn't important. Heck, the fact I was running around naked was probably enough to clue him in.

I held up my hands. "Werewolf, yes, but I wasn't spying on you."

"So, you just coincidentally happened to rent Bill's basement apartment? Why? You got a fetish for shit holes or something?"

"Not quite. But I wasn't there to spy. I was keeping an eye out in case..."

"For fuck's sake!" Winston interrupted. "Will you stop sucking this guy's dick and gut him already."

Ed quickly glanced behind him before once again focusing on me. "Who are you talking to?"

"I ... I'm not talking to anyone," I replied nonchalantly. "Why do you ask?"

Too bad Winston wasn't getting the hint. "Fucking hell. If you're going to be a pussy then I'll do it myself."

Unsurprisingly, my body once again began to go numb from brain chemicals. We were already in deep enough do-do, so I tried to stop it – a feat made somewhat easier since it was daylight. "You need to knock it off."

"Give me one reason I should, pupcake."

"Oh, I don't know, maybe because he's got a gun pointed at our face!"

"Gods damn you're a bitch. Like that'll stop me."

"Do you really want to test that theory out?" Ed replied, staring at me curiously as he patted the chamber of his weapon. "Silver slugs."

"Wait, you know about that?" I asked.

"Um, yeah. It's only in every freaking werewolf movie ever made. Not to mention silver tends to be pretty handy against all sorts of nasty fuckers, so I figure why not you guys as well."

"But where did you get them?"

"Pop knows a guy. Let's leave it at that. So how about it? Are you ready to surrender, or do you need a minute to talk it over with whoever else is in there with you?"

"There's no one else..."

"Don't bullshit a bullshitter," Ed interrupted. "For starters, you used the phrase *our face*. Second, this isn't my first multiple personality rodeo. Although in your case it's somewhat less subtle than I'm used to seeing."

I debated denying it further, but what was the point? Winston was eventually going to say something whether I wanted him to or not. On the upside, I doubted Ed would be sharing my revelation with Hobart anytime soon.

Speaking of my alter ego, he'd apparently given up on forcing us to transform, so now was probably the time for me to try and tip the odds of survival in our favor. "You might not know this, but..."

"We've already established I do. You're the guy from Bill's apartment. Mike, right?"

"Yeah, Mike…"

"Walden," he finished, his eyes opening wide in surprise. "Shit, I thought you looked familiar. Now I remember. Back in grade school the kids all used to call you Mike Hunt."

I nodded. "Yep, that's me. Although, I never understood why you guys called me by my middle…" I trailed off as sudden recognition dawned. "Never mind. I just now got the joke."

Ed shrugged. "Happens to the best of us, man."

"What joke?" Winston asked.

"Never you mind," I muttered, more than aware we were still on the ground with a gun pointed at us.

"Is it because of how much you suck at hunting?"

"Um, yeah. Let's go with that."

Ed watched our exchange with a curious look. "Anyway, as I was saying, small world."

"Tell me about it," I replied. "But that's not what I meant. What I was trying to say is back when Jacob, your dad, got chased off by the pack, the others I mean…"

He narrowed his eyes. "What about it?"

"Near the end, just before he got away. There was another werewolf, different from the rest, one who helped him out by clearing a path. Ask him about it. That was me."

Ed didn't seem particularly convinced, but fortunately another voice picked that moment to speak up.

"Different how?"

I turned to find the front door open and Jacob Vesser standing just inside. He was burly and muscular where his stepson was a string bean on legs, not that such things mattered in the world of the weird. More importantly, he was similarly armed, holding a Winchester rifle while a heavy caliber handgun hung at his side.

Guess I couldn't blame either of them for being over-prepared.

"Um, it was, I mean *I'm* brown," I said. "My fur that is. Anyway, I tossed some of the other werewolves out of your way. Oh, and then I waved as you guys drove off."

Yeah, that had definitely sounded better inside my head.

The older of the two men stepped from the house, well, older in appearance anyway. If what they said about vampires was true then I had no way of judging how old Ed actually was. Well, okay, I'd seen him growing up, but I dunno, maybe vampires were able to regress into a larval state in order to fool people, like in that *Dragonball Z* cartoon. Although I seemed to recall those being androids not vampires, but whatever. Just because something wasn't in a movie, didn't mean it was impossible.

I pushed aside that heaping helping of brain salad, for now anyway, realizing I had far more important matters to worry about.

Jacob appeared to think it over for a minute or two before he said, "Let him up."

"You sure, Pop?"

"I ain't sure about much these days, Eddie, but I'd prefer we not start shooting people just for showing up at our door minus their knickers."

"I disagree. That's actually the perfect time to shoot them, but your call. Besides, I'm getting tired of staring at his dick." He made eye contact with me. "Not that I was. Anyway, you heard him. You coming in or are you just gonna keep lying there like some weird-ass lawn ornament?"

I was about to take him up on his offer when Winston decided to add his two cents. "Are you seriously going to make nice with these assholes?"

This time I didn't even pretend. "As a matter of fact, I am. Now would you'd kindly shut up?"

"Is the other guy gonna be a problem?" Ed asked, taking the barrel of his gun off me but keeping it at the ready.

"No."

"Try me and find out, fuck nuts," Winston added.

"No!" I repeated. "Trust me, it's cool. He talks a big game but I've ... mostly got it under control."

Left unsaid was that only held true while the sun was shining. Afterward, well, hopefully we'd have reached an understanding by then.

There I was, once again wearing another man's clothes. I swear, it was starting to become a habit. I really needed to make it a point to start seeding hidey holes around town with clothing bundles.

Regardless, I felt better once I was no longer dangling in the wind. Alas, being a nudist wasn't something I'd ever be comfortable with. Maybe it was time to start investing in extra stretchy underpants.

As for Winston, I tried reasoning with him as I got dressed, telling him he needed to chill out, especially since the alternative was a fight we couldn't win. He'd taken an instant dislike to Ed for some reason, but that seemed to get through to him ... for the moment.

Several minutes later found us gathered around Jacob's dining room table as he brought out a fresh pot of coffee. Despite his hospitality, I noted both he and his son made it a point to keep their weapons within reach. I tried not to take any offense while hoping my inner wolf did the same.

"You're Ginny and Lloyd's boy, right?" Jacob asked, fixing me a steaming mug.

"Yes, sir."

"They're good people."

"They've always spoken highly of you too, sir." I took a sip then had to resist the urge to slurp it all down, not realizing until that moment how empty my tank was. Safe to say, it was probably best for me to focus on other things for the time being. "So, I gotta ask. Are those guns really loaded with silver, or were you just trying to scare me?" It probably wasn't the best ice breaker but I'd had a long day.

"Silver jacket over a lead core," Jacob said, "but just as good from what I've heard." He glanced toward Ed who nodded in turn.

"Let me guess," I replied. "Barley Hills?"

"What about them?"

"That's where you got them, right?"

Jacob raised an eyebrow. "Why in hell would Mennonites sell me silver bullets?"

"Because they're werewolf hunters, so I just kinda figured..."

Judging by the looks on both their faces, I'd just spilled the beans on our sister town's little secret. *Oops. Slick move, Mike.*

"Hold on," Ed interrupted. "Are you saying they know about ... guys like you?"

"What do you think, scrotum for brains?" Winston replied.

Crap! "Sorry. That wasn't me."

"Yeah, kinda figured." He pointed toward his ear. "The *other guy* talks with a different cadence ... among other things."

Jacob let out a chuckle. "You don't need super powered ears to figure that one out."

"So, anyway, Barley Hills, really?" Ed continued. "Goddamn, I guess Bill wasn't making shit up after all."

Jacob glanced his way. "Making what up?"

"Remember the big shootout that was in the news right after Kara and I ... well, while we were still in Cali?"

His stepdad nodded. "The one we're not supposed to know Billy was a part of?"

"Exactly. He was telling me how at one point he saw a bunch of Amish dudes up on the rooftop shooting up the place."

"That was them," I confirmed.

"Goddamn. For real? And here I thought maybe he'd gotten his ass kicked a little too hard. Either that or that thing in the Hudson fucked him up more than he was letting on."

And suddenly he had my full undivided attention. "Thing in the Hudson?"

"Some big-ass monster," he replied dismissively. "They're calling it Leviathan. Guess I owe him an apology. Bill, not the big-ass sea monster."

"Leviathan?" I repeated, an uneasy feeling stirring in the back of my mind. I knew it typically implied something large and frightening, but there was an older meaning behind the word, one on the tip of my tongue.

"Yeah, after they got out of Brooklyn they got attacked by..." He trailed off. "Hold on a second. Bill mentioned one of the werewolves helped them against the rest. Was that you?"

I was about to answer when his words finally registered. "Wait. *He told you this?* Are you saying they got away from that thing?"

He shook his head. "Just him and Sally. She's..."

"The one with the glowing eyes," I interrupted. "What about the others?"

"They were all captured." His eyes narrowed. "Including that werewolf."

I probably should've said something, but my mind was suddenly back on that dock in Manhattan. *Leviathan.*

Too bad my distraction gave Winston an opening. "Not exactly, shit breath. The pink-skinned dipshit here was the one who got caught, not me."

I forced myself to focus before he could say anything else. "He's right... sorta. That monster, it got *me* too." I really didn't want to feed my inner beast's ego, but fair was fair. "The only reason I was able to get away is because of Winston."

"Winston?" Jacob asked.

"My inner wolf," I explained. "Werewolf that is."

"So, you're a werewolf," Ed replied, "but that part of you is somehow also a separate personality named Winston?"

Before I could answer, I found myself leaning across the table, my face directly in front of Ed's. "You got a problem with that, fang fucker?"

Out of the corner of my eye, I saw Jacob reach for his rifle, but Ed held up a hand. "It's cool, Pop. Like I said, not my first time dealing with a guy with demons running around his head."

"Please tell me that other person had a happy ending," I said, forcing myself to sit back down.

"Depends on your definition of happy, although technically it didn't actually end." He leaned back, took a sip of his coffee, and sighed. "Five years of normalcy, of thinking it was over, only to learn that whatever had been inside some of us was still there, waiting for a chance to wake up again."

I thought back to the ritual. "You may not believe this, but I understand what that's like."

"I had a feeling you might. Call me crazy, but I'm

gonna go out on a limb and guess a population of were-wolves didn't spontaneously spring up in Harris County overnight."

I nodded. "You wouldn't be wrong."

"So where have you guys been all this time?"

I considered telling a lie, but what was the point? "Here, going about our lives."

"What about during the full moon? Or are you saying half the town spends one night a month chained in their basement like BDSM gimps?"

"I ... really hope not. The truth is, I don't think anybody in Harris County was sprouting fur and a tail until a couple months back. Don't get me wrong, I'm pretty sure we were all born like this. We just didn't know it."

He raised an eyebrow. "A couple months? You mean when magic returned?"

"Yeah, or so I've been told."

"Then that means something must've changed," Ed surmised, "between back then and now."

I nodded but said nothing, curious if he had any insight I didn't.

"I guess that makes sense. There's been all sorts of weird shit getting shaken up as of late. No offense."

"None taken," I said before Winston could chime in.

"So, if what you're saying is true," he continued, "and you only recently discovered you were werewolves, then I guess the bigger question is – why the fuck do you guys all seem to have a bug up your ass when it comes to *me*?"

"You?" I replied, caught off guard. "I have no idea what you're talking about."

"Really? You're saying you have no idea why your furry buddies seem hellbent on continually harassing Pop and my friends?"

"No ... I mean I guess I kinda do, but it has nothing to

do with you. Hobart... He's the pack leader, by the way. Anyway, he's obsessed with some vampire he calls the..." I trailed off as a glimmer of insight slowly began to seep into my thick skull. "No way! Are you saying you're...?"

"The guy everyone keeps calling the Progenitor for some reason? Apparently so, and trust me, I'm not any happier about it than you are."

31

THE NOT-SO-GREAT SATAN

"**W**ait," Winston said. "*You're* the guy who's got Hobart acting like a bitch in heat at a packed kennel?"

"I ... think so," Ed replied tentatively.

His response didn't matter because Winston had already dissolved into laughter.

It took some effort for me to speak between his guffaws. "Sorry ... that was ... the ... other ... guy."

"Thanks for clarifying."

"He does have a point, though," I said, managing to regain control of my mouth. "You're the all-powerful vamp trying to enslave us? Hobart's words, not mine."

Ed shrugged. "Not quite. Honestly, I'm in the same boat as you. Prior to six weeks ago, I had no idea you guys were even real."

Myra had said pretty much the same thing, but considering she wasn't the most stable of individuals, it seemed wise to get a second opinion. "Are we just talking about Harris County right now, or..."

"No. I mean werewolves did not exist *period*, as in anywhere."

"Seriously?"

"As serious as this weird shit can be," he explained. "And this wasn't just gossip among the newbs either. This was considered established fact by old-as-fuck dickheads for whom the French Revolution was a fond memory. Hell, I can personally attest I saw some shit during the Strange Days that still keeps me up at night. I'm talking slime covered dinosaurs, shape-shifting rock monsters, and worse. But not a single werewolf in sight. And yet, according to you anyway, they've been here all along..."

"Not realizing we were monsters," I finished for him.

"Exactly," he said. "In a world of fucked up shit, that's ... extra fucked-up."

Jacob leaned back in his chair. "It's funny. I always thought Harris County had an air of uniqueness to it, but I didn't realize how much."

"Tell me about it," Ed replied. "Oh, and just for the record, I'm not here to enslave shit. If you really want to talk about that sort of thing, I'm happy to direct you toward a little psycho named Gan."

"Gan?" I asked.

"Short for Gansetseg. She's Genghis Khan's granddaughter, basically a three-hundred-year-old nutcase with a rage boner for subjugating the world. Pretty sure Bill's been trying to tell this Hobart guy about her every time he shows his ugly mug."

I grinned sheepishly. "Sounds about right for him. He's the sort who can be real stubborn once he gets a burr up his behind."

"Which is about a million times nicer than I would've put it."

"I don't understand, though. You say you're the Progenitor but none of the rest is true. So then what are you, and more importantly, what are you doing here?"

"That last one's a chicken and egg problem, son,"

Jacob replied. "Only reason my Eddie is here is because Hobart's *people* started in with me first. He's just being a good son and helping out. As for that slavery nonsense, don't ask me. I have no idea where that oversized fool got it from."

I couldn't help but wonder if Myra was to blame. Seeing as she'd known she was a witch her whole life, she'd almost certainly had more contact with the ... err ... supernatural community at large. As for where she got her information or how she'd come to share it with Hobart, I couldn't say.

"Gods, can you imagine Hobart pissing himself over this puny shithead?" Winston remarked, still way too amused to grasp the seriousness of the situation.

"Thanks," Ed replied dryly.

"You'll have to forgive him," I said. "He hasn't much experience with any social cues that don't involve murder." Then, before we could change topics, I added, "But I do have to ask why they call you the Progenitor. It's the sort of title which brings to mind..."

"A lot of ominous shit?" he interrupted. "Trust me, I get it. Here's the thing with the vampire nation, though. Those fuckers absolutely love meaningless titles, especially ones that let them use chumps like me as their own personal scapegoat."

"But Progenitor implies you're the first..."

"I am, but not the way you're thinking. Believe me, if I was actually the first vampire none of us would be having this conversation. I actually had the displeasure of meeting her and that woman was crazy evil with a capital holy shit. Forget whatever Hobart thinks. Harris County would be nothing but a fucking crater if anyone here had so much as looked at her the wrong way. As for me, I'm just a guy who's stuck dealing with shit I don't want to deal with."

"Okay, then why do they call you that?"

He let out a sigh. "You saw me outside, right?"

"Kinda hard to miss the asshole pointing a fucking gun at my face," Winston spat.

"Sorry about that. Crazy times and all. Anyway, you may have noticed the sun shining down on us, yet me not turning into a living tater tot."

I nodded. "The thought had occurred to me."

"Well, this is why." He pulled down the collar of his shirt, revealing a burn on the side of his throat in the shape of a hand. "Through a series of unfortunate events way too bizarre and traumatic for me to get into right now, I became the first vamp who can also enjoy the occasional beach day."

"Hence the Progenitor title?"

"Sorta," he replied. "See, there's a catch. Normal vamps tend to breed like rabbits. I mean, not actually *like* rabbits, but if you get bitten by one, there's a good chance you'll become one too. At that point an extra-dimensional spirit will meld with your body and voila – instant vampire."

"Extra-dimensional spirit, gotcha." I actually didn't but filed it away for later. Who knows? Maybe that explained my own internal intruder.

"Not so with this new breed," Ed continued. "I'm the only one who can spread this ... virus I guess. All the other *neo vamps* – that's what Bill calls them – are sterile for some reason. You'd think this would be a good thing, but since walking around during the day without turning to dust is big on the vamp wish list, that gave them the excuse to not only tag my ass with a stupid name but also milk me for my spit."

"Which is the only thing that can make more of what Eddie is," Jacob explained.

"Pretty much," his stepson acknowledged, "which

includes upgrading existing vamps to the latest software patch."

"Hold on," I said. "You can do that?"

"Are you kidding? It's the whole fucking reason magic is back. Remember that Gan nutjob I told you about? Technically, she should be dead, same way every other vamp over a century old bit it when magic went bye-bye. But because I was forced to bite her, she's like me now. Not only can she spend her afternoons sunbathing as much as she pleases, but it somehow allowed her to survive long enough to figure out a way to bring magic back and fuck us all in the ass with it."

If that last part was true, his description was more apt than he realized. Without magic, the fine folk of Harris County would've never discovered their fondness for howling at the moon. Hobart would've never started his war against Jacob. Myra would ... well, let's not go there. And I would've never gotten zapped by a psychic dinosaur, meaning I wouldn't have a psychotic werewolf running loose in my brain.

All the same, I couldn't really blame Ed. If anything, it sounded like he was as much a victim as anyone else. And though I had no way of knowing another man's mind, I found myself choosing to believe him.

"So yeah," Ed continued, "if you know any damsels in distress hoping the sun is their salvation against the evil undead, just know there's a good chance they're screwed. And yes, even though that might tie back to me indirectly, the vampire nation hasn't given me much choice when it comes to being their poster boy for noontime walks in the park. Don't even get me started on that enslavement bullshit. I couldn't even begin to tell you where anyone got that idea."

"Instinct."

"Huh?" Ed and I both replied, which sounded weird coming from me as it had been Winston's response.

"Can't you sense it?" Winston asked, although I had a feeling it was directed toward me. "Oh, who am I kidding? Of course you can't."

"Anyone else find it strange when he does that?" Jacob replied.

I raised my right hand just as my other half started in again.

"You," he said to our undead host. "You're damned lucky the pupcake was around when you *greeted* us out there because my first, second, and third inclination was to show you your own guts. But do you know what the funny thing is? It had nothing to do with you shoving a gun in my face." He let out a chuckle. "Don't get me wrong, I'd happily fuck your shit up for less, but it runs deeper than that. It's like the second I saw you, all I wanted to do was paint the ground with your innards. Still do if we're being honest, and this is after realizing you're no threat to a kitten, much less me."

His threats hung heavy in the air, but I was suddenly struck once again by those fleeting memories of our time in the New York underground. "The sewers," I said. "You felt it there too, didn't you?"

He nodded, meaning we both did. "Yep. One sniff of those fanged fucks and all the hairs on the back of my neck stood up. Good thing for them I was a little distracted."

"Distracted?" Ed asked.

"Long story, none of it your business." My left eyebrow rose. "I smelled it on them, knew it in an instant. But you..."

I sniffed the air, not noticing much outside the smell of fresh coffee. My human nose was only a fraction as powerful of what I was capable of, but it was still like I was the only person in the room. Although in this case I realized it was nothing supernatural, especially since this was the second time in as many days that I'd been ambushed by it. "Scent control spray?"

Ed touched his finger to his nose. "Bingo. Pop hoses us down with that crap at least three times a day."

Jacob chuckled. "Can you blame me?"

"All right, let's back up a second," Ed said, steering us back on track. "You said your ... *dislike* of me was instinctual but didn't say why."

"Don't know why," Winston replied. "It just is. Those suckheads in the sewer were the first I'd ever seen."

Ed shook his head. "That's not true. We met back in..."

"I meant as myself, without any influence from pupcake here. And no, don't ask. Anyway, it's not like they were threatening me. I just knew what they were and that I wanted to tear them to shreds." I cocked my head to the side. "This feeling is practically etched into my bones, and it tells me your kind aren't to be trusted."

"And Hobart is?" I replied.

"Fair point." He looked Ed in the eye. "Here's how it is. My gut is telling me I should eat your face, shit it out, and slap it on you backward. *But* I've got bigger problems right now, which means I'm willing to not gut you if you'll help me gut Hobart instead, once he gets here."

"What do you mean *once he gets here*?" Jacob asked.

Oh crap. I'd been so caught up in this Progenitor stuff that I'd almost forgotten why we were there to begin with.

"Why do you think I was out there in the middle of the day?" Winston continued. "Hobart and his pack bitches are on my tail, through no fault of my own of course."

"Through no fault of...?"

He kept talking over me, though. "Far as I can tell,

they backed off right before I got here, but that doesn't mean the ass-licker is gonna give up so easily."

"Wait," Ed replied. "You *led* them here?"

"Well, technically the pupcake did. But whatever. Bottom line is, it's only a matter of time before Hobart gets over whatever flea's crawled up his ass and kicks the front door down. So, what do you say, oh mighty *Progenitor*? You ready to join me in this fight or what? Not that you have much choice in the matter."

32

REMEMBER THE ALAMO

"I honestly can't tell whether you're some kind of masochist or just that stupid," Ed groused. "And for the record, I'm talking to you both."

I could understand why he was a little testy. Not only had we invaded his father's home, but we'd led the barbarians right to their gate.

Sadly, there wasn't much I could do to make the situation better, other than keep Winston from making whatever retort he was trying to force from our lips.

Interestingly enough, the only one who didn't seem on the verge of losing their mind was the home's owner.

"Calm down," Jacob said after a few moments, the parental authority in his voice unmistakable.

"Calm down? Did you hear this fucker, Pop?"

"Ain't nothing wrong with my hearing, boy." He got up and emptied his mug into the sink. "This isn't anything we didn't expect by coming back. It was bound to happen sooner or later, and you know it."

"I was kind of hoping for later."

"Won't lie, me too. But wishes ain't horses. And it's not like we aren't ready for some trouble."

"*Some* being the operative word," Ed replied. "The question is how much?"

I was about to offer my opinion, but Winston spoke up first. "All of it."

"Wait," I replied. "What do you mean?"

"Exactly what I said. That fat fuck's had all the opportunity in the world to storm in here while we've been drinking ... whatever this shit is." He indicated the mug in front of us. "But he hasn't."

"Why do you think that is?" Ed asked.

"Because deep down he's a fucking pussy. He doesn't know what's going on in here and it's still daylight out, so he has to rely on his bitch's magic. I'm willing to bet that's got him all twitchy inside."

"He means Myra," I explained. "She's a..."

"I know what she is," Ed replied. "Bill and I had a run-in with her back in Brooklyn. Go on."

Winston scoffed. "Like I need your permission. Anyway, this is no longer the easy hunt he was expecting, but he can't let the others know because it'll make him look weak and pathetic."

"Okay and how exactly does that translate into *us* having to fight him?"

"Simple, twig dick. We might be fine for now. But I'd bet my tail he's whipping the whole gods damned pack into a froth so they can be up our asses like pups in a den the second the sun goes down."

Ed turned to his stepfather. "If that's the case maybe we should make ourselves scarce while we have the chance."

"I'm not running," Jacob said. "Not again."

"I was afraid you'd say that."

"Wouldn't do any good anyway," Winston replied. "Hobart's a fucking idiot, but he's not a *complete* fucking idiot. Don't doubt he's left one of his ass sniffing buddies behind to keep an eye on the place. We run and he's gonna know. Besides, it's not like we'll get far with all that magic shit keeping us penned in."

"There's a quarantine in place," I explained.

"I've heard," Ed replied. "Let's just say the supernatural underworld isn't shy when it comes to gossip."

Unfortunately, Winston had a point. Jacob might be able to get away but there was only so far the rest of us could go. Worse, I doubted anyone here knew exactly how far that was. One step over the line and *Zzzap*! However, there was one place within reach, especially if the coast was clear enough for us to make it.

"What about Barley Hills?" I asked. "They're within the quarantine zone."

"Hmm, we lead Hobart to those straw-hat wearing hicks, then wait for them to wipe each other out." Winston shrugged. "I could get behind that plan."

"Not quite what I meant, and now that you mention it I'm not sure I like this idea anymore."

"I'm not sure I liked it to begin with," Jacob remarked. "I've never had issue with any of the folks there, but they keep to themselves. How do we even know they'll help us?"

"Did you miss the part about them being werewolf hunters?"

"Nope. Heard you loud and clear, as well as the part about you being a werewolf yourself."

"Fair point, but we ... sort of have an arrangement. They know me over there."

"And what are their thoughts on vampires strolling into their quaint village?" Ed asked.

"I ... it didn't come up in conversation."

Jacob shook his head. "I'm more curious as to what

could cause an entire town to drop everything and devote their lives to fighting monsters."

"What do you mean?"

"You said so yourself. You didn't know what you were." He hooked a thumb Ed's way. "At least not before Eddie's friends brought magic back."

"I already told you, that wasn't us."

"I get what you're trying to say," I replied, interrupting their sidebar. "But this isn't a new development for them. From what I've been told, they've always been werewolf hunters."

"That means they knew about you before any of you did."

I gave him a single nod.

"And that doesn't strike you as seriously problematic?" Ed replied.

"Yep. Pretty fucked up if you ask me," Winston remarked unhelpfully.

"I am definitely *curious* about it," I added, being diplomatic. "But I'm sure they have their reasons."

"I don't give a fuck about their reasons." Ed got up and looked out the window, as if to make sure the front yard wasn't swarming with monsters. "I'm more interested in the fact they've been aware of you guys for however long, but somehow nobody else seems to know shit about it."

Jacob chuckled. "Maybe someone else does know. They just aren't talking."

"That's exactly what I mean, Pop." Ed blew out a breath through gritted teeth. "I doubt a group of trigger-happy farm boys just happened to settle down next to Werewolf Central by accident. That's the sort of coincidence you only find in *Hallmark* movies and shitty horror novels. It means one of the big factions had to know, whether it was the vamps, the Magi ... or even the fucking Feet."

"The feet?"

Ed smirked at me. "Bigfoot. Believe it or not, they used to be one of the major players in the supernatural world. And yes, that sounds crazy to me too, but it's true. Problem is, they were big, dumb, and mostly hated the fuck out of people. So I'm not sure I buy them setting up a bunch of yokels to protect humanity from the werewolf threat."

"So that leaves..."

"Too many unknowns to risk it," Ed interrupted. "We could stroll into Barley Hills looking for help, only to find ourselves in deeper shit than we already are. I'm not going to chance that, not until we know more."

"Agreed," Jacob said, before turning my way, "but for different reasons. I understand you know these people, Mike, and if you say that's good enough then I have no reason to doubt you."

"But..."

Jacob held up a hand toward his stepson. "But I also don't fancy bringing my fight to another man's door. What's done here is done, but I don't care to make it worse than it already is."

I nodded after a moment, the rebuke clear as rain. Much as I liked the idea of having the hunters as backup, our host had a point. I'd done enough to endanger innocent bystanders for one day.

"All right," I said. "We can't run and Barley Hills is a no go. So where does that leave us?"

"In deep shit with one paw tied behind our back," Winston replied.

"Maybe not as deep as you might think," Jacob said, crossing his muscular arms.

"And how do you figure that, old timer?"

"Simple. We've got weapons, ammo, and a few other

surprises. Not to mention, my Eddie's no pushover in a fight."

I couldn't stop Winston's subsequent laughter, although to be fair the look on Ed's face said he didn't share his stepdad's faith in him.

Wonderful.

"Besides, this is my land," Jacob continued, ignoring my alter ego. "I know it like the back of my hand. That means the best ways in and the best ways out, as well as chokepoints we can defend. Last time those sons of bitches caught me by surprise, but now we have a couple hours to prepare. So, what say we stop lollygagging and make use of them."

Jacob's inspirational words left me envisioning a montage of us concocting all sorts of makeshift traps meant to confound Hobart and his pack, like that old show *The A-Team*.

Reality turned out to be somewhat more sobering, though, as a good chunk of that first hour was spent on the phone taking care of something long overdue.

I was already racked with guilt at having dragged Dallas into this mess. Therefore, I did what I should've done the moment Myra brought me back home. I called my parents.

Thankfully, Dad picked up on the second ring, telling me I wasn't too late.

I quickly learned that Myra had done more than simply *borrow* his car. She'd also used her magic to scramble his brain. Dad was able to recall lending his Ford out but couldn't recall to whom. Nor did he have any knowledge of being contacted by Hannah and told I was back. My call was a complete surprise to him.

Too bad it wasn't entirely a happy surprise. What should have been a tear-filled reunion in person had been denied us by circumstance and a witch who didn't believe in consent.

As much as I would've loved to have talked to him for hours, I was forced to cut things short and get to the point.

If the gloves were indeed off, as I had to assume they were, then it was only a matter of time before Hobart paid my folks a visit to recruit them into whatever evil he had planned for tonight.

Fortunately, it didn't take much convincing. And while Myra might've still been joyriding in Dad's car, he had an old UTV out in the garage. Though Ed's distrust of Barley Hills was apparent, I still considered them friends. More importantly, they were the only place I was aware of that was within the quarantine zone yet outside Hobart's reach.

So, hoping I wasn't making a big mistake, I told him to grab Mom, head there, and throw themselves on Isaiah's mercy. Even if the overseer felt the need to lock them up for everyone's safety, it was still better than having to worry whether they were among the monsters we'd soon be facing.

I wished them both my love before hanging up with tears in my eyes, much to Winston's chagrin. On the upside, my endeavors on the phone proved more fruitful than Ed's, who returned to us grumbling about voicemail and nobody picking up. I wasn't sure who he'd been trying to reach but it seemed a safe bet that last minute reinforcements were not in our future.

That sobering realization out of the way, we got to work cleaning and loading Jacob's not inconsiderable arsenal of handguns and hunting rifles. We then stashed them in various hiding spots throughout the house and surrounding yard. All the while, Ed pulled double duty as lookout, his nose seemingly almost as sharp as my own but without any need to transform in order to use it.

The hours passed quickly, too quickly. Before we knew it the shadows had grown long and the sun hung low in the sky.

It wasn't too long after when the first distant howls reached my ears.

33

COLLARED AND CORNERED

"**I**'m not wearing this."

"Yes, we are."

"No fucking way," Winston stated.

"Seriously, what's the problem?"

"The problem is my name ain't Fido and I'd sooner shove dog treats up your ass than beg for them."

"Technically it's *our* ... butt," I said, fighting with my left half to tie a bandana around my neck while not making much progress. "We already agreed to this."

"Wrong. *You* did. I didn't agree to shit."

"It's to keep us from getting shot by accident."

"Fuck that. Either of those assholes takes a potshot at me, and what I do to them won't be accidental."

I shook my head, attempting to keep my temper from fraying. "You're not going to do anything to either of them."

"Really? Are you gonna stop me?"

"If I have to, yes. You've already caused enough problems today. You're the whole reason Hobart is after us. If you hadn't pulled the *crap* you did, we could have..."

"Are you still whining about that? You can't possibly be

stupid enough to think we could've trusted that worm-ridden flea biter."

"I'm not, but it could have bought us some time to plan. Now we have no time at all, while you, rather than be reasonable, are throwing a freaking tantrum."

"Am not."

"Enough."

"But..."

"Enough!" I snapped. "We can talk about this later, *if* we survive. But I swear if you do *anything* to make this situation worse than it already is, I will head back to Barley Hills and ask Isaiah to give me every single recipe for werewolf roofies he has on file. Are we clear?"

"What the hell's a roofie?"

"Wait. You don't know?"

"Why would I? Have you roofied anyone as of late?"

"What? Of course not!"

"Then how the fuck would I know? If you haven't seen or interacted with something since I've been awake, then I have no clue. That means I have no idea what a roofie is. Luche libre midget porn, on the other hand..."

"I clicked on the wrong link ... *once*."

"Sure you did. Whatever keeps the ticks from biting."

"Okay, forget about roofies ... and everything else you just said. I need you to behave, for now anyway. *Please*."

He let out a sigh of disgust. "The fucking things I do."

There was silence for a few moments but then I felt myself once again in full control, allowing me to loosely tie the bandana, leaving plenty of room for once we transformed.

"Maybe you have a set between your legs after all," he said. "A tiny, inadequate set."

I took the *compliment* for what it was then stepped out the front door into the night air, where Pop and Ed were making final preparations for the siege to come.

"Do you guys always do that?" Ed asked, as I slipped the rest of my borrowed clothes off and placed them to the side.

"You heard us?"

He pointed at his ear. "Loud and clear. Trust me, it's not always a blessing."

"So you guys have enhanced hearing like us," I replied, trying to act nonchalant despite being naked save for a handkerchief around my neck. "What else?"

He grinned. "Our sense of smell is pretty good too. Oh, and being able to see in total darkness definitely doesn't suck."

I let out a chuckle. "Gotta wonder what else we have in common."

I'd meant it as a joke, but the look on Ed's face said otherwise. "More than I think either of us know, at least judging by what Bill discovered when he took a drink from one of your fur friends."

"He did? What happened?"

Ed turned toward the tree line, cocked his head, then apparently determined the coast was still clear. "Long story, but Bill's a special kind of vamp. And I don't just mean he's a dumbass who needs constant supervision. He can do things the rest of us can't."

"What sort of things?" I asked.

"For instance, if he drinks another vamp's blood he can temporarily absorb their power." He let out a sigh. "Used to be real handy back when you couldn't throw a rock without hitting some centuries-old asshole. These days, not so much. But anyway, it's a power that only works on other vampires, or so we thought."

I wasn't so dim as to not pick up the hint. "You mean he...?"

"Changed," Ed affirmed. "But not all the way. It was

more into some gimpy halfway form. Twice as ugly but too slow and ungainly to be useful."

"What does that mean?"

"Fuck if I know. Christy, she's the witch we had looking into it, is currently trapped in another dimension." He shook his head. "And yes, that's a long story too."

"I bet it is." Tempting as it was to ask him about it, the hour was growing late. Suffice to say, I didn't think I'd ever stop being amazed by the supernatural underworld that existed alongside mankind.

Heck, if there was an answer to the mystery behind the ritual as well as the hunters of Barley Hills, it was almost surely to be found within the wide world of the weird. But now was not the time for unsolved mysteries. We needed to focus on the task ahead. "Just remember, I won't be able to talk to you guys in my other form."

"Sure I can," Winston replied. "Not my fault these two morons won't be able to understand it."

"Isn't that the same problem just stated differently?" Jacob asked.

"Potato, po-tah-to," I replied.

"Is that supposed to make sense?" Winston remarked.

"Someday it will, maybe."

"Whatever the case," Jacob continued, "keep that bandana on if you can. Eddie can see in the dark just fine, but you're all gonna look alike in my scope." He patted the high-powered rifle in his hands, loaded with silver-plated rounds as were Ed's weapons.

Sadly, while that wasn't the sum total of their silver arsenal, it was the majority. Most of the weapons we'd stashed around the property were loaded with regular shells.

They'd still hurt like the dickens, but not nearly as much. Heck, outside of lucky shots, it would probably take between five and ten normal rounds to equal what one silver bullet could do.

With any luck, we wouldn't need to test that theory. My hope was that the first few minutes would prove decisive enough to end this, especially if the pack witnessed some of their fellows burning from the inside out.

In truth, I didn't want to see that happen. Sure, some of them were Hobart's buddies during the day, but most were our neighbors, folks just trying to eke out a living in this crazy world.

They didn't deserve to be maimed or killed, not when they were being forced to follow the orders of a man who most certainly didn't have their best interests at heart.

Once again, though, I didn't have an easy way to differentiate dominated friend from actual foe. The sad truth was we couldn't afford to pull our punches. If we did, we'd be as good as dead. That was the stark reality of what we were facing.

It filled me with regret as well as no small amount of anger, but that anger was focused solely on Hobart, Myra, and their lackeys. Heck, I couldn't even really blame Winston. There was no doubt he'd upped the timetable of this showdown, but I couldn't fool myself. What was about to happen here was probably inevitable. Hobart had made it clear on the night when he'd threatened to chew my balls off.

At least here, now, I had the upside of not being alone. I knew Jacob to be a good man. As for his son, I chose to believe he wasn't out to rule the world or enslave anyone. I'd seen his friends in action back in Brooklyn, and there'd been no doubt they'd been trying their best to minimize casualties amongst the innocent bystanders.

That wasn't something monsters did.

Many of those we'd be facing tonight were likewise decent folk, but they wouldn't be in control of their own faculties. And that meant we needed to first survive them as beasts before we could deal with them as people.

Just the thought of it made me sick to my stomach. But, rather than puke, I instead opted to go numb. It was time to change into my other form. Mike Walden, trash collector, wasn't needed tonight.

It was Winston the werewolf's turn to take the wheel. With maybe a little help from me in the backseat.

As usual, the subsequent sneezing fit wasn't fun, especially since it drew a few muffled chuckles from the Vessers.

Once it passed, though, it was like being blind and then granted sight anew as all my senses ratcheted up to supernatural levels. Within seconds, the darkness retreated, sounds became amplified, and all the scents painted a vivid picture of my surroundings.

It also didn't hurt that I had a better view thanks to the extra foot in height.

"*Much better,*" Winston grumbled.

I couldn't disagree. With the sun having set, that bizarre tingling was no more. If anything, it felt right, natural even to be in this form.

We stood tall and stretched. Then my alter ego had to ruin the moment by turning to our two companions. "*Oh, and just for the record, if either of you teat suckers so much as point those boom sticks in my general direction, I will tear your fucking heads off and shove them so far up your assholes you'll be shitting eyebrows.*"

What came out instead was a series of chuffs and grunts, which neither Jacob nor Ed mercifully understood. Both stared back at me as if seeking clarification.

Rather than let on Winston was being a jerk again, I merely flashed them both a thumbs up.

Do you have to be that way?

"*Just getting a few things off my chest before the fun starts.*"

We have very different definitions of fun.

That out of the way, I took hold of the Remington pump action rifle Jacob offered me. Normally it would be too small to effectively use in this form, but he'd taken the time to file off the trigger guard, leaving plenty of room for my sausage-sized fingers.

It felt tiny in my hands, but I knew it would pack plenty of punch once the time came, something even Winston couldn't complain about.

Speaking of which...

I detected a subtle change to the scents in the air, barely perceptible but there nonetheless – one that left a slight tingle in my nose.

Myra!

"Over there," Ed cried, pointing.

"*Way ahead of you, pipsqueak*," Winston replied.

A ways off, the distance hard to gauge due to all the foliage, I spied a glow among the treetops maybe fifty feet off the ground. It was yellowish, oddly comforting, and growing brighter by the moment.

Soon, despite the numerous obstructions blocking the way, it became clear what it was. The moon – a miniature version of it anyway, one way too close to the surface of the Earth to ever be real.

The actual full moon was still weeks away, meaning Hobart needed Myra to initiate a mass change among the pack. Sadly, unlike earlier, it would now be that much easier to keep them in their alternate forms.

"I don't care how many times I see illusion magic," Ed remarked. "It's still kinda fucked up."

"Won't disagree," Pop replied.

Winston let out a soft growl. "*You shit sniffers have no idea.*"

Be nice.

"*I was talking to you too, fucknuts.*"

What did I do this time?

"*For starters, not paying attention. Your mount buddy's spell, there's something different about it.*"

How do you know... I paused mid-thought as the answer hit me. I took another breath, letting it flow over my heightened senses. Unfortunately, I still couldn't find any trace of what Winston was talking about. I said as much.

"*That's because you fucking suck at this. Something is different, though. Trust me.*"

So what's different about it?

"*Do I look like I know how magic works? I'm just telling you it's changed from earlier. I don't know how, but we need to be ready for some fuckery.*"

We have to tell Ed and his dad.

"*Have fun figuring out how. Me, I'm gonna focus on staying alive. I'd suggest you get your snout in the game and do likewise.*"

Sure enough, I caught the sound of footfalls racing our way. They were joined by snarls and growls mere moments later.

"They're coming," Ed cried. "Everyone get ready."

"*Fucking amateur,*" Winston snorted. Before I could think of any way to quickly convey a warning to the Vessers, Winston took a hard right toward the tree line.

Much to my shock and amazement, my inner wolf didn't immediately go rogue and do his own thing. Instead, we raced to a small clearing about twenty yards into the woods, just as we'd planned, and stopped there.

We were atop a small rise, giving us the high ground. Not only that, but the woods to the south of us were relatively sparse here, offering a reasonable line of sight for one gifted with superior night vision. Unseen to anyone not in the know were about three dozen rounds of extra ammo hidden about the area, all within easy reach.

There wasn't a great deal of cover directly ahead – good for us, bad for them, assuming Myra wasn't part of this first wave.

That was unlikely to be the case, though, as she'd not only have to contend with us, but the pack too as they weren't overly picky about their targets once they got their dander up. It was perhaps the lone plus in our favor of them all becoming mindless beasts in their other forms.

Such worries became moot mere moments later as my eyes and ears picked up movement ahead. Three werewolves made up this first wave, no doubt meant to test our defenses – all of them racing my way with reckless abandon.

Remember the plan. I'm in charge of the gun. You take over when they either get too close or we run out of ammo, whichever comes first. I left out the slim hope that this fight would be over before either of those occurred.

"Keep treating me like your fucking dog. See where it gets you."

Despite Winston's obstinance, I felt him cede control. I raised the rifle, small and almost laughably fragile in my hands, and took aim.

It almost wasn't fair.

Between my enhanced senses, effectively making my eyes a living night scope, and the werewolves barreling toward us with zero stealth or strategy, it was like shooting fish in a barrel.

I just hoped none of those fish were named Dallas.

Sadly, I had no way of knowing and Winston wasn't offering any insight. So, rather than continue torturing myself, I said a silent prayer and pulled the trigger.

34

SMART WOLF / DUMB DOG

My first shot missed by a country mile, thanks in part to me totally forgetting how much louder guns sounded when you had supernatural hearing.

That one was my fault. I'd gotten too caught up in the weeds to remember the reality of the situation. Heck, if I'd been smart, I would've asked Jacob if he had any ear plugs I could borrow. Mind you, unless they were werewolf-sized I'm not sure what good they'd do me.

Maybe once this was all over, it was time to invest in a 3d printer and see if I could make it a homebrew project. Heck, I could even make it a side business here in Harris County, serving the local paranormal populace.

And yes, it *was* a strange thing to focus on as the gunfire reverberated painfully within my ears while my nostrils filled with the stench of rifle discharge.

Trust me, not a delightful combo.

Ahead of me, two of the werewolves that had been closing in threw back their heads and howled, no doubt *enjoying* the loud report about as much as I had. The third, however, a werewolf with bald patches on both shoulders, dove for cover behind a tree.

I raised a curious eyebrow just as Winston said, "*Be sure to let me know when you're done being a fuck-up so I can take over.*"

That was just a warning shot.

"*Well, consider this my warning. I'd better start seeing some blood, otherwise I'm heading out there and unzipping their guts my way.*"

I considered a few rude responses but forced myself to focus instead. The two howling wolves had stopped their caterwauling and were once again on the move. As for the third...

There was no sign of it. Maybe my shot had scared it off, although I highly doubted it. Regardless, I needed to focus on the targets I could actually see.

I quickly lined up my next shot, my amped reflexes making the action smooth as butter. This time I braced myself against the sound before pulling the trigger.

Boom

It was like a hand grenade went off inside my head, but I managed to not flinch. The werewolf I'd been targeting, however – a male judging by his clearly visible ... *thing* – did more than flinch as the bullet tore a hole in his side.

"*Again!*"

Much as I didn't care to indulge Winston's bloodlust, he was right. This was no time to debate or argue. So, I chambered another round and fired. This time my shot hit the wolf dead center in the chest.

The werewolf let out a pained yip, not exactly doing wonders for my morale, then he fell backward, disappearing into the brush. I had no idea whether he was wounded or ... *worse*, but I couldn't afford to give in to my humanity right then.

The second werewolf, a female, had been slowed by

the sound of my subsequent shots but not nearly as much as she'd been by the first. She too was barreling toward me with teeth bared.

It wasn't in anger or revenge, though. She hadn't even given the downed wolf a second glance. No, these were the actions of a mindless beast following the orders of its master.

Speaking of which, I noticed movement to my left – my eyes pulling double duty as my other senses were currently overloaded.

It was the third werewolf, the one with the patchy shoulders I'd momentarily lost track of. He'd somehow managed to circle around, closing the distance between us.

"This fucker's too smart for his own good."

Winston was right. Both the remaining werewolves were converging on my point at the same time, but I judged this one to be the more dangerous of the two. Not to be sexist or anything, but even if he'd simply gotten lucky using the undergrowth he was still larger and likely stronger. It was a clear choice.

I turned that way, simultaneously keeping track of the female as she closed in. That turned out to be sooner than expected as she launched herself at me while still a good twenty feet away.

It might as well have been a mile.

I merely stepped back out of the way as I raised my rifle toward the other werewolf, preparing to fire as soon as I had a clear...

What the?

Quicker than I would've imagined a dumb animal capable of responding, *Shoulders*, as I deemed the large male, reached out and grabbed hold of the female before she'd even landed. He dragged her between us in the split second before I fired.

The she-wolf let out a howling scream as she was gut

shot, the patchy fur on her abdomen instantly stained red with blood.

How did he do that?

"Stop thinking, pupcake, and keep shooting!"

I racked the next round but hesitated as the larger of the two beasts held his wounded companion in front of him like a living shield. It was almost as if he knew what he was doing.

That's when he began to chuckle. It sounded like an out of tune rock tumbler but there was no mistaking the sound. It was in stark contrast to the injured werewolf he held. She was clearly in pain but struggling far more like a trapped animal than a person.

I...

"Fuck this deer shit! I'll do it myself."

Winston abruptly wrested control, pulling the trigger. It was sloppy, the attack of a newb who didn't have the slightest clue about firearms. However, both our targets were at point blank range so it's not like he had much chance of missing.

The bullet slammed into the she-wolf's upper thigh, eliciting a snarling yipe from her.

Sadly, her pain didn't dissuade Shoulders in the slightest. He started advancing upon us, continuing to use the she-wolf as an inhuman shield.

I didn't know who this werewolf was, other than he clearly wasn't Hobart, but he was impossibly smart. And I don't mean dog smart. What he was doing was a conscious act of maliciousness that could only be ascribed to a person.

But how?

I must've thought that part louder than intended, because Winston immediately picked up on it.

"Seems pretty obvious to me, pupcake." Rather than expound upon his statement, he instead pulled the pump

and chambered another shell. Guess he'd been paying more attention than I'd given him credit for.

Boom

This time my flinch had nothing to do with the sound as the she-wolf's snout and a good chunk of her face disappeared in a spray of flesh, bone, and gristle.

Oh my god!

My abject horror was ignored, though, as Winston chambered yet another round. Shoulders appeared to have been temporarily blinded by the backsplash of blood, and my inner wolf was seemingly more than happy to take advantage of it.

All that changed in a hot second, though, as gunfire erupted from back in the direction of the house. Jacob and Ed had entered the fray. Shoulders turned his head that way, taking his eyes off us just long enough for Winston to apparently decide on a change in strategy.

He spun the rifle in our grip, then stepped in swinging it like a baseball bat. The stock collided with Shoulders' head. The sheer force of the impact destroyed the weapon but that didn't matter. It had served its purpose. The big male dropped what was left of the she-wolf and staggered backward, momentarily dazed.

I balled my fist, assuming the plan was to knock him out, but Winston had other ideas. We stepped in close and then, before I could protest, clamped our jaws onto the other werewolf's throat.

No, don't! I was too late as a geyser of hot blood instantly filled my mouth. *Gross, gross, gross! Wait, what in the name of...*

All thoughts of jumping into a steaming hot shower ended in that moment. Heck, it was like the world itself ceased to exist. I wanted to hate the taste washing over my tongue but found I couldn't. If anything, it filled me with a longing hunger for more.

More! My teeth dug in even deeper, but this time Winston had nothing to do with it.

The blood, it was ... utterly intoxicating.

I couldn't explain it, other than my mind might've still been human but my body had suddenly gone all in on the whole alpha predator transformation. I knew full well my senses of sight, smell, and hearing increased dramatically when I changed, but what was happening with my taste buds was on a whole other level.

To date, I hadn't eaten much in my werewolf form. It simply hadn't occurred to me. Usually, I'd grab a bite at home, preferring not to *wolf* it down, then I'd transform and head out on patrol. Sure, I'd popped a few berries here and there, but it's not like I'd spent my evenings hunting rabbits and squirrels. But this...

I wanted to do nothing less than tear Shoulders apart and savor every last bite. Crazy enough, this was like the exact opposite of how that potbellied pig had tasted to my then human taste buds. That had been the height of disgusting, but this was almost intoxicating.

I was suddenly reminded of Mom's friend Margie. Dad was right. There was no such thing as a vegan werewolf. Not when fresh meat was so delicious and...

Just then, right as the first delectable chunks hit my stomach, I abruptly pulled back. Flesh gave way to teeth as we quite literally ripped the other werewolf's throat out.

The utter savagery of this move should've horrified me, but I was more focused on the fact that Winston spat out the savory hunk of meat in our mouth.

I was eating that, jackass!

"*Focus, idiot.*"

But...

"*We don't have time to lose ourself to the hunt, and by we I mean you.*"

That's not...

"Get it together, you shit eating witch fucker!"

Winston's words managed to cut through the haze, or at least his insult did.

I shook my head. Mere moments had passed, no more, even though it felt like hours. Shoulders stood there, a look of surprise upon his canine face as his ruined throat continued to gush blood. Then he collapsed into a heap next to the body of the she-wolf.

Both lay at my feet unmoving, an easy meal for me to...

Winston slapped my side of our face, sending streams of foamy drool flying. *"I said knock it off, pupcake! Gut assholes now, snack later."*

I...

"Need to stop fucking off?" he interrupted. *"You might want to get with the program since these fucks were just the opening volley."*

The heady feeling from the blood began to pass, slowly leaving me once again able to think clearly. *What ... what the heck was that?*

"That was you learning what real *food tastes like."*

It was...

"Pretty gods damned awesome, right?"

Bloody disgusting is more like it, I lied, daring a glance down at myself and then immediately wishing I hadn't.

Talk about a rush. I couldn't help but wonder if this was how sharks felt during a feeding frenzy. If so, then maybe it was a good thing the Vessers, Jacob anyway, were back defending the front yard.

Guess that explained why werewolves were such ... animals. Speaking of which, I needed to get my head back into the game. I looked at the downed werewolves, noting the blood as it continued to weakly pulse from Shoulders' throat.

Is he...?

"*Dead meat?*" Winston replied. "*Probably. Just don't get any ideas. We don't have time for a snack break.*"

But what about...?

"*I said no.*"

I'm not talking about that. Is it me or was he acting a lot smarter than he should've been?

"*Noticed it too, eh?*" Winston replied.

But how?

"*Seems pretty obvious to me. Told you something was different with your mount bitch's spell.*"

Myra's spell? The spurt of blood slowed to a trickle and then finally stopped. Next to him, the she-wolf likewise lay unmoving. Though I couldn't be one-hundred-percent certain, not with our strange physiology, my gut told me these two wouldn't be getting back up again.

All of a sudden, the coppery taste on my tongue was considerably less appetizing, but I forced myself to focus nonetheless. *Are you saying Myra somehow made them smarter?*

"*Not all of them, obviously. But if there's one smart crotch licker, I'd bet there's a few more.*"

How is that even possible?

"*Fuck if I know. Magic probably.*"

Ask a stupid question. *How many do you think...*

"*I'll stop you right there, pupcake. I have no fucking idea, on any of it. All I know is what I can see, hear, and smell. And right now none of that is any good. So we can either stand here admiring my handiwork or we can get back into the shit before the almighty Progenitor ends up with a new asshole chewed into his backside.*"

He was right. We'd taken down three of Hobart's pack, but my nose was telling me that was just the warmup round. If we were to have any hope of surviving the night, this was one fight where we'd have to go the distance.

35

THE QUICK AND THE UNDEAD

I tried not to think of the people beneath the fur as I headed back toward Jacob's house.

Of far greater concern, as I tried to convince myself, was the fact that one of them had been a lot smarter than the rest. How smart, I didn't know, but I had a sinking suspicion Myra had cracked some code that allowed them to think as freely as Hobart and me. Seems I was right to be worried about what she'd managed to accomplish while I was gone, just not in the way I assumed.

Alas, none of my worries were going to be addressed by mere speculation. So instead, I focused on the task ahead – stopping about halfway back and kicking over a rock lying next to a white birch.

Beneath it lay a bottle of scent control spray as well as a Ruger Super Redhawk loaded with 454 Casull rounds, both of which I'd placed there earlier. I picked them up, taking a moment to admire the weapon. My father had always wanted a gun like this for his semi-annual hunting trips but there always seemed to be some bill in need of paying.

Heh. Of course, that was before I'd *inherited* my ill-gotten stash from the Chadworths. Probably not the best use of the money, but there were plenty of worse ways to spend it.

"*Are we gonna pick our teeth with that or just stand here looking stupid?*" Winston asked, dragging me from my thoughts.

I could understand his skepticism. Much like the shotgun, the weapon was almost comically small in my hand. On the flipside, it was loaded with rounds powerful enough to stop a buffalo, leaving me curious how that would translate to angry werewolves.

"You fuckers looking for the Progenitor? Well, here I am!" Ed cried from up ahead as the gunfire petered out. It was the agreed upon signal that it was time for the next phase of this deadly tower defense game we were playing.

Snarls and growls rose up in response to his challenge as I quickly hosed myself down with the contents of the spray bottle.

"*Huh,*" Winston huffed. "*Didn't think he had the balls to do it.*"

It was certainly a bold move on the vampire's part, painting a target on himself, despite it being part of our plan. The question now was whether it would prove to be a wise decision on our behalf.

I made my way to the corner of the large metal prefab that served as both Jacob's workshop and garage. Peering around the edge, I spied his front yard.

Ed stood alone in the center of the gravel driveway, casually reloading his weapon. There was no sign of his father, once again part of the plan.

The stench of smoke mixed with blood hit my nostrils, obscured before this moment by the plentiful carnage Winston and I had unleashed. Seemed Ed and his dad had likewise been successful against Hobart's first wave.

I spied four downed werewolves. All had wisps of smoke and sputtering flame rising from wounds on their bodies. Score one for silver bullets.

Do you think they're dead?

"*Don't care,*" Winston stated, empathy an alien concept to him. "*And neither should you.*"

I hated to admit he was right, but every werewolf we took out of this fight helped to even the odds a little. Still, I couldn't help but wonder who'd be waking up tomorrow to find their spouse, sibling, or, God forbid, child wasn't coming home.

As horrific as the thought was, if we lost it would be *my* parents waking to that awful revelation instead. That's what it really came down to, us or them. And, much as I didn't want any of this, I wasn't ready to call it quits just yet. I liked being me and had every intention of seeing where this little adventure called life ultimately led. I only hoped it wasn't to my own personal Custer's last stand.

"I know you're out there somewhere, Vesser," Hobart's voice whispered into my ear, nearly causing me to jump out of my furry skin.

I spun, weapon raised, certain I'd find him right behind me. In my haste, my index claw slipped off the trigger, preventing me from opening fire and giving away my position. Good thing too because there was no one there.

And yet it had sounded as if he'd spoken from right beside me.

"I'm standing right here, asshole," Ed shouted back.

"Ain't talking to you, boy," the pack leader replied, his voice as clear as if he were standing next to me. "Mind your betters. I'm looking for your pop."

What the? My hearing was good, but this was totally off the charts.

"*Where the fuck is he?*" Winston grumbled.

It's gotta be Myra's magic, I thought back. *She's throwing his voice like some kind of amped up ventriloquist.*

"*I have no idea what that is, but I'll take your word for it. Seems your mount buddy is full of tricks today.*"

Please stop calling her that.

"*Fine. Once I gut the bitch I'll stop mentioning her all together.*"

I let out a sigh as I tried to focus on my other senses.

"Here's the deal, Vesser. Give me the Progenitor. Mike Walden too. I know he's there with you, so no use lying about it. Tell them to surrender and this'll all be over. We'll leave and won't bother you again. You have my word."

Despite my ears telling me Hobart was within spitting distance, my nostrils painted a completely different picture. Though I couldn't quite pick him out from the crowd, there was a large group of werewolves maybe a hundred yards deep in the woods – far enough back to be effectively invisible even to my enhanced eyes.

Not coincidentally, that was also roughly right about where the fake moon was now hovering.

It was the bulk of the pack, all of them transformed and exuding enough violence I could smell it through the pores of their skin.

That's gotta be where Hobart is. If we circle around and come up behind them, we could end this before...

"*We're both torn limb from limb? Not likely, pupcake.*"

You don't know that.

"*The hell I don't. You're probably thinking that ass licker is standing all the way at the back. Problem is, you're also a fucking idiot. We follow your lead and we might tag the witch, but I guarantee Hobart's at the front of the pack.*"

I took another sniff. Once again, it painted a clear picture of the forces aligned against us, albeit not *that* clear. *How do you know?*

"*Because he's a Dominant. That's what we do, even sniveling cowards like him. He doesn't have a choice in the matter, not when they're like this. Can't you smell it?*"

He was talking about their current mood and the barely restrained rage I'd sensed. *He's ... just barely able to hold them back.*

"*Look at you becoming a little less stupid,*" Winston replied with a chuckle. "*Yep. He let it get too far, riled them up, and now they want blood. And if they don't get it, he's just as likely to be on the menu as the rest of us.*"

Unsurprisingly, there came no answer from Jacob as Winston and I quietly discussed things. I figured that was it with the talking, but Hobart was apparently game for one more try.

"Last chance, Vesser," he called out again. "No harm will come to your boy. We'll keep him fed and safe. You have my word. But we can't have him running free. We won't be hobbled by him and his kind, not ever again."

I couldn't help but notice he hadn't extended the same courtesy to me.

"First off, I'm not your pet goldfish," Ed called back. "Two, you can go fuck yourself. And three, if you had any balls you'd be saying that to my face."

"Oh, I'll say it to your face all right," Hobart snarled. "*Not that you'll have one for much longer.*" The way his voice abruptly changed told me the rest of him was as well. Guess now the talking was over.

A long, low-pitched howl rose up from the woods. There was no need for Myra to magically amplify it. It was easy enough for all to hear and, though I didn't speak werewolf, the meaning seemed clear.

The main event was about to begin.

An angry chorus of snarls and growls filled the air. It was accompanied by the sound of branches and saplings snapping as the pack tore through them.

They were on the move, all of them this time.

I stood at the far edge of Jacob's garage, waiting with gun in hand. At the speed the pack was moving, it would only be a matter of seconds.

Patience.

"Don't give me that shit. You're the one holding the peashooter."

Out on the front lawn, Ed stood his ground defiantly, or at least that's how he probably hoped he looked. In truth, he was holding his shotgun like a life preserver in the middle of the Atlantic.

Can't say I blamed him.

I'd originally volunteered to be the bait, but Jacob had rightly pointed out, much to Ed's chagrin, that his stepson didn't have a werewolf half with a fondness for chaos.

Speaking of which, the first of the pack burst from the tree line. However, rather than acting as a focused front, they were growling and snapping at each other just as much as anything else.

Hold...

"You don't need to keep saying that."

I'm talking to myself, okay? Grrr. As much as it helped to be able to communicate, I kinda hated the fact he could hear my thoughts.

Refocusing on the task at hand, I saw two werewolves step in from either side of their more chaotic minded fellows. Using their bodies, they effectively kept the pack moving in a straight line, like border collies herding sheep.

It was a smart tactic, too smart.

I made a note of them. They would need to be among our first targets, just as soon as…

That's when it happened, almost as if Jacob too were reading my thoughts.

Before the pack could make it halfway to where Ed stood, the yard lit up like Christmas as every floodlight attached to the house turned on simultaneously – all of them pointed directly toward where the attack was coming from.

Confused growls and yips rose up as all the werewolves currently on the move were temporarily blinded, their night vision effectively ruined.

So, of course, that's when I lifted my gun, took aim, and fired.

Nor was I alone.

36

AND IT WAS GOING SO WELL, TOO

The upside of excellent night vision is fairly obvious. When you can see in the dark then you have the advantage over *everything* else that relies on sight.

The downside, however, whether natural or electronic, is that all it takes is a bit of bright light to screw it up. In a hot instant you can go from seeing everything in clear relief to blind as the proverbial bat. And go figure, either Jacob really enjoyed his front lawn looking like the surface of the sun, or he'd been preparing for a moment just like this.

Either way it worked. With Ed's back to the floodlights, his previous status as an easy target instantly changed, putting him in the perfect spot to pick off angry werewolves who currently couldn't see a damned thing.

That was good for us, but the fact I was nearby to back him up was even better. However, the chef's kiss was the upstairs window where Jacob had stationed himself, hiding until the perfect moment.

All three of us opened fire at once.

Ed and Jacob still had some silver rounds, although whether it was enough to finish the job was up for debate.

Regardless, two of the smart wolves immediately went down, both with smoking holes in their sides and abdomen. The pair of werewolves closest to Ed likewise decided to lay down and *play dead* after he blasted them point blank with his shotgun.

That left me to pepper their flank – an easy enough thing to do. Far as I could tell, Hobart had sent the remainder of the pack in, so it was like shooting giant, hairy fish in a barrel. I would've had to close my eyes and aim at the sky to have much chance of missing.

The downside was I emptied all six chambers in short order.

Though I was firing some seriously heavy rounds, ultimately my part served more to distract them than anything else. And it worked too. When our first volley was all said and done, another half dozen werewolves, probably a third of Hobart's remaining forces, were either out of the fight entirely or at least no longer an immediate threat.

Not bad, but it wasn't nearly good enough.

Even as Jacob and Ed continued to fire, the pack began to acclimate to the bright lights. Worse, I saw two more wolves drag their wounded brethren from the ground and use them as shields the same way Shoulders had.

Suffice to say, werewolf or not, it was shocking to see some of them acting so callously *inhuman.* It was like Hobart had purposely commanded them to be the biggest jerks imaginable. That of course assumed he was commanding them at all.

I raised a fuzzy eyebrow as that thought sank in.

Ordering around a pack of animals was probably comparatively easy once you established yourself as *top dog.* But I had to guess it would require a lot on Hobart's part to impart the same willpower over thinking creatures – quite possibly more than he was capable of.

Unless...

That's when the final piece of this puzzle fell into place.

These smart wolves. They're Hobart's friends, his lieutenants.

"*Ya think?*" Winston replied.

Gotta be. That's why only a handful of them are smart. They're the ones Hobart doesn't need to worry about, the only ones probably happy to be here.

Winston let out a grunt of acknowledgement.

Sadly, we didn't have the luxury of discussing this further as the pack was once again rapidly advancing on Ed.

At least he wasn't being stupid about it. The second Ed was out of bullets, he turned and ran – his speed impressive despite his lack of canine physiology.

Better yet, he kept his wits about him, sprinting around the side of the house instead of directly into it. It kept the fight firmly outside where Jacob could hopefully continue to pick off our foes.

While a few glanced in the direction I'd fired from, most of the pack followed after Ed, turning to track him almost like a flock of birds. I tried not to be insulted that he was obviously still their number one priority.

Most was not all, though.

One werewolf broke off from the rest, dragging another with him as he raced toward the house at breakneck speed.

Crap!

We'd guessed this might happen, but it still didn't make me happy knowing what we needed to do next. This was no time to deviate from the plan, though.

You're up, Winston.

"It's about gods damned time."

The sharp crack of steel meeting flesh was no surprise as we raced toward the house, nor were the angry cries of pain coming from inside.

I wasn't sure if one or both the werewolves that had gone after Jacob were the smart variety. But even if they were, neither had bothered to slow down and check things out before plowing through the front door.

"Hah! Now you assholes know how it feels," Winston chuffed in amusement.

I tried not to share in his glee but didn't admonish him either.

We'd prepared for the eventuality of the pack storming Jacob's home, laying traps accordingly – including the sort that Winston and I had the displeasure of *sampling* barely a day earlier.

Slowing down werewolves was one thing, stopping them altogether was on a whole other level. The first floor was riddled with booby traps, many of which would've easily deterred human intruders. To monsters like me, though, they might as well have been set by that kid from the *Home Alone* movies.

Ed was fast, but it was only a matter of time before he was caught. We needed to make sure Jacob remained safe then get back to helping his son. If one part of our defense fell, the rest would almost certainly follow soon after.

Outside of downed werewolves, the front yard was now empty. With us all but invisible to the pack's sense of smell, it was the perfect time to make our move.

We barreled forward full-tilt, Winston now in the driver's seat.

Just remember where we placed those…

I didn't get a chance to finish as he launched us recklessly through the battered opening that used to be Jacob's front door.

I had a moment to take in the two werewolves inside the foyer. One was screeching his head off, having been hit by a spring-loaded two-by-six covered in razor wire. The other was caught fast in a bear trap. He was bent over attempting to pry the jaws open when he saw us.

The second wolf's eyes opened comically wide in the split second before we slammed into them both like a freight train. Then the two not-so-immovable objects met the irresistible force that was Winston and me.

It was no contest.

Flesh tore and bones snapped as we plowed into the surprised duo. It wasn't particularly pleasant to see, hear, or feel, but they served to break our fall as we skidded across the front hallway into the living room and onto the plywood *nail boards* that had been laid out on the floor.

The exposed points of dozens of nails and screws burrowed into flesh as we came to a halt, eliciting more cries from the two werewolves. And one from me as well as we tried to get to our feet, only for the palm of my left hand to come down hard on a nail. It hurt but was minor compared to the injuries sustained by the two monsters we'd tackled.

The first was missing long strips of furry flesh, rendering it a bloody, howling mess. As for the other, another of Hobart's friends, not only was it lying on its back on the bed of nails, its leg – still caught in the trap – had been shattered by the impact.

I tried and mostly failed to not be skeeved out by all the carnage but held it together best I could. *All right, we just need to make sure they can't cause any more…*

My alter ego was not in a listening mood, though. He

lashed out at the first wolf with our claws, erasing its throat in one savage slash and reducing its mewling cries to choked gurgles.

"*Much better,*" he said with a cruel chuckle. "*Now I can hear myself think again.*"

Holy crap!

"*Unfortunately, I can still hear you too.*"

The other werewolf grumbled something at us in response despite clearly being in pain.

"*Oh yeah? Say that again, you ball-licking piece of shit,*" Winston responded in kind.

The other werewolf muttered something else unintelligible, a questioning quality to its vocalizations.

"*First off, I ain't him. Secondly, fuck you and the tail humping witch you rode in on.*"

He balled our right fist and drove it hard into the wolf's jaw, breaking it and dropping him like a bad habit.

Whoa. Did you...

"*Don't act so surprised. I can't kill all these fuckers. Hard to lead a pack when you're the only one left in it.*"

Not that. You actually understood him?

"*Of course,*" Winston chuffed. "*Shit, I was more surprised the fuckhead understood me back.*"

Okay, so what did he say then?

"*Something about thinking twice before mouthing off to his betters.*" He kicked the downed werewolf in the ribs. "*Ain't that right, Jeb?*"

Wait, that's Jeb?

"*Is there an echo in here, pupcake?*"

If so, it was promising news. Jeb was Hobart's right-hand wolf, one of the crew who'd waylaid us earlier. He was a small-minded bigot and very much Hobart's biggest supporter regardless of whatever skin he was wearing. With him out of the picture, our job would be that much easier.

"Guess you were right about Hobart's ball buffers getting all the brains," Winston remarked.

Was that a compliment?

"Not really."

Didn't think so, I thought with an unseen smirk before adding, *You shouldn't have knocked him out. We could have asked him how Myra was able to...*

ZAAAAP

Speak of the devil... Alas my train of thought immediately derailed as I was enveloped by a cloud of crackling blue energy.

I fell to the floor twitching, landing halfway on the nail board and puncturing my body in a dozen different places – not that I could feel much of anything with my nerves lighting up like Christmas.

I managed to turn my head just enough to see the witch in question standing in the doorway, a nimbus of purplish energy surrounding her.

Guess we'd both been too distracted to notice her bringing up the rear.

"Hey there, lover." She was sweating profusely, having obviously expended a lot of power. Nonetheless, she still had enough left to throw an unhinged grin our way. "Color me impressed. Just the three of you chuckle-fucks against the entire pack, yet here you are making a go of it. If that don't have Hobart's knickers in a bunch, I don't know what will. But me and the big dog still got us an agreement. And that means I can't have you gumming up the works. I'm sure you understand."

She stepped into the living room, carefully avoiding the few traps left unsprung.

"You fucking bitch," Winston growled as she drew near.

Myra inclined her head quizzically. "I'm gonna do you a favor and assume those were some profound last words." Then she turned her head and let out a shrill whistle.

Her call was answered by snarls. Moments later, two more werewolves, both male, appeared in the doorway, their muzzles dripping with foam. They saw Myra and immediately leapt at her, causing my own heart to leap into my throat.

Sue me. Sure, we weren't even remotely on the same side these days, but it's not like I wanted to watch as she got torn limb from limb.

I needn't have worried, though, as both monsters were rebuffed by the purplish glow around her, some sort of defensive magic.

She let out a pained sigh, then hooked a thumb in my direction. "Over there, you two numbnuts."

Sure enough, both wolves slowly turned my way, their nostrils working overtime at all the blood that had been spilled.

It forced me to remember my own reaction at getting a taste just a short while ago. And that had been with me in full control of my faculties, something neither of these werewolves clearly was.

As they closed in on me and Winston, both of us still helpless to do anything about it, I couldn't help but wonder if this was how the Chadworth's pet pig had felt in its final moments.

37

DOG EAT DOG

The only upside to our predicament, if you could call it that, were the two werewolves Myra had summoned. Let's just say they were definitely not of the smart variety.

One kept lapping up blood from the nail board – yiping every time it pierced its own tongue. The other stopped at the living room entrance to scratch its back against one of the room's support beams.

The look on Myra's face said she wasn't particularly impressed. "Get him, you fucking idjits!"

Thankfully, for all her magic, her ability to actually control them was apparently nil, small comfort as I lay there twitching.

"*I told ... you. Should've ... let me ... gut ... the ... bitch,*" Winston managed to sputter through clenched teeth.

For once I didn't put up an argument. *I'm open to suggestions. Any ideas?* My body might've been tased, but fortunately my thoughts were still able to reach Winston.

"*Muh-maybe. Work ... with ... me ... here.*"

"I really hope you're not begging for mercy, Mike," Myra replied with a grin, "because I don't speak mongrel."

We weren't, not that I could say anything. Besides, I was still trying to figure out what Winston had meant. Sadly, his meaning didn't become any clearer as my right palm came down hard on two nails.

Ow! Watch it.

"*I ... said ... help me!*"

As he continued to put pressure onto our impaled hand, it finally hit me. He was attempting to roll over, so we could get back to our feet. Only problem was our muscle control was severely limited thanks to Myra's stun spell.

Wait a second...

Or at least that was the case for us individually.

Before now, Winston and I had mostly either worked against each other, or grudgingly ceded control so one of us could take over. But what would happen if we truly tried working together? There was only one way to find out.

I'm with you. Let's do this.

"*About ... fucking ... time!*"

Between the pain of my punctured flesh and every muscle in my body contracting uncontrollably, it was a struggle to cry out in pain much less do anything else. However, slowly we began to move as Winston and I both focused on the same task at once.

The feeling of being tased was nowhere close to pleasant but, as my inner wolf and I synced our efforts, the tremors seemed to grow less intense. It was like we were sharing the effects, which subsequently lightened the load for each other.

I had no idea how such a thing could possibly work. All I knew was our focus, combined with our formidable werewolf constitution, served to help us roll off the damned nail board. Then, as we placed both hands on the floor, we slowly began to rise.

Sure enough, the smug grin on Myra's face evaporated. Even better, the sweat streaming down her brow told me she didn't have much left to augment her attack.

"I'm ... gonna ... enjoy splitting you down the middle."

Though Winston's words were still alien to Myra's ears, the rumbling growl that escaped our lips was quite clear in its intent.

Credit where credit is due, Myra was no dunce. In the next second she stopped shocking us, a most welcome improvement. However, before shutting down her spell completely, she shot two bolts of blue energy into the behinds of the two misbehaving werewolves she'd brought along.

Both let out a yip before ceasing their nonsense. Snarls once more escaped their lips, especially from the one who'd been busy licking the bloody floor. With Myra still safe behind her magical force dome, they both turned their attention toward the only other foe left standing – me.

Had Myra not clearly overexerted herself, I'm sure she'd have stuck around to watch the festivities. She seemed to have a screw loose about such things. I still wasn't sure if her recently returned magic had changed something within her, or if it had always been there, but either way it was rapidly becoming difficult to reconcile her with the woman I'd not so long ago considered spending the rest of my life with.

Such introspection could wait, though, as she turned and hightailed it out the front door. The two werewolves spared her a glance before refocusing on Winston and I.

Under normal circumstances, I didn't hate our odds against them. Winston's strength combined with my insight had already proven a formidable, if messy, combination against these brainless brutes.

Sadly, it was all either of us could do to remain upright. Myra had hit us with enough juice to turn my body's nervous system into a jumble of useless spaghetti. While I could feel the effects of the spell starting to subside, it was happening way too slowly to mount an effective defense in these close quarters.

Running was out of the equation as more gunshots rang out from upstairs. The beasts winced at the sound before looking up toward the ceiling. Even if I managed to escape, Jacob was still up there. And if he was continuing to provide cover fire, then that meant Ed was still in the fight too.

Leaving offered no guarantee either of these monsters would follow. Winston might not have cared if Jacob lived or died this night, but I did. Regardless, I doubted we'd get very far anyway.

The werewolf furthest away continued to cock his head, as if slowly realizing someone was upstairs. As for the one closest to me, the same one who'd been licking rusty nails, he let out a low bubbling snarl as long ropes of drool dripped from his maw.

Eww, and here I thought Spud was gross.

"Really? That's the best you've got right now?"

Sorry, wasn't talking to you. Still getting a handle on this psychic communication thing.

Winston let out a snort. "*Yeah, well if you want to keep breathing I'd suggest you get a handle on fighting instead, because you're gonna fucking need it in about two seconds.*"

Me? I thought you were...

"*Shut up and listen,*" he interrupted. "*I can't believe I'm saying this, but I need you to take over for a minute or two.*"

You do realize this is the worst time in all of history for a smoke break, right?

"What's a smoke break?"
Never mind. What do you need to do?
"Just trust me on this one, pupcake."
Trust you? I...

There was no time to finish that thought. Drooly the werewolf rushed me, mouth wide open. I recognized the bloodlust in its eyes. It was probably the same look I'd had on my own face barely twenty minutes earlier. Except in this case, I sincerely doubted he was going to come to his senses at the last second.

A part of me was tempted to steer him toward the two werewolves already littering the floor, both of them a much easier meal in the making. And yes, it was vile of me to even think, but altruism is apparently the first thing out the window when a quarter ton of monster is bearing down on you.

In that same instant there came a subtle feeling of my muscles going slightly limp, as if they were no longer receiving proper instructions. Winston had put me back in the driver's seat. Pity I had no weapon in hand, nor was there time to search one out in the various nooks where we'd stashed them.

I barely got my arms up in time, bracing myself against the other werewolf as it plowed into me. Normally, that should've been enough to stop it in its tracks, but I was still recovering from Myra's assault, so the attack forced me backward.

Ugh!

To make matters worse, my head also began to throb for some reason.

Do werewolves get migraines?

No answer was apparently forthcoming, and it's not like I had any idea. Besides, I was too busy coming to the realization that my legs weren't in much better shape than the rest of me. I quickly overbalanced and went down onto my tail, quite literally.

The snarling beast came along for the ride, snapping its jaws like a rabid dog as I tried to fend it off.

ARGH!

Unfortunately, as I worked to keep its teeth from taking my face off, that left the rest of it free to claw the crap out of me. There was no rhyme nor reason to its attack. It snapped and slashed with reckless abandon, turning me into a bloody mess in short order. Nor was my plight made any easier as the strange thrumming inside my skull continued.

At least only one of the werewolves was raking us over the coals, so far anyway. If its buddy joined in, however, that was it. They'd tear me limb from limb.

Speaking of which, the tremors in mine were finally starting to abate, allowing me more control as I tried to avoid becoming this thing's dinner. Too bad my recovery was coming too late to make a difference.

My arms and torso were a mess of cuts and slashes. All the while, I'd done little more than hold this monster at bay. It was a far cry from the seemingly easy wins Winston had managed so far in this fight.

That probably had something to do with his methods being far more brutal than my own, something I'd have no choice but to accept if I wanted to survive...

The throbbing in my head picked that moment to mercifully end. Good timing, as I was finally starting to regain enough control to fight back. As the werewolf continued its efforts to shred my flesh into confetti, I slid my hands ever closer to the sides of its head.

One good twist. That's all I need.

I tried not to think of whoever the person was beneath all this fur and fury, instead focusing on the fact this is what Winston would've done in my stead, if he wasn't off doing whatever it was he'd ditched me for.

I swear, he'd better not be taking another nap.

My grousing thoughts trailed off as something massive loomed over us. I looked up to find the other werewolf had finally joined the fray.

No!

However, instead of dogpiling me like his buddy, he instead yanked his companion's head back, pulling him from my grasp. Then, before Drooly could respond, the second werewolf raked its claws across the beast's throat – ripping out his windpipe in one savage movement.

What in God's name?

Blood rained down upon me, forcing me to close my mouth lest I lose myself to the bloodlust again.

In that same moment, I felt Winston once again grab hold of his side of the steering wheel. He was back, although in time for what I couldn't say.

"*Not too shabby,*" he grumbled. "*Now sit the fuck down like a good doggie before I fucking make you play dead.*"

There's no need to be a jerk, I replied. *I did the best I could considering the circumstances.*

"*Wasn't talking to you, pupcake.*"

"*Then who?*"

"*Him, obviously.*" He pointed at the other werewolf. "*Or don't you recognize your best buddy in the whole world?*"

Best... Wait! That monster is Dallas?

38

WITH FRIENDS LIKE THESE

I watched with amazement, and no small amount of horror, as the werewolf, his fur practically matted to his body with blood, proceeded to obey Winston and plop his butt down onto the floor as if he were a labrador retriever.

Are you saying that's Dallas?

"*You going deaf on your side? Yes, that's your asshole buddy with the stupid name.*"

His name isn't... I paused to collect my thoughts before a dozen questions all came racing out at once, something I doubted Winston would be appreciative of. *You're sure?*

"*Is there an echo in here? Of course I'm fucking sure.*"

But how?

"*Shut up and take a sniff.*"

Rather than argue, I did, finding the air absolutely saturated with the smell of blood, viscera, and weapons discharge.

"*Deeper than that. C'mon, you can do it.*"

I didn't appreciate his mocking tone, but I tried anyway – letting the scents of the area wash over my olfactory nerves. The stench of blood was so heavy, intoxicatingly so, almost too heady to ignore.

No! Ignoring the saliva starting to drip from the side of my mouth, I powered through it, seeking out the kaleidoscope of odors I knew existed underneath it all.

There!

Pushing past the overpowering smells on the surface, I finally found the rest, so many scents it would've blown my human mind. My wolf brain began to catalog them all – wood, grass, trees, metal, furniture polish, leftover coffee grounds, the stew Jacob had been simmering for dinner, all of it.

I then turned my attention toward the werewolf still sitting there as if waiting for a biscuit. I recognized dirty fur, sweat, saliva, a bit of pee, and that was it. Except it really wasn't. There was another scent below even those, a lingering one that caused me to wince as it hit my nostrils.

"*There you go,*" Winston said. "*Recognize it yet?*"

It's...

"*The shitty, rancid ass smell that follows your friend everywhere.*"

I was going to say Dallas's cologne.

"*What's cologne?*"

It's something humans spray on themselves to smell better.

"*Offhand I'd say he failed pretty fucking hard, but that's beside the point. What matters is this is our guy, or your guy anyway. Personally, I still think he's an expendable dipshit.*"

When did you realize it was him?

Winston shrugged, meaning I did. "*Pretty much the second he walked in the door with your mount buddy.*" He let out a huff of laughter. "*Got to hand it to her. When it comes to being petty as fuck, she doesn't miss a thing.*"

Couldn't argue with him. As for that first point, it reinforced how much more adept Winston was in this form. All of this came instinctually to him, whereas for me

... well, let's just say constantly overthinking the situation was doing me no favors.

One thing I could do better than him, though, was show gratitude. *Thank you. It means a lot that you...* Freed wasn't quite the word I was looking for, as Dallas began scratching himself with his back paw. *Um, what did you do to him?*

"*What does it look like? I dominated him, of course. He's one of* mine *now.*" Before I could comment, he continued. "*It's like I said earlier. Hobart's offer weakened his hold. With everything that's gone on since, I doubt he had much chance to work on reestablishing their bond. Between that and knowing your friend would be fighting against his control, however pathetically, it didn't take much effort to recruit him.*"

Recruit him?

"*Exactly!*" He chuckled again. "*Don't believe me? Check this out.* **Roll over, you dumb fuck!**"

I winced as I somehow *felt* Winston's order not only with my ears but *inside* my mind as well. It was like those five words had taken on a power all their own. It reminded me of that first encounter with Hobart where for a second I'd almost been compelled to obey him.

As for Dallas, he immediately dropped to the floor and began rolling around in the blood and gore spilled by no less than three werewolf bodies.

Stop that!

"*Want me to make him speak next?*"

No!

"*You take all the fun outta life. Oh well, guess it's back to the basics.* **Enough of that shit. Get out there and gut those teat suckers!**"

In a hot second, the look of contentment vanished from Dallas's face, replaced instead with an angry snarl as he rose from the floor.

No. I didn't want this. Not for him.

I didn't have time to reason with Winston. I merely reacted. "***Stop!***"

However, instead of merely thinking it this time, the words actually came out of my mouth, albeit unintelligibly, but it was more than that. Once again, I felt the command deep within, seeming to resonate inside my very bones.

I could only stand there slack-jawed, unsure of what I'd just done. All I knew was that Dallas stopped growling like some Cujo-wannabe and went back to standing there as if he didn't have a care in the world.

How did I...

"*Did you just fucking countermand my order?*" Winston demanded, a deep growl rising from my own throat.

I don't know.

"*Because holy shit,*" he continued, "*gotta admit, I did not expect that from a pupcake like yourself. I'm almost impressed you figured it out.*"

Figured what out?

"*Wait. You didn't do that on purpose?*"

I ... no, not really.

"*Scratch being impressed. Oh well. Guess even a blind wolf occasionally finds a squirrel.*"

This was getting us nowhere. Something significant had just happened, but there was no time to dwell on it, much less play *Twenty Questions*.

Make him change back, then tell him to get out of here, I said before Winston could once again try to send Dallas off to his death.

He responded with laughter. "*No can do.*"

Why not?

"*Because I don't fucking want to, that's why!*" He took a breath then continued. "*We could use another set of paws and you know it.*"

But...

"And even if I wanted to, which I don't, that's easier said than done with your mount buddy's spell still out there. If I force him to change, he's liable to turn back anyway. And even if he doesn't, how far do you think he's gonna get with Hobart's personal bitches running around like the entire yard is made of rabbits?"

More shots rang out from upstairs as if in confirmation of this. They resulted in a pair of pained yips from somewhere outside. Unfortunately, it was also followed by a dry click then Ed's voice, both easily picked up by my sensitive ears.

"Shit, I'm out!"

"What's it gonna be, pupcake?" Winston asked. *"We can stand here debating this, or we can accept your friend's obedience with good cheer and get back out there before Hobart scarfs down that bloodsucker like a shit sandwich."*

There was no arguing and Winston knew it. I was stuck between a rock and a hard place. However, there was one thing I could do to mitigate things a little. *Give me control.*

"And why would I do that?" he replied.

It'll only be for a second. I trusted you, now it's your turn to trust me. It was probably petty, but I added, *Unless you're too scared.*

Winston let out a low growl, but then I felt my left side relax.

I didn't waste time with platitudes. Instead, I used the time to untie the bandana we still wore. Then I stepped up to Dallas, hoping he didn't decide to bite me just for the heck of it, and retied it around his neck.

There. If we're going to use him, then the least we can do is ensure he doesn't get shot by mistake.

I expected Winston to protest, but instead he let out a deep laugh.

"Look at you, pupcake. Like I said, maybe you've got a set after all."

A tiny, inadequate set?

"Exactly."

I couldn't help but smile. *All right. What say we get out there and do what we can to ruin the rest of Hobart's night?*

"Just his night?" Winston replied. *"You gotta think bigger, pupcake. I say we ruin the rest of his life instead, as short and painful as it's gonna be."*

39

THINNING THE HERD

Despite Winston's protests against wasting more time, we took a few moments to reset some traps before heading outside again.

Jacob had almost certainly heard the ruckus on the main floor and was probably debating the wisdom of relocating. Being he was the ... *squishiest* member of our team, I wanted to ensure we gave him as much head start as possible.

That done, I cautiously moved through the first floor to the kitchen and its large picture window overlooking the backyard. Now that I wasn't busy being attacked, I took the time to open the top cabinet and retrieve the revolver stashed there earlier – a loaded Smith & Wesson .44 Magnum.

Jacob had no shortage of big bore handguns. Considering his son's bloodsucking proclivities, I doubted this little hobby of his was mere coincidence. Nonetheless, I wasn't about to look this gift cannon in the mouth.

I took a moment to rue the fact my werewolf form didn't come with pockets for spare ammo, like some kind of were-marsupial. Then I turned my attention toward the backyard. It took my sharp eyes maybe two seconds to figure out our next stop on this lethal tour de force – Jacob's *shed.*

In the hours before the attack, Ed had explained it was originally built as a guest house. But, as life moved on, it had been relegated to storage instead – containing the myriad memories families tended to accumulate over the years, as well as a bunch of useless stuff that should've been earmarked for a yard sale. Considering it was currently surrounded by monsters, though, it was also a safe bet that's where Ed was holed up.

It was his fallback point as the walls were thick, the windows small, and everything was further fortified by all the junk inside. Regardless, it wouldn't keep a determined group of wolf beasts at bay for long.

Fortunately, Ed wasn't dealing with the *full* pack, otherwise he'd have already been overrun. Scanning the yard, I saw that a few had indeed been felled by sniper fire. As for the rest, it seemed like maybe half the remaining force was starting to lose focus and sniff around elsewhere.

In short, they were acting like wild animals.

No real surprise. Ordering them to attack a visible target was one thing. Having them lay siege, however, was probably asking more than their attention spans were capable of. Even with Hobart's lieutenants there to help keep them in line, it was still a lot of *cats* to herd.

Unfortunately, I had a feeling their focus would quickly return once we rejoined the fray. I stated as much.

"*No shit,*" Winston replied.

So, what do we do?

"*Simple. We send your idiot friend to gut the witch. Once that's done, Hobart won't be able to keep more than a handful of these crotch sniffers in their true forms. The rest... If they're smart they'll run.*"

That was certainly ... an idea. However, pitting my

best friend against my former girlfriend wasn't something I could get behind. Despite everything, I didn't want to see Myra killed. Call me a softy if you will, but making murder my go-to solution for all of life's problems felt like a slippery slope that ended with me becoming a true monster.

Equally important was the fact that, tired or not, Myra was still dangerous. With Dallas little more than a mindless beast, there was a very real chance things could end badly for him.

However, that didn't mean I saw no use for him in the coming conflict.

Too risky, I countered without elaborating. The last thing I needed right now was another argument. *He should stay here in case Hobart sends anyone else after Jacob.*

"*Let me get this straight. I finally recruit us an ally worth a shit and you want him to play guard dog?*"

We need to keep Jacob safe. It's the only way to win this.

"*And that pack of mutts pissing in the grass outside?*"

I glanced down at the handgun. *We'll figure something out.*

"*Really? That's your fucking plan?*"

I'm serious, Winston.

"*Fine.*" He let out a sigh of disgust then said, "*I see how it's gotta be.*"

Rather than say more, Winston turned back toward the living room and called for Dallas. A moment later, my friend came loping into the kitchen like an obedient dog, the illusion further cemented by the bandana still around his neck.

A part of me felt bad using him at all but come tomorrow he'd at least know I'd had his back.

"*All right, here's the deal, Fido,*" Winston said. "*You need to...*" I once again felt a resonance deep within as he prepared to dominate my friend in no uncertain terms.

"...*Get out there and play the part of the rabbit for those brainless chuckle fucks.*"

What?! *That's not what I...*

There was no time to argue. Instead, I tried to recall how I'd used that same power earlier – a moment of pure panic in which I'd somehow gotten Dallas to...

Oof!

Winston backhanded my side of our face, scattering those thoughts to the wind.

Before I could recover, Dallas launched himself through the window, sending shards of glass flying everywhere and making enough noise to wake the dead.

Werewolf heads perked up as he landed on all fours then let out a high-pitched snarling howl. I had no idea what he was saying, if anything, but there was a defiant tone to it, no doubt intended to get their attention.

I was immediately glad I'd given him my bandana, because I had a feeling more than werewolf eyes were turning his way.

Then, before anyone could respond, myself included, my friend rose to his hind legs and took off running like a bat outta hell.

Most of the werewolves that had been idly sniffing around took off after Dallas, but I was too angry to care.

Why did you do that?

"*Because you were about to countermand my order,*" Winston said, "*not that it would've worked. Anyway, be thankful I didn't carve your fucking face off instead.*"

Not that! We agreed Dallas would...

"*I didn't agree to cat-shit, asshole, and since I'm top canine of this pack what I say goes. Consider yourself lucky I met you halfway.*"

You sent him out there to die!

"*Only if he's a slow runner.*" Winston let out a snort. "*Relax, pupcake. Soon as they're outside your mount bitch's range, they should all revert.*"

And what if they hit the quarantine barrier before then? I countered. *Did you think of that?*

"*As a matter of fact I did. I just don't give a shit. That's their problem, not mine. Now do you want to stand here whining about it all night or take advantage of the fact the odds just got a shitload better for us?*"

Before I could answer, a shot rang out from upstairs. Guess Jacob agreed with Winston's logic.

I turned to see a spray of blood and smoke erupt from the arm of a werewolf still laying siege to the shed, causing it to let out a squeal of pain.

A low-pitched growl came from another – a large, black furred, beer-bellied werewolf. Hobart! At his command, the rest raced to the far side of the structure, putting the building between them and Jacob's keen eye.

Much as I didn't want to admit it, Winston was right once again. The odds, while not great, had taken a turn in our favor. According to my ears there were still three ... no, make that four left to contend with, but it was still much better than the numbers we'd started against. All the rest had chased after Dallas.

Winston's strategy had been sound. Mind you, that didn't make me happy.

I'd mistakenly begun to think we'd come to an understanding, that we were ... well, a team. I saw now he was still every bit the wildcard. Won't lie. He was lucky we shared the same body, otherwise the Smith & Wesson in my right hand might've been too tempting to ignore.

"*I'll add this as a bonus, just in case you haven't figured it out yet,*" Winston said as if sensing my smoldering anger. "*The only ones left are Hobart and his personal ball fondlers.*

So, no need to get your crotch hairs in a knot over whether they deserve what they're about to get. Unless, that is, you'd prefer we wait here picking our ass until the others get bored of chasing your friend and come back."

Once again, his logic was hard to argue against. There would be a reckoning between us, of that I silently promised. It just wouldn't be right now.

Winston apparently took my silence as agreement. *"Good. Then let's stop wasting time and start wasting fuck-heads instead."*

Fine, but we need to be smart about it, not rush in like...

Like we were apparently doing anyway.

In that same instant he used our powerful legs to launch us out the broken window, hurtling us a good twenty feet into the backyard. Just as quickly as we landed, we were on the move again, racing toward the shed and the sounds of battle coming from the far side where Hobart and his crew were trying to break in.

Rather than go around the structure, however, Winston instead continued to pick up speed. Our legs tensed just as I realized what he was doing. Instead of engaging our foes on the ground and risk being surrounded, he was going for the roof instead – giving us the high ground and a chance to pick off one or two before they knew what hit them.

I readied to start shooting as we leapt, our momentum carrying us easily high enough for the angled roof.

It was a solid strategy, even if Winston couldn't be bothered to let me know about it first. That was fine. I could improvise in a pinch.

BOOM!

What neither of us could do, sadly, was dodge a bullet midair.

In Winston's haste to take the battle to Hobart, he'd forgotten we were no longer wearing the bandana that signified us as friend not foe. The fact we'd raced into the fray at full speed had almost certainly not helped.

Sadly, playing the blame game was a moot point as fire erupted from my side, figuratively and literally as a silver slug punched a hole through my left kidney.

The Magnum went flying from my grasp and an unearthly screech escaped my lips, one born of both the personalities inhabiting this monstrous body I called my own.

Then, rather than touch down gracefully upon the rooftop as planned, we slammed into the rafters and fell, landing in a bleeding, burning heap upon the hard ground.

40

ALL THAT GLITTERS

In the movies, silver tends to kill werewolves easy peasy. One minute they're invincible monsters, the next the credits are rolling as the survivors limp back to town. Real life was not only a lot messier, it was considerably more painful too.

In truth, being instantly killed would've been a small mercy – quick and relatively painless, like swatting a fly. Instead, it was more like someone was pouring salt into my wounds accompanied by a lit road flare. It's like a silver bullet looked at the amount of pain a regular bullet caused and said, "hold my beer."

Perhaps this was a bit of twisted poetic justice, considering the werewolves we'd been forced to shoot in self-defense. If so, my alter ego wasn't being particularly gracious about it.

"*I ... am .... gonna ... fucking ... kill ... that trigger happy ... old ... fuck,*" Winston half grunted, half whined.

I would've tried talking him down, but it currently felt like a thousand cigarettes were being stubbed out in my side all at once.

That wasn't the worst of it, though.

Even now Jacob was probably watching us from his makeshift sniper nest, debating whether to fire again. He had to be running desperately low on silver by this point, but Winston and I were an easy target. With nothing to easily distinguish us from the rest of the pack, there was no good reason he shouldn't put a slug into our noggin for good measure.

Unfortunately, I had no way of letting him know it was me. I couldn't even tell where he was hiding as he could've been holed up behind any of the several open windows on the upper floor. My only consolation was knowing that, had I not given Dallas my bandana, it could be him lying here right now instead of me. Although, damn it all, but feeling my blood boil from the inside out, I couldn't pretend I wouldn't have made a different choice if given a do over.

There *had* to be a better way of doing crap like this.

Forcing myself to focus, as much as I could anyway, I tried to see how bad it was. The bullet wound wasn't easily visible from my line of sight, but the shower of sparks shooting out like a roman candle gave its location away. Sadly, there was no front exit wound to be seen or felt, meaning Jacob's slug was still merrily chewing up my insides.

We need ... to get ... the bullet out, I managed to think.

Winston's response was a growl, somehow encapsulating both agony and annoyance in one hitched breath.

Before either of us could say more, though, another sound caught my ear, easy to miss against the ruckus of splintered wood on the far side of the building. It was the soft click of metal sliding against metal ... a door opening.

I inclined my head to look while Winston bared our teeth in a snarl, not that there was much threat behind it.

Sure enough, the soft patter of footsteps in dirt

followed, again just barely audible as a wiry form stepped around the corner of the shed.

"*Ed,*" I tried to whisper. Unfortunately, it came out more as a hacking bark, one that caused him to wheel in my direction and point his shotgun directly at my face – the most unpleasant stroll down memory lane imaginable.

Despite my size in my werewolf form, the barrel looked mighty big indeed from this distance. Needless to say, so far, my foray into the backyard could have gone smoother.

Thankfully, vampiric night vision was all it was cracked up to be because, rather than blow a hole through my face, Ed lowered the barrel.

"Mike?" he hissed.

Winston's response was another low growl.

"Yeah, yeah, and the other guy too."

I took control and managed a nod, which seemed to be all the answer Ed needed. He dropped the barrel toward the ground then turned toward the house and waved, hopefully cluing in his dad to stop filling us with silver slugs. That done, he leaned down and took a closer look.

"Shit. Pop got you good. Why the hell did you take your collar off?"

"*Collar?*" Winston growled.

Knock it off. He's on our side. Or have you forgotten the reason we're here?

"Never mind. I retract the question. It's not like I can understand you anyway." Ed offered his hand instead. "Come on, let's get you up. Trust me when I say that staying here is a bad idea."

He glanced back toward the shed just as there came a

godawful racket from the far end. If Hobart and his crew hadn't gotten inside before, they were now.

Rather than risk Winston being obstinate at the worst time imaginable, I grabbed hold of Ed's outstretched hand. If asked, I would've said that a string bean like him would've had zero chance of hauling someone my size back to his feet, but human logic didn't apply where creatures of the night were concerned.

"Pop's got a first aid kit inside," Ed said as he yanked me from the ground. "We just need to be quiet about..."

"*Grarraggh!*"

Sadly, being pulled to my feet while my insides were on fire wasn't conducive to stealth. I wasn't sure whether the cry was Winston's or mine. Heck, maybe it was from both of us. Whatever the case, I couldn't clamp my mouth down fast enough to stop the yelp that escaped.

In response, the commotion coming from the shed instantly ceased.

Ed met my gaze and mouthed, "*We need to move, now.*" Well, okay, he may have thrown in a few expletives too.

Winston cocked our head to the side, no doubt unfamiliar with the finer points of lip reading, but I got the gist well enough.

Give me control, I told him in no uncertain terms.

I slung one arm over Ed's shoulder, letting him take some of the burden off, then I clamped my other hand over the still sizzling bullet wound – trying to ignore it was like stoppering a boiling tea kettle with nothing but my palm.

I gestured toward the house, hopefully conveying I was as ready as I was going to get.

Ed helped me get moving, but not before muttering, "Someone really needs to get you guys a werewolf-sized *Speak & Spell.*"

I was in no position to disagree.

41

CUTTING EDGE

This was not good.

If our ambush had worked, this battle would've been over. Instead, thanks to some unfortunate friendly fire, I was barely in any position to walk, much less fight.

Ed was still in decent shape but I didn't like his odds against a quartet of smart werewolves, including their leader. The only factor currently in our favor was that Jacob was still somewhere above, hopefully waiting to plug the first monster who dared make an appearance.

"*We need to fix this now*," Winston growled, "*because I seriously doubt fuckface here can win this on his own.*"

Ed glanced at us, one eyebrow raised. "Just so you're aware, I still have no clue what you're saying."

"*Wasn't talking to you, squirrel fucker.*"

Let's get inside, I replied, changing the subject. *See if Jacob has forceps, disinfectant, maybe a needle and thread.*

"*What for?*"

So we don't bleed out.

"*That's what you're afraid of? Gods damn it, you are an embarrassment to my body.*"

Before I could respond, there came a commotion from inside the oversized shed – the sound of multiple vocalizations, almost as if they were ... arguing about something.

"The fuck?" Ed whispered, echoing my own confusion.

In the next minute, one of the werewolves came rushing out the front door, staggering to maintain his footing as if he'd been ... *shoved.*

"*That cowardly piece of shit,*" Winston muttered.

I was about to ask what he meant when two thunderous reports rang out from directly above us, loud enough to almost make me forget the burning agony in my side. Almost.

The werewolf jerked twice as one slug hit his arm while the other punched a hole high up in his chest. He let out a high-pitched yipe right before lifting his good arm to shield his face, a very human gesture.

In that moment I understood. Hobart must've ordered one of his men to step outside and see if the coast was clear. However, since Myra's spell had somehow allowed them to retain their intellect, his lieutenants weren't as quick to obey as they might otherwise have been. Go figure, but the downside to increased intelligence was a decrease in their willingness to eat a bullet for their *lord and master.*

Realizing this, he'd resorted to doing things the old-fashioned way – picking a *volunteer* and pushing his butt out the door like a sacrificial lamb.

Although perhaps *sacrifice* was putting it too strongly.

Rather than drop as so many of his fellows had done, the werewolf remained standing. The scent of his blood hit my nostrils but there was no fiery discharge as there'd been from my own wound.

The beast raised his head curiously, as if realizing that was the worst of it. Then, despite his wounds, he began to chuckle, the sound like scraping the inside of a cement mixer.

"Shit," Ed remarked. "Pop must be out of silver."

"You mean that pup of a bitch used his last silver bullet on me?" Winston grumbled.

I ignored him, gesturing toward Ed's weapon with a questioning grunt.

He raised his shotgun in the direction of the werewolf as he whispered out of the corner of his mouth, "Best not to ask."

Great. He was out too. Guess that explained why he'd slipped out the door rather than blast Hobart and his buddies point blank.

The wounded werewolf chuckled for a moment longer, then it looked up at something over our heads. Its eyes opened wide and it threw itself to the side with frightening speed just as another shot rang out.

"Fuck, they spotted him," Ed hissed, backing up a step. "We need to move."

Unfortunately, I had little shot of outrunning a toddler much less a pack of supernatural wolf monsters.

"We aren't going anywhere," Winston replied, as if sensing my concern. *"Pussies run from fights, not Dominants."*

Or maybe not.

I was tempted to remind him the only reason we'd made it this far was because we'd had the good sense to run earlier, but that felt like pouring salt into our wounds, and my side already hurt badly enough as is. Instead, I thought back, *Please tell me you have a plan.*

"Watch and learn, pupcake. Oh, and try not to bite my tongue."

Why would I bite... "AIEEEEE!"

All coherent thought scattered to the wind as Winston took his claws and sliced into our side. This was no mere flesh wound either. He dug deep, like he was carving up an extra tough side of ribeye.

What ... are you ... doing?

"*Shut ... the fuck up,*" Winston said through gritted teeth. "*I'm ...trying to ... focus here.*"

Ed looked back at us in that moment, seeing Winston fileting our body like a fish. "Jesus fuck, dude!"

Won't lie. Had I been capable of speech, I would've shared a similar sentiment.

Smoke, sparks, and blood – so much blood – poured from our side but still Winston continued to dig in like a determined Jack Russell Terrier. Then, just when I thought there was no possible way this could get any worse, he jammed our left hand into the grotesque wound he'd created. It made the pain of getting shot seem like a pleasant memory.

At that moment I would've gladly accepted the blissful nothingness of passing out. Too bad my werewolf constitution was made of sterner stuff.

Ed kept shifting his attention between me and the werewolf still trying to draw Jacob's fire. "Seriously, Mike. What the fuck?"

I wished I could've told him, but I had no clue why Winston was busy committing half-assed seppuku on us.

However, that question was answered moments later as he mercifully pulled his hand free. The utterly mind-consuming agony made it hard to think and I found myself blinking away tears of pain, but finally I saw the reason why.

In his hand, the blood still sizzling off the metal, was the silver slug we'd been shot with.

I'd love to say it made me feel better, but now there was a gaping wound in our side big enough to stuff ... well, a fist into. And yes, I could feel every excruciating square inch of it as...

Except I realized that wasn't quite true.

The pain was still there, believe me it was hard to miss, but it was now slightly muted, at least to the point where I didn't want to curl up into a fetal ball and cry for my mother.

It took me a moment to realize what was going on as I was still traumatized from *gutting* myself, but then I felt my insides start to shift and rearrange. Not only had Winston sliced us to ribbons but he'd initiated the change without giving me so much as a heads up.

Don't get me wrong, the momentary relief brought on by the flood of brain chemicals was nothing short of miraculous. However, I couldn't help but notice he was changing us back to a human at the worst possible moment.

"*Nrrrrr ... no!*" I managed to cry just as we reached the bizarre halfway stage between man and monster.

That finally caught Ed's attention. "Now?! Have you lost your fucking split-personality mind?"

He wasn't wrong as the wounded werewolf chose that moment to barrel forward. But he wasn't aiming at either of us. Instead, the beast leapt, soaring ever higher, no doubt in a bid to reach the second story window.

Ed spun and tracked him, his vampire reflexes impressive. He raised his shotgun and fired with almost no hesitation. Sadly, there hadn't been time to properly aim. On the upside, his target wasn't exactly tiny.

The blast hit the werewolf's leg, causing it to spin out of control just as another shot came from above. I wasn't sure whether Jacob's round hit or not, but the werewolf slammed into the siding before falling to the ground in a heap.

There was no time to celebrate, though, as there came a loud rending *crack* from inside the shed. Another of the remaining werewolves stepped out. Unfortunately, I couldn't tell if it was Hobart or not, as he was using the heavy front door, freshly torn from its hinges, as a makeshift shield.

He was followed by his friends. One was using an old metal wash tub to protect himself while the other was holding a canoe as cover. Jacob might've been out of silver but these guys weren't taking any chances.

Before I could shout a warning, Winston took control, pausing the transformation where it currently was. "*Listen up, suckhead. I need you to keep these fuckers busy for a minute or two.*"

Ed turned partially toward us. "What for?"

"*Stop asking stupid questions,*" Winston ordered, "*and fuck their shit up!*"

As if in response, more shots rang out from above, Jacob letting loose as this was obviously the end game. There was no point in holding back any longer. Wood splintered and metal clanged as the high bore bullets struck home. I had no doubt most penetrated the pack's makeshift armor, nonetheless it didn't appear to be slowing them down.

Ed shook his head. "Whatever you're gonna do, fucking do it already." Then he turned to face the wolf holding the door as it closed in.

Rather than blast it, though, he spun the shotgun in his hand and wielded it like a baseball bat instead. Guess that also explained why he'd been hiding in the shed.

Mind you, out of ammo didn't mean out of *options* when it came to creatures of the night.

The werewolf, its vision obscured, didn't see the attack until it was too late. Ed hit him dead on, splintering wood and sending the beast flying.

Unfortunately, that still left two more for him to contend with.

Too bad there wasn't much I could do to help as

Winston picked that moment to recommence our change back into a human.

I wanted to scream, tell him he was crazy for doing this now, but then I realized his gambit. The change brought with it a massive healing surge, one that had already saved our butt this day.

Unfortunately, with the rush of brain chemicals fading, there was nothing to mute the torment of flesh and muscle knitting itself back together.

As the two werewolves tackled Ed in a flurry of fangs and fur, I was powerless to do anything other than be overcome by a blinding haze of agony.

42

FIGHT OR FLIGHT

Silver was like a one-two punch when it came to werewolves. On the downside, it chemically reacted with our blood in a way akin to mixing potassium with water, or so my high school chemistry teacher had taught us.

But there was an even *downerside*, too, as we were coming to realize, one that seemingly lingered after the silver was removed from the equation.

It apparently messed up something with our ability to heal. It was as I'd said. This curse hadn't come with an instruction manual.

Case in point, the healing surge the change brought on should've gone a long way toward closing the gaping wound in our side, if not outright taking care of it altogether. Instead, we finished the transformation in only slightly better shape than we'd started.

The worst of the bleeding had stopped, but it left an ugly open wound filled with raw and tender flesh.

And hey, go figure, now that my nerve endings no longer had the benefit of supernatural toughness, the pain

329

jumped from an eleven to roughly a forty-six, causing me to collapse into a quivering heap.

It had been a good plan on Winston's part, but whatever luck we might've enjoyed this night had up and abandoned us.

We weren't the only ones in dire straits, though. Ed wasn't faring much better. He was backpedaling across the yard, attempting to fend off one werewolf holding a canoe and another wielding a wash basin as a shield. He was still swinging his empty shotgun to keep them at bay, although by now it was little more than a twisted tube of ruined metal.

It was a scene that would've been pretty hilarious in a movie. Pity this was real life.

Unfortunately, any chance of a save from above was cut off prematurely as the shed's door came flying toward the house – slamming into the upper floor and sending wood and glass flying.

Hopefully Jacob hadn't been hit by the makeshift missile, not that I had much chance of checking on him.

A growl from close by clued me in that I probably needed to worry more about myself. The first werewolf out of the shed, the one I'd mistakenly thought was down for the count, was crawling my way. He was an absolute mess, bleeding from several wounds and missing most of his left leg below the knee, but the damned thing refused to quit. Knowing werewolves as I did, I had no doubt he was still more than a match for me in my human form. Unfortunately, running away was not really an option.

"What ... the fuck?" Winston cried. "Why didn't ... that work?"

"It's the silver," I told him. "It ... messed us up worse than ... I thought."

"I'm so gonna gut that old bastard."

I was far more worried about us being the one gutted,

more than we already were anyway, as the injured werewolf continued inching toward us. The poor bastard couldn't have had much left in him, yet his red eyes continued to glare with murderous intent.

Or they did until a massive, furred foot lashed out and kicked him in the face, sending him flying into the siding, where this time he finally fell still.

I looked up, hoping against hope that perhaps Dallas had circled back to help us.

No such luck.

It was the werewolf who'd been using the door as a shield – his massive size, pitch black fur, and prodigious beer gut confirming his identity in a hot second.

Hobart had decided it was time to step in and finish this personally.

I fully expected the werewolf leader to tear my head off my shoulders and be done with it. Or, barring that, to sink his teeth into my crotch and chomp off my family jewels.

Honestly, I wasn't sure which I preferred least.

However, rather than finish me off, Hobart's flesh began to shift and reform – his body growing smaller with each passing second until he stood there fully human and naked as the day he was born.

"Sorry, Larry," he said to the unconscious wolf, "but it's like I told you. This one's mine." He turned back toward me with a smirk. "Evening, Mikey."

"Right back at ya, fuck face," Winston replied.

"Damn, son. I don't know where you got this sudden influx of piss and vinegar, but I like it. Suits you. Hell, it almost makes me sad it's come to this."

I felt Winston about to say something else, but I bit down on my tongue, shutting him up. I was beginning to see the writing on the wall. It was time to salvage whatever dignity I could.

"Let my friends go and ... I won't fight you." I clamped down with my teeth to keep my inner beast from adding his two cents.

I had no desire to die, but there was also no lie behind my statement. The simple truth was I had very little fight left to give. We'd done our damnedest. Heck, we'd done better than we had any right to ever expect, but I was beginning to realize this outcome was inevitable. The odds were too stacked against us. Maybe if we'd had more time to plan.

We hadn't, though. At least this way maybe I could save a life or two.

"The hell you won't," Hobart replied with a smug grin.

Or not. "Excuse me?"

"You heard me, boy. You and me are going to settle this the old way. I don't care what shape you're in. It's gone too far for anything less." He lowered his voice, not that it probably made much difference to the creatures still battling less than a dozen yards away. "Much as it pains me to admit, you and old Jacob put up a lot more fight than I'd anticipated. Hell, credit where it's due. It was pretty goddamned impressive, like watching a one-legged whore play hopscotch. But therein lay the problem. You understand where I'm coming from?"

I didn't, but Winston apparently did.

"It's because I made you look like a weak-ass pussy boy."

It wasn't a question.

Hobart's eyes narrowed. "Something like that. Goddamn, it's plain as day you still don't know shit about being a Dominant, but..."

"More than you might guess, ass face."

As I struggled to keep Winston from mouthing off

further, Hobart continued. "Maybe that's true. You did manage to steal your friend away from me, after all, although I'm thinking it was more luck than anything else. Back to what I was saying, ignorant or not, I'm guessing you've figured out I can't abide anyone making me look bad in front of my people."

He glanced over at where Ed was just barely holding his own against the two monsters nipping at his heels. The vampire had obviously been in a scrap or two in his time, as he was doing a decent job at keeping himself from being flanked. All the same, it was obvious he wasn't much of a fighter. It was only a matter of time.

"Don't get me wrong," Hobart said, watching the fight with detached amusement, "folks like Doug and Emmett over there ain't the problem. They both know what side of their bread is buttered, especially now that Myra figured out a way to keep their wits about them after the change. Too bad it takes a lot out of her. Hell, I reckon she'll be in bed for the better part of a week once this is over."

He shook his head then turned back toward me. "The problem is all the rest. A man knows who signs his paycheck, but a dumb brute only knows who can whip his ass and who can't. And if they doubt me for even a second, then all the mind mojo in the world ain't gonna do shit to keep them in line."

His words echoed everything Winston had said, not that it was of any help to us now. Nonetheless, I tried to push my despair away long enough for a quick look around, hoping to find something, *anything*, that could forestall Hobart's plans for us.

Unfortunately, the gun I'd dropped earlier was nowhere to be seen, nor was there anything in reach save dirt, splintered wood, and shards of broken glass too small to be useful.

Hold on.

I spied one item that had potential. There was an old planter situated near the back corner of the house, maybe thirty feet away. Inside lay a loaded .45 buried in the dirt, one of the many surprises we'd hidden throughout the property.

Sadly, it might as well have been ten miles away for all the chance I had of getting to it before Hobart was all over me like a new suit.

"I suppose that's enough jawing," Hobart said, perhaps sensing my desperation. "If it makes you feel any better, I'm of a mind to let Jacob walk away from this, so long as he promises to keep his nose outta my business going forward."

"What about...?"

"The Progenitor?" he interrupted. "No can do. He's got to die, but I think you knew that already." He let out a disgusted sigh. "Ain't gonna lie to you, Mikey, not in your final moments anyway. He ain't what I expected, not after everything I heard. Still, why take the chance? Worst case, one less bloodsucker in this world. I doubt anyone will take me to task for that."

"But..."

"But nothing! That's enough. Ain't no weaseling out of what comes next. You had your chance, but the time for talk is done."

This was it. I wasn't sure how he was going to do it, but my odds of stopping whatever came next were close to zero. Winston's silence on the matter told me he'd come to the same conclusion. All we could hope was that Hobart made it quick.

"On your feet, son."

"I ... I don't think I..."

"I said on your feet!" he barked, making it a point to say it extra loud for any ears listening.

He gripped one meaty hand beneath my armpit and

heaved me up, the pain more than enough to keep me from offering any further protest.

At last, I stood on wobbly legs, barely maintaining my footing, but somehow I managed to not topple over.

"That's better," Hobart said. "Now change."

"What?"

"You heard me. We're gonna settle this like men. And in case it's not crystal clear, that means we're gonna settle it *as* monsters."

43

DOGGED DETERMINATION

"Um, I don't suppose I could have a few minutes to get ready?"

Hobart narrowed his eyes. "Nice try, kid, but I don't think so. See, I'm guessing you've got weapons stashed in every damned nook, cranny, and gopher hole between here and Canal Street. Hell, I'm half-surprised you ain't got one jammed up your ass too."

"Huh," Winston remarked, as if he wished he'd thought of that first.

"No way I'm letting you slink off," Hobart continued. "You've played enough games for one day. Now it's time to shit or get off the pot."

I was tempted to point out there was little chance of me getting off the back porch much less any pot but held my tongue.

"Now *change*," he barked, just as his own voice started to get all gravelly. "*You try to run or hide, and I'll gut you like the coward you arrrrrrgh.*"

He transformed as he spoke, his final word being lost as his features became too monstrous for human speech. That was okay. I got the basic gist.

So too apparently did Winston.

"Run?" he replied. "And risk your fat ass dying of a heart attack as you try to follow? No thanks. I'm gonna rip off your balls for all to see then swallow them like the tiny, dried-up kibble they are."

What? Guess he still hadn't accepted our fate. No matter. "Actually, scratch that. We ... I won't be doing anything of the sort."

Hobart's eyes momentarily opened wide in confusion, but that quickly gave way to a low snarl. The meaning was clear. He thought I was stalling. I needed to change now otherwise we weren't going to get a chance to do anything but bleed out.

I clamped down on my tongue as I tried not to think of the check Winston had just written with our mouth that our body had little hope of cashing. Instead, I tried to focus, gazing past Hobart and toward the rapidly fading illusion of the moon that still hung over the trees. It was almost fully transparent by then, with the stars behind it now clearly visible. Myra was almost at the end of her magical rope. A few more minutes and it would be gone all together.

That wouldn't save me from Hobart's wrath, but if Ed could hold on long enough then he might have a chance. There was no way Hobart could fight me, even injured as I was, while maintaining the focus necessary to keep his remaining lieutenants from reverting. And even if he could, without Myra's spell they'd be little more than wild animals.

Mind you, first I had to survive long enough for that to happen.

So for now, I willingly succumbed to the flickering glamour, along with its nearly irresistible pull to let go and surrender to the beast within.

"Oh yeah, that's the shit," Winston muttered as our

body was once again flooded by a stew of brain chemicals, dulling the awful pain enough so I no longer felt as if I'd keel over.

Next came the change as my entire body rearranged itself in unnatural ways. Sadly, that included a massive sneezing fit as my fur grew in, rattling my insides enough to almost double me over. Just my luck I hadn't remembered to take my allergy pills during my brief layover at home. I swear, the universe was having too much fun kicking me while I was down.

Mind you, none of that slowed my transformation in the slightest.

Hobart went from glaring down at me to staring me straight in the eye as my body grew to match his. Heck, I might've even had an inch or two on him, although he made up for it in girth around the middle.

Sadly, while I might've normally considered my odds against him to be okay-ish, the gaping hole in my side said otherwise.

Speaking of which, the pain once again took hold as the rush of brain chemicals faded. It wasn't as bad as before, no doubt thanks to my now supernaturally augmented constitution, but it still felt like someone had stabbed me and was having a grand old time twisting the knife.

I dared a glance down to find the wound in my side only marginally smaller than it had been before I'd changed back. The sides had closed up a little but it was still big enough to stuff my wallet into, had I been carrying... *Ooof!*

Hobart barreled into me as I was doing my wellness check. Guess he hadn't been kidding about ixnaying any prep time.

I was lifted off my feet like I'd been hit by a runaway bus. My momentum was momentarily slowed as I slammed into the back of Jacob's house, knocking the wind out of me. But then came the sharp *crack* of what I hoped was wood as we plowed straight through the outer wall.

I caught a brief glance of an upended dresser then I was tossed flat on my back. Amazingly enough, though, the landing was far softer than I'd been expecting. No wonder. I'd fallen onto a bed in what appeared to be a guest room.

Sadly, my soft landing was in for a rude awakening as Hobart leapt atop me snarling and clawing.

Clunk!

Then, just to add insult to injury, the bed frame collapsed beneath us as I doubted it was built to handle half a ton of werewolf tussling atop it.

"*Get off me, asshole,*" Winston snarled. "*You're not my type.*"

I personally doubted there was much we could do to rectify this situation as Hobart's claws turned our chest into a bloody mess of crisscross scratches, but I'd underestimated my feral half.

Rather than fight against our foe's superior leverage, Winston instead ripped a large handful of stuffing from the ruined mattress. He managed to fend off Hobart's claws just long enough to shove it all straight into the werewolf leader's gaping jaws and as far down his throat as he could manage without losing a hand.

Hobart's eyes opened wide as he began choking on memory foam.

Good idea!

"*Less ass-kissing and more helping,*" Winston replied, grabbing the fur on our foe's head and managing to drag him off us.

My other half was right. I needed to get my head into the game. The time for grousing was over, along with any chance of a quick, painless death. It was either fight or accept what was sure to be a horrific end. In that moment, the choice seemed an easy one.

There was nothing left but survival of the fittest. Now to hope this was a case where two minds were better than one.

The traps in the living room! We can use those.

Winston grunted acknowledgement as he rolled us off the mattress before Hobart could recover.

Rather than waste time standing up, we scrambled out the bedroom door on all fours. It hurt like hell but was a lot quicker than lurching down the hallway.

"*Too slow, pup-licker!*" Winston called back.

Do you think he understood you?

"*Fuck if I care.*"

A fair enough sentiment. That said, we stood no chance in close quarters. But with some space at our back and maybe some improvised weapons, our odds would almost certainly improve.

Or perhaps it would've been the case, had there not come a deafening roar from behind us, one that stopped Winston dead in his tracks.

For one horrifyingly long moment I feared Hobart had somehow managed to *dominate* my other half, as we slowly began to turn around.

What's going on? Are you okay?

"*Did you hear that fucking bitch?*" Winston replied. "*Nobody calls me a coward.*"

Seriously?!

On the upside, Winston wasn't being mind controlled. Less good was he'd been easily baited.

I was forced to assert myself, steering us back in the direction of the living room – a feat made slightly easier since the gaping hole in our body was on his side.

"*What the fuck are you doing?*"

Sticking to the plan.

"You're actually gonna let him get away with calling us that?"

He could call me his Aunt Gertrude for all I care. I paused for a moment, realizing I needed to take a different approach if I didn't want him fighting me every step of the way. *I meant, we have a better shot of making him eat those words in the living room.*

I swear, dying was bad enough, but getting killed because my werewolf half had an inferiority complex would be downright embarrassing.

Fortunately, it's not like we had far to go.

Far less fortunate was me forgetting about the mess we'd left behind. As I rounded the corner into the living room, moving as fast as I could, my hands slipped on the blood-soaked floorboards, sending me tumbling butt over teakettle.

Guh!

Not only did it hurt like the dickens, but I just barely avoided impaling myself on those nail boards again. To make matters worse, I came to a halt face-to-face with one of the werewolves we'd been forced to put down.

Unlike what the movies would have you believe, my kind didn't automatically revert upon either death or incapacitation. Such a thing didn't happen until the full moon set or whatever spell was keeping us furry ended.

No doubt about it. The local emergency room was going to be a very busy place once the sun came up. The coroner's office too, sadly.

Knock it off. Now's not the time for this crap.

"Who are you talking to?" Winston asked.

Myself.

"Why?"

I don't know. It's just something humans do.

"And yet you idiots are somehow the dominant species."

Our back and forth was cut short as two shots rang out from upstairs. Since neither perforated me where I lay, I had to assume Jacob was back to doing what he could to help Ed.

As refreshing as that was to know, I realized I'd led Hobart to a spot where, if he defeated me, he'd be in prime position to easily hunt Jacob down. Sadly, there was no time to rethink this plan. Instead, I pulled myself painfully back to my feet before grabbing one of the sprung traps and snapping it off at the base.

"*Huh, maybe you're not so useless after all,*" Winston grumbled as he tested the weight of the razor wire bound board.

Care to do the honors? I asked, just as Hobart charged in after us.

"*With pleasure.*" He let out a throaty chuckle as we swung the multi-edged weapon.

Hobart was no fool, though. He was ready for our ambush, raising a furry arm to block the attack.

Winston surprised me, however, by pulling the blow at the last second. Rather than strike with full strength, he slashed the razor wire across Hobart's flesh instead. It didn't do a lot of damage, but I bet it sure as heck hurt.

"*Grarrrrr!*"

Before Hobart could counter, Winston reversed course, raking the board across our foe's sizable chest, effectively using it as a giant cheese grater. Flecks of blood flew in every direction, not that anyone would've noticed in the already gore-splattered room.

Hoo boy. This was one mess that wasn't going to be fun to clean.

More importantly, it kept Hobart off balance, causing him to stumble into one of the werewolves we'd laid out earlier. It was Jeb, Hobart's right-hand wolf. If that wasn't poetic justice, I didn't know what was.

Now!

We lowered our head and shoulder-checked the burly Dominant, sending him sprawling butt-first over the body of his chief lieutenant only to land squarely atop a nail board.

Hobart squealed in pain as a dozen metal points bit into his keister.

"*Slap this on your ass too, teat fucker.*" Winston lifted the razor board high and prepared to bring it down, this time with everything we had left.

Too bad our opponent was far from out of it.

Before we could knock some sense into him, he kicked out with a clawed foot. There wasn't much leverage behind it, but he didn't need a lot to get the job done. Between the blood-slicked floor and our own weakened state, he managed to knock our right leg out from beneath us.

We staggered backward, the situation not helped as Winston and I somehow managed to flail in opposite directions as we both fought to maintain our footing. Realizing we were going down hard if I didn't do something, I took control, dropping our makeshift weapon and grabbing hold of the entertainment center to keep from falling. My quick thinking saved us from another nasty tumble, if just barely.

Regrettably, it wasn't quick enough.

Hobart was already back to his feet, contemptuously kicking his lieutenant out of the way. He was dripping blood from a dozen spots but seemed too angry to care as he came at us.

In the ensuing panic, Winston and I wrestled for control of our body, both of us trying to mount a defense but doing little more than sending conflicting signals to our arms and legs. The result was less than impressive as Hobart first nailed us with a contemptuous backhand, followed by a right cross to the jaw that sent us flying.

Oof!

Time almost seemed to slow, allowing me a brief montage of the living room's ceiling, followed by the ruined doorframe, then the stars above as we were launched into the front yard. Guess we were fated to end this evening's *festivities* in the same place we'd started.

I landed hard in the dirt, dazed and with the wind knocked out of me. Presumably the same was true of Winston since we shared a set of lungs.

Much as I wanted to lie there and enjoy the night sky, I managed a glance back in the direction we'd come, seeing Hobart's massive frame step through the open doorway.

On the upside, we'd managed to lead him away from Jacob. Pity it came at the cost of placing our odds of survival somewhere between slim and none.

44

JUST ANOTHER MANIC MOONDAY

As Hobart advanced on us – taking his sweet time since he currently held all the cards – Winston shared his thoughts on our teamwork so far.

"*I take it back,*" he wheezed. "*Stop helping.*"

Everyone's a critic.

"*I'm not joking, pupcake. Sit back and shut up, otherwise I'm carving you outta me once this is finished.*"

It was very *optimistic* thinking on his part. I was tempted to point out he hadn't exactly been batting a thousand either. However, the last thing we needed was an argument right as Hobart was preparing to twist our fool head off. So, for now, I once again took a back seat, essentially acting as the Dr. Stein to Winston's *Firestorm*. Not that I expected him to know who either of them were.

My alter ego's first action was to clamber back to our decisively unsteady feet. In response, the werewolf leader chuffed something at us.

"*I don't think so,*" Winston replied. "*I'm not finished yet, you furry fuckhead.*"

Hobart let out a deeper, decisively less amused snarl in response.

"Oh yeah? Why don't you come over here and say that to my face?"

Guess that answered whether they understood one another, leaving me to wonder at the rest of their exchange as I was the only one left uninvited to this werewolf *Duolingo* party.

Now wasn't the time to worry about the nuances of lycanthrope linguistics, as the leader of the Harris County pack took Winston up on his offer, abandoning his lazy gait and charging full speed at us.

I fully expected to be bulldozed again, but Winston surprised me. Rather than meet our foe head on, we side-stepped at the last moment. It wasn't particularly nimble nor nearly as quick as we could normally move, but Hobart wasn't exactly a prima ballerina in his wolf form.

As the massive beast raced past us, Winston turned with him, taking a swipe with a clawed hand. Hobart saw the attack coming and moved to dodge but was a hair too slow, resulting in his left ear being sliced clean off.

The werewolf Dominant let out a high-pitched yipe, but my inner beast wasn't done yet. Before Hobart could turn to face us, Winston leapt upon his back.

He slung one arm around the big werewolf's neck then wrapped our legs around his ample midsection piggyback style. The swift, savage movement not only hurt like hell but the fresh heat blooming from my side told me we'd ripped ourselves open in the process.

Just great.

However, wonderful as that might not have been, Winston made up for it by clamping our jaws down onto Hobart's shoulder.

The werewolf Dominant screamed in pain, but I barely heard him as my mouth filled with the savory goodness of piping hot blood.

Oh God!

Though it had been less than an hour since I'd almost lost myself to the headiness of bloodlust, it somehow felt like years instead. It was as if I'd forgotten how utterly intoxicating it tasted in the short time that passed.

So good! Want more!

"*D* ...*n't* ... *lose* ... *yer..elf* ... *idiot!*"

I had no idea what Winston was grumbling through clamped teeth, nor did I care. Whatever it was, I was certain it was unimportant in that moment. What mattered was drinking my fill of the savory red deliciousness, especially since I'd lost so much of my own. Heck, it was only natural I replenish...

My jaws began to unclench as we started to pull away from Hobart's succulent flesh.

Nuh... "*No!*"

The words slipped from my mouth as I fought back, refusing to let go. Why would Winston do that to me? What would possess him to deny me the blissful nectar of the gods?

"*Grrrarrr... Get off!*"

What? It took me a moment to realize the words hadn't come from our own mouth.

Hobart? Had I just understood him?

Whatever. It didn't matter, not so long as the taste of his blood and flesh continued to slither down my...

I was rudely denied eating my fill as Hobart reached back, grabbed the fur at the scruff of my neck, and tossed me over his shoulder like a sack of week-old garbage.

I landed hard on the driveway gravel, but the impact barely registered as I was too caught up in licking the last of the blood from my lips.

Winston tried to take control, but I fought him, refusing to budge until I got every last...

URGH!

Hobart's slammed his fist into my jaw, instantly erasing the haze of bloodlust that had claimed me. Unfortunately, the blow also erased a good deal of my teeth too as a haze of pain descended instead.

I rolled to the side coughing out blood that probably wasn't his, but he wasn't finished yet.

"*Stupid son of a bitch,*" Hobart growled, his voice still understandable. "*I'm gonna krrrgrrraaaagh!*"

And then suddenly it wasn't, as his words were once again replaced by unintelligible snarls.

What the heck?

Sadly, the meaning was still crystal clear as he kicked out with a clawed foot that tore our midsection to ribbons and once again sent us flying.

We landed hard, leaving a smear of blood behind as we skidded to a halt in the grass.

"*You ... fucking ... id...*"

The rest of whatever Winston had to say was lost as our stomach heaved from the violent attack, forcing us to vomit its bloody contents upon the ground.

Long moments passed, then there came the sound of cruel laughter from above as Hobart's foot slammed into our back, sending us crashing face-first into a puddle of our own sick.

It was about as pleasant as you can probably imagine. No doubt about it. If we somehow managed to survive this, I was spending a solid week in the shower. Sadly, that was easier said than done.

My arms began to flail seemingly of their own accord as I continued to retch, telling me Winston was doing his damnedest to retake control.

I didn't offer any resistance as my head finally started to clear. Regrettably, along with clarity came the realization my uncontrolled bloodlust had, in all likelihood, killed us both.

Perhaps if Winston had warned me first I could have...

No. This wasn't his fault, I ... *OOF* ... considered as Hobart kicked us over onto our back.

While my inner wolf was apparently able to handle the taste of blood, something about it, at least in this form, caused my human mind to go all cuckoo for *Cocoa Puffs*. It was like conscious thought fled to the wind, leaving me little more than a shark in a feeding frenzy.

It made me wonder if Hobart had a similar reaction to this ... feral addiction. A shudder passed through me as I realized that if he decided to test it out by taking a bite, neither Winston nor I were in any shape to fend him off.

Mind you, it's not like we were doing particularly great against him as it was.

"*Guh*!" Case in point as he stomped down hard on our chest, once again driving the wind from our lungs.

Or maybe not.

Whereas I wasn't able to do much more than wheeze in response, Winston managed to grab hold of Hobart's leg, digging his claws in as he tried to fend off the attack. Alas, there wasn't much behind it. Wounded, bleeding, and with lord knows how many internal contusions, even now I found myself growing woozy from blood loss.

Considering the way Hobart easily yanked his foot from our grasp – earning little more than superficial scratches in the process – told me Winston wasn't faring much better.

Gah!

We caught another contemptuous kick, this time to the jaw, leaving us flat on our back with tongue-hanging out, unable to do anything more than stare up at the sky. On the upside, the view was nice.

This far from town, the stars seemed to shine twice as brightly, almost as if the Milky Way was a living thing unto...

A light drizzle began to rain down upon our face, odd as the sky was quite obviously clear. But then the reality of the situation hit home a scant second later.

Hobart was peeing on us.

Eww! Did I say a week in the shower? Make that a full month with a gallon of bleach.

"*Y-you ... fucking... Oh fuck, I got some in my mouth*!"

Needless to say, since we shared the same tongue, I found myself longing for the blissful taste of blood, or even that pig. Sadly, there didn't seem to be much either of us could do about it, save lie there and be pissed upon beneath the...

Wait ... the stars!

"*Wh-who gives a fuck?*" Winston sputtered, trying to talk from the corner of our mouth lest we get another taste of golden shower.

I can see them. The full moon. It's gone! I grinned despite our *unfortunate* situation.

We'd done it. We'd held on long enough to exhaust Myra. Without her magic, the pack would quickly revert back to their human selves. So long as Ed was still alive, that meant the tide was about to change, for him anyway.

As for us, I was just about done for, but a pyrrhic victory was better than none at all. Now to hope Ed and Jacob had enough left in them to fend off Hobart once he was finished with us.

If not...

He must've noticed the wistful look on my face because the werewolf leader abruptly looked skyward, letting out a confused growl as he finally realized the absence of a full moon.

He glared down at us again, pure hatred showing in

his red eyes, then, even as he continued *raining* on our parade, he threw his head back and let out a howl that filled the night air.

What's he doing?

"*Letting the others know,*" Winston said, his voice barely audible against Hobart's howl. "*He's telling anyone left this fight is over … and that I lost.*"

I had to take his word for it as my tenure for understanding werewolf had been all too brief. All I saw was him howling like a madman, or wolf, while completely … ignoring us!

It's not over. Not yet.

"*Enough. I can't believe I'm saying this, Mike, but we need to face facts. I … we lost.*"

Had Winston actually called me by name? If so, things must've truly been dire. Nonetheless, despite wanting to give up earlier, I now found myself refusing to accept our fate, finding a well of resolve deep inside I didn't even know was there.

I doubted it was enough to win, but maybe we could still claim our pound of flesh.

Give me control.

"Why? *There's no use fighting him.*"

Just do it!

I put as much force of will as I could into that thought, fearing it still wouldn't be enough. But then it happened. I felt my limbs go limp, letting me know they were mine to command.

Not that I had much left to command them with. My arms felt like lead and my head was swimming … and not just from being peed on. But I had enough for one final act of defiance, something that would hopefully leave a *lasting* mark.

I raised my head, unsure if our foe would even understand me.

Whatever. He'd get the point soon enough.

"*Hey, Hobart,*" I called out, catching his attention as his howl finally came to an end. "*Piss on this!*"

Then, as his eyes opened wide in both surprise and terror, I reached up and drove my claws straight into his still leaking crotch.

45

NUT ALLERGY

My attack didn't have a lot behind it. But it didn't need to as it turned out some areas of male werewolf anatomy were slightly more *vulnerable* than others. It was a dirty, underhanded cheap shot on my part, not to mention gross as can be. But, after getting bounced around by Hobart and nearly gutted in the process, I figured Winston and I deserved to go out in one final blaze of glory.

Not to mention, it was satisfying as all heck – an attack our foe was unlikely to forget anytime soon.

Even Winston seemed surprised, our jaw dropping open in apparent shock as I buried my claws knuckle-deep into Hobart's *wolfhood*.

A high-pitched shriek escaped the pack leader's throat, as if someone had left the door to Hell wide open. It wasn't human sounding in the slightest, but its meaning was clear – what I was doing hurt like the dickens.

Unfortunately, gratifying as pruning Hobart's shrubbery might have been, it didn't come with a second wind. Thus, I had no defense left as he kicked me in the face, sending us tumbling end over end away from him.

That was it, my last act of defiance. I didn't even have enough left to try and slow us down as we skidded to a halt. All I wanted to do was close my eyes and pray whatever happened next was quick. But apparently that wasn't to be.

"*H-holy shit,*" Winston chuffed. "*You actually got one.*"

Huh?

As we lay there barely able to move, Winston resumed control and lifted my right hand – now slick with Hobart's blood and still clutching...

What in God's name is that? I asked, spying the fleshy *souvenir* I'd taken with us on our brief journey across the yard.

Winston let out a tired chuckle. "*I'll give you one guess.*"

Oh no.

"Oh yes!"

So freaking gross!

"*Yep. Now eat it before he can do something about it!*"

What?!

"*You heard me. Open wide.*"

No!

"*Why not?*"

Because it's one of his freaking balls, that's why!

"*Stop being such a puppy. Eat it now, before he can stop us.*"

Winston tried to stuff the bloody testicle into our mouth, forcing me to take control of our other hand to fend off the one trying to feed me Satan's bonbon.

"*What the fuck, asshole?*"

Do not put that into my mouth!

"*Why not?*"

Because I don't want to chew on Hobart's balls! That's ... not something sane people do.

"*I'm not people. I'm a Dominant.*"

Bully for you, but I have to live in this body too.

I clamped our lips shut as he tried to force the fleshy blob into our mouth like it was the last chicken nugget on Super Bowl Sunday. The result was us wasting what little energy we had left fighting over where to store Hobart's family jewels. Needless to say, playing *keep away* with a torn off testicle was a poor use of what little time I'd bought us.

And sadly, that time was up.

Just as I was a hair's breadth away from being forced to sample the werewolf version of Rocky Mountain oysters, Hobart grabbed hold of the scruff of our neck and dragged us to our feet.

Before I could even comprehend that our foe was clearly back in the fight, he slammed his fist full force into our stomach.

Gurrrg!

Winston and I doubled over retching, not that there was anything left to puke at this point, but the pack leader refused to let us fall. I briefly registered the combination of embarrassment, pain, and sheer rage in his eyes, then mine were blackened as he drove his fist into our face before doing it a second time for good measure.

Ugh!

Hobart let go long enough to box our ears, reducing all the myriad sounds of the forest to little more than a dull throbbing in my head.

What followed was more a drunken bar fight than two wild animals going at it, as punches, slaps, and elbows plowed into me with reckless abandon. The assault was relentless. There was no sign of Hobart's former arrogance as he mercilessly beat Winston and I to the brink of unconsciousness.

There came the sharp crack of bone breaking, although by then I had no way of telling if it was my jaw or

Hobart's fist. Everything was a dull haze of pain, literally the only thing keeping me from blacking out.

Then, just when I thought it couldn't possibly get worse, Hobart grabbed our head and yanked it to the side, exposing our throat. Neither Winston nor I had anything left to stop him with. Heck, I probably couldn't have formed a coherent thought had I tried.

All I could do was close my eyes and wait for the end as his fetid breath washed over us, telling me we were seconds away from his fangs tearing into our...

A muffled roar broke the momentary impasse, sounding like thunder as heard by a child with his head hidden beneath the blankets. Something red hot stung the side of my face, telling me this was it, that Hobart had closed in for the kill.

So then why was I still alive? And why didn't it hurt more?

I managed to crack one eye open, only to find our foe unmoved from where he'd been. He stood there, mouth open and eyes wide, but this time it wasn't with rage so much as ... surprise?

Call me crazy, but that was probably because *his* throat was somehow now a bloody, ruined mess instead of my own.

What the hell?

Before I could even begin to question this bizarre turnabout of luck, wisps of smoke and sparks joined the blood gushing from the wound in his neck.

Sparks?

Hobart backed up a step, clutching at the gruesome injury. With him no longer holding us up, Winston and I stumbled then fell to our knees. However, I barely noticed, trying as I was to make sense of what had just happened.

He ... he's been shot. With a silver bullet.

I glanced back toward the house, but there was no sign

of either Jacob or Ed. No real surprise. I doubted there'd been enough time since Myra's spell ended for them to clean up their own mess, much less rush to my aid.

There was one other problem with that theory. With my back to the house, they'd have needed to shoot through me to get to Hobart. Clearly that hadn't happened, especially since the brief view I'd gotten of his mangled neck suggested an exit wound.

I reached up with a shaky hand and touched the side of my face, feeling blood oozing from the furrow made when we'd been grazed.

He was shot from behind. But by who?

Any attempt to make sense of this was interrupted as Hobart toppled over onto the ground – sparks and smoke continuing to rise from where he'd been shot.

His body convulsed for several long seconds, then he took one last gurgling breath before falling still. Hobart Callahan, Dominant of the Harris County werewolf pack, was dead.

Mind you, Winston and I didn't seem far behind as the only thing we could do to celebrate this strange turn of events was collapse into a heap.

The sound of shifting flesh and muscle caught my attention. It was Hobart's body changing back to his human form.

For one panicked moment I was certain he was going to heal and be right back at it with us, but it soon became evident that wasn't the case.

With no moon in the sky or conscious will to maintain its wolf form, his body was reverting. The glazed, unseeing look in his eyes when it was finished told me as much.

"*Let's … get over there … and gut that fucker … just to be safe*," Winston croaked, his voice barely a whisper.

It was obviously not necessary, not that we had the strength to do so anyway. Besides, I had no interest in fighting my alter ego over Hobart's remaining testicle. *I … have a better idea.*

With that, I focused on initiating our own transformation. Winston was either too tired to fight or simply didn't care at this point. Either way, the glorious numbness of an endorphin rush filled us in the moments before our fur receded and our own body rearranged itself.

When it was done, the hole in our side not only remained but was still painful as all heck. However, I was happy to find some of the damage inflicted upon us during the battle had healed. I still felt like I'd gone ten rounds with an angry grizzly, but at least we didn't seem to be waiting for the Reaper to pay us a visit. It was nothing a buttload of stitches, a lot of antibiotics, and maybe a blood transfusion or two wouldn't fix.

What can I say? My mama raised me to be an optimist.

"It's still fucking cold being you," Winston weakly groused.

"Our pants are inside if you want to get up and find them," I replied.

"Maybe in a few minutes."

"That's what I thought."

I was about to say something else when movement registered in the corner of my eye. I turned my head to see the vegetation at the far reaches of Jacob's flood lights swaying in the non-existent breeze.

Huh?

My heart leapt into my chest as one of the bushes stood up and began ponderously moving our way, but then realization hit. It wasn't some nightmare straight out of *Day of the Triffids*, merely someone clad in a ghillie suit.

As for who was skulking about in such an outfit, the high-powered rifle in their hand was a dead giveaway – one of the hunters from Barley Hills.

Guess that answered who had shot Hobart. Mind you, happy as I was for the save, it didn't tell me what they were doing in Harris County.

My meeting with Isaiah Hood had ended with the impression I still had their trust, albeit tentatively. But now a tiny pang of fear began to inch its way up my spine as the voice in the back of my head started to question whether I'd been wrong.

I opened my mouth, hoping to shout a greeting and dispel those worries as the hunter shouldered their weapon. But I quickly bit my tongue as they drew a wicked looking hunting knife from their side, never breaking stride as they continued toward us.

"Fuck me," Winston croaked. "What now?"

I couldn't disagree as I was forced to wonder what else this accursed night had in store for us.

46

EXIT WOUNDS

Under normal circumstances, fighting off a single human wasn't particularly daunting, especially if they were obliging enough to put their hunting rifle away first. However, despite the change from werewolf to man having pulled me back from death's door, I was still pretty much lying on its front porch.

Not only was I badly injured but my tank was on empty, and there was no food in sight, at least none that didn't require resorting to cannibalization. Thankfully, even the thought was once again repellent now that I was back in my normal skin. Heck, it almost seemed downright absurd how the taste of blood had driven me so crazy only a short while ago.

That was neither here nor there, though, as I was currently far more worried about being gutted like a fish.

I tensed up as the ghillie-suited figure drew near, but then they stopped as they reached Hobart's corpse. The lone hunter knelt over his body for several long seconds, as if examining it.

It seemed painfully obvious he was done for, but perhaps that wasn't the case for the newcomer as they raised their hunting knife right before burying it nearly hilt deep into Hobart's still oozing throat.

Holy crap!

"You seeing this shit?" Winston asked, sounding nearly as freaked out as I was.

"Kinda hard to miss." My response was a mere whisper, fearing that we were about to be next.

I watched with a combination of surprise and terror as the camouflaged hunter continued to hack with the business end of their weapon, as if Hobart wasn't dead enough for their personal edification.

The crazed butchery continued until, at last, they pulled the bloodied knife free, taking a moment to clean the blade on the grass before standing up again.

"Much better," they, or should I say *she,* said, surveying her gruesome handiwork.

My eyes opened wide at the familiar voice. "Hannah?"

She reached up and removed the suit's headpiece, proving me right. Hannah Hood, one of Barley Hill's best werewolf hunters and daughter of its overseer, stood staring at me for several long moments before finally breaking out into a grin.

"I'm glad to see ye alive, Michael." She paused before adding, "Ye too, Winston."

"Uh, thanks," I replied, utterly dumbfounded. "So ... um no offense, but what are you doing?"

"Talking to a man wearing no britches, quite obviously." Hannah pulled open the front of her suit, revealing a satchel. She opened it and removed a coarse looking bedroll which she then tossed my way. "Here. Wrap that around yerself awhile. It'll make this conversation a wee less awkward."

"For which one of us?"

She didn't answer, merely waited for me to cover up, a feat made more difficult thanks to Winston's *help.* Finally, after what seemed far too long, my pertinent bits were hidden from view, leaving me sitting on the lawn looking up at her expectantly. "Better?"

"Much, thank ye."

"So back to what I was saying. Care to tell me what you're doing? Not that I'm complaining, mind you, but it seems a bit overkill to keep ... beating a dead horse."

"He's not a horse," Winston said. "And she's not..."

"It's another figure of speech," I interrupted before turning my attention Hannah's way again. "Anyway, I think you got him."

She cocked her head. "Got who?"

"Hobart ... with your first shot. So, there's no need for ... whatever this is."

"Ye must be mistaken, Michael. I didn't shoot this man."

"You didn't?" I immediately looked around, wondering how many more hunters were about to come pouring out of the woods. If so, that might not bode well for those of us who'd just barely survived this battle. "Then who did?"

A moment passed in which Hannah did nothing but meet my gaze. Then Winston replied, "She didn't kill him."

"I know what she said, but then who...?"

"Me, obviously. I killed the fucker. Gutted the shit outta him as a matter of fact."

"What? No, you didn't."

"Yer other half gets it," Hannah said with a smirk.

"Gets what? I'm sorry, but he was clearly shot from behind."

"For fuck's sake," Winston cried. "Could you for once try pretending to be more than a semi-evolved ape?"

"I don't understand."

"The pack," he explained with a sigh of disgust. "I'm

in charge now, whether those kibble lickers like it or not. But..."

"The transfer of power will go a lot smoother if they think yer the one who vanquished their leader," Hannah finished for him. "Which ye obviously did. Come and see for yerself."

I raised an eyebrow. Then, curious as to what she meant, I slowly and painfully got to my feet and lurched over. The gristly sight was more than enough to turn my stomach, but somehow, I managed not to retch. Guess I'd been desensitized by all the blood and guts this night.

I wasn't the only one, as Hannah stood by casually as if desecrating a corpse were an everyday occurrence for her.

Note to self: try not to get on her bad side.

Speaking of desecrating, I looked closer, specifically at the wound in Hobart's neck, which Hannah had made larger as well as considerably uglier thanks to her ministrations.

"See?" Winston remarked. "Tore his fucking throat right out, just like I remember doing. Get it now?"

"I ... suppose it looks that way, if you squint."

Hannah stepped next to me. "Mind ye, it won't stop any of yer kind from smelling the bullet residue."

Winston nodded. "True, but since I'm the only Dominant left in town that shouldn't matter. Just means we need to dispose of the *trash* before next moonrise."

"My thoughts exactly."

"Wait," I said. "And you're okay with this?" Hannah opened her mouth to reply but I held up a hand. "I meant Winston."

He shrugged. "Not how I would've preferred it, but that grey-haired shit kicker had to go and shoot me. Anyway, a dead asshole is a dead asshole far as I'm concerned. As for how he got that way..." He trailed off as we once more turned toward the huntress.

She in turn mimed zipping her lips.

"But why?" I asked. "And how did you even know to be here?"

She gestured around us. "The why is simple, Michael. The whole of Barley Hills will rest more soundly knowing the pack is now in ... *suitable* hands."

"Meaning mine," Winston explained.

"Of course," she said, the subtle sarcasm in her tone flying right over my other half's not-so-furry head. "As for the how, ye didn't think I'd let ye waltz back into this den of monsters alone, now did ye, at least not without checking up on ye?"

I was about to respond when her words sunk in. "Hold on. *You'd let me*? Does your father know you're here?"

She smiled at me, the simple emotion lighting up her face despite the heavy camouflage. "You have yer secrets and I have mine. Perhaps 'twould be best if we kept them between the two of us."

"Three of us," Winston corrected.

"Of course. My apologies, *yer Lordship*."

"Hmm, I kinda like that."

Flattery aside, her meaning was clear. Loose lips could sink both our ships. Although, I had to wonder if that was all there was to it. Nonetheless, I was grateful she'd thought to keep an eye on me, doubly so since we'd be dead if not for her.

"I meant what I said earlier, pupcake," Winston said after a moment. "I like this one. So, if you're ever in the mood to mount ... mmmphrhhh."

I clamped a hand over our mouth, cutting him off before he could say something that might embarrass me ... *more*, or insult the heavily armed werewolf hunter barely two feet away.

"So, um, anyway," I stammered once Winston got the

hint, "consider it a deal. We'll keep your secret if you promise to do..."

"I've got an even better idea," a crazed voice interrupted, one even more familiar to me. *Myra!* "The best kept secrets are the ones cunts like you take to the grave."

We both spun in time to see the crimson-haired sorceress step from the tree line, a look of red-hot murder gleaming in her eye, quite literally.

Before either of us could react, the reddish glow spread to Myra's body and then to her outstretched hands.

"No! Don't..."

I was too late in my warning as she launched a blast of fiery death directly at us.

The only thing I could do was shield Hannah's body with my own. Sadly, my injuries coupled with my now human form proved too much. I barely managed half a step before the magical hellfire engulfed us both.

I was knocked to the ground, feeling the awful sensation of my skin heating up in the space of a second. I opened my mouth to scream as the temperature became unbearably hot and then...

The red glow abruptly vanished, allowing the coolness of the night air to once again wash over me.

What...

"The fuck?" Winston sputtered, echoing my thoughts.

A shrill cry from next to me served as a reminder that we hadn't been the only ones targeted.

Hannah!

I sat up, still surprised to find myself in one piece, but for the moment I was far more worried about the huntress who'd unexpectedly come to our aid. I fully expected to find the worst had happened but instead found her merely patting her hands against a few spots on her suit that had begun to smolder.

I'd seen Myra's spell before. It was lethal battle magic, yet what had happened was more akin to sitting too close to a campfire. I was too amazed to still be alive to question why.

"Are-are you all right?" I asked, crawling to Hannah's side.

She nodded, looking as surprised as I felt. "Singed my eyebrows, but that seems about it."

Somehow the eldritch attack had left us no worse off than an extra five minutes spent under a tanning bed. It made no sense, unless...

Hannah raised an eyebrow, no doubt thinking the same thing. "No offense to ye, Michael, but I didn't realize yer other half could repel magic like that."

"Wait, you thought that was me? I figured you had some anti-magic doohickey stashed on you."

She shook her head, letting out a nervous chuckle. "Our mystics are good, but not *that* good."

"Then what the heck just happened?"

Had Myra pulled her punch, perhaps on account of our past relationship? But if so, then why even bother scaring us if she was just going to...

That thought scattered to the wind as Winston began to laugh.

"Something funny?" I asked.

"Just the realization that witches are no smarter than the rest of you monkeys."

"Meaning what?"

"Meaning your mount buddy, stupid."

Oh crap. "Um, she's not..."

Winston kept talking over me, though. "The bitch was too tired to keep that fake moon of hers in the sky, so I doubt she had anywhere close to enough to blast us to pieces like she wanted."

Huh. Actually, that made all the sense in the world. Heck, Hobart had even admitted how much the smart wolf spell took out of her.

Winston nodded as if sensing my thoughts. "She might be angry as a wet cat over the death of her puppy pal, but that doesn't mean she's ready to piss with us big dogs."

Tempting as it was to agree with this rare bit of insight, I doubted my ex was about to give up so easily. However, as I turned back toward where she'd launched her spell, I saw nothing but trees waiting for us. Myra was already long gone.

I considered giving chase, for maybe a moment or two, but sat back down instead – something even Winston didn't seem inclined to protest.

Fine by me. We had plenty of our own wounds to lick, figuratively anyway, as well as friends in need of being checked on. Once that was done then we could take some time to marvel at the fact that, against all odds, we'd won.

It might not have been how either Winston or myself had envisioned it, but the end result was what mattered, even if it was best we kept the truth to ourselves.

As for the rest, figuring out how to deal with the pack, or with Myra for that matter, well, that could wait for some other night when both me and my inner wolf once again felt the call to run through the dark woods surrounding Harris County, a little town with a big secret – yet one I was happy to call home.

THE DOGGONE CONCLUSION

"I swear, Mike, it's the damnedest thing. Most days this town is so quiet, I'm lucky if I write up a horsefly for speeding. But this past week, I dunno. It's like all our bad luck has come due. Three fatal accidents. A few more gone in their sleep. And now I gotta send a man out to Callahan Hauling because it sounds like old Hobart's left town in the dead of night."

"I hear his business hasn't been doing well," I replied, doing my best to ignore the bead of sweat sliding down my face. "Or at least that's what the rumor mill says."

Sheriff Deke Haskell nodded. "So I've heard. Still, it's a damned shame to see a man with such deep roots make off like a thief in the night. Hell, he might be a bastard, but I'm sure folks would've been happy to help if'n he'd asked."

I shrugged. "Maybe. Guess he just ... panicked." *Kind of like how I'm about to.*

"Sure sounds like it." Deke shook his head. "Oh well. What's that saying about trouble coming in threes?"

"Then let's hope that's the end of it, Sheriff."

He waved me off. "I'm standing here in my shorts and

bathrobe. I think we can dispense with the formalities. Anyway, you sure picked a hell of a time to get back from vacation."

"As Stucky keeps reminding me."

"I bet he has." Deke let out a laugh. "So how was the big city anyway?"

I carefully considered my answer. "Definitely not boring."

"Well, be sure to tell me all about it next time. Don't want to keep you from your job."

"Will do, sir." I threw him a nod then started to turn away.

"Oh, and Mike?"

"Yes?" Outwardly I remained calm, but inside I wanted to scream. My folks had been big *Columbo* fans back in the day, and this was usually the point where he put the squeeze on the guilty party.

"I appreciate you holding the truck. Last thing I need is the missus chewing me out for letting the trash pile up."

I could've almost wept with relief. "No problem whatsoever, Sher ... Deke. We gotta watch out for one another."

I let out a nervous sigh as I quickly carried the bin to the truck, emptied it, and started up the compacter. Running into the sheriff during my rounds had been unplanned, more so since he'd been in the mood to discuss the recent spate of local *tragedies*.

Much to my surprise and relief, though, his tone had been more that of a concerned neighbor than someone who was about to call for a statewide manhunt. Regardless, I'd expected my first day back on the job to be stressful, but this was pushing the envelope even for me.

"Shithead's lucky he shut his trap when he did," Winston muttered. "One more word and I'd have gutted him like..."

"What did I tell you about talking like that at work?" I hissed, keeping my voice as low as possible. "Or talking at *all* for that matter."

"I don't answer to you, pupcake. Besides, this is your fucking job, not mine. I mean, why am I even back here smelling this shit? We should order your asshole friend to switch places."

"We don't get to order anyone around during the day, or until the next full moon for that matter. Until then, this is how we earn our keep."

I quickly shushed him as Dallas picked that moment to pop his head out of the cab.

"Yo, Mike, Stucky needs us to take a detour to Chaney Road."

"Oh?" I replied as nonchalant as I could.

He grinned sheepishly for some reason. "Yeah. Got … a call about a last-minute pickup, and since we're running a bit ahead…"

"Not a problem." A route change was no big deal. Not to mention, I was in no position to complain after my two-and-a-half-week *sabbatical*.

I nodded my acknowledgement before climbing onto the side rail and throwing him a wave, hanging on tight as we started to move again.

The cool breeze kept the *fragrant* scent of the truck's contents at bay, giving my nostrils a few moments of peace as I reflected on recent events.

Hannah had made herself scarce following Myra's aborted attack, leaving me to stumble back to the house to see how Ed and Jacob were doing.

Turned out reality had other plans, though, as

Winston and I sat down to catch our breath first, at which point we'd promptly passed out.

I'd awoken some time later to the stench of warm, fetid breath upon my face. Cracking one eye open, I'd nearly peed myself at the massive canine face taking up nearly my entire field of vision. However, a quick tongue bath confirmed it was merely Spud wishing me a good morning. Not only was I back in my apartment, in my own bed, but the hole in my side had been stapled shut.

To say I'd been pleased as, well, an excitable pitbull was no understatement. Winston too apparently, as the subsequent threats he threw Spud's way were somewhat less ornery than usual.

Before I could begin to wonder whether it had all been a bad dream, my eyes had fallen upon a letter left on the nightstand.

It was from Jacob.

He let me know that he and Ed had fared well in the final minutes of the battle, especially once Myra's moon spell fizzled. Though he hadn't gone into detail, he made it clear that once Hobart's minions reverted, it was short work for his vampire stepson to send them packing with their proverbial tails tucked between their legs.

They'd found me not long after. With a hospital out of the question, for a variety of reasons, they'd patched me up best they could and brought me back home.

The note ended with him telling me not to worry about either of them, that I should rest up and then come visit once I was back on my feet.

Safe to say, not worrying was out of the question, but Jacob hadn't been kidding with his orders. I'd tried to get up, only to realize I was one big pile of bruises and abrasions. With the silver in my blood still affecting my healing, I was roughly in about as good of shape as if I'd been hit by a bus.

When next I'd awoken, it had been to more familiar faces, albeit ones considerably less fuzzy. Dallas had come to check on me, and he'd brought my parents along. Talk about sights for sore eyes. I swear, I would've cried like a baby had I not been certain Winston would've said something crass.

After hugs, kisses, and lots of doting, I brought them up to speed on everything, minus a few *minor* details. Then it was Dallas's turn to do the same.

Turns out he'd led the pack on a merry chase. They'd all finally reverted in an open field nearly a mile away – mercifully well within the quarantine zone, whether through luck, instinct, or a bit of both.

Better yet, the others had been none the wiser as to what had transpired that night, with one exception. Upon waking, they all somehow knew. Whatever hold Hobart had upon them, whatever grip he'd had upon their lives, was now gone. Both my parents were able to confirm they too had felt it all the way over in Barley Hills. They explained it as a heaviness inside of them, one they barely even realized was there, had suddenly disappeared.

None of the others knew how, why, or that I'd even been involved. They simply understood something had changed and they were now free, which of course prompted me to bite down on my tongue to keep Winston from commenting to the contrary.

We both knew the pack couldn't be allowed to remain uncollared, but that was a discussion for another day.

On that note, it took another full day for the silver to work its way out of my system, during which Dallas acted as my eyes and ears in town, learning what he could.

Sadly, it wasn't all good news.

Of the werewolves we'd managed to take out of the

fight, roughly half succumbed to their wounds before reverting back. Most were those struck by silver bullets, making me grateful Winston had performed impromptu surgery when he had.

Unlike my happy reunion, there were families in Harris County now missing loved ones. All were in the know about who and what they were, as well as the risks that came with our rather unique lifestyle, but that didn't make it any easier.

All of that and more would have to be dealt with once I finally worked up the nerve to face them as their new Dominant. But with the next full moon a few weeks away, it gave me some breathing room to think about what to say, as well as hopefully figure out some compromise with Winston.

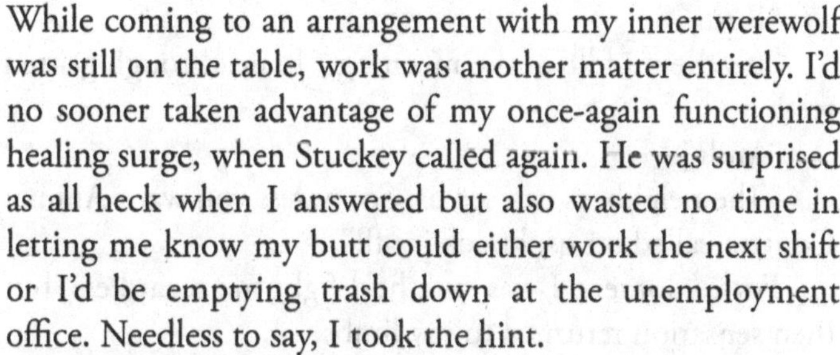

While coming to an arrangement with my inner werewolf was still on the table, work was another matter entirely. I'd no sooner taken advantage of my once-again functioning healing surge, when Stuckey called again. He was surprised as all heck when I answered but also wasted no time in letting me know my butt could either work the next shift or I'd be emptying trash down at the unemployment office. Needless to say, I took the hint.

Can't say it bothered me much, as there was a certain Zen that came from the simplicity of my job, putrid smells aside.

Speaking of which, I pulled myself from my reverie as the truck turned onto Chaney Road.

We slowed down just as we approached an all too familiar building.

Oh no. You have gotta be kidding me!

Sadly, there was no denying it as the big vehicle came

to a halt. Dallas threw me an apologetic grin from the side mirror before pretending there was something interesting waiting for him on the dashboard.

The reason why was obvious. We were at Myra's place.

Figures.

"No fucking way this is a coincidence," Winston muttered. "Be ready."

"For what?"

"For anything, stupid. Or have you forgotten about her magic?"

"Trust me, that would be hard to forget... Wait, what are you doing?"

A familiar numbness settled over my extremities. Realizing I was moments away from busting out of my coveralls in broad daylight, I made it a point to stomp on that real quick. "I repeat, *what* the heck do you think you're doing?"

"Getting ready to shred a witch in need of shredding."

"No!"

"But..."

"It's the middle of the morning," I said through gritted teeth.

"And?"

"The neighbors can see us. So, unless you want Animal Control called on us, knock it off!"

For a moment I was sure he'd fight me regardless, but then sensation returned to my limbs.

"It's your funeral."

I was tempted to correct him that technically it would be *our* funeral, but that seemed like a can of worms best left unopened. Besides, those same rules applied to Myra. It's not like she could just hex us in the middle of the street on a workday.

Hopefully.

Holding onto that thought, I walked to her bin like

this was any other property and pulled out the two bags waiting inside.

I'd no sooner gotten them free of the can when movement caught my eye. I looked up and spied the curtains swaying, as if someone had been peering out at us. Then both trash bags simultaneously burst apart, dousing my legs in garbage water and skeeving the utter crap out of me.

As we stood there reeking of fish guts and spoiled mayonnaise, Winston had only two words for me.

"Told ya."

I stopped home after my shift for an extra-long shower before hopping back in my Jeep. Mom and Dad were expecting me for dinner later, but first I owed Jacob and Ed a visit. It had only been a few days, but was way overdue, nonetheless. After all, I'd brought a war to their front door. Seemed only right to thank them, as well as offer my help with any repairs.

It didn't hurt that they were also the only people in town I could truly be myself around.

I pulled into the driveway, surprised to find it looking so ... normal. That's when I spotted Ed. He was standing outside the garage, saw in hand and a pile of boards and molding at his feet.

He waved as I came to a stop. "Look what the cat dragged in."

"Say what?" Winston immediately growled.

"Chill out. It's just..."

"Let me guess. Another stupid human saying?"

"More or less," I mumbled, climbing from the driver's seat.

"I see you're finally back on your feet," Ed said, walking over.

"You too."

"Vamp healing is nothing to sneeze at. Also doesn't hurt that Pop didn't shoot me."

"Yeah, about that, asshole. I'm gonna..."

"Let bygones be bygones," I interrupted, before quickly adding, "So, how goes it?"

Ed let out a laugh. "About what you might expect. No rest for the wicked."

"Oh?"

"Yep. Go figure. I've got supernatural stamina and a landlord who's not shy about abusing free labor."

I couldn't help but smile. "Werewolf stamina ain't too bad either, that is if you need some help."

He shrugged. "I'm almost done out here. Pop's got me doing all the shit work while he makes it look pretty. Although, if you want to head in, I'm sure he could use a hand ... or paw."

"Can do." Heck, I'd even picked up a pair of super stretchy spandex bike shorts in case any heavy lifting was needed, figuring these fine folks had seen enough of me naked to last a lifetime. Winston wasn't too happy to be wearing them, but he could suck it up as we were most certainly in their debt.

All thoughts of under garments trailed off as I turned toward the house, noting that barely a blade of grass seemed out of place on the expansive lawn. It was hard to believe the difference from the battleground of blood and bodies the yard had become on that fateful night.

Bodies. What happened to all the... "I don't mean to be rude, but..."

"You're wondering how we cleaned up the mess so quickly?"

It was a cold way to refer to the lives we'd been forced

to end, but I guess I couldn't fault him. "Something like that."

"No, it's more than that, pupcake," Winston said, sounding almost impressed. "Take a sniff."

I did, smelling nothing but grass and sawdust. *That can't be right.*

"All right, teat sucker, spill," Winston said, almost as if reading my thoughts. "How'd you do it? This place should reek of death, but it doesn't. So, what's the deal? Did you eat all those fuckers by yourself or did you have help?"

What?! "You can't just say things like that," I cried.

"Why not?"

"Because it's ... rude."

"You humans are all fucking idiots. You know that, right?"

If Ed was insulted, he didn't show it. Instead, he replied, "For the record, I didn't eat *any* of them because that would be fucking gross."

I was tempted to agree but the memory of how the taste of blood had affected my wolf form told me that perhaps it was best to sit this one out.

"Then how?" my alter ego demanded. "You got an industrial sized woodchipper out back you've been hiding?"

Horrified as I was at Winston's lack of tact, Ed actually laughed. "Not quite. Let's just say we have a mutual friend who *knows* some people."

I raised an eyebrow. "Friend?"

"Sally," he explained. "She's the one..."

"With the glowing green eyes," I interrupted. "Yeah, I remember."

"Good. Anyway, back in the day, before magic got destroyed that is, she and her coven kept a crew of *cleaners* on retainer."

"I'm gonna assume we're not talking maid service."

"Not quite. These are the sort of people who make problems go away, no questions asked. Anyway, turns out Sally held onto her old contact list. Long story short, in the interest of none of us going to jail, I gave her a call and ... let's just say I owe her one."

I took a moment to digest this. "And they just came out and did *all this*?"

"And more before they left."

"Left? But...?"

"When I said people, I wasn't kidding," he replied. "Seems the quarantine doesn't affect humans, no matter how questionable their moral fiber."

I remembered my earlier conversation with Sheriff Haskell. "What exactly did they do with the ... victims?"

"Their best, to make it look like either an accident or natural causes that is." Ed turned my way. "And before you ask, I specifically requested they be respectful about it. There's no need to cause any more grief than we already have."

I considered that many of the fallen were people I'd known. "I appreciate that."

"I don't. It's more than the fuckers deserved," Winston opined.

"Ignore him. He's..."

Ed waved me off, having come to understand that Winston could be *difficult* at the best of times.

"Seriously, though, thank you."

"It's fine," he said. "We needed to cover our asses. Besides, I knew some of them too. It was ... the least I could do for them."

The uncomfortable silence that descended told me it was probably time to change the subject. "Does it ever get easier?"

Ed inclined his head. "We talking home repairs, or everything else?"

"The latter."

"Not really. But that's a good thing. Keeps us from becoming monsters, like our buddy Hobart. Because believe me..."

"He's not my buddy, ass biter," Winston warned.

Ed held up his hands. "It's a figure of speech, *Werewolf of London*. What I mean is, he's not the only fuckhead out there who's drunk on his own power. So no, it doesn't get easier, and it's probably not going to get *better* anytime soon either."

I couldn't help but feel a chill at his tone. "What makes you say that?"

He looked around, as if making sure his father wasn't in earshot. "Because shit's only getting worse. And I'm not talking about you and your furry friends either. No offense, but you're not the only *things* that have seemingly appeared from out of nowhere as of late. Heck, you're not even the weirdest."

"Dare I ask?"

"You're probably going to wish you didn't, but we're talking evil leprechauns, giant mutant cockroaches, and of course big-ass sea monsters in the Hudson."

"Leviathan." I'd meant to add it only for context, but in that moment something finally clicked inside my head, connecting dots I should've realized much sooner. "It's from the Bible, isn't it?"

"What's a bible?" Winston asked.

I ignored him. "I knew I'd heard that name from somewhere."

Ed shrugged. "Hey, at least your first thought wasn't a crappy eighties horror movie."

I barely heard him, though. "It was ... a mythical beast that even the angels were supposedly afraid of."

Ed chuckled but there was no humor behind it. "Not so mythical I'm afraid."

It took a moment for all this to sink in, but once it did I was left utterly gobsmacked. "Something big's going on, isn't it? Out there in the world, I mean."

He nodded. "I believe the phrase you're looking for is ... *biblical proportions.*"

"I still don't know what a bible is," Winston opined.

Ed let out a sigh before adding, "To put it into perspective, if this were *Ghostbusters*, Egon would be giving us a speech about nine-hundred-pound Twinkies right about now."

"I don't know what the fuck any of that is either," my inner beast groused.

To me, however, it suddenly all made sense.

No wonder we'd felt such overwhelming terror back in those sewers. What we'd smelled in that place had imparted a sense of something both ancient and alien. If Ed wasn't pulling my leg, and I had no reason to believe he was, then that meant the creature that mind-zapped me was both impossibly old as well as incalculably powerful.

Winston had been wise to run for his life.

It forced me to wonder what else was waiting out there in the big wide world of the weird. More importantly, it made me realize that, however much I wanted to bury my head in the sand and worry about nothing but my friends and family here in Harris County, it might not be possible.

True, for the moment we were stuck, trapped by a magical barrier because someone somewhere had concluded we were a threat, an almost laughable idea compared to a biblical era horror lurking in the Hudson.

But if whatever was happening out there was as big as Ed suggested, then I might have no choice but to get involved, terrifying as that concept might be.

Heck, the fact the past few days had left me with more questions than answers might necessitate that alone. I still had no clue as to the actual history of Harris County, how the supernatural world could have no knowledge of my kind, or even why Hobart had been so obsessed with Ed when, far as I could tell, he was just a guy looking out for his old man. Then there'd been Winston's instinctive aversion to vampires, when I didn't even know they existed prior to a month ago.

It was a lot to deal with for a guy who just wanted to get back to his life collecting trash in rural Pennsylvania. I might've been a werewolf, as well as the new Dominant of the local pack, but right at that moment I felt very small – a speck of dust caught up in a hurricane.

Still, crazy as it all might be, it was nothing that was going to be fixed today. No. Right then, we had more down-to-Earth concerns to worry about, something I allowed myself to take comfort in.

A time would almost certainly come when I'd be forced to contend with all the unknowns in my life, but for now, I turned back toward the garage to grab a load of freshly cut molding.

There was work to be done. More than enough to keep me busy for the time being.

As for the future, Winston and I could wait until the next full moon to see what surprises it might have in store.

THE END

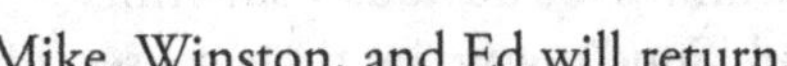

Mike, Winston, and Ed will return.

BONUS CHAPTER

Hellhounded
Howling Mad Monsters, Book 2

"One more time, boy. You can do it!"

I tossed the tennis ball, only to watch it bounce off the top of Spud's head and go rolling away into the grass. It was finally at that point that he seemed to notice it, happily trotting over to pick it up.

"Are you ready to accept it yet, pupcake?" Winston remarked.

"Accept what?"

"The sad truth that it's time to put the snack down for good."

"What? No! Why would you even say that?"

"Look at him. He's obviously suffering."

I glanced Spud's way in time to see him drop the tennis ball so he could bark at a bird flying by overhead. "How exactly is that suffering?"

"Of course, he doesn't realize it. He's a brainless fuck-wit. But trust me. If I were that stupid, I'd be begging for someone to put me out of my misery."

"For the last time, I'm not..."

"You say that now," he interrupted, "but let's see what you think in a couple hours, especially once you get a little taste."

A shiver ran down my spine at the implication. Tonight had all sorts of potential for murderous mayhem. The full moon would be high in the sky and the pack would be running free in the woods surrounding Harris County. Or that would be the case if Winston and I weren't around to hopefully wrangle them. Well, okay, more Winston than me. I still wasn't entirely sure how this whole werewolf domination thing worked and my alter ego was being less than helpful in educating me.

The problem was, lives were at stake. First and foremost, obviously, were the non-werewolf denizens of Harris County who made up the vast majority of our sleepy little town. However, they weren't the only ones at risk.

If I was going to assume leadership of the pack, then that meant assuming responsibility for their safety as well, mostly since Winston seemed as if he could care less about that part.

Tonight was potentially a dangerous time for them. On one side, the forest would no doubt be patrolled by our sister town of Barley Hills, secretly a rogue Mennonite sect of werewolf hunters. Their intent was to keep the pack contained, but with an arsenal of silver weapons at their disposal accidents could easily happen.

Then there was the quarantine. Far as I'd been able to ascertain, it encompassed both towns, the area in between, and roughly a mile radius on either side. Any werewolf stepping outside that zone would face lethal consequences of a magical nature.

The area itself was large enough for the pack to run and hunt, but the issue lay in the fact that, aside from Winston and myself, all the rest would effectively be mindless beasts, far more ferocious than Spud but not much smarter.

We were the only werewolf able to remain in control of our actions, and even that was potentially tentative, as my inner beast had seen fit to remind me. As I'd learned a few weeks back, my werewolf form had one significant weakness. For some reason, the taste of blood sent me into an uncontrollable feeding frenzy akin to a land shark.

Despite Winston's disregard for pretty much all human life, including my own, he'd been the only one able to snap me out of it last time. And that had only been because we'd been fighting for our lives. I could easily envision him letting me chow down on my own dog for no other reason than his own sick and twisted amusement.

Too bad for him, I'd assumed as much well in advance, making arrangements while he napped. Speaking of which, my contingency plan was right on schedule as the sound of a vehicle pulling into the driveway caught my attention.

"Who the fuck is that?" Winston remarked, noticing it as well.

"That's for me to know and you to get all huffy about." I didn't wait for a response, whistling instead for Spud to come over. Then whistling again, then a third time, until the stubborn canine finally realized I was calling for him. He trotted over without a care in the world so I could snap his leash on.

We walked around the garage to find I was right. A bright pink van with *Trina's Top Doggy Day Spa and Kennel* printed on the side was parked waiting for us. A petite brunette waved to us from the driver's seat before climbing out with safety harness in hand.

"I repeat, what the fuck?"

I shushed my inner beast before stepping forward.

Harris County didn't have any posh boutique businesses such as Trina's, but that wasn't the case three towns over. Normally that would be a problem for a guy stuck in a magical quarantine, but fortunately Trina's also provided door to door service. Cost me more than I was comfortable admitting, but it was worth it knowing Spud would be enjoying a night of pampering far from the potential chaos of either werewolves or werewolf hunters.

"Master Spud Walden, I presume," the driver said cheerfully, setting eyes on the heavyset pupper wagging his tail next to me. "Trina Hartberg at your service."

"Master? What kind of dipshit are..."

I covered Winston's rudeness with a cough. "Sorry. Must be something in the air."

If Trina was insulted, she didn't show it, kneeling until she was at Spud's level. "Ready to go, big guy?"

"Go where?" Winston asked, refusing to take the hint.

"To the best gosh darned doggie hotel this side of the Steel City," Trina said, seemingly happy to break into her spiel despite having already cashed my deposit.

"Doggie hotel?" my inner beast replied before I could grit my teeth against further outbursts. "The fuck? That a nice way of saying you're taking him to be gassed?"

Trina laughed, probably assuming Winston was joking. "Don't listen to this big meanie," she told Spud. "We're going to have a great time. First we'll trim your nails. Then you'll get a bath with our special avocado shampoo. Afterward, we'll brush you all nice and shiny. Then you can run in our playground until it's dinner time. And do you know what's for dinner? Oh, I'll tell you. It's a special mix of turkey, chicken, lamb, and rice, with all the vitamins a good boy like you needs to grow up big and strong."

"Wait, are you fucking serious?" Winston replied.

Sadly, I couldn't step in and stop him, not without looking like a major weirdo.

"Of course," she said. "It's all in our brochure. Satisfaction guaranteed."

"And do you have any of this dinner on you? Because it sounds pretty good."

Wait, what?

"We do sell it by the can, but alas it's for doggos not people."

"That's okay because I ain't people."

Crap! I shoved the leash into Trina's hand and forced out the biggest laugh I could to keep Winston from saying anything else, continuing to chortle even as he tried to force more words out.

The look on Trina's face told me her professional veneer was being pushed to the breaking point, not that I could blame her. I probably sounded like an absolute loon. But it was far better than letting on I was a werewolf with a split personality.

Needless to say, she loaded Spud up double time before getting back in and throwing the van into reverse. Close of a call as that had been, it was a relief to see him off. Now to hope she didn't call animal control on me for being a nutjob.

Sadly, my brief moment of contentment came to an end as Winston smacked me upside the head. "What the heck, dude?"

"Don't *what the heck* me, pupcake. The fuck do you think you're doing?"

"Sending my dog somewhere safe for the night."

"Who gives a fuck about that? I'm talking about the avocado shampoo, whatever the fuck that is, the brushing, and those fancy dinners while I'm stuck eating that shit you forced me to choke down last night."

"There's nothing wrong with frozen pizza."

"Gods damn, I am so tempted to gut your half right now."

"Which would probably kill us both."

"Maybe, but it's almost worth finding out for certain."

I quickly headed back inside to continue our *polite conversation,* lest my landlords look out their back window and see me arguing with myself like a madman.

"All I'm saying is I don't see why your pet snack gets decent grub while I get garbage," Winston continued to grouse as we stepped into my apartment.

"Because that's dog food," I pointed out. "And as you are so fond of reminding me, you're not a dog."

"What kind of fucked up world do you human apes live in where dogs get a succulent screaming little lamb, while a Dominant such as myself is forced to eat a soggy piece of dough from your heat box."

"Microwave," I corrected. "And they're not feeding Spud an actual lamb, especially one that's still screaming."

"Why not? That's half the fun."

I let out a sigh. Most of my time with Wiston was spent arguing over stupid things, such as why he wasn't allowed to kill everyone who looked at us funny, while the rest entailed explaining the finer details of human existence.

In some ways it was like playing host to a murderous toddler. Winston couldn't read, yet anyway, and had no patience for TV, much less the internet. So I ended up being his personal Wikipedia for every question that crossed his furry mind, of which there was no shortage.

Guess it was time to explain how processed pet food worked, lest he force me to sample some to satisfy his personal curiosity. "You know those cans in the cupboard that Spud gets?"

"The ones full of crud that looks and smells like shit?"

"Exactly. Well, if you were to check the ingredients, you'd find... Holy crap!"

Before I could launch into my tortured soliloquy on dog food, a blinding flash of light filled the living room. I backed up, blinded, until my butt hit the screen door. A real pity I hadn't properly latched it, as I subsequently tripped over the threshold only to go tumbling down half a flight of stairs butt over teakettle.

Ow.

I crashed onto the landing at the spot where it wrapped around the garage I lived over, lying there dazed on my back for several long seconds.

"Get your ass up, you fur-addled fool. We need to talk."

I shook my head to clear out the cobwebs, realizing in a hot second that hadn't been Winston's voice.

"Fuck me," he growled. "It's..."

"Myra," I finished, finding her at the top of the stairs, a look of annoyance on her face as if I'd inconvenienced her by nearly breaking my own neck.

Sadly, any retort I might have as to her violating my personal space would have to wait. "Behave," I muttered beneath my breath.

"This ain't no time to be lying around talking to yourself," Myra responded. "Now get your butt up here pronto."

Won't lie. Was almost tempting to let Winston take control. But no. That wasn't who I was, or who I wanted to be.

Besides which, I had no interest in scrubbing blood out of my carpet.

So instead, I pulled myself to my feet and limped back upstairs, finding Myra pacing in the living room.

"So what's it gonna be, witch?" Winston barked the

second I was back inside. "You here to fight, or is this just a shoe call?"

"A what?" she replied.

"Are you here to fuck with me or..."

Crap! "Sorry," I blurted out. "Booty call. The phrase is booty call."

"That's a stupid..."

"Thing to say, by a guy who ... um ... just hit his head in a fall."

Myra cocked her head for a moment before scoffing, "You wish."

I didn't, but saw no reason to antagonize the situation further.

"And no," she continued. "I ain't here to fight neither. Listen, I know things didn't end well between us last time."

"You tried to kill me."

"Tried and failed," she corrected. "And it's a good thing too because what's coming is bigger than either of us."

Winston started to respond, but I clamped down tight and mumbled, "Go on."

"It's the Magi. I've heard through the grapevine they've been debating what to do about their little quarantine."

"And?"

"And it ain't good. There's trouble brewing out there between them and some jackass claiming to be a demigod."

"Wait. A demigod? What's that got to do with us?"

She waved me off. "Nothing, except they can't afford to keep one eye on us while they deal with this problem."

Uh oh. "I assume this doesn't mean they're planning on letting us go."

"Oh, they are. They're letting us go ... in about a million fucking pieces. Because if we don't come up with some way to stop them, our precious little town is going to become a precious little smoldering crater."

To be continued in...

HELLHOUNDED
Howling Mad Monsters – Book 2

Coming soon!

AUTHOR'S NOTE

There's something satisfying about writing an entire novel stemming from a joke told maybe ten years ago. Allow me to explain.

One of the core tenets of my *Tome of Bill* series, as some of you will no doubt remember, was that, despite vampires, witches, and god knows what else all being real, werewolves were not. They were imaginary boogeymen to the actual boogeymen.

Well, at one point fairly early in my journey I joked on social media that someday I'd introduce werewolves into that universe, and it would only be fitting for me to do so in the same way I'd introduced ToB's main character Bill Ryder. In his case, it was a book titled *Bill The Vampire*. So, going with that theme, I suggested that such an intro-duction would be titled something unassuming, like *Mike The Werewolf*.

My readers thought it was funny and so did I. But in my case, I kept that little tidbit in the back of my head, knowing one day I might want to revisit it.

As it turned out, werewolves never did rear their ugly heads in the original *Tome of Bill*, but with the creation of its sequel series *Bill of the Dead* came the opportunity to change things up. And one of those opportunities was to ask myself, "What if werewolves have been around all this time but something happened, however long ago, to convince even the immortal predators of the night that they were nothing but a myth?"

Obviously if you've read this far, you know that's a mystery I heavily hinted at in this book, not to mention within the pages of *Bill of the Dead*. In fact, that's where Mike's first appearance stems from, specifically book-2 *Everyday Horrors*.

If you've read it, awesome! If not, well, you are more than welcome to, but it's not an absolute necessity. I tried to add appropriate context here to that much wider world, and my plan is to continue doing so as these stories don't exist in a vacuum. That said, while reading both series is intended to paint a broader picture, I have no interest in forcing the issue. My goal is to serve you a full and satisfying meal regardless of where you choose to dine. The only difference being the perspective of the characters and their individual experiences.

In laymen's terms, they only know what they know and no more.

Regardless, I hope you enjoyed the inaugural adventure of Mike and Winston, as well as the addition of Ed, Bill Ryder's often kidnapped friend and former roommate. My hope is that we'll be seeing much more of them all in the coming years. Until then...

- Rick G

ABOUT THE AUTHOR

Rick Gualtieri lives alone in central New Jersey with only his wife, three kids, and countless pets to both keep him company and constantly plot against him. When he's not busy monkey-clicking words, he can typically be found jealously guarding his collection of vintage Transformers from all who would seek to defile them.

Defilers beware!

Also by Rick Gualtieri
THE TOME OF BILL
Bill the Vampire
Scary Dead Things
The Mourning Woods
Holier Than Thou
Sunset Strip
Goddamned Freaky Monsters
Half A Prayer
The Wicked Dead
Shining Fury
The Last Coven

BILL OF THE DEAD
Strange Days
Everyday Horrors
Carnage À Trois
The Liching Hour

FALSE ICONS
Second String Savior
Wannabe Wizard
Halfhearted Hunter
Deviant Dark Dryads

HIGH MOON
The Girl Who Punches Werewolves
The Girl Who Fights Witches
The Girl Who Hunts Fairies
The Girl Who Defies Fate